TALENT

Also by Howard and Susan Kaminsky
(writing as Brooks Stanwood)

The Glow
The Seventh Child

TALENT

HOWARD & SUSAN KAMINSKY

BANTAM BOOKS
NEW YORK · TORONTO · LONDON · SYDNEY · AUCKLAND

This novel is a work of fiction. Any references to real people, events, establishments, organizations or locales are intended only to give the fiction a sense of reality and authenticity. Other names, characters and incidents are either the product of the authors' imaginations or are used fictitiously, as are those fictionalized events and incidents which involve real persons and did not occur or are set in the future.

TALENT

A Bantam Book / August 1989

Library of Congress Cataloging-in-Publication Data

Kaminsky, Howard.
    Talent / Howard & Susan Kaminsky.
      p. cm.
    ISBN 0-553-05371-X
    I. Kaminsky, Susan. II. Title.
    PS3569.T3342T3 1989
    813′.54—dc19   89–113
                                    CIP

Bantam Books are published by Bantam Books, a division of Bantam Doubleday Dell Publishing Group, Inc. Its trademark, consisting of the words "Bantam Books" and the portrayal of a rooster, is Registered in U.S. Patent and Trademark Office and in other countries. Marca Registrada. Bantam Books, 666 Fifth Avenue, New York, New York 10103.

For Jessica

PROLOGUE

Though the staff writers' meeting for *Tinseltown P.M.* was scheduled for nine-fifteen in the morning, it didn't start until almost ten. The conference room at the Burbank lot faced down a row of sound stages that spilled out onto the "New York" street. By the time Mel Starr, the executive producer of the daily half-hour syndicated show, arrived, all who were gathered for the meeting could read the preceding week's Nielsen rating written on his face.

"That bad?" asked Gloria Raymont, a short, heavyset writer.

"Worse." The tall, balding producer settled into the chair at the head of the table, dropping a folded piece of paper onto it. "If these numbers were my vital signs I'd be lucky to be in a coma," he said.

"How long do we have?" asked Shep Fairman, a writer who had a mortgage so large he sometimes felt like a Third World debtor nation.

"That's too damn negative a question for me even to answer," said Mel Starr. "What we have is a chance. The production company is giving us a one-hour special in prime time to get some new people to watch. Now you've supposedly been thinking about ideas for the past week, so let's hear them. And they had better be good. Jim?"

"Reece Albright's just gotten out of the Betty Ford Clinic," answered Jim Tindal, the youngest writer on the staff, who was always reminding everyone of that fact.

"So what? There are more graduates of that place than Hollywood High," Starr snapped back.

"Yeah, but he's written a screenplay about the place that everyone says will get him at least a nomination. Spielberg might direct. And he's ready to talk about everything. The coke, the crack—you name it."

"Who gives a shit what a writer has to say," answered Starr with the slightest of smiles. "And nobody knows who the hell he is."

"What about doing a piece on one entire class at the Ford Clinic? You know, those who made it, those back on the stuff," said Jim, still pitching.

"Sounds like a Donahue show. Gloria?"

"Remember Vera Boland?"

"The kid in the sitcom? That must be a hundred years ago. What was it called?"

"The Nuggets. And it's in reruns. Ran on NBC for six years. Now she's become a militant lesbian teaching up at Amherst. Lives with a woman who looks like a linebacker. But Vera is still a knockout. She's dying to get some publicity for her group, something called 'Daughters Yearning to Know Equality.' Get it?"

"Get what?" yelled Starr.

"D.Y.K. . . ."

"The censor will love that," Starr interrupted impatiently. "But maybe it's worth ten minutes. Work it up and let me see it tomorrow. Now come on. I want something bigger. Much bigger. I want heat. Real heat. Money. Power. Love. All you've been giving me so far is the standard drug and weirdo sex crap that's covered to death by the *Enquirer.* Come on now. Stretch yourselves. Let's get going."

The room was quiet for what seemed a long time before Barry Hooper, a young producer who had joined this entertainment Titanic only a month before, said, "I think I've got something."

"Don't be shy, Barry. Lay it out."

"Allison Morton."

"Gus Morton's niece? At Universal Talent Management?"

"That's her. She's beautiful. Young. Twenty-five or -six. Smart. She's a lawyer, and a lot of the heavyweight people in town say she can hold her own with them. She can't keep herself out of *Women's Wear Daily.*"

"She sounds like a fucking fairy tale. But where's the *shvitz,* for Christ's sake?" yelled Starr.

"One," said Barry, rapping his hand against the conference table, "we have power. There's a takeover struggle going on at U.T.M. that makes Carl Icahn's raids look tame. And it's this young, beautiful girl pitted against a couple of the roughest sharks who swim in that particular sea. Two, she's had an incredible affair with a New York playwright that's now on the rocks, and she's carrying a torch for the guy that could light up Ellis Island. And, to top it off, a friend of mine at L.A.P.D. says this gal has more than enough reason to look behind her back."

"Meaning what?"

"Someone has tried, and I mean more than once, to knock her off."

"I'm beginning to smell something here. Think she'll talk?"

"No way. But we don't need her. We've got so many angles and so many others who will talk that we don't need her cooperation. It's all there for the picking."

"I think I like it. It could be our set piece. Work with Gloria and get me a treatment by the end of the week. I finally feel some decent ratings on the horizon," said Mel Starr, as he lit his first Monte Cristo of the day.

PART ONE

1

Allison Morton opened her eyes. The room was dark, not a hint of light, and a cold breeze blew in the window. The chill must have awakened her. No need to get up, though, or even think about it. She pulled the blanket around her shoulders and shifted her position, but after only a few minutes she realized she was not slipping back into wooly oblivion. Instead, her mind was busy, filling up with images of herself: shaking hands, answering the telephone, sitting at a desk in an office she didn't recognize, one that was bright and airy and had a marvelous view of the Hollywood Hills. The faces of the people around her were indistinct, but she could see her own clearly: smiling and happy. Very happy.

Suddenly panicky, she snapped back to the present and fumbled for the switch on the light next to the bed. Even though it made no sense, she wondered if she had somehow missed the alarm. She blinked at the momentary unfamiliarity of her room in Gus Morton's Bel-Air house, where she had not been since July, when she left to travel in Europe. But of course she had not overslept. It wasn't yet five. She double-checked the setting on the clock—still seven-fifteen, still ready to ring—and turned off the light, though she doubted she could get back to sleep. This was the day she had been preparing for all her life. On this September day, she would cease being just Allison Morton, Smith, B.A., Harvard Law graduate, and become, in addition, Allison Morton, legal counsel for Universal Talent Management. Well, actually, the most junior counsel of a staff of eleven.

Allison had been hearing about the talent agency, which her uncle, Gus Morton, owned, since she was a child. At the end of World War II, so the story went, while Gus was debating whether to return to college on the GI Bill or find a job so he could get his hands on some money, he got a telephone call from an army buddy named Owen Lloyd. Owen used to claim he was an actor in civilian life and now, out of the blue, here he was with proof that it was true. A producer wanted to sign him to a regular spot on one of those radio variety shows that keep on running forever, and Owen asked if Gus would represent him. Even then, it was obvious to anyone who stopped to think about it that Gus Morton could sell anything, but it had never occurred to Gus to sell people's talent. He made the deal for Owen, an extra-good deal, and the rest, as Gus loved to joke, was history. He had a rough start, but it too just became part of the Gus Morton legend: his first so-called office, which was a closet masquerading as a room three floors up from the Carnegie Deli; his first secretary, who was really just the receptionist for the dentist next door and who picked up his phone during her lunch hour; his first dry spell, which immediately followed the Owen deal and lasted so long he nearly quit his new profession. But he did not. And soon, one success bred another, and he was in the business he was destined for. It took less than ten years for him to become an important agent and then, inevitably, the most important agent of all.

Allison was the daughter of Gus's brother, Teddy, and the sole member of the next generation to carry the name Morton. Gus doted on her and, as soon as she was old enough to know what an agent was, he began to groom her for a place in the company. He told her about the deals he was making and why. He encouraged her to read *Variety* and *The Hollywood Reporter*. She always asked questions about what she read in the two trade papers, and he in turn taught her how to look between the lines. During each of her summer vacations, he found her a job in a different area of the agency. As a file clerk in the rock music division, a travel booker for the concert division, a reader in the literary department. She thrived on it.

Now, as she lay in the dark that was beginning to turn to gray, she wondered again where Gus intended to start her off. Contracts would be logical, she thought—there never could be enough lawyers to keep up with those—but despite her nudging, he had not given her a clue what he had in mind, nor had Diana Paget, who headed up the legal department. The furthest her uncle would go was to say that he had a surprise for her.

Allison reached over and turned on her bedside light. Quarter past five. If she made herself a cup of tea, she might be able to concentrate on something other than questions that couldn't be answered. She could polish off the current issue of *Vanity Fair* and at least three or four chapters of the Trollope novel she had begun when she and her best friend, Cynthia Traynor, were traveling through the Greek Islands. Later she still would have time for a long shower and a real breakfast of fruit and coffee in the garden next to her room.

The guest wing of the house was its own kingdom, stretching off in the opposite direction from Gus's quarters. It consisted of three generous-sized suites, the most luxurious of which was Allison's. At the center of the house, beyond the sweeping marble-floored entrance hall, was a spacious living room with a half-dozen different sitting areas and a commanding view of the city and, next to it, Allison's favorite room, a large, oak-paneled library, lined floor to ceiling with books and memorabilia and furnished with overripe, vastly comfortable armchairs and couches, in addition to Gus's gleaming partner's desk, whose work surface was always cleared for action.

Everywhere, in all the rooms and in the halls that connected them, were pieces from Gus's eclectic furniture collection—secretaries, highboys, tables, chests, armoires, consoles, benches, chairs—all periods and all styles, with a slight preferential nod toward Art Deco and Wiener Werkstätte. Each piece was more choice than the next. One of his special prizes was a Jean-Michel Frank desk in shagreen over a delicate rosewood frame, which he kept in his bedroom. Although all the pieces were of top museum quality, Gus insisted on using them, living with them, and so they were always piled high with books, vases of flowers, odds and ends—and other collections. Collections of bronze heads, Japanese netsuke, ivory elephants and crayfish, Buddhas, and, lately, brass compasses. His other enduring passion, in addition to furniture, was art, and though Allison herself was not yet a collector of anything, one of the other lessons she had learned early from Gus was, never worry about having the right place to hang a picture or put a piece of furniture. Buy it anyway. The right spot will make itself known.

Now, as she slipped along the guest-wing corridor, past a grouping of Sargent watercolors, through the entrance hall with its Jasper Johns, Lichtenstein, Newman, and Bartlett canvases, into the library and beyond it through the pantries to the kitchen, the house breathed silently around her. Even Maria, the cook, was not yet in her domain. After the quick shriek of the teakettle, she glided in bare feet back to her room, placed the pot of tea and cup on the table next to one of the most inviting chairs, and opened her magazine. It was only then that she acknowledged a feeling of . . . what? uneasiness? Yes, that was the feeling that had begun sneaking up on her ever so quietly. She hadn't felt this way since childhood, facing the first day in a new school. She held her hand out straight in front of her and observed the small tremor, then pressed her hand into her chest. She did not really need this confirmation, but, yes, her heart had picked up some extra beats and was beginning to race rather hard. She had to admit it to herself: she was scared.

—Scared? her calmer self demanded. Isn't that too grand a word for first-day-on-the-job jitters?

—Of course I'm scared. Why shouldn't I be? Who says I can handle it?

—Don't be ridiculous. Weren't you in the top ten percent of your class? And made *Law Review*? And had to fend off the job offers? There were more than a few.

—Well, yes, that was flattering, but that's the point in a way. Instead of having to compete with everybody else for one of those plums, I was just *handed* this job. I didn't have to do a thing to get it.

—You know Gus would be crushed if you didn't join the agency. It's what he's wanted all along. More than anything.

—I suppose so, but it makes me feel . . . well . . . sort of . . . programmed.

—Oh, give yourself a break. If it doesn't work out, if you don't have that certain something, *then* you can get some mileage out of your law degree. It won't go away.

—Okay, okay, you win. Enough!

Enough indeed, thought Allison, putting down her teacup. She would have her shower now, and then begin the day all over again. Calm, confident, and ready for anything.

Gus Morton took a deep swallow of cappuccino, leaned his head against the bed pillows, and considered whether to have a second piece of toast. Unbuttered.

Gus was a pioneer of good health. His family's history of heart failure had propelled him into watching his diet as far back as the late 1950s, when the only other people who knew anything about the subject of nutrition were college students who elected it because it was a gut course. He did the easy things first, giving up ice cream, skipping the pleasures of hard sweet butter, which he used to eat by itself in sandwiches and slather on top of everything else, especially those little red and white radishes from France. These days Albert, his houseman, kept him honest in the mornings, with breakfast trays full of fresh fruits and juices, five-grain breads, and bran cereals. Even though he cheated occasionally, Gus had become something of an expert on diet and exercise, assiduously following every new development until he was so well-informed that he had startled more than one world-class heart surgeon with the extent of his knowledge. At a recent benefit, the starstruck head of cardiac surgery at Cedars-Sinai was dying to hear what it was like handling a Robert Redford or a William Hurt, but all Gus wanted to talk about over dinner was the latest research in treating blocked arteries with medication versus bypass surgery.

Gus decided against the piece of toast and pushed the tray across the linen coverlet to the edge of his bed. It was six in the morning, time to make his telephone calls to the East Coast. As he finished his coffee, he looked through the tall double windows at the foot of his bed across the lawn to the pool and to the sculptures surrounding it, just emerging now from the night's darkness—the silvery David Smith, the Richard Serra arc.

His first trip to Europe, courtesy of the U.S. Army during World War II, had shown Gus a side of himself that he had had no idea existed. In the great museums of France and Italy, he discovered he possessed a discriminating visual sense, and the more he learned, the surer he became of his instinct for line, color, and composition, for originality, and most of all, for quality. When the agency began to grow, Gus began to collect.

Now, for a moment, he studied the de Kooning painting he had hung opposite a shaped Elizabeth Murray canvas. Though he liked to change the placement of his art from time to time, he always wanted that particular de Kooning here in the bedroom with him. His eyes traveled around the room, scanning these and the other paintings and pieces of furniture. As a mental exercise, he started to calculate their worth, but quickly abandoned the effort. With auction prices in an upward spin, it could be nothing but a wild guess.

He reached for the telephone on the table next to the bed and settled it on his lap. He ran his right hand through his thick charcoal-gray hair, then shook his head and rubbed his eyes. He would be sixty-eight in two months, though anyone meeting this vigorous, exceedingly attractive man for the first time would think he was ten years younger, even on this morning when he had been awake since four o'clock. The cause of his fitful night's sleep was herself asleep in the other wing of his house. Allison . . . his thoughts lingered on her for a moment. Allison was his only blood relative and the person dearest to him in the entire world. Today, an occasion he had anticipated for a long while, would be her first day working full-time for Universal Talent Management—called U.T.M. by everyone in and out of the industry—Gus Morton's personal creation, the biggest and most powerful talent agency in the world, and a business which he intended one day to leave to his niece.

Reluctantly Gus forced Allison from his mind. He had a wonderful surprise planned for her later in the day, but there was no time to savor it now. Charlie would be picking him up as usual at seven, and he was running late. Before he showered and dressed, he wanted to speak to two of his top people who had flown to New York the day before for the opening of a new musical. A budget-buster, and virtually a family affair. U.T.M. represented two of the three producers, the director, the two stars and one of the main supporting actors, the lighting designer, and the lyricist, not to mention the hugely successful book on which the play was based. The opening had been delayed three weeks by a second act that needed reworking, set machinery that didn't function, and a pair of co-stars who liked each other about as much as the State Department cared for Qaddafi, but word was, everything had come together in the end. Gus would wait until he had spoken to Ben Wildman and Lee Simons before he believed it.

First he had one other quick call to make. A piece of unfinished business.

"All right, Frank, what's it going to be?" he asked without preamble when the phone was picked up on the third ring. As he intended, he had caught the producer—one of that small breed who pride themselves on living in New York though all their work is in L.A.—before he left for his office.

Gus smiled as he listened to the predictable sputter from the man at the other end of the phone. "Frank, I'm not the one keeping you from signing Jamison, and you know it," said Gus. He paused for an exquisitely calibrated moment and then went on. "No, we won't sign a postcard without my definition of gross. I've given you a concession on price that's so good, if it ever gets out people will be calling my agency the United Way. I hope you realize that." He paused again. "Well, Jamison loves the script and your director, so I'm willing to stretch, so much so that the Lakers will be after me to play center. Don't push me too far, though."

As the other man spoke, Gus buffed his neatly trimmed nails against the lapel of his silk robe. "No, Frank, I can't give you until the end of the week. I got another script he likes almost as much, and they're pressing me hard. *And* on my terms. Anyway, if we don't wrap this up, it'll fuck up your squash game."

As deals went, this wasn't big stuff. Don Jamison had been a star since the Metro contract-player days and Gus had been his agent all the way. He was only one of six actors and directors whom Gus personally handled. But he was slowing down, and the good parts were not coming around as frequently as they used to. Jamison was right about this role. Though not the lead, it was a part with enough meat on it to feed a hungry dog and set him up for more than a good shot at an Oscar nomination. Jesus, Jamison would have *two* death scenes. Both better than Brando's in *The Godfather*. But Gus knew that if he didn't get Jamison's standard deal on the movie, the word would get out and he'd have more trouble next time. And Don Jamison was special to him. Gus didn't want him subjected to the cold surgical hands of the deal-making vultures in this industry. Jamison had class. He deserved better and Gus would get it for him.

"You heard my terms, Frank. You want to give me less, there's no deal. Take a little from Rogers. I know what you're paying the kid for this. It only goes up his nose anyway, you know. With Jamison in the package, you have a chance to get your tux dry-cleaned so you can walk on stage and grab that piece of gold plate you'd sell your mother's pacemaker for. Now tell me, what're you going to do?"

Gus listened for a few moments, then picked up a notepad and pen. "Good man, now you're talking," he said, writing down a few lines. "That's it. Exactly. You've made the right decision. Have the contracts in my office by Thursday. Okay, Friday it is. I always knew you were a smart boy, Frank. Give my love to Rosalie and the kids." He placed the phone back on its cradle as gently as a lover touches a woman's hand in the morning.

Smiling, Gus kicked back the covers and climbed out of bed, letting the robe drop off his shoulders and onto the floor. No matter that U.T.M.'s 10 percent of the deal he had just concluded would barely register on the agency's monthly profit and loss statement. He still felt a jolt of satisfaction. It was the kind of deal he was known for, tough but fair, played out according to a code of behavior that was distinctly old-fashioned. Gus cared passionately for the bottom line, but he also cared how he got there, and it amused him that for the pains he took he was dubbed "eccentric." He had long ago discovered that he was smart enough to dictate his own rules. The fact that the rules he chose were strictly honorable was viewed by others as a personal peculiarity bordering on the irrational.

He switched on the speaker phone, dialed Ben Wildman's number in the New York office, and, naked now, moved over to the wall of closets, to the section where his shirts were ranked by Albert according to their predominant color. He wanted to wear something with a touch of burgundy in it today, maybe one of the new batch of Turnbull & Asser shirts that had arrived from London last week. The phone was answered on the second ring.

"Hello," came the voice over the speaker.

"Good morning, Ben," said Gus.

"How are you, chief?"

"Terrific." Gus paused. "Lee, are you there?"

A wet, rasping cough that sounded as if it had been dredged up from a riverbottom came in response. "Barely," said a woman's petulant voice after a moment. "I feel like Pol Pot's been working me over. Really, Gus, why did you make us come into the office at this ungodly hour? We were out partying at Elaine's until . . . what time was it, Ben?"

"I don't know about you, but I got back to the hotel at three-thirty."

"All right, you two," said Gus, "give it to me straight. How did it go over? If it's good news, stretch it out. If it's bad, keep it crisp. You know who said that? S. J. Perelman. Now that was one smart cookie."

"*Gus* is the one who's a smart cookie," said Ben, placing the phone back in its cradle.

Beyond the office where he and Lee Simons sat, the noises that signal the beginning of the business day had replaced the dead quiet of a half hour earlier. U.T.M. occupied two floors at 30 Rockefeller Plaza. The theatrical and literary divisions of the agency had grown so rapidly that they had put the squeeze on those in the company who used the space only on an occasional basis, but Ben, who was a snob about addresses as well as about people and just about everything else, would have been horrified if Gus had decided they should decamp to larger quarters in one of the dreary buildings along Sixth Avenue, or, God forbid, downtown. Rockefeller Center was part of Ben's New York image.

When Lee did not react to his comment, Ben bubbled on. "I'm constantly amazed by him. He never misses a thing. Just a few weeks ago we were discussing the score, you know, those bars at the end of the first act that Alan changed, and I realized then that Gus knew it better than Alan, the whole score, and Alan wrote the damn thing. Gus is so quick about everything."

"Oh, sure," said Lee, exhaling an exaggerated cloud of smoke from her cigarette before stubbing it out. She was short and thin in an undernourished way, with blunt features that looked like a cartoonist's rough sketch of a face. "He's quick to throw up smokescreens too. I hope you noticed he mentioned everything but what's on his mind. How long do you think she'll last?"

"Who?"

"Who's asleep in Gus Morton's house right now and about to embark on a career guaranteed to head in only one direction?"

"Allison?"

"Who do you think I'm talking about? Fergie?"

"Allison's as bright as anyone I've ever met. She's just like Gus," said Ben, picking up and squeezing the small pink rubber balls that he called spaldeens, which he always carried with him to strengthen his grip. He was irked at having his morning exercise routine upset by the phone call. His hotel had a gym, but he had had to skip his daily thirty minutes on the stationary bicycle and half of his bench presses.

"Jesus Christ!" Lee went on. "It's one thing to spout the party line, but to take it up the ass . . . Ooops! Pardon me."

"Enough with the gay jokes, Lee. I am what I am."

"She *is* bright, but big fucking deal. Do you know how many spoiled brats from Harvard Law have been in and out of U.T.M. in the last couple of years? It's not as if they're in short supply. Only, *their* last names haven't been Morton."

"Lee . . ."

"Ben . . ." mimicked Lee in a whiny voice. "And would you cut it out with those—if you'll excuse the expression—balls. You're making me nervous. Though I'll grant you it wouldn't take much today to fucking unhinge me."

Ben gave Lee a nasty look and put the two balls down on the desk.

"Thank you, darling," Lee gushed. "You know that old saying, don't you? If it floats, flies, or fucks, rent it. Well, add lawyers to that. Especially a certain young thing who happens to have been born with a golden spoon in her mouth *and* in her ass. She's going to be eaten up! Putting an innocent like that in our business is a joke. And if Gus thinks that for even one moment I'm going to work for her—"

"Take it easy, Lee. Don't kid me, or yourself. You're not going to work for another agency. Where else would you get such a good deal?"

"Lots of places, but don't let yourself forget one important thing: Gus is not immortal. What happens the day he can't work anymore?"

"Exactly what we've always talked about. We'll run the show."

"Yeah, I guess so, but that bitch of a niece had better not throw anything out of whack." Lee lit another cigarette and stood up. "I'm going back to the Sherry for a few hours. Where's our lunch date with that twerp novelist Gilliam wants us to meet? The Four Seasons?"

"Right you are. In the Grill. Twelve-thirty. But stay and have a cup of coffee. I was about to ask the receptionist to make some for us."

"No, thanks, Ben dear. Nothing personal, but I need some more sleep *and* a little something else that, if I'm not mistaken, will be waiting in my bed for me. Ciao." Lee gave a short, suggestive laugh, turned on her heel and disappeared.

In the silence that ensued, Ben picked up the spaldeens again and started rhythmically squeezing them, counting to ten, then pausing, then counting to ten again, as he thought about what Lee had said. Gus Morton was everything in the world to him. He was Gus's oldest employee and had worked for Gus since his early twenties, almost thirty-five years now. He was proud of the association and of what the length of it said about his value to the agency, and he knew everyone at U.T.M. considered him to be Gus's second in command.

The distance between them, however, was greater than Ben's position suggested, for after all these years, he still hero-worshipped Gus. And emulated him—without, as he was all too aware, entirely pulling it off. Gus Morton was precise and understated in his custom-tailored suits, but Ben could not resist buying what was newest and trendiest in clothing and then flaunting its cost. One way or the other he always contrived to let his jacket flop open or his tie twist around so that the expensive designer labels could be read. He had had some success in modulating his New York accent, but just as he was intoning Noël Coward British, his Bronx adenoidal beginnings tended to pop out for all to hear. Although his barber was a master at creating subtle hair pieces to disguise his thinning growth, his manicurist did him in by finishing his nails with a too-visible layer of polish that made them gleam like a store mannequin's. The one area in which he indisputably outshone Gus was in physical condition. It was his obsession, and in this realm he had transformed a naturally unimpressive body into a model of physical fitness. He would be the first to say it had made all the difference to his private life.

Whatever his personal traits, however, Ben was *the* mainstay of the agency. He was a masterful negotiator, a compendium of information on all aspects of the business, and, maybe most important, absolutely loyal to Gus. Wasn't it time—past time, to be honest—for Gus to reward him for his service to the agency?

The thought of what had not yet occurred was a small but intolerable splinter of dissatisfaction under Ben's skin. Gus had made him promises, hinted broadly more than once that Ben was in line for the title of chief operating officer, but that had been over a year ago and he had said nothing to Ben since. So what that he was executive V.P.? Lee had the same title, as did Diana Paget and Parker Welles. Ben had hoped that he wouldn't have to remind Gus of their conversations, but he knew now that he must, that he would, and what better time could there be than now, with Allison joining the agency? Yes, he would talk to Gus—maybe even tomorrow, when he was back in L.A.

Buoyed by his resolve, Ben focused his gaze admiringly on his flexing arm muscles. Some people teased him about his tenacious dedication to exercise but really, he asked himself now, only half-jokingly, what was wrong with looking one's best?

At precisely seven, Gus settled himself in the backseat of his white Rolls and waited for his chauffeur, Charlie Horner, to hand him his briefcase. Though Charlie was almost six feet six and weighed in at more than 250 pounds, he slid gracefully and quickly into the driver's seat. Before he put the car in gear, he patted his chauffeur's cap to make sure it was secure. He had lost all his hair when he was in his forties and, still sensitive about it, always wore a hat of some kind to hide his baldness.

The white of the automobile was not a standard tone but had a subtle blush of pink in it that made it a little softer and warmer than other whites. L.A. car buffs called it "Gus Morton White," though few could have known that Gus's inspiration for it was the hint of pink that appears in the innermost center of a white peony. A small funky body shop that Charlie had discovered in the Valley had mixed up one sample after another until Gus saw just the shade he liked, and from that time on each new car he bought received coat after coat of his signature white lacquer.

Before pulling out of the driveway, Charlie took a peek at his boss in the rearview mirror. *The Wall Street Journal, The Los Angeles Times,* and *The New York Times,* neatly folded and waiting for him as they were each day, remained on the seat beside him, untouched. Often Gus liked to schmooze with Charlie on the short drive to the office, about the Dodgers, the Lakers, or the Rams, about whether Hagler was too old to come back, about what movies Charlie had seen and liked, and occasionally about the past, for he and Charlie had shared a lot together. Today, though, Charlie knew, even before Gus greeted him, that this morning would not be a time for talk. It was Allison's first day at the agency, and Charlie knew better than most people just what that meant to the boss.

He and Gus went back to World War II, when one day it had fallen to Gus, who was an officer in the same company in Anzio, to drag Charlie's enormous, beefy frame to safety from the ditch where he lay, shot through both legs. Sometime in the year after the war ended, this grateful ex-infantryman, still only a teenager, showed up on Gus's doorstep, insisting that the man to whom he owed his life give him a job to do—anything at all; he didn't care if he earned any money for it, just so he could start paying Gus back. Charlie ran messages, subbed as a janitor, even took stints answering the phone in Gus's two-bit office above the deli, but as U.T.M. prospered, his rightful role became clear. From then on, it was

Charlie who was at the wheel of the ever larger white cars in Gus's fleet, and soon Gus never rode in a car that Charlie Horner didn't drive. Whether in Los Angeles or New York or London. Gus kept identical cars in all three cities.

Big-hearted, faithful, loyal, Charlie over the years had been a witness to Gus Morton's professional and personal life—his life with brother Teddy and Teddy's awful wife, Françoise, with Gus's first and only wife, Laura, later with Diana, and always with Allison, especially Allison. He remembered the first time Gus had laid eyes on the infant Allison, the party in New York on her first birthday, the first time Teddy and Françoise left the little girl alone for a nice long visit with her uncle Gus in California.

And Charlie remembered that snowy drive to Allison's school, the first year she attended it—in the late 1960s, it must have been—for the kindergarten Christmas pageant. It marked Allison's debut as an actress. She played an angel.

The snowstorm had started early and by midmorning a carpet of white, thick as a fist, covered the streets and sidewalks of New York. Charlie drove up Madison Avenue with particular care. Not only was the road devilishly slippery, but the Eldorado was brand new, so new that the surfaces of its sleek white exterior shone like beacons through the soft tumble of flakes that was fast making the air as dense as a steambath.

North of Eighty-sixth Street, Charlie gently applied the brakes. Two cars in front of the Eldorado had not been able to make it up the slight rise in the road and had brought all traffic to a stop. Charlie, his attention free to wander, listened discreetly to the voices in the backseat.

"But I don't see why we need O'Brien. There's nobody he handles that we don't. Actors, directors, writers, musicians. You name it, we've got it, and more and better. What's so special about him?" That was Teddy Morton, Gus's older brother. Decent, but unimaginative.

"Television, that's why. For reasons one to one hundred. O'Brien is shrewd. Got into packaging early. Only he needs more talent to package with. So do we, but we've got one big advantage. We've got the money to convince him it's time for him to pull up a chaise in Boca Raton and let us run his show. The price we pay him will look like peanuts in a couple of years." That was the boss speaking, of course.

"You really think so?"

"Would I say so if I didn't? Look, Teddy, I want to expand. O'Brien is small, just a boutique, but his clients are gilt-edged. I can use them. And also, it'll be one less agency to compete with. Don't you see? I want to build the biggest talent agency in the world. And I'm not going to let anyone, *anyone,* stop me. I don't care if his name is Lastfogel or Mao. Why should a few guys have it all to themselves? But, Teddy," Gus's voice softened perceptibly, "you don't have to concern yourself with any of this. Just watch out for the concert division, all right? What's the problem there, by the way? I saw we lost out on that new piano whiz—what's his name, you know who I mean—and you don't look too hot lately. Are you all right?"

Teddy's reply was lost in a cacophony of whirring tires and blaring horns as the traffic gave signs of opening up. Charlie, his eavesdropping time over, checked the cars behind him in the rearview mirror, catching one more glimpse of the boss and his brother. They had the same wavy black hair and the same strong, muscular build, but everything else about them was different. One of the differences was the gaudy-looking woman wedged between them, Teddy's wife, Françoise.

"We'll be no more than an hour, Charlie," Gus said when they pulled up in front of Allison's school. He was followed out of the cocoon of warmth in the car by Françoise. Swirls of vibrant red hair snaked out from beneath her large fox hat, which resembled a scaled-down version of the headpieces worn by the Queen's guards. She tottered in the snow on heels the size of a man's span until her husband grabbed her by the elbow as he emerged last from the car.

"Oh, my shoes!" she complained in a grating voice, winning from Gus a look of disgust mixed with rampant dislike as he watched her pick her way over the snow to the sidewalk. "Let's not stay more than half an hour, all right, Teddy?" she went on obliviously. "I don't want to be late for my lunch date at Côte Basque." This time it was Teddy's turn to look fed up, and then the heavy red door closed behind the unhappily matched threesome. . . .

"Charlie. *Charlie!*" Gus Morton's voice was insistent, startling the other man from his daydreaming. He turned around and looked at Gus quizzically.

Gus laughed. "You know, it really is very comfortable here, I'd never dispute that, but unfortunately I don't get as much work done in the car as I do in my office."

"Oh, sorry, boss," said Charlie, his large face reddening as he realized he must have been daydreaming. How long had they been sitting here in the Rolls, he wondered, as he hurried around to open the back door for Gus.

"Where were you, my good man?" said the boss with a grin. And then, at seven-twenty exactly, as on every day, Gus Morton pulled open the heavy, black glass doors of the U.T.M. Building and disappeared from sight.

"Good morning, Gus darling." The tall blonde spoke in a low, sensuous voice as she leaned down and brushed her lips against Gus's. "I've missed you."

Diana Paget put her portfolio down on the ivory inlay of Gus's desk and walked over to the sideboard to pour herself a cup of coffee. It was only a few minutes past eight, and this would be the first pot of the day brewed by Gus's secretary, Lillian. For all his concern about good health, Gus had been unable to break his coffee habit.

Diana was in her late forties and still lovely, with a figure as strong and graceful as when she had graduated from Stanford Law. She had joined U.T.M. immediately after Stanford and for the last dozen years had run the legal division. She had been playing in the men's league well before it was customary (without losing a drop of her femininity), and anyone sitting across from her at the negotiating table knew what to expect: a gritty clear-headed opponent who knew motion picture and theatrical law cold. She and Gus had been lovers for years, always together on the social circuit, on weekends, and on most nights, when Diana stayed with Gus in Bel-Air rather than at her own house on Mulholland Drive. Last night and the night before, the first time Gus had seen Allison since her trip to Europe, had been exceptions.

"Would you like some more coffee?" Diana asked, holding the pot up to Gus. She was wearing an Ungaro in a small black-and-white checked pattern with a straight skirt and fitted sleeves. Draped over one shoulder was a folded scarf of the same fabric, lined in red, which added a dash of drama.

Gus leaned back in his moroccan leather chair and nodded, and Diana, refilling his cup, continued, "Where would you like me to begin?"

"Start easy and work up."

Diana laughed. "You're not going to be thrilled with anything I have for today, though I do see a bit of give on Skip Frank's vacation request. Shall I lead off with him?"

Gus nodded, and Diana sat down and pulled a list of notes from her portfolio. Her progress report on contracts, litigations, and any other pending legal matters was always on Gus's early morning agenda, for no matter how much time they spent alone in each other's company, in town or at one of Gus's houses in Trancas, Palm Springs, or Sun Valley, they never discussed business. Gossip, yes, and plenty of overheated exchanges about who liked or did not like a movie, play, or book involving one of U.T.M.'s clients and why, but nothing more substantive. Maybe he went overboard on the subject, Gus freely admitted, but he swore he did not know a single couple who had survived working together unless they drew a firm line between their business and their personal lives. Nothing was so important that it couldn't wait until the next day. The new contract for Skip Frank, TV's number one daytime talk-show host for three years running, was a case in point. The negotiations were not leisurely, but each side was taking its time. Gus was more than certain that U.T.M. would prevail in the end, and then what did it matter that it might have been wrapped up a few weeks sooner?

Diana brought Gus up-to-date. Gus had wanted the network to double Skip's salary and in addition give him ten weeks off instead of six. For several months the network had flatly declined to discuss these terms and then had approached them only on a kind of ad hoc basis, grudgingly granting him an extra three weeks' vacation this past summer, but at last the impasse was showing real signs of thawing.

"They're within an inch of our salary demand now, and I know we can push them over," said Diana, "but they claim they can't go beyond eight weeks off. They got too much flak this year from the local stations, they said. But I don't believe them. I went over this again with Lee on Friday, and she agrees. I think it's just the hardheadedness of the new management. They're testing us."

"You're right, I'm sure of it. Tell them this. Tell them I know what Skip's electrocardiogram and blood-sugar count look like. They don't. He *needs* ten weeks off a year. It's not negotiable. One little thing, darling. I don't want any more coffee, but could you get me a glass of Pelligrino with lots of ice?"

As soon as Diana handed him the glass, he almost drained it. "Is it hot in here or is it me? Okay, what's next?"

"The *Farfel and Company* spin-off."

"Don't tell me Friedman hasn't come around yet."

Diana shook her head. "No, he hasn't budged, and he's getting a little nasty. Nasty and cocky. I suspect he figures Ronnie is expendable and that the show will work just as well with another actor, but he's wrong, I think."

Andy Friedman, the producer of *Farfel*, which was firmly positioned in the middle of the Nielsen top ten for the second year running, was riding high, but so was its star, a comic named Ronnie Whitlaw, whose sudden elevation to pop star rank had been long overdue. Now Friedman wanted to do a spin-off of the original show, which made sense, but he was having difficulty making one important connection that Gus Morton insisted on. The lead character of the spin-off would be based on a character Ronnie had been using in his nightclub act for years. Ronnie, Gus reasoned, deserved an exec-producer credit and more than a decent piece of the action on the new show.

"Hang in there, sweetheart. Friedman seems to be having a little trouble with his ABCs. Explain to him that (A) he's looking at more than one hundred million in syndication rights if Ronnie plays in *Farfel* for three more years; (B) he's kidding himself badly if he thinks the show will last without Ronnie; and (C) either Ronnie gets a real taste of the spin-off or I yank him from *Farfel*. Immediately. How's that sound?"

"Sounds good to me. But I'm not a twerp named Andy Friedman, who thinks now that he drives a Rolls he's ready for a cabinet appointment."

In quick succession, Diana presented Gus with the latest developments on a three-picture deal with Warner for Reno Taylor, which was right on target as to money and the star's rights of approval, but which still didn't give the actor a shot at directing the third picture; Metro's continued refusal to do a negative pickup on a picture U.T.M. had packaged because the videocassette rights had been sold off in advance; NBC's interest in buying Clayton Ryder's music publishing company, but only if all his future work was included in the deal; and on and on until Diana stopped talking, closed her notebook, and looked up.

"Is that it?" asked Gus.

"For now it is." Diana looked at her watch. It was only eight-thirty. "Time for some small talk?" she asked, smiling.

"I'd love it, darling, but I'm expecting Parker soon. And I've got a little thinking to do."

"About Allison, by any chance?" said Diana, standing up.

"Why do you say that?"

"You're as jumpy as a cat."

Gus shrugged. Diana waited for a moment, but when it became clear that he wasn't interested in talking about Allison or about anything else and that he wanted to be alone, she left his office.

As she walked back to legal, she thought how much things were going to change now with Allison at the agency. Diana had been dreading this day for so long, it seemed as if it had been there, waiting, all her life. It wasn't enough that Allison had come between her and Gus in so many ways since the beginning; now Diana's professional life with Gus would change too. Why kid herself? She knew she was important to Gus, but only *after* Allison, whose every mood and need preoccupied him. Oh, if he only felt that way toward her. Maybe if they had married, as Diana had thought they would so many years earlier, it would be different. But that had not happened. Perhaps Gus just didn't want to share Allison with anyone. Perhaps the little bit of Gus that was Diana's alone would now be lost. A storm of thoughts roiled through her, and almost every one started with, "If only . . ."

As he watched Diana depart, Gus wondered what he would do without her in his life. He loved her so much. Why didn't he let her know that more often?

When she had come to work for him, he had fallen for her, immediately. Heedlessly. He was twenty years older than she, and married, but that didn't matter. There was no chance of his marrying her—how could he have divorced Laura, lying unconscious in a hospital bed, there because of his own selfishness?—and later, when Laura died, he still had made no move. What a mistake, and how it had complicated things between Diana and Allison. It crushed him that Diana viewed Allison as a rival for his love, but she had forgiven him for so much over the years that he knew he must forgive her this.

Gus buzzed Lillian. "Ring Parker, will you, and tell him I can't see him now, but could he make it around nine-thirty instead. After Allison."

Allison . . . Effortlessly, Gus conjured up his memory of the moment he had known that his deepest wish, that she join the agency, might come true. He and his good friend and client, Oscar Buckman, were attending a performance of *Three Sisters* at Allison's school. It had been on a spring evening nearly ten years ago.

" 'Where? Where is it all gone? Where is it? Oh, my God, my God! I've forgotten everything. . . .' "

Allison Morton, in the role of Irina, the youngest of Chekhov's sisters, moved stage left into the arms of her sister Olga. In spite of her stage tears, she looked thoroughly enchanting in a long pale green dress with a high neck, her thick black hair swept away from her face and held back in a loose knot.

" *'I've forgotten . . .'* " continued Allison, heartbroken, " *'it's muddled in my head. . . . I don't remember what* window *is in Italian, or the ceiling there . . . I'm forgetting everything, every day forgetting, and life slips away and will never return, never, we'll never go to Moscow . . . I can see we'll never go!'* "

"Depressing, isn't it?" said Gus Morton, as he and his guest stepped out into the cool evening air a few minutes later for the last intermission.

" *'Amo, amas, amat,'* " said Oscar, quoting the third sister. "Masha gets to me with that remark every time I see the play. Best role, I think. But Irina's no walk-on either."

"I don't know if you've seen more of these school productions than I have, but what I wonder is, why can't they have a little more fun? Last year it was, God help us, *Winterset.*"

Oscar groaned.

"I see you agree," continued Gus. "All I ask for is a little Neil Simon. Well, maybe that's going too far. Even Tennessee Williams would be a good change. At least he's lively."

"More impenetrable these days, I'd say."

"True, but I'd take a shouting match any day over all these tears."

"You might, but not the rest of the good folk in the audience. Remember, it's bad form to raise your voice. This part of the world still takes its Emily Post seriously," said Oscar, laughing as he lit his cigar.

The cigar smoke was like a flare, alerting anyone who had missed it that the only director ever to win two Academy Awards and four Tonys was present. Oscar was one of Gus's oldest clients, and when Gus learned over lunch one day at 21 that Oscar frequently weekended with friends on Lake Waramaug, near Allison's boarding school, he prevailed upon him to join him at a performance of the school's spring play. Allison, who was in her junior year, was passionate about a career in acting. Already she was lobbying Gus to let her forgo college in favor of enrolling with Lee Strasberg in New York.

As the lights flickered for curtain time, Gus caught a glimpse of the head of the drama department huddling with two assistants at the other side of the lobby. They had their eyes firmly on Oscar.

"Don't look now," said Gus, "but if we don't hurry back to our seats, you're going to get an invitation to speak to the cast after the performance."

When the final curtain had fallen and the players had wrung every last drop of applause from the partisan audience, Gus and Oscar strolled out into the night air again. Oscar relit his cigar, and the two men walked slowly around the courtyard in front of the auditorium, stretching their legs before Gus went backstage to see his niece.

"I'm so proud of Allison," said Gus. "She didn't flub a single line."

"You know, I don't believe I've seen her since she was twelve. She's become a real beauty."

"Thank you. I agree. I'm her legal guardian now, by the way. Her mother remarried and disappeared to Switzerland after Teddy died. I would have paid her to do it, but fortunately she came up with the idea herself. Now, Oscar," said Gus, seizing the man's arm, "I need your opinion. Your honest, objective opinion. Allison's fascinated by acting. She's grown up with it, and she wants it for herself. Tell me what you really think. Has she got the talent for it?"

"Well, she has some talent. . . ."

"No," said Gus impatiently, "I'm not interested in 'some.' I mean real talent. We both know what a brutal profession it is. Can she make it?"

Oscar stopped walking and drew on his cigar thoughtfully. "I owe my career to you, Gus," he said after a moment. "You were the first person to have confidence in me. And you've never wavered. You always found work for me. Good work. And when it counted most. You remember that bad patch of mine. When was it? Twenty-five years ago? Seems hard to believe now. But my point is, I don't want to jeopardize our relationship. For anything. Promise me you won't be hurt if I tell the truth."

"Of course," said Gus quickly.

Oscar slowly blew a ring of smoke into the cool night air. He tapped a large ash off the end of his cigar and watched it disappear into the gravel driveway before he looked up.

"I wouldn't say Allison has no talent," he began carefully. "She has . . . a little. But for the big time? No. No way."

"Oscar, that's the best news you could have given me!"

Oscar Buckman, startled, looked at Gus in bewilderment. "What do you mean?"

"I mean," said Gus exultantly, "that I've always wanted to bring Allison into the business. I never thought she could act worth shit, but I didn't know that for sure. Now, thanks to you, I do. Now she has no excuse not to come into the agency after she's finished her education." Gus glanced at his watch. In his pocket he felt the new, tissue-wrapped charm he had for her bracelet. The Greek masks. "I'm going backstage. I won't be long."

"Let her down gently," said Oscar wistfully.

"What do you think the definition of a doting uncle is? *Me.* But not to worry, I have no intention of spoiling this evening with any heart-to-heart talks. . . ."

The intercom button on Gus's phone gave a short ring, interrupting his reverie. It wasn't nine yet, but he thought it must be Allison.

"Send her in," he said before his secretary spoke, and then he stopped to listen. "All right, tell Harrison I'll see him, but it'll have to be brief. What a way to begin the day."

2

___

At five minutes to nine, Allison walked into the lobby of the Universal Talent Management Building. As she waited for the elevator, she smiled at a couple of young women about her age, whose faces she recognized, then glanced at herself in the mirrored wall beside her as soon as they turned away. Her handsome gold link choker, long black hair, and deep tan complemented her new gray Armani suit perfectly, she thought, and the short skirt showed off her legs to advantage. She had struck just the right note, she was sure of it. Tailored but stylish.

As she got off the elevator on the executive floor, she almost bumped into Diana Paget. The two women hugged each other closely, with smiles and cries of delight. If either one of them was asked, each would maintain that they were the best of friends. In fact, they were bound together, like a delicately balanced sauce, by the person at the center of both of their lives: Gus Morton.

"You look marvelous, dear," said Diana, squeezing Allison's hand. "Are you excited?"

"Of course. Can't you tell?"

Diana nodded. "I'll see you later, all right?"

As Allison stepped into Gus's outer office, a burst of loud laughter echoed from behind her uncle's closed door.

"Harrison Rappaport," said Gus's secretary, Lillian, smiling at Allison. "He should be leaving soon."

Before Allison could sit down to wait, the door to Gus's office was flung open. "Allison, honey!" shouted Gus delightedly, as if her appearance outside his office were completely unexpected. He kissed her, then turned to the short, bearded screenwriter who had followed him out of his office. "Harry here has just come up with a brilliant idea. It's going to make *L.A. Law* look like a cable access show. The networks will kill for it."

Rappaport received the tribute silently, as his due. Allison watched him tug on his beard as contentedly as a cat licks its chops. Gus slapped him on the shoulders, propelling him forward as he congratulated him. "I'll talk to you this afternoon after I make that call we spoke about. Lillian, see Harry to the elevator, please."

Gus ushered Allison into his office and shut the door behind them. "That little *vunce*. He *is* talented. No question about it. But so sanctimonious and pleased with himself! He never refers to what he's writing as simply a 'script.' God forbid! It's always 'the work.' Still, he has a popular feel in his gut as good as Betty Crocker's, so until he loses it, I'll just have to listen to him with the attention of a Boswell. Enough of that egomaniac. How do you feel now that you're here?"

"Wonderful."

"You know, Allison, darling," said Gus, taking her hands in his, suddenly serious, "I'm so proud of you. You've never ever let me down."

"I hope I never do."

"You're going to take to the agency beautifully. You have it in you to become a great agent. You're bright. You're strong. You're independent. People naturally like you. *And* you have it in your blood. I believe that with all my being."

"I've waited for this day for a long time, Uncle Gus."

"So have I, darling."

He held her hands tightly for emphasis, then suddenly the phone on his desk buzzed. "Of course. Send him in," he said into the receiver.

A middle-aged man with a burly physique, sallow skin, and straight dark hair edging into gray entered the room. He was in shirtsleeves and his double-knit pants were creased. He seemed out-of-place in this elegant setting, but he moved forward confidently.

"Good morning, Mr. M. You wanted to see me?"

"Yes, Mario. I want you to meet my niece, Allison. Allison, this is Mario Petrucelli. You're going to be working for Mario."

Allison stared at her uncle. Something was dreadfully wrong.

"Mario runs the mailroom," said Gus. "He's brilliant at it. It's the best in the business. No—in the world! And it's the heartbeat of the agency. There's no place like it for learning U.T.M. inside out."

"But, Uncle Gus . . ."

"Don't say it. You have a law degree. And you'll do lawyer's work. Later. When you're ready. And you'll make yourself ready by working your way out of the mailroom. And the knowledge that you'll take out with you will be indispensable."

"But, Uncle Gus—" Allison began again, shocked. Was this the surprise he had told her about?

"Allison, I don't want to hear another word," Gus cut in sharply.

"Everybody starts in the mailroom. Everybody. It's a U.T.M. tradition. I'm amazed you didn't guess I had it in mind for you."

Allison turned and followed Mario out of her uncle's office, too stunned to speak. She felt . . . betrayed. Yes, betrayed was the word. And by Uncle Gus!

"Our operation's in the basement," said Mario as they waited for the elevator. She noticed his undershirt, outlined beneath the thin fabric of his shirt.

"I hope you don't mind if I make an observation, Allison," he continued in a friendly fashion, his eyes slipping from her face to her linen jacket and back again. "I don't think you should wear fancy . . . I mean, dressy clothes like those. Or that kind of jewelry. It's pretty hard to stay clean doing the kind of work you'll have to do. So, unless you want monster dry-cleaning bills you'd be smart to look at what the others are wearing. You'll get some good ideas from them."

The doors of the elevator opened and Allison stepped in behind Mario without a word. The slow, inexorable descent to the building's basement seemed to take forever. When the doors finally parted again, Allison, feeling more depressed and alone than she ever had before, followed Mario Petrucelli, her new boss, into the mailroom.

3

That first day went by with an excruciating slowness intensified by the humiliation Allison felt. In addition to the permanent members of the mailroom staff, there were twenty others like herself, she discovered—young, aspiring trainees, starting out at the bottom, being tested by a job that bored them as much as summer work had during high school.

What added to Allison's discomfort was the realization that the entire mailroom crew knew who she was. She was sure some of them were smiling behind her back. Several times that day she had to steel herself against going to her uncle's office and telling him she couldn't handle this. She couldn't believe he would do this to her. She was a lawyer! Top 10 percent at Harvard! How could she learn the business by operating a postage meter, sealing scripts in Jiffy bags, and pushing a wire mailcart from office to office? And running errands—twice that day, for one young agent alone, Rob Loomis, who wanted the frames on his sunglasses changed and then, at ten minutes before five o'clock, his car washed.

"Make sure you go to the brushless place on Melrose. The finish on my Lotus is as sensitive as a baby's tush," he said, smiling as he tossed the keys to Allison.

Just as Allison was about to leave with Loomis's car, Mario Petrucelli called her over to his old-fashioned clerk's desk in a corner of the mailroom.

"It's Mr. M., I mean, your uncle," he said, handing her the phone.

"How's it going?" asked Gus, his voice brimming with affection.

"Well, I guess . . ." she said, trying to think of something positive or at least neutral, because what she really wanted to tell her uncle couldn't be said in front of Mario.

"First days are always a little strange and exciting. Though it's frowned upon to leave early on the day you start, I have a little surprise for you. Why don't you meet me in the lobby in five minutes?"

Another one of his special surprises? thought Allison grimly. Maybe he now wanted her to put on a pair of coveralls and start cleaning the building! Her anger and mortification were still so strong that the idea of even seeing him made her wonder if she could control her rage. When she met with him next, she decided, it would be with a clear head and firm resolve. She couldn't stay in the mailroom a day longer, but telling him that would have to wait till she felt calmer.

"I can't meet you now, Uncle Gus. I have to take Rob Loomis's car out to be washed," she responded in a flat tone. The absurdity of the statement made her want to laugh. Gallows humor at best.

"Really? Well, I believe I can still pull a string or two around here. Put Mario on the phone. I imagine that this once he can find someone else to handle Rob's car. But no one can accuse you of not taking your job seriously," he said with obvious pride.

As Charlie chauffeured the Rolls along Sunset Boulevard a few minutes later and then up into the hills above it, Allison's uncle inundated her with questions about her first day at U.T.M. The listlessness of her answers seemed not to register on him. The "surprise" was probably drinks and dinner at a quiet restaurant and yet more discussion of her career start in the mailroom. Would this day ever end?

And then she realized that the car was stopping. They had pulled into the driveway of a rosy-pink Spanish stucco building.

"Well, what do you think?" asked Gus as they got out of the car.

"It's nice." She looked around for signs that this was a restaurant. It sure didn't look like one.

"I would think that someone seeing the very first house she owned would be a little more . . . well, excited," he said, putting a ring of keys into her hand and hugging her.

"Oh, Uncle Gus!" Allison finally managed to say. The frustrations of the day still hung over her, and the joy she knew she should be feeling about this beautiful house—*her* house—curdled in her stomach. The idea that she was now the owner of what had to be the finest house belonging to anyone who worked in a mailroom anywhere in the world seemed more comical than anything else. She knew her attitude was insufferable, but she couldn't help it.

The house was built on three levels that tumbled down the hillside to a spacious deck overlooking one of the most spectacular views of the city that she had ever seen. The house's previous owner, Gus told her, had moved to Rome. With Allison in mind, he had had his eye on the property for years, he said, but the woman had resisted selling it. Finally persistence and good luck had paid off. As Allison walked through the place with him, struggling silently with her bad humor, the house began to win her over. She found herself being charmed by its proportions, its unexpected angles and subtle colors, and by its former owner's taste in furnishings. The honey-colored Mission-style rocker, the bright Navaho rug draped across the sofa, the loosely slip-covered, sand-colored sofa and armchairs were all pieces that Allison could live with happily until she made it over for herself. On the dining room table an exquisite raku bowl held a large bunch of Shasta daisies. A bottle of Lillet rested in a crystal bowl of ice, and on the counter were fresh coffee beans, oranges, and a loaf of fresh-baked bread, the makings of her first breakfast. In the bedroom, the clothes she had left at her uncle's that morning had been hung in the closet and neatly arranged in the drawers of a low, spacious pine bureau. He had thought of everything!

Come on, brighten up, Allison chastised herself. *This should be the happiest day of your life. As soon as Uncle Gus understands how you really feel about the mailroom, the whole dreadful episode will be over.*

"I love it, Uncle Gus. All of it," she said with real delight.

"Well—my little tour isn't quite over yet. You know what one of the saddest sights in L.A. is?"

"I haven't a clue," she answered, recognizing the mischievous glint in her uncle's eyes.

"It's people sitting on benches waiting for a bus to come. I always thought it was a fitting subject for Hopper to paint. This really is a car town," he concluded, as he walked her out the front door and over to the driveway to a set of garage doors.

"What am I supposed to do now?" Allison asked.

"Nothing, until we get these doors open." He grinned as he turned a key on the side of the garage that raised the doors.

There, nestled into one of two parking spaces, was what was obviously Gus's pièce de résistance: a gleaming new red BMW with Allison's initials painted in silver enamel on the driver's door.

"Uncle Gus!" She was truly speechless with pleasure. He could take her breath away with his instinct for exactly what would please her most.

"Give it a whirl, honey," he said, handing her the keys. "I'd love to go for a drive with you, but I've got to head home now. I'll see you tomorrow."

The first thing Allison wanted to do before taking the car out was to change her clothes, shed the elegant silk and linen that reminded her of where she had spent her day and where she would be going tomorrow, but as soon as she stepped into the bedroom, she dropped onto the bed— just for a few minutes of rest, she told herself. The tightness that all day long had held her with the grip of a large boa constrictor, joined now by the giddy excitement of the last half hour, had drained her of energy, and within minutes she fell into a dreamless sleep as empty as the screen in a theater after the audience has gone home. Only the persistent ringing of the phone next to her bed brought her out of it. Eight-thirty. She had slept for over two hours.

"Hello," said Allison, her voice thick with sleep.

"Hi there, superagent. I called your uncle's house and Albert gave me this number. Well, how was it, the first day at work? Line up any flicks for Kevin Costner? Or are you setting up another tour for The Boss?" laughed Cynthia Traynor, her voice full of the humor and friendship that had helped Allison through countless bad times during college and law school.

"Cyn . . . God, it's good to hear from you," Allison said, coming to.

"Well, don't keep me dangling. How's it going? Tell me *all* about it. What does your uncle have you doing? I want to hear everything. I can't begin to tell you how *te*dious it is at this pres*ti*gious Wall Street law firm. I spent the whole day reading securities cases, looking for a precedent that you couldn't squeeze a termite through, not even a particularly small termite."

"Well," answered Allison, haltingly. "The first day at a job is never the most interesting." That, she thought, was the understatement of the year. "I'm familiarizing myself with contracts." Sure, by putting them in envelopes and licking them closed. "I doubt if I'll get into any good stuff for a while." Another great understatement. Allison looked up at a mirror on the opposite wall. The thin smile that had incongruously appeared on her face would never have fooled her friend. And, at that, she confessed to Cynthia the truth about her job.

"I'll call you again tomorrow," said Cynthia after listening to Allison's catalog of woes. "Better yet, you call me. Got to run now. It's late. Have to be in by seven tomorrow to ferret out more nuggets of legal trivia. One is judged here, as you well know, by one's staying power. Put in the hours, is the motto of an associate. Hang in there, Allie, and don't forget to call. Bye."

The next morning, wearing a plain blue skirt and a simple cotton blouse, with no jewelry but a narrow silver and ivory bracelet and a pair of Peretti stud earrings that she had had forever, Allison set off for her second day in the mailroom. It was every bit as demeaning as the first day. This time she was sent by Ben Wildman's secretary to his house because he had forgotten his cigarette lighter. The secretary repeated the instructions twice, as if Allison had just waded across the Rio Grande that day. Because Ben Wildman's maid was out sick, the secretary almost made Allison take an oath on a Bible that she wouldn't forget to double lock the front door and reset the burglar alarm. Allison had known Ben since childhood and was fond of him, but that didn't make the job any easier to take.

On the third day Allison fell into conversation with a tall young man named Gary while he showed her the procedure for sending packages by Federal Express. Gary, who blow-dried his hair and dressed with a pure preppiness that bordered on parody, told her that he too was a holder of a graduate degree, an M.B.A. from Wharton no less, and had been in the mailroom for almost nine months. The conversation sent a chill down Allison's spine. That night, though she had planned to go out to see a film—anything to get her mind off the mailroom—Allison abandoned the idea and settled into the Trollope, some French bread that was as hard as a cop's nightstick, and a can of Campbell's Vegetarian Vegetable. When the phone rang, she picked it up on the first ring.

"Hi, honey. Everything okay with the house?" asked Gus, his voice brimful of love that not even the coldness of a phone could dispel.

"The house is great, Uncle Gus."

"And the car? How's it running? It seemed a little small to me, but Diana assured me it's both chic *and* safe."

"The car's great also, Uncle Gus. Just great," said Allison, managing to hold her tongue.

"I'm getting terrific reports on you, honey. The entire office is tickled pink that you're starting out like everyone else. You don't know what that does for the morale. To see my only relative working in the mailroom, even though she has a law degree," he said, the pride in his voice suddenly making Allison unsure of herself, "I can't begin to tell you what it means to me."

"But that's just it, Uncle Gus. Wouldn't I be more help if I started— somewhere else?"

"Definitely not. Keep your eyes open. Learn who's imaginative, who has compassion, who's organized. It's the best background you can get. No college can give you that 'fly on the wall' view that you can get from roaming around doing your work."

"But how long will I be there?"

"Don't worry about that. Just learn. I'm going to Chicago tomorrow morning, so I've got to get to bed. Be back the next day. Remember what I said about learning. And don't forget I love you."

It was a few moments before Allison realized that her uncle had hung up. With a deep feeling of hopelessness, she laid out her clothes for the next day, set the alarm, and went to bed.

4

Somehow Allison got through the rest of the first week. Though Gus invited her to spend the night at his beach house in Trancas that Saturday, Allison begged off. She was in no mood to meet new people and field the inevitable question: "What do you do?" Instead, she slept late, talked on the phone with Cynthia, rearranged drawers and closets, and went to the beach on her own.

The beginning of the second week started the way the first had ended, with mindless duties and chores. Allison had to stand in line for two hours at the motor vehicle bureau to get license plates for Lee Simons's new, baby blue Mercedes. Lee Simons was the hottest female agent in the business. It seemed as if not a week went by without Lee bringing a new actor or actress into U.T.M. In the past half-dozen years her clients had won more Oscars and Emmys than anyone else's in the business. Still in her midthirties, she was short, thin as a whippet, and aggressive enough to hold her own in a room full of lobbyists. She had had her colors done and dressed in a palette that was circus bright. Her jewelry was as tasteless as it was costly. Her license plates had to be applied for in person, because Lee Simons wanted something special for her newest toy. First Allison had to look up the name the agent wanted in a massive compendium of plates already in use, but Lee Simons was in luck. It seemed no one else had thought of, or wanted, SHTUP.

Twice a day Allison drove to Malibu to feed a Persian cat named Points, which would eat only freshly ground liver. Its owner, Jack Epstein, one of the top people in the agency's television department, had a maid, but he insisted she couldn't be trusted with the care of Points. Of course, thought Allison, only a lawyer could handle that kind of job.

The other trainees in the mailroom were courteous to Allison but more than a bit standoffish because she was Gus Morton's niece. Everybody, that is, except for a tall young man with black hair and matching eyes that were luminous and the size of Greek olives. His name was

George Bellamy. Because of her deep funk, Allison parried all his attempts at friendship.

"You look like the sprout type," George Bellamy said to her late one morning in the mailroom.

"I beg your pardon?" Allison said archly.

"You know, whole wheat bread milled by ex-hippies who don't eat anything but organic greens. That kind of thing. You really look like the health-food type. I mean that in a complimentary way, of course."

"That's interesting," said Allison, in a tone that suggested the opposite was true.

"I'm not really into that kind of stuff myself, but there's a place a couple of blocks from here called The Cornucopia. I thought maybe you'd like to grab a bite with me there. I'm sure I could find something I could put down," George said, smiling agreeably.

"Well, I'm actually in the mood today for a terrible carcinogenic hamburger backed up by a large plate of fries and an intensely chocolate malted."

"There's a great place for burgers—"

"Another time," Allison said, as she turned around and pushed her mailcart out of the room.

But George Bellamy wasn't the sort to give up that easily. Two days later he asked Allison if she liked jazz, because he had two passes that night to a club on the Strip. Allison, who loved jazz, told him that the most modern composer she listened to was Prokofiev.

Despite her desire to have nothing to do with anyone in the mailroom, there was something about George Bellamy's smile that was so natural and free of guile that it almost made Allison smile too. Why was she being so hard on him? A little friendship might make it easier to endure this strange form of hazing that her uncle was inflicting on her. Since George was going through it too, at least she wouldn't feel so alone. She made up her mind that the next time he asked her out, she would accept. Happily.

The next day Allison went out of her way to ask George a question about Xeroxing a script to which she already knew the answer. Just to show him she was now friendly. She smiled brightly as she waited for him to explain, but all he did was nod at a sheet of paper taped to the wall.

"The directions are right in front of your nose. I assume you can read. Right, barrister?" There was no return smile as he quickly turned away and left the mailroom.

Whenever George was looking the other way, Allison studied him. Though his mouth was as delicately molded as that of a figure in a Renaissance painting, it was capable of bursting into the sunniest of smiles with barely any provocation. His skin, a shade deeper than almond, seemed to glow from beneath. Though he wasn't muscular, he held himself with a bearing that was graceful without hiding his strength. Allison knew instinctively that the thick black curls capping his head would feel like the coat of a beautiful and slightly dangerous animal. He had wanted to be friendly to her. And what had she done? Treated him as if he were carrying a new social disease! There was nothing to do about that now. She obviously had hurt his feelings past the point of his ever being interested in her again.

So that Friday, after two full weeks in the mailroom, two mind-numbing and demeaning weeks, Allison looked forward, if that was the way to describe it, to another lonely weekend that would prepare her for another work week that she would give anything to avoid.

Since parking spaces in the big lot next to the building were assigned to executives, Allison walked slowly around the corner to where she had left her car on the street that morning. *Great,* she thought, as she saw the parking ticket stuck under the BMW's windshield wipers, *my luck is still holding.* She collected the ticket, unlocked the door on the driver's side, and got in. After glancing at her makeup in the rearview mirror, she turned the ignition key and heard . . . nothing. She checked to see if the transmission was in park and tried again. Still nothing. Okay. Decision time. Do we laugh or do we cry? Laughing would show greater strength of character, she guessed, but, dammit, she really wanted to just cry.

"Will you promise me that if I try to be a good Samaritan, I won't get my head bitten off?"

George Bellamy, his incredibly black eyes bunched in a tight squint against the late afternoon sun, stood on the sidewalk looking at Allison.

"Promise," she answered softly. "I'll go you one better. I'll buy you a drink of your choice, anything except a Harvey Wallbanger because I can't abide the name, if you get this thing running again."

"Well, let's see if a misspent youth devoted to a passionate affair with grease and gears will pay off in a free drink."

George disappeared under the hood for what seemed only a moment before signaling with his arm for Allison to start the car. And, just like that, it sprang to life.

"That will be one glass of champagne, madame," said George Bellamy, wiping his hands on a handkerchief. "This grease monkey doesn't work cheaply."

"I'm a woman of my word. Where do you want to go?"

"Where else but the Polo Lounge for two of L.A.'s rising young

mail—er, talent agents. Also, the guacamole is both fantastic and free."
He slid into the bucket seat next to Allison. "I suggest we use this little
number of yours, since no self-respecting Beverly Hills denizen would
even allow his maid to drive my wheels."

"A mechanic of your ability deserves a chauffeur of my unique talent," said Allison, laughing. And, as they continued to joke, Allison and
George drove down Wilshire toward the Beverly Hills Hotel.

Later that night, after several margaritas, which seemed a much better accompaniment to the guacamole dip than champagne, followed by
two huge platters of spaghetti puttanesca at Dan Tana's, which George
insisted on paying for, Allison dropped him back at his car, parked two
blocks from the U.T.M. Building.

"I have a question to ask and then a confession to make," George
said.

"The confession first, please. I haven't heard a good one since my
second year of law school."

"No," answered George firmly. "The question first."

Almost absently, he ran his hand slowly up and down the warm skin
of Allison's forearm.

"Okay. Question away."

"You won't think I'm weird or anything like that if I don't make a
pass at you now, will you? I really like you. Have since the day I saw you
looking like sadness personified, standing there getting instructions on
how to use the postage meter that first day you were in the mailroom.
You really did look miserable." George smiled, continuing to trace delicate, invisible lines back and forth on Allison's arm. "So what I'd like to
do is pick you up tomorrow and, I hope, spend the day with you. We
could go to the beach or drive out to the desert or—"

"Done. You've got yourself a driving partner, provided we split the
gas and everything else."

George nodded.

"Well?" asked Allison after a long moment.

"Well, what?"

"The confession. I'm waiting."

"Oh, that," George answered with a small laugh. "Promise you
won't be mad?"

"Promise."

"Well, this little beauty you're driving has no problems. You really
didn't require Bellamy's Road Service."

"What do you mean, George? I'm not following you."

"What I'm trying to say is that I . . . I disconnected one of the battery cables during lunch and then waited for you to leave this evening. I guess you'd call me a calculating good Samaritan. You're still not mad?"

"Of course not. We met, didn't we? And that's what counts, isn't it?"

"Nothing could count more," George said and then quickly kissed her. His lips, warm and dry, brushed hers for an instant. "Tomorrow at ten?" he asked as he got out of Allison's car.

"Ten-thirty."

"See you."

"Hey," Allison yelled after him as he walked away. "You don't know where I live."

The laughter came back to her clear and happy from the darkness of the street. "You think a car tamperer wouldn't know the address of the tamperee? 'Night. See you at ten-thirty."

5

That weekend Allison and George didn't go to the beach or out to the desert. Instead they drove around L.A. looking at houses designed by Frank Lloyd Wright in Hollywood and Los Feliz, ate sushi at a lunch counter in Little Tokyo, scoured the stacks at Tower Records, and talked. And talked and talked.

"I always knew deep down that I would get into show business, somehow," said George. "I realized I didn't have the talent to perform or write myself, but I figured I had something else. Instincts and stamina. I'm not afraid of working hard. I'm not going to let anything stand in my way. Not anything. I know I can make it. Even in the past six months in this damned mailroom I've learned an incredible amount. I read every memo that passes through my hands, pick up as much as I can about deals that are in the works without being accused of snooping, and I eavesdrop like crazy. I'd wiretap the phones if I thought I could get away with it! I want to find out everything I can, as fast as I can. I'm positive I'll be out of the mailroom soon and on my way."

George's excitement was contagious. When he talked about the business, it consumed him. It was easy to see that it was the most important thing in his life. For Allison, on the other hand, it had always been a given—the glamour, the power, all of it. She had been trained to take her place in it, close to Gus. It was the expected order of events for her. For George, it was different. Making his way in the business would be an act of will. Seeing things from his perspective made everything seem fresh and new and exhilarating. Maybe this was exactly what her uncle hoped would happen when he insisted she take her turn in the mailroom. If, like the others, she had to pay dues to become a member, she wouldn't be blasé.

Allison talked about her childhood in New York with her father, who had been gentle and sweet and whom she had loved, and with her mother. Teddy Morton had died of a massive heart attack shortly after she turned nine, and trying to describe him now to George was a bit like picking a figure out of a foggy landscape. There were touchstones to her memory of him—skating in Rockefeller Center, ice cream at Rumpelmeyer's, cuddling in his arms for bedtime stories—but if it were not for the photograph of him as a young man that she had on her bureau, she might have had difficulty remembering exactly what he looked like. The photo, her favorite, showed him in hiking gear standing on a mountainside filled with flowers; ironically, it had been taken the summer he met her mother, Françoise. Allison had learned only many years later how that meeting had come about. Every summer Teddy, who was in charge of the agency's classical music division (and himself was a gifted oboeist), scouted for talent in Europe, moving along the circuit that extended from Glyndebourne to Salzburg. At a reception following a concert in Nice one year, he had been introduced to Françoise, a young, well-born French actress. By the time he realized she was not French but from a dirt-poor potato-farming family in Canada, certainly not that young, and a lousy actress for extra measure, he didn't care. He was mad for her. Latching on to Teddy was the one successful thing Françoise had ever done. Although she still maintained the fiction of being an actress, every now and then winning bit parts in various New York–based TV series, what she had become in reality was the petulant and indulged wife of a moderately successful, moderately rich businessman.

About her mother, Allison did not say much to George, for it was still painful to accept how little she had meant to Françoise. Françoise had never seemed to need her the way Allison knew she needed her mother. Or once had. After Allison had spent a lonely year with her following Teddy's death, Gus had brought her to California to live with him until she was old enough to go to boarding school. Françoise apparently did not object to losing her daughter to Gus, for soon afterward she married a Swiss restaurateur and disappeared from Allison's life. Almost disappeared. Over the years, there were occasional reunions, but these grew increasingly awkward.

George's family was as straight-arrow and upper middle class as you could find. "The right house, the right station wagon, even our dog, Honey, a golden retriever, was right," he told her. "I guess Mom and Dad slipped up with three children. The really right number is two point three." He had gone to prep school outside of Chicago, where his family lived, and then east to Brown, followed by two years at the Yale Drama School.

"I dated a fellow at Brown once," Allison said, as they sat on her deck watching the sun, balanced on the horizon like a ball on a string, dropping through a sky tinged with a hint of night and scrubbed free of clouds. "His name was Rick Harrell. I think he was the same year as you. Did you know him?"

"Harrell? Sounds familiar, but I don't remember him."

As Allison talked about the weekends she had spent at Brown with Rick Harrell and asked George questions about what it was like for him there, she started to develop a very odd feeling. Listening to his comments about those four years, she could not keep the idea out of her mind that maybe . . . well, he seemed to remember so little of the place. Perhaps he had had an unhappy time at college. That would make a person repress lots of things. That was not uncommon, after all. Had to be that. Because there was no artifice in George. Everything he was was right there in the openness of his face.

On Sunday night, the third evening in a row that they had spent together, Allison thought that George would again give her a chaste kiss before he left for his apartment. But this time his lips didn't touch hers lightly and then depart. Instead, he pressed them against Allison's so tightly that if she hadn't felt the way she did for him, she would have cried out in pain. Without a word, they undressed each other and made love, their hands never once leaving each other's bodies, right there on a yellow kilim that suddenly felt soft as down. Later, a few hours before dawn, they stumbled together into Allison's bed.

"Damn," grumbled Allison, as she reached over and silenced the alarm. It seemed like only minutes since they had gone to bed.

"What time is it?" asked George, sitting up, looking alert and rested.

"Too early. We can get another hour's sleep easy," she answered, already squirreling her way back under the covers.

"No, we can't. Anyway, I have to go home to get a clean shirt. Remember, we're not going to get out of the mailroom faster by showing up late."

"Okay, you win. But at least you don't have to look so wide awake and purposeful at this ungodly hour. And how about a kiss?"

"That's easy," he said, bending over Allison and kissing her gently. "You free tonight?" he asked as he started to put on his clothes.

"Sure. No, darn it! It's Monday, right? I'm having dinner with Uncle Gus. But why don't you come along? I'm sure he wouldn't mind."

"I can't, Allie. I want to prove myself to him before he knows anything about my feelings for you. Can you understand that?"

"Yes. Actually, I was sort of hoping you'd say that."

"How about one more kiss for the road?" George asked, reaching out for Allison. "We won't be able to do this in the mailroom."

"Or the hallways," said Allison, as their lips broke apart.

"Right. At U.T.M., we're both struggling—"

"And competing," she added, smiling.

"Absolutely. In the race out of the mailroom, it's every man—"

"*And* woman—"

"Well, you get the idea. I think it wouldn't be out of line for us to have an occasional lunch together at Hamburger Hamlet though."

"So long as we're chaperoned by some of our colleagues from postage stamp central. Well, conspirator, until we meet again."

As Allison watched George walk down to the driveway and get into his battered Datsun, which looked as if it had just won an important off-road race in Baja, she suddenly realized that she was looking forward to going to work. And later, as she showered, the happy sound she heard was her own singing.

6

The party Friday evening to celebrate Arnie Lemay's promotion from the mailroom was held at his small apartment on Fountain Avenue. The apartment, in a large, rococo building dating from the late 1920s, had fallen on hard times since its days of grandeur, and like aberrant cells, the once spacious apartments had divided and redivided to produce a multitude of studios with high ceilings and bits of glorious plaster detail. Starting on Monday, Arnie, now forever free of his mailcart, would begin his next step up the ladder as secretary/assistant to Brit Canfield. Canfield, an ambitious young agent in the film division, had discovered last year's beautiful blond thing, who seemed to have an aptitude for comedy and was already being hailed as the new Monroe. Arnie, who had been in the mailroom for just under a year, made his escape by calling Brit Canfield's attention to a young actor-comedian whom he had seen at a small improvisational club in the Valley. Canfield concurred with Arnie's judgment and, within two weeks of signing the new client, landed him a supporting role in a new Sidney Lumet film.

The entire mailroom crew, plus girlfriends and boyfriends, hungry actor and writer buddies, and assorted others from remote corners of the industry were crammed into the single room under a canopy of smoke as dense as any smog alert the City of Angels had ever experienced. Some were dancing, but in the cramped space, what they were doing looked more like the jerking and swaying of subway riders in a crowded car.

"You look a little less than happy, love," whispered Allison, as she and George tried to move rhythmically to a song by a group that sounded like Philip Glass at his hypnotic worst.

"You want truth or party talk?"

"That sounds ominous, George."

"Hey, Allie Cat," he said, pulling her closer, "my funk has nothing to do with you. You're the best thing that's happened to me since I came out to this big parking lot. It's this damned party."

"What's wrong with Velveeta on rye crisp? Or warm Blue Nun? Of course, not everybody appreciates air quality that rivals Mexico City's. But this is a party, after all."

"Arnie's out, but where am I? I'll be running that postage meter until I get my pension. Maybe I should start thinking about being a real estate agent. There's a lot more of them. And they don't have to start out in a mailroom."

"You're terrific. Don't ever forget that. You'll get out soon. You're going to be a great agent."

"That's easy for you to say, Allie. Your uncle's not going to let you rot in the mailroom. Your passport out is there for the taking."

"I resent that, George. You have no right to bring my uncle into this. Suddenly I'm thinking maybe I don't know you at all."

"I didn't mean that. I was off base. I'm sorry."

"Okay, but let's leave. I don't really feel like celebrating either."

A thick heavy front, gray as cat's fur, had hung over the L.A. basin all day. A misty rain that was perfect for ferns made the night sky seem like a bell jar. Allison, who always felt more the Easterner, more the out-sider, when she was unhappy, drove west on Sunset. George, slumped in the seat beside her, stayed deeply and sadly wrapped in his thoughts. It was only when Allison turned off on Stone Canyon Road that he sat up.

"Where we going?" he asked abruptly.

"The only place to be on a night like this. The bar at the Bel-Air Hotel. A roaring, *real* wood fire and a tundra-dry martini. How's that for ad copy?"

The parking attendant took Allison's car with the mild disdain reserved for those pitiful enough to show up in anything less than a Rolls. As they walked over the narrow footbridge that spanned the pond in front of the hotel, Allison stopped for a moment and peered into the gloomy broth of night air that swirled above the still waters.

"There." She nudged George. "See it?"

"See what?" he asked, as he too stared down into the darkness.

"The swan. Haven't you ever been here before?"

Then George saw it, gliding so effortlessly it barely left a knife edge of a ripple in the water. He turned and followed Allison into the hotel's quiet, elegant bar. After the bartender had taken their order, Allison grabbed George's arm.

"On the way over here, I kept thinking about Arnie," she said. "And about you and me. And I swear I think I understand something I didn't before. It's so simple."

"What're you talking about?"

"Getting out of the mailroom, of course. Arnie'll make an okay agent, though not as good as you or I. But he's got his chance. He found the agency a new and probably lucrative client. Whether that actor sailed up to him out of the blue like the swan out there or whether he searched him out doesn't matter. He found him. And U.T.M. signed him."

"Baby, what do you think I've been trying to do? I've been beating the palm trees for something, anything, anyone. I'm not fussy. Just desperate!"

"Nothing like a little desperation to lend an edge to things," said Allison, laughing at George's gloomy expression.

"You can kid around. You've been in the mailroom . . . how long?"

"Twenty-five days, and I've hated every minute of it. Except for you, of course."

"Let's drink to that," said George, smiling again. He reached for one of the icy martini glasses the bartender had just placed before them. Droplets of water like perfect beads of caviar dotted the rims.

"Of course, luck has something to do with this," said Allison, "but I refuse to believe you and I can't find two people out there that U.T.M. would love to have on their client list. Two real, live clients with our names on them. One for you. One for me. And then, goodbye mailroom."

"Great idea. So what do we do?"

"I'll tell you," said Allison, and she hurriedly ran through what she'd been mulling over for the last hour. They would devote not just some but all of their free time to searching for talent. They each would concentrate on what they knew and liked best. George, who loved pop music, would cover rock, punk, soul, country, and blues, and Allison, the theater and writing scene. *And* they would do it together.

"We'll keep each other company. I'll go to clubs with you, you'll come to plays with me. Then when we bomb out, at least we'll have the consolation of having spent the time together. Who knows, it might even be fun."

And for a while it was. Every week they studied the local papers and trades for theater groups and rock clubs. They tried every trick they could think of to get a head start on other agents, from pumping actor and musician friends for leads to showcase presentations they could see during rehearsal to scrutinizing neighborhood bulletin boards for mimeographed announcements of shows that not even the underground press reported. Whenever possible, they tried to make the evening a doubleheader—a play first, then a club date.

In the weeks that followed, they saw one bad group and one bad play after another, usually at the rate of two a night. And then it happened.

George struck gold at Vinyl, a small, seedy club off Ventura Boulevard. The group was called Totaled. They made their entrance onto a darkened stage lit by flashing strobes, to the accompaniment of an eardrum-piercing soundtrack of a monstrous car crash, followed by cries of pain mixed with the wail of ambulance sirens. The lights came up on four bleached-blond men in blood-splattered paramedic whites. As soon as they got into the music, however, the compelling, hard-hitting sound made their theatrics superfluous.

When the set ended, George rushed backstage. A ponytailed roadie guarding the dressing room waved him on when he heard George was from U.T.M. The members of the group were flopped on a sofa and chairs in various stages of exhaustion. George identified himself as an agent from U.T.M. and began raving about their sound. They listened briefly, then ignored him. The drummer rolled a joint and started passing it around. George was rattled.

"Gordon send you?" Terry, the lead singer, finally asked.

"Gordon?"

"Gordon Fox, man. Who else?" said Terry, inhaling on the joint. "You know, Gordon Fox of U.T.M. *Our agent*. Don't you jokers over there talk to each other?"

"Sure, Terry. They talk to each other. Ten percent of the time," said the drummer, with a stoned giggle.

George retreated down the hall, laughter cascading behind him. He couldn't believe it. The agency had already signed this group, and he hadn't even known it. "Watered down Beach Boys," was the only reason he gave Allison for not pursuing them. He was too embarrassed to say more.

Although Allison cheerfully accompanied George during the first month of their search, by the second she found herself making excuses not to go. She detested the decibel level of rock. Allison had dragged poor George to her share of wasted evenings too. Latino proletariate drama groups, experimental workshop productions of restoration plays in modern dress, even a Jewish senior citizen mounting of *No Exit*. They had been told that the director, a social worker with a theatrical bent, was a find. He wasn't.

One evening she and George drove to the Valley to catch a group called Autism. The group consisted of five women dressed in black spandex, high boots, and leather aviator helmets. The audience, half of whom looked like family, responded ecstatically. Allison found the music loathesome.

At intermission Allison turned to George and said without preamble, "This is it. I've had it."

"They are pretty bad, aren't they?"

"Bad is a relative term, George, but these ladies are distant relatives."

And then, after assuring each other that their own relationship was as good as ever, they decided to look for talent independently for a while. Together neither of them had gotten anywhere at all. When they both had free evenings, they would see each other, of course.

The next week, for the first time in almost two months, Allison indulged herself in some thoroughly unproductive evenings. She dined at Angeli's with a friend from New York, caught up on a couple of movies she had missed, and went to the kind of cocktail reception at USC Law School that she normally declined, just because she hadn't been to a real party for so long. She spent the weekend at her uncle's beach house. There were no guests, and Allison was able to sun, swim, and read with no thought of her career.

Looking around on her own for a client did not change her luck immediately, but finally, two weeks later, she thought she had a winner. After stopping on impulse one evening to scan the student bulletin boards at UCLA, she noticed that the film society had a current program of short films by new filmmakers and that one was about to be screened. It was an unmemorable piece of business, but in it was a charming, fresh young actress named Clara Rivera. She discovered that Clara lived in Venice and arranged to meet her for a drink near the office. She liked her at once. She was only a year younger than Allison and talking with her gave Allison a tiny window into the life that might have been hers if she had had any acting talent. It wasn't an easy life. Clara scrambled, and then scrambled some more. She auditioned continually, waited on tables at a Mexican restaurant, and camped out in her married sister's spare bedroom. Allison borrowed a tape of the little bit of TV work she had done and viewed it in the office after work. She was good. Very good. Without any guarantees, Allison made a date to talk with her about the agency representing her.

When Allison arrived at the Venice address, a woman who looked as if she must be Clara's sister opened the door. Allison introduced herself.

"Clara's not home," said the sister.

"Well, how soon do you expect her? I could wait."

"No, you don't understand. She's away."

"But we made a date. I'm sure she wouldn't have forgotten."

"You didn't spot it, did you?" said the sister almost to herself. She glanced behind her into the living room, where Allison could see two small children watching television. "Clara's in the hospital," she said. "She gets very depressed. Medication doesn't seem to help much now. She's had to be hospitalized more and more. I'm so afraid she's going to have to give up acting. It makes me heartsick. It's her whole life." Her eyes began to fill with tears. "I really have to get back to the children. I'm sorry."

It wasn't until after Christmas that Allison finally hit pay dirt.

One morning, Lee Simons called her out of the mailroom. "You're from New York, Allison, so you'll be able to understand what this means to me. I'm going to give you two words. Ready?" asked Lee, her wet, red lips smiling almost lewdly.

"I think so."

"Corned beef."

"Corned beef?"

"You know what it's like when you really want a good New York corned beef sandwich. That's what I need now. A nice, thick corned beef on rye. No, two corned beefs on rye."

Allison stared silently at Lee Simons. The thought of this stick of a woman cramming two overstuffed sandwiches down her gullet, leaving a trail of lipstick prints on the bread, almost made her gag.

"There's only one place that gives the Carnegie a run for its money, and that's Canter's. I don't care what people say about Nate 'n Al's. The only snag is, they don't deliver."

Allison, no surprise, was given the assignment to make the trip for Lee to the delicatessen. L.A. was in the midst of a heat wave, and it was just Allison's luck that the air-conditioner on her car was busted. As soon as she had finished her corned beef mercy mission, she looked for a place to stop for something cool to drink. She spotted a small diner on Fairfax, pulled into its parking lot next to a red Porsche, and ordered a lemonade with lots of ice.

She opened her newspaper to an article she had started reading that morning. She was only a few paragraphs into the story when she heard a familiar voice. She looked around, and then she saw him. Felix Godwin. *The* Felix Godwin. The darling—and scourge—of any movie director foolhardy enough to cast the English actor in a role. He was box office gold, but just having him on the set spelled trouble. He had a reputation for being an insatiable womanizer and a man with only two hobbies: coke and booze. His temper was legendary. Allison had read in one of the gossip columns that he had fired his last agent a year ago and had vowed never to hire another. Certainly he looked tame enough now, as he joked with the short order cook and waitress.

Somewhere in his early forties, he was tall and thin, almost gaunt. His fine, even features were beginning to show signs of coarsening from the pounding surf of years of pub crawls and debauches. His red hair tumbled down over his collar, and his face hadn't seen a razor in days.

"Thanks, love," he said to the waitress as she placed a plate of eggs in front of him. "Got to eat this fast. I have a date with a chap I met last week. He's got some Regimental Highlanders. Wants to trade them. They have incorrect legs. Very rare."

Allison watched surreptitiously as Godwin began to consume his eggs while he scanned the pages of a magazine. She thought of the famous story about Sue Mengers catching the attention of an actor she wanted to sign by dropping her business card into his soup as she passed his table at Sardi's. Instead of being outraged, the actor was charmed and subsequently became a client. Allison could think of no way to introduce herself to Godwin, clever or otherwise. Her only hope was to arrive at the cash register at the same time he did, but before she could even ask for a check, Godwin threw down some bills, waved goodbye, and departed. When she stepped outside, Allison noticed at once that the red Porsche was gone.

That evening her uncle called. He was flying to London in the morning on unexpected business, but he would be back on the weekend. He and Diana would be driving to Palm Springs for a golf tournament on Saturday.

"Think about joining us, honey. Haven't seen much of you lately."

"I'll let you know, Uncle Gus." She loved the comfort of his house in Palm Springs, but golf bored her. "What's Felix Godwin up to these days?" she asked.

"Godwin? He's just finished shooting a Western in Spain. It's a big summer release. Why?"

"Someone showed me a script the other day that would be perfect for him," answered Allison, inventing madly.

"Well, good luck," said Gus, laughing. "But don't waste too much time on him. I tried to sign him on several occasions, you know. He's a nut case. No telling what he'll do. Thinks agent means agent of the devil."

Every lunch break during the next week, Allison drove past the diner, Mabel's, in the hope of seeing Godwin's Porsche again. She had become determined to acquire him as a client. Maybe *she* was the nut case.

One Friday, as she rushed out of the mailroom at lunchtime, George Bellamy cornered her in the hallway. "You've been acting very mysterious lately," he said in a bantering tone. "Got a new boyfriend, Allie Cat?"

"Several," Allison said jokingly. "Just to keep you on your toes."

"Watch out, or you'll make me jealous. What're you really up to though? Are you on to somebody for the agency?"

It struck Allison that George's questions were more pointed than friendly. He sounded threatened.

That afternoon, Allison spotted the Porsche again, parked in front of Mabel's. When she walked into the diner, she saw Godwin sitting alone at the counter. She took a seat several stools away. He was reading a tissue-thin, airmail edition of a British newspaper, and there was a stack of other magazines and papers at his elbow.

Allison dawdled over a sandwich, trying to screw up the courage to speak to him. Fifteen minutes passed, then twenty. Finally she had no choice but to return to work. As she stood up, she tried to read the titles of his magazines. She was able to make out two. *Sight and Sound*. That figured. *Miniature Warfare*. What was that?

Allison had just turned the key in the ignition of her car when the front door of Mabel's swung open and Felix Godwin emerged. She watched as he crossed the street and entered a doorway next to a dry cleaner. She waited until she was confident he wasn't coming right out again and then walked over to the doorway. A small, hand-lettered sign above the doorbell read LITTLE WARS, LTD. She was puzzled for only a moment and then she understood exactly what it meant. And what she must now do.

After work that day Allison went to a hobby store nearby that advertised itself as *the* headquarters in Los Angeles for miniature soldiers. Allison had read about wargaming a couple of years earlier in the lifestyle section of *Newsweek*. The competition pitted individuals or teams against each other to fight battles with miniature soldiers. The military engagements were based on actual battles. The participants were sticklers for verisimilitude. Uniforms, artillery, and topography had to be exactly right, whether the battle was Waterloo or Dien Bien Phu. The storeowner seemed thrilled at the prospect of a new enthusiast. He implored Allison to buy not one but two introductory guides, as well as the latest copies of each of the monthly magazines published. She recognized one as the new edition of the magazine Godwin had been reading in the diner. He gave her the names of two clubs that might have openings for new members and a typewritten hotline of people willing to advise over the phone on tactics and strategies. In the middle of tallying her purchases, he darted to the rear of the store and returned with a small bag of unpainted metal figures.

"This'll hook you. A Napoleonic starter pack. No charge. It's on the store."

That evening Allison pored over the material she had purchased. By the time she was ready for bed, she had formulated her plan. It was wonderfully simple.

The next morning, Saturday, traffic was light. Allison arrived at the building across from Mabel's before ten. She parked the car and rang the bell for the wargamers' club. Nobody answered. As she started back to her car, a man beckoned to her from the window of the dry cleaner.

"You looking for the joint chiefs of staff?"

"Who?"

"You know, the military. The game players."

Allison nodded.

"They usually don't start fighting World War Three until noon, but you're in luck. The guy in charge of the place just called me. He lost his key. I keep his spare. He said he'd be by for it pretty soon."

About half an hour later, a tall, balding man appeared carrying a shoe box under his arm. Allison explained why she was there, and the man motioned her to follow him upstairs. When he unlocked the door, she took two steps into the room, then stopped and stared.

There before her was a large battlefield spread over half a dozen Ping-Pong tables pulled together in the center of the room. Hundreds and hundreds of tiny figures ranged across a hilly terrain sculpted from sand, clay, and crumpled fabric. The figures were set down in intricate formations. At the end of the battlefield that was nearest the door, twenty or thirty knights on horseback were poised to sweep down a hill, flanked on both sides by several times as many archers, bows drawn. She followed the direction of their charge and saw that at the end of the hill another group of small warriors was breaking ranks and fleeing.

"It's fantastic," said Allison, a little awed.

The man walked over to the middle section of the battlefield and gingerly put the shoe box down on the edge of the table. He reached inside it and held aloft a brilliantly colored miniature horse and rider.

"These troops," he said, "are French reinforcements. Beauties, aren't they? I finished painting them last night."

The man took a tape measure from one pocket and a diagram from another and, leaning over the table, calculated the exact placement of the first of his new men. "Now," he said over his shoulder, "when do you want to join?"

"Today. Immediately."

"Immediately! Are you kidding? I'm sorry, dear, but that's impossible," said the man, straightening up. "Can't take in new members in the middle of a battle. Too disruptive. And we'll be fighting this one for a while. We're just getting into Crécy. A lovely engagement. The English still celebrate it. A glorious victory. Fought in 1346," he added, noticing her blank expression. "At the beginning of the war. The Hundred Years War, that is. Come back and see us in . . . four months. Well, try us in three."

Sitting in Mabel's ten minutes later with a cup of coffee, Allison consoled herself on her aborted scheme to meet Godwin. She thumbed idly through one of the wargaming magazines she was carrying with her. A double-page spread of British guardsmen in bright red and black caught the attention of the short order cook on the other side of the counter.

"You too?" he asked.

"Excuse me?" said Allison, looking up.

"I don't know what it is turns you people on to those little lead soldiers. You've seen Felix Godwin in here, right? Well, he's a fan too. Spends days at it. Absolutely fanatical. Me, I can't stand anything longer than a game of Monopoly. The short version. You know, where you deal out the properties."

As the counterman rambled on, Allison thought of another way to approach Godwin. She would make *him* take the initiative. Arrange it so he introduced himself to her rather than the other way around. It depended only on his being as observant as the short order cook.

Starting that Monday, Allison began to have lunch every day at Mabel's, regardless of whether the red Porsche was parked out front. She wanted to be accepted as a regular. A few days later, Godwin was leaving as she arrived, but early the next week her timing was perfect. She just had given her order when she saw the actor enter the diner. Calmly she put down *The Hollywood Reporter* and picked up her copy of *Model Maneuvers*. It was the latest issue. She held it so that Godwin couldn't miss seeing the title if he looked in her direction. And it worked. Within a few minutes he got up and asked to borrow the magazine from her. She had finished her sandwich and was drinking her coffee when Godwin slid onto the stool next to her.

"I see you're a freak, too, luv," he said pleasantly.

"A what?"

"The little blokes. Miniatures. You're into wargaming, aren't you?"

"I sure am," she answered with enthusiasm. "I love it."

"How long you been a devotee?" Godwin asked.

"Six, seven years. An old boyfriend got me into it."

"You've got something to thank that lad for. Belong to a club here?" he asked.

"Not yet. I've only been out here a couple of months."

"What's your favorite engagement?"

"Vicksburg," Allison answered, thinking fast. She had seen a newspaper article on it recently.

This launched Felix Godwin into a detailed analysis of Grant's assault on the city. All Allison could do was nod occasionally and murmur "of course." Finally Godwin stopped and smiled slyly at her.

"You're very smart, but your quick study was a little too quick. How long did you say you've been interested in wargaming?"

"Six or seven years," Allison answered uncertainly.

"Really?" said Godwin. "Wouldn't six or seven days be more like it? Or maybe even six or seven hours?"

"Okay," said Allison, laughing. "You're right. I admit it. I'm a total novice, but I want to learn."

"You just happened to stop by Mabel's. . . ."

"Yes, and I—"

"Just happened to notice a wargamer on the premises, so you decided to stick around."

"Right again. I confess to it all."

"I think you know my name, but I don't know yours." After Allison introduced herself, Godwin continued. "Well, Allison, this is your lucky day. We get under way at the club in ten minutes. Come and watch for a while. At the very least, you'll pick up the ability to say 'of course' at the right moments when we have our next *chance* encounter."

"I'd love to, Mr. Godwin, but—"

"What's this Mr. Godwin stuff? The name's Felix."

"I've got to get back to work now. I'm already late. But can I have a raincheck?"

"Sure. Where do you work?"

"U.T.M.," she said, not thinking.

In the silence that followed, Allison realized her blunder.

"U.T.M.," Godwin finally repeated, with a look of distaste. "You mean that bloody fucking talent agency?"

Allison nodded glumly.

"So, the little lady is an agent. I should have guessed."

"But I'm not an agent. I'm only in the mail—"

"I don't want to hear your excuses, kiddo. But I will make you an offer. If you ever decide to go respectable and leave that line of work, then we'll have our raincheck." He handed her back the magazine and patted her on the head dismissively. "See you around sometime."

Allison returned to Mabel's every day thereafter until she saw him again. On the first occasion, he was sitting in one of the booths with another man, but the next time she saw him he was by himself. He stood up and came over to her.

"If you never speak those three initials again, there's a chance we could be friends. There's something refreshingly eager about you. Is that a deal?"

"Deal," Allison said quickly.

In the weeks that followed, Allison arranged to run into Felix a number of times. He was good-natured enough to maintain the fiction that these meetings were accidental. He seemed genuinely to like her. He told her about his childhood in Surrey; his love for games of all kinds, and how it had been nurtured by his father, a world-class backgammon player; and, on one hungover occasion, about his palimony troubles with an ex-girlfriend of long standing. Sometimes they talked about the business, with Felix doing most of the talking then. The only time Allison actually pitched the agency to him, he listened politely, then shrugged.

"Come and see me when you're out of the mailroom," he said with a wink.

"But you're my ticket out of it!"

Felix laughed. "As if I didn't know, kiddo. But I like the fact that you're honest."

Finally Allison shared her secret with George. She had become friendly with Felix Godwin. She thought there was a chance—only a remote chance, unfortunately—that she could sign him for the agency. Certainly he hadn't say yes, but he hadn't said no either, in so many words. Once when she was having a late dinner with George at Primi, she saw Felix sitting at a table nearby and introduced the two of them.

Several days later she saw him again at Mabel's. When he saw her come in, he brought over his cup of coffee and sat beside her at the counter. "Still looking to travel?" he asked casually.

"Travel where?"

"Up the corporate ladder, where else?"

"Are you saying what I think you're saying?" When Godwin nodded, Allison threw her arms around him. "You're fabulous," she said. "You won't regret this, I promise."

"I've never regretted a thing, and my face is beginning to show it. Actually, this is probably the sanest decision I've ever made. You're smart, honest, a lawyer, and your unc' owns the bleeding works. But what I like most is that all my old pals will think I've rounded the bend at last. That I'm absolutely committable. Signed with a wench who's still in the mailroom. Imagine the publicity! And garnered without the help of Stolichnaya, Colombian flake, or sexual scandal. I love it."

Allison was ecstatic. It was the break she had been waiting for. She would prepare a contract immediately so that they could meet to review the terms before the end of the week. Felix suggested his house in case his lawyer wanted to be present.

The morning of their meeting, Felix called to postpone it until the following day. When he telephoned the next day to postpone again, Allison grew uneasy. No, Felix assured her, nothing was wrong. His lawyer was still out of town.

That evening, at a small dinner Gus was giving for his client Oscar Buckman, she almost told him what was about to happen. She drove over to his house directly from the office in order to speak to him privately, but before she had a chance, the guest of honor arrived, and there was a flurry of kisses and greetings. Allison had not seen Oscar since she had been in boarding school.

When Allison departed, before the movie Gus was screening, it was still so early that she decided on the spur of the moment to drive to Felix's to drop off the contract, which she was still carrying in her briefcase. She found the house easily and parked out front. The lights were on downstairs, but the house had a quiet air. It wasn't until she had rung the bell that she heard the sharp staccato of a woman's laugh and the low throb of music.

"Somebody get that door," she heard Felix say. A few moments later, the door swung open, and she was face to face with George Bellamy.

"George! What are you doing here?"

Then Allison was shocked into silence. Behind George she could see Felix in a short white terry cloth robe, giggling convulsively, half supported by two nude young women. Godwin looked up and saw Allison.

"Come in and join the party," he said to her. "I've been given lots of splendid goodies. My mate, George here, has done a great job of catering the powder and"—he pulled the women closer to him—"these little lovelies. Georgie boy is the kind of bloke I need to have around. He's a marvel. He takes care of *everything*. Isn't that right, girls?"

Without a word, Allison turned and ran toward the car. George followed her. Everything had become very clear.

"Don't blame me, Allie," he said, grabbing her arm and forcing her to stop. "Felix came after me. It was his idea."

"Like hell it was, you lying creep. He's a decent human being. Screwed up, but decent. He wouldn't do that to me."

"Listen, I'm the right kind of agent for him. You're not, and he knows it. We speak the same language."

"Some excuse, you son of a bitch. The bottom line is you stole my client. How could you!"

Allison tried to pull away from George, but he held on to her with a fierce determination.

"Try to understand, Allison. Not everybody has an Uncle Gus. I've been in that mailroom for almost a fucking year."

"And you deserve to rot there. Let me go, dammit."

George released her arm.

"You disgust me," said Allison. "And I thought I knew you. Thought you cared for me. I don't believe what's happening." She looked at him coldly, then slapped him hard.

"Take the long view, Allie," said George, rubbing his cheek, as he watched Allison get into her car. "U.T.M. is still going to wind up with Felix Godwin. Isn't that so?" he shouted after her. "Uncle Gus is still going to be pleased. Right?"

Allison, shaking with anger, accelerated sharply away from the curb. Wait until Uncle Gus heard about this. Then George would see how far it got him. She pushed down on the gas pedal as she rounded the corner and headed downhill. Lights from houses exploded into her line of vision like fireworks as she flashed by them. Her eyes stung with tears. She felt wrapped like a mummy in a suffocating cocoon of fury, and in that instant the sound of a blaring horn penetrated her consciousness. Headlights were coming straight at her. Horrified, she pulled the car back to her side of the road and braked to a stop, then rested her head on the steering wheel and let herself cry.

A cold rage had overtaken Allison by the time she got home. She picked up the phone and dialed her uncle's number. What George had done violated every principle Gus stood for.

Albert answered the telephone. "Your uncle and his guests are watching Mr. Caine's new film. Do you wish me to interrupt him?"

"No, but ask him to phone me after everybody leaves."

She sat outside on her deck, taking short, angry slugs from a large glass of cognac. She was too exhausted to think about what had happened or why she had been foolish and naïve enough to let it happen, and before fifteen minutes had passed she crept inside to the telephone, asked her service to hold her calls, and fell into bed.

The next morning at exactly eight, Allison walked into Gus's outer office. Though he always arrived earlier, this was the start of his official workday. Lillian nodded at Gus's closed door: "He should be free soon."

Allison flipped through the pages of one of the magazines on the table by the sofa, then picked up another. She did not want to have to make small talk. Suddenly the door to the office opened, and there stood Gus, grinning broadly, his arm around George Bellamy.

"Allison! What a wonderful surprise. Shake hands with U.T.M.'s newest agent. George has pulled off the coup of the year. He's signed Felix Godwin. I'm staggered. God knows how many times I've tried to land him myself."

Allison stared at the two of them. She couldn't have spoken if she'd had to.

"This feat calls for something special. We're going to skip the secretarial apprenticeship for George. After a coup like this, it's straight to agent. The last time I had the pleasure of doing this was for Lee Simons, twelve years ago."

Her uncle's voice seemed to pull away from Allison, like a train moving off down a tunnel. It was only when Gus led her into his office that she realized George was gone.

"You look ill, Allison. Are you all right?" asked Gus, holding Allison's face in his hands.

"I'm fine. Just fine," she answered in a hollow way that sounded to her as if she were speaking from another part of the room.

"Albert told me you wanted to speak to me last night. I phoned, but your service said you weren't taking calls. Was it anything important?"

"No, Uncle Gus, it was nothing. Nothing at all," Allison replied, knowing for the first time that no matter what her uncle felt for her, or she for him, she would have to get out of the mailroom on her own. And, yes, she would have to deal with George Bellamy on her own too.

7

That day no one in the mailroom could talk of anything but George Bellamy.

"You got to hand it to George," said a tall, smiling redhead only two months out of USC. "If you work as hard outside this place as inside, it'll happen. The credit's totally his. He did it all by himself."

Allison couldn't stand either the talk or the speculative looks, some not so disguised, directed at her. Who knew? Maybe they thought she had slowed George down. She barely made it through lunch before telling Mario that she felt the flu coming on and had to get home to bed.

She spent the afternoon on her deck sunbathing, while she came to terms with what had happened. Her uncle was not going to give her a break, but that was fine. She didn't think she could bear a future of having to apologize for who she was and whom she was related to. If she wanted to become an agent, she had to make it on her own. Nobody was offering an outstretched hand, unless it was a hand poised to slap her down. Maybe this business was no more cutthroat than others, but try telling that to George Bellamy. As for George, she knew that given time she would catch up with him and then would pass him by. Not because her last name was Morton, but because she was smart and had her own way of doing things. She could be herself *and* succeed.

Later that afternoon, Cynthia Traynor called. Mario had told her Allison was home sick.

"Home recovering, is more like what I'm up to. But not from the flu. From George," said Allison with a short laugh. And she described George's treachery.

"Look at it this way," said Cynthia, after the two friends had spent a satisfying half hour excoriating George. "As Gertrude Stein said, 'A shit is a shit is a—' You get the idea. Think positively. What if you hadn't found out what a creep he was for another six months? Think of the time you've saved."

．　．　．

In a few days the excitement over George Bellamy's sudden ascendancy died down in the mailroom and Allison and the others settled back into the routines of the job. During the evening, she threw herself into the pursuit of talent with an intensity that made her past efforts with George seem amateurish. She searched for something, for anything, that would hasten the end to her servitude in the mailroom. Story ideas, new personalities, fresh combinations of known quantities. She sat through dull plays and unfunny nights at the comedy clubs, kept up as much as possible with scripts under consideration for agency clients, and read through magazine after magazine, looking for she didn't know what.

One evening after an hour spent fruitlessly skimming through her ever-growing stack of current and not so current publications, Allison decided to treat herself to a long, luxurious bath. She splashed some bath salts into the tub, ran the water as hot as she could take it, and eased herself in inch by inch until only her head and hands protruded. Beside her were a glass of iced Perrier and a few selections from the reading stack, in case she had the energy for them. On top was a recent issue of the alumnae magazine from Smith, an item she usually tossed into the wastebasket as soon as it arrived. In her present state of frustration, though, she decided even it deserved a look. And, unexpectedly, she was right. What she found inside made her sit up straight. It was a short piece about Lavinia Tedesco, who had graduated from the college in the 1950s, gone on to a brilliant career as a playwright and novelist, and, now that Allison thought about it, hadn't been heard of for a number of years.

Allison's attention was caught and held by a single sentence. "Since I don't have an agent, and never have had," Tedesco had written, "I handle all my business affairs myself." Allison lingered over the sentence, teasing herself with the possibilities, but it was Tedesco's address that crystallized her thoughts. She lived in Carmel, just six hours up the coast.

Allison climbed out of the bathtub and toweled herself dry. She tried to remember what she knew about Tedesco, who was one of those famous graduates, like Mary McCarthy at Vassar, whose association with the college gave the other alumnae personal comfort, almost as if she were kin. Only a few years after she had graduated, Leland Hayward had taken a chance on her first play. It had been a smash. Audiences loved it. Critics praised its witty but powerful dissection of family life. A second play followed soon after, also a hit, and then a third and a fourth. Allison had read the first three when she was in college and had been knocked out by one, *The Season for Loving*.

For a while, Tedesco must have been everyone's darling. She was hailed as the new Lillian Hellman. Her plays were performed around the world, including behind the Iron Curtain. Then, just as she must have had theatergoers and producers begging for more, she changed directions. About fifteen years ago, Allison guessed, though she was fuzzy on the chronology, Tedesco stopped writing plays and turned to novels. She produced a massive two-volume saga about Romanian immigrants settling in the mining country of Pennsylvania, based on her own family background, Allison supposed, then reversed herself again, this time to write a short and fiendishly clever suspense novel. Allison recalled a savage attack on her in *The New York Review of Books,* taking her to task for her lapse in seriousness. Her sales just kept on increasing. Allison had devoured her last novel, *The Question Is,* but that had been published almost five years ago.

"What do you know about Lavinia Tedesco?" Allison asked Cynthia, as soon as she could pull on a robe and dial New York.

"What are you talking about, and do you realize it's almost midnight here?" asked Cynthia wearily.

"I do, but I figured you'd be up."

"You know all too well the hours I keep. Tonight I didn't leave that damned place until after ten. But what's this about our star grad?"

"Do you remember any of her stuff ever being filmed? I can't, but I may be pulling a blank."

Cynthia thought the answer was no, though she wasn't positive. She remembered that someone had bought one of the books, but that Tedesco had script approval and the film finally hadn't been made. She was a lot more sure, however, about Lavinia Tedesco's personal life.

"Where've you been, Allie? Don't you read *People?* I can't believe you don't remember what happened. But you were so out of it at law school. A real grind. She married a West Coast poet who used to hang out in Big Sur. Everything was very lovey-dovey. The perfect December romance. She was about fifty or a little older, I'd guess. What happened was, one night, one of those miserable foggy nights, they were in a terrible automobile accident. On the Coast Highway. She was driving. He was killed. She was in critical condition, but she made it. Ever since, though, I hear she's been outdoing J. D. Salinger. A total recluse."

The next day, Allison bought all of Tedesco's plays and novels. Then she read through the clipping file on the writer in the UCLA library. She didn't learn a lot more than Cynthia had told her. Tedesco made no public appearances. Though her publisher had recently announced that she had nearly completed a long and important new novel, Tedesco would neither confirm nor deny it.

By late morning on Friday, two days later, Allison was on her way to Carmel. She had made up her mind. She was going to bring Lavinia Tedesco into U.T.M. Tedesco would be her first client.

She had no problem finding the house where Tedesco lived. Everybody knew where it was. It was almost a tourist attraction, the next stop after the bar that Clint Eastwood frequented. It was a low, sand-colored house several miles outside of town, set back from the road and perched on a cliff above the ocean like an osprey nest, ringed by wind-stunted trees and fields.

Since it was still early in the afternoon, Allison decided to give it a shot then and there instead of waiting until the next day. She had concocted a story about being sent to see Miss Tedesco by the alumnae magazine. The short article on her had created so much interest, so many people had written in asking to know more, that the magazine wanted to do a full-scale interview. Would Miss Tedesco consider it? The whole thing seemed flimsy even to Allison, but she knew she was good at charming her way around people.

She was turned down cold in less than one minute. And not even by Lavinia Tedesco. A plump woman wearing a maid's uniform came to the door. The answer was a firm no that sounded as if it had been given many times before.

Saturday morning Allison sent what she thought was a really sweet handwritten note, a "fellow alumna" kind of appeal, admiring but not too grossly flattering, and again she got a no. Next she tried parking across the road from Tedesco's driveway, with the notion of waylaying the writer as she was on her way out. She had hardly opened her container of coffee and a newspaper before a patrol car pulled up. A young officer asked to see her license. He looked at it without comment, then told her to move on. Miss Tedesco had complained.

By Sunday, Allison was almost ready to give up, when she had a nutty idea. At boarding school, one of her teachers had introduced her to birding and the habit had stuck. She never went anywhere without a copy of Roger Tory Peterson tucked in the trunk along with a pair of binoculars.

She'd do a stakeout. She felt ridiculous, as if she were taking cues from a caper film, but it seemed her only chance. So, very early Monday morning, she parked her car out of sight in a dead-end road she had spotted earlier and crept through the field in front of Tedesco's house until she was as close as she dared to go without risk of being seen. And there she stayed all day, except for calling in sick to Mario and taking a break for a sandwich, flopped on her stomach, binoculars trained on the house.

For a while she thought she was going to strike out with this gambit too. Tedesco drove off early in the morning, before eight, but she was back by nine. Otherwise nothing happened. A dry cleaner made a delivery to the house, and a van from a video rental store. Sometime in mid-afternoon, a short, burly man, who was probably the maid's husband, emerged from the house and returned an hour later with a load of groceries. But what Allison hoped would happen did not. The couple never left Tedesco alone. Perhaps because she still was not completely well. Allison had been surprised to see from her outpost how badly the writer limped. If the couple didn't get out of the way, she would never have an opportunity to approach Tedesco. Allison went back to her motel at the end of that day totally dispirited.

Tuesday morning she saw Tedesco drive away from the house at precisely the same time as she had the day before, ten minutes to eight. Of course. She must have a regular appointment somewhere at the same time every morning. The next day, following through on this idea, Allison parked her car out of sight and waited for Tedesco. When the writer drove by exactly on schedule, Allison pulled out and followed her into town. She stopped in front of a low white building: FIT FOR NOW. A health club. That made sense.

Allison had to wait one more day before making her move. She bought a tanksuit at a small shop and took out a trial membership in the health club. When the writer arrived the next morning, just as the club opened, Allison followed her inside. After putting on her bathing suit, she looked for Tedesco in the swimming pool, but it was deserted. The surge of relief she felt was so great that she almost changed her mind and left. Tedesco's writing, which she had read and reread all last week, had really impressed her. And she thought, *How ballsy can you get? This woman wants her privacy. Let her be.*

But Allison stayed. She couldn't stop now. She looked into a room filled with gym equipment. Not a soul. Then she noticed a door to a sauna. She pulled the door open, and her eyes met those of Lavinia Tedesco. It would have been difficult to say who was the more surprised.

Tedesco, who had been lying nude on one of the benches, hurried to cover herself with a towel. Allison looked away from the long, horrible scars that the older woman's towel didn't quite hide. She felt embarrassed by her own good health. She knew she had done the wrong thing. She had gone too far. All she wanted to do now was get out of the sauna. Disappear.

"No, stop," said Tedesco, as Allison turned to leave. "Don't go, but shut the door."

Tedesco was still struggling with the towel, trying to cover more of her shattered body. Allison watched mutely. It occurred to her that the writer came here early because no one else was around to see her.

Tedesco looked up again at Allison. "Aren't you the young woman who came to my house the other day? And then parked out front? You *are!*"

"Yes," Allison blurted.

"Well, what do you want from me?"

"My name is Allison Morton." Allison paused, disgusted by her own pushiness, wavered, and then continued. "I really did go to Smith. But the alumnae magazine didn't send me. I'm here entirely on my own. All I want is to talk with you."

"About what?"

"About—" Allison hesitated. "About representing you. I work for Universal Talent Management. The agency."

"And that's why you trapped me here? Do you think this is a proper place to discuss business?" said Tedesco, the anger rising in her voice.

"No, of course not. But will you see me this afternoon at your house? Five minutes is all I ask. I won't bother you ever again. I promise."

Tedesco assessed Allison slowly and silently, then nodded. "All right. Four o'clock this afternoon. Now leave me alone."

That afternoon the two women sat on a stone terrace facing the ocean while the maid served tea. Now that she was in command again, her wounds hidden from sight, except for a jagged claw mark of a scar on her neck, Tedesco was surprisingly gracious. When five minutes and then ten minutes passed with no sign from Tedesco that her time was up, Allison relaxed.

"You like movies," she said, remembering the video delivery truck. "It's criminal that none of your plays or novels has been filmed."

"It would have been 'criminal' if they had been," said Tedesco dryly. "I'm thinking of *The Season for Loving*. My one experience with the movie people. A studio bought it, but then, thank God, the screenplay was so vile that the whole business collapsed."

"You just haven't encountered people who share your sensibilities, that's all," said Allison. "Give me a chance. *The Question Is* begs to be filmed. Give us a crack at it. We won't even take a commission."

"But what's in it for you then? And don't think that means I'd let you do whatever you want with it—put any actors in it you chose. I can't stand Hollywood's box office fixation."

"Don't worry. You'll have full approval. That'll be part of the deal,"

Allison answered. "Just the knowledge that we represent you will bring other writers to us."

Tedesco rose abruptly. Reaching for the cane looped over her chair, she limped over to the parapet that edged the terrace on the ocean side and sat down, beckoning Allison to follow. Something in her manner suggested that she wasn't closing the subject, just backing off momentarily. She started to talk about other things. About Carmel, her immigrant parents' feelings for America, her writing. She confirmed that she was just finishing a big, new novel. She talked for an hour and then she stood up again.

"All right," she said. "I'll give you *The Question Is* on a trial basis. See what you can do. If you can put together the right kind of movie, I insist you take a commission. Whatever is customary. And one last thing. I want a guarantee in writing that you personally, and only you, will handle the negotiations."

"Well, that's very nice of you."

"I'm not trying to be nice," said Tedesco, smiling. "Just trying to ensure accountability."

"Okay, fine. But there's one more thing, Miss Tedesco."

"Lavinia."

"Remember the story I made up about the alumnae magazine?"

"Of course, I saw through that immediately."

"Well, I have something else to confess."

"And what's that?" asked Lavinia Tedesco, her calm gray eyes fixed steadily on Allison.

"I'm not an agent yet. I work in the mailroom at U.T.M. But if I sign you up, I'm sure they'll make me an agent. Absolutely."

"Why, that's even better, Allison," the writer responded after a moment. "It'll be a first for both of us."

8

Gus carefully twisted the thick cork on the chilled bottle of Roederer Cristal, 1972.

"Allison, do you know what I call this sound?" Gus asked as the cork came out with a sharp pop. "I think of it as the finger snap of success. And I can't tell you how happy you've made me." He slowly filled the Baccarat flute that Allison held up by its stem.

After Gus filled his own glass, he put his arm around his niece and led her over to a small framed photograph that hung, incongruously, between a whimsical Klee and a large somber Rothko.

"Do you remember when I first showed you this?"

"I was very young, Uncle Gus. Maybe seven or eight."

Allison edged closer to the faded black and white photograph. Two little boys, both in sailor suits, sat self-consciously in a small pony cart, with a solemn-faced man and woman standing stiffly beside them.

"You know, Allie, I still remember the day this picture was taken. What an occasion it was for Teddy and me. Our dad was usually too tired to go out. He worked six days a week, long days, but this was a treat. A *whole* day at Luna Park. I wasn't able to sleep a week before. And now, whenever good things happen, I like to stand in front of this photo and it's almost as if, and I know this sounds corny, but it's almost as if my folks and my brother share it with me."

Gus put down his glass and pulled Allison close.

"You've done well. And," he held her at arm's length and smiled, "as of this moment you're no longer in the mailroom."

"Oh, Uncle Gus, thank you. Now I'll be able to show you what I can really do."

"Starting tomorrow morning you'll report to Lee Simons as her new secretary/assistant. I've already spoken to Lee and—"

"What did you say, Uncle Gus?" Allison almost shouted.

"Well, I spoke to Lee and she thought it was going to work fabulously."

"But I thought you were going to make me an agent," Allison said, barely in control of her voice.

"Don't you understand that you of all people can't skip any steps? You have to do more because of who you are. And because of what you're going to become. I'm sixty-eight, and I won't be around forever."

"But you made George an agent. Right from the mailroom."

"You were absolutely on the mark about him. He's a natural. He's going to become very important someday. And I think that's not too far off."

"What else can I learn typing letters for Lee Simons? And making appointments for her with her manicurist?"

"I know Lee is a bit . . . well, maybe she's not refined. But she has the best deal-making sense I've ever seen. And her ability to sign talent can't be touched by anyone, except perhaps yours truly," answered Gus, a smile playing at the corners of his mouth.

"I can't work for her, Uncle Gus. I just can't."

"Well, it might create a little problem," he said slowly, "but I think I can finesse Lee. I'm sure I can arrange for you to assist Ben Wildman instead. You know how long Ben's been with me."

"But that's not what I mean."

"Ben knows more about this business than almost anyone. You know, years ago I used to call him Univac Wildman. He can give you the deal points in a memo made back in sixty-th—"

"I won't do it, Uncle Gus. I've already served my apprenticeship in this company. You're going too far. If you only knew about George Bellamy and his signing . . . but that's beside the point. I just won't do it."

"You've got to trust me, Allison."

"I already have."

They stood opposite each other for what seemed like minutes before Lillian knocked softly and entered the office.

"Simpson and Bruckheimer are outside for their eleven o'clock."

"I'll be with them in a moment, Lillian," Gus answered, his gaze still fixed on Allison.

"Well, Uncle Gus?" Allison asked after the door closed, not allowing her eyes to retreat from his.

"I'll expect to see you tomorrow morning in Ben Wildman's office," Gus said as he turned and went to his desk.

Allison started to answer, but she knew the vow she was about to make was better left unspoken. She would never work for Ben Wildman or any other agent in the firm. And nothing her uncle could say or do would change that. She turned, placed her champagne glass down carefully, and walked out of the office.

9

"Can I come see you for a moment?" Ben Wildman asked Gus over the phone several days later.

"I'm busy, Ben. Can't we deal with it on the phone?"

"It's about Allison."

"What about her? Still got the flu?"

"I guess so. At least she called in this morning and *said* she was still sick."

"It's that season. A lot of it's going around."

"Maybe," Ben said, and then hesitated before he spoke again. "But I saw her this morning. Having breakfast at the Polo Lounge."

"So? She's probably feeling better. She'll be in tomorrow."

"She was having breakfast with Mike Ovitz."

"What?"

"You heard me. Mike Ovitz. And I don't mean some accountant from Pasadena by that name. I mean Ovitz of Creative Artists Agency. Jesus, he just wooed over two of our top kids from the rock department."

"Get in here fast, Ben." Gus jabbed at the phone button to signal Lillian.

"Yes, Mr. Morton?"

"Get Allison on the phone for me. Try her at home."

A minute later Lillian walked in with Ben.

"She wasn't there, Mr. Morton. The service said she's out of town."

The next day Gus was told by Lee Simons that she had seen Allison having dinner at Spago with Jeff Berg, head of International Creative Management. Feelings of betrayal and profound sadness coursed through Gus. That evening he tried to reach Allison a half-dozen times, but she wasn't in. He even insisted that he and Diana drive up to Allison's house after dinner to make sure something awful hadn't happened to her. The place was quiet and undisturbed—and dark. Clearly nobody was at home. What was going on? After all these years of planning and dreaming, could she possibly be . . . But the thought was too painful to follow to its conclusion.

Though a weekly staff business lunch was scheduled for the following day, Gus instructed Lillian to cancel it. He had to get away from the office. He needed time to himself and wanted to have lunch alone.

Charlie Horner could tell when the boss didn't want to talk, so the drive to La Scala was a silent one. Gus mumbled his thanks to Charlie as he stepped out of the car and entered the cool, dark restaurant. Jean, the owner, showed Gus to his customary table, a banquette in the corner.

"The usual, Monsieur Morton?"

"No, Jean. Not today. I need something a little stronger. Give me a Bombay martini. Very dry. With no fruit."

After the drink arrived, Gus sipped it morosely, the chatter from the other tables as remote as the sound of crickets in the night. It was only after his second drink that he pulled himself out of his thoughts to scan the room. He planted an automatic smile on his face as he nodded to the various studio and network executives, actors, and directors who were scattered throughout the restaurant between tables of overdressed "lunching ladies." And then, in a corner, he saw Allison. He started to get up to walk over to her, to clear up this whole crazy business, when he saw who was seated next to her. Norman Brokaw! Brokaw was a nice man, and Gus always enjoyed talking to him whenever they met at parties and screenings. But Brokaw was one of the heads of the William Morris Agency. And they, more than any other, were U.T.M.'s chief rival. What was Allison doing? Selling an option on her birthright before she had the good grace to bury him? It took all his willpower to keep from rushing across the room. No. Gus Morton couldn't do that. Moving rigidly, as if he were wearing a back brace, Gus got up from his table and walked out of the restaurant.

"That was fast, boss," Charlie said as he held open the door of the Rolls.

"She's in there, Charlie. Sitting there talking to Norman Brokaw. Did you hear me, Charlie?"

"I heard you." The big man looked at Gus in the rearview mirror. "Back to the office?"

"Yes. I mean, no. Stay here. But pull back a little."

Almost an hour later, Allison walked out of the restaurant with Brokaw. Gus watched the two talk animatedly while the valets retrieved their cars. Brokaw's arrived first, and after shaking hands with Allison he got into the tan Mercedes and drove off.

"Now, Charlie. Pull up!" Charlie had rarely heard that kind of urgency in the boss's voice.

"Allison!" Gus called. "Could I speak to you, please."

"Why, Uncle Gus. How are you?" she answered, a huge smile lighting up her face.

"Come with me," he said. "I'll give you a lift."

"But the man is getting my car."

"Charlie, take care of Allison's car. I'll meet you at the office," Gus said as he got out of the back and took over the driver's seat.

"Sure, boss," Charlie responded, clearly unhappy that Gus was intending to drive the Rolls.

"Don't worry, for Christ's sake. You think I'm going to wrack it up? I drive very well and you know it," he called to the retreating chauffeur. Actually, Gus couldn't remember the last time he had driven, but it was something you didn't forget how to do. Like riding a bicycle.

"You know, I've been thinking about your reaction to becoming a secretary," Gus finally said to Allison when they were halfway to the office. "Maybe you're right. I think you are ready to be an agent."

"Uncle Gus, I love you!" Allison yelled as she reached across the seat to hug him. Gus instinctively pulled at the wheel, almost sending them into the path of an oncoming truck.

"Jesus, that was close," he said, breathing heavily. "Let's curtail the celebrating until we make it to the office. I've got to give Charlie a raise. This isn't a piece of cake."

In his office, Gus uncorked a bottle of champagne. "I want to hear your ideas about where you want to start. You should spend a bit of time in each division, including legal. Maybe you ought to start there, in fact. But first," Gus poured champagne into two glasses and clicked his against Allison's, "first there's something very important I need to know."

"What's that?" she asked, grinning.

"Lunch with Brokaw. Dinner with Berg. Breakfast with . . . whomever! What the hell have you been up to with the competition? I've been half out of my mind the last couple of days worrying about the job offers they must be making you."

"What offers?" she asked innocently.

"Come on, 'fess up. You've made it. You're an agent now, so stop torturing me. What in God's sake were you doing?"

"They asked me the same thing, too," answered Allison, now laughing so hard that tears came to her eyes. "I'm sorry, but it *is* funny. You see, I called all of them saying that *you* had to see them immediately. About something very important and," she lowered her voice, "something secret. An important industry piece of business. So important that they had to break whatever they were doing to see you. Then, of course, I showed up instead, saying something even *more* important had come up that kept you away at the last moment, but since they were there, I wanted to tell them about a surprise birthday party I was planning for you. One that would coincide with the major donation you're making to the L.A. County Museum. Those Newmans that you're giving them next month. At least that part is true. Actually, they were all very charming. I had a great time."

All Gus could do was stare at her. And then he started to laugh. And laugh. And laugh.

10

Gus Morton pressed his lips together in a determined effort to be serious, swung his golf club high above his shoulders, and then forward in a long but jerky arc. Raising his head, he watched the ball speed down the fairway—and into a thicket of trees and bushes 150 yards ahead. As it disappeared from sight, he broke out into a big smile, as if his bum shot were something to cheer about. "So, darling," he said gaily, turning to Diana, "is that ball number three or ball number four that I've lost so far?"

"It's the sixth, boss, if you really want to count," said Charlie, answering for Diana. He had parked the golf cart on the edge of the course at a discreet distance, but in the quiet of the late afternoon he might as well have been standing beside them.

"And it serves me right."

"Right," said Diana, taking a practice swing with her club now that it was her turn.

"That little devil, Allison," said Gus, who seemed only to be going through the motions of a game of golf. He could talk of nothing but his niece. "I still can't believe she had me convinced she was going to work for the competition. The Morris office. Not to mention—"

"Hey, Gus, give me a break," interrupted Diana. "I'm just as thrilled as you are that you've worked out everything with Allison, but even if you don't care what you shoot today, which is very unlike you, I do. How am I supposed to concentrate?"

"Sorry, darling, I'll shut up. Promise."

Diana stepped up to the tee and in one perfectly timed and coordinated motion drove the ball within yards of the green.

"I love to see you pull off a shot like that," said Gus, kissing her lightly on the forehead. "You're much smoother than I am."

"Stop trying to flatter me, you old duffer," said Diana, though it was obvious she was pleased by his compliment. They handed their clubs to Charlie and started down the fairway.

They almost never rode in the cart except at midday when the weather was oppressive. Nonetheless, Gus insisted on its presence. Beneath the jaunty striped canopy were fresh towels, a freezer chest stocked with cold drinks, and, most essential, a telephone. Gus could not tolerate being out of reach of a telephone, no matter where he was, whether outdoors, en route somewhere, or ensconced in one of his various houses, each of which boasted so many extensions that when the phone rang it set off a cacophony like the barking of an excited pack of dogs. He was impervious to Diana's teasing on the subject.

"And what if she'd gone to work for C.A.A.? God, what a catastrophe. Think of it, Diana—Allison working for Ovitz. He's as bright as anyone out here, but I'd rather have her working for the Ayatollah. Well, almost," continued Gus, picking up where he had left off a few moments earlier. "She's such a sly one. Reminds me of the time when she was three years old. Did I ever tell you that story?"

Diana nodded wearily. Gus seemed not to notice.

"I used to wear a ring in those days. A garnet, bought it in London after the war, and it fascinated her. She was always reaching for it, and so one day I took it off and gave it to her to play with. Sure enough, she hid it, and then she pretended she'd forgotten where. I turned the house upside down. Nothing. Then I had an idea. I decided to give her something else and follow her, figuring she'd go to the same place where she'd put the ring. Makes sense, right? I took off one of the cuff links I was wearing. They were real beauties. My favorites at the time. Art Deco. Gold and black enamel. And then, just when I was supposed to be trailing her to her cache, I got distracted. The phone rang, and by the time I got back to her, the cuff link had disappeared, too. Well, I was damned aggravated, as you can imagine, but she kept playing innocent. Just couldn't remember where she'd put it. I decided I had to make it worth her while to 'find' my ring and cuff link, so I bought her a gold charm, a little teddy bear with ruby eyes, which is how that bracelet of hers began, as you know, and I asked Teddy to bring her over to my house for another visit. I showed her the charm and asked her if she wanted to make a trade, and right away she gave me this little smile and reached into a plastic purse that she never went anywhere without in those days, and there they were, just where she'd put them in the first place. The ring and the cuff link. The little devil. What do you think of that?"

"What do I think?" said Diana. "I think she knew very well that she had her uncle wrapped around her tiny finger."

"Oh, come on," laughed Gus. "At age three?"

"Absolutely. But tell me, where'd you finally decide to start her off? What comes first?" asked Diana, falling in with Gus's preoccupation.

"Well, maybe the TV department, maybe film."

"That sounds right. Now, what do you want to do about your ball? It was just about here that it disappeared." Diana pointed at the undergrowth.

"I'm certainly not going to go looking for it, if that's what you're asking," said Gus. "I'll happily take the stroke. Charlie, toss me a new ball and my nine iron."

This time Gus succeeded in hitting the ball straight, landing it just off the green, close to Diana's. "Yeah, I think that's what I'll do," he went on, after they had walked for a distance in silence. "I'll start Allison in TV, then move her to film. I want her to get a taste of everything that's important, and most of all, I want her working closely with me. I want to be able to throw things at her that it took me twenty years to learn. I want her to be right in the middle of things, where there's no telling what will come up. After all, I'm not getting any younger, and I want to be able to teach her everything I know."

"And then what, after film and TV?"

"Well . . ."

"Well, in other words, when does she work for me?" asked Diana. She took an iron from Charlie and started lining up the ball for her approach shot.

"I've been thinking about that some more. You run a wonderfully tight ship there, darling. I don't want to give you a swelled head, but just the other day one of our competitors was grousing about how lucky we are to have such a great legal department. Best in town, he said, though I knew that already."

"Oh? Who said that?"

"Gaines, in fact. And he dispenses compliments like the Klan hands out Torahs. But, you know something, I'm not so sure I see Allison spending time in legal after all."

Diana looked up. "You don't? But that's what she's trained to do. Aren't you being a bit capricious?"

"No. Not at all. It just depends on how you look at it. As I see it, Allison already *is* a lawyer. It's not something she needs to be coached in. But she does need to pick up some skills that can't be learned in law school. The sorts of things I learned as a kid in the streets. Staying cool. When to take chances. How not to tip your hand. You know the kind of thing I mean."

Instead of answering, Diana bent over her ball again. She wasn't sorry to lose the services of Allison, but she was angry that Gus hadn't told her he had changed his mind. The legal department had always been part of his plan for Allison. It would have meant more work for Diana to have a junior lawyer under her, but it might have been a way for them to get to know each other better. *Like* each other better. Wasn't that what she really meant? But Diana doubted it would have turned out that way. The chance that she would overcome her wariness of Allison, who was the real focus of Gus's life, was practically nonexistent. Probably it was better this way. But what would the others at U.T.M. think? Would it seem to them that Gus didn't trust her with his cherished heiress? No, his explanation that Allison was already a lawyer would satisfy everyone.

When Diana looked up and saw Gus waiting for her to take her turn, she swung too quickly—and sent her ball into the sandtrap. She took her sand wedge from Charlie and walked down into the trap to size up the position of her ball. The lie wasn't as bad as she had thought it was going to be. She should be able to put it near the pin. She set her feet and took a few practice swings. She tried to fix her mind on the shot and nothing else. Then, just as she thought she was ready, Charlie's voice penetrated her consciousness.

"Boss, it's Allison on the phone."

Diana stepped away from the ball and looked at Gus.

"Sorry, darling," he said over his shoulder, already retreating to the golf cart. "I took Allison to a meeting this morning with Murdoch. I gave her this number. I'll only be a minute."

Diana nodded silently. As she watched him pick up the phone, his face shining with pleasure, she felt as certain as she ever had of anything that it had been Allison's idea, not Gus's, that she skip a stint in legal. Allison had once again wrapped her uncle around her little finger.

And then something else nudged at the edge of Diana's consciousness, something that made her feel uneasy, a memory from long ago. Though she had witnessed countless telephone conversations of Gus's over the years, this time there was something special in his expression and in the way he cradled the phone receiver under his chin and tilted his head to one side. It took her back to another telephone call on another occasion, many, many years earlier. That conversation had taken place in Gus's office on a wonderfully clear, sunny Friday afternoon that would turn out to be one of the bitterest, darkest days of her life.

Diana Paget, only one year out of Stanford Law, stood in Gus's office waiting for his okay on a new contract with NBC for one of the agency's top writing clients. As legal's most junior member, she was seldom entrusted by the chief lawyer, Henry Quincy, with anything important enough to demand Gus's personal attention, but on this contract she had gotten lucky, and her luck was still holding. Not only had Quincy asked her to see it all the way through—his two main associates were both out sick with a virulent new flu, and the work had backed up terribly—but when Diana arrived at Gus's office, his secretary was nowhere in sight. This was more than Diana could have wished for, for what the chief lawyer did not know, and what she hoped no one else in the firm knew, with the exception of Teddy Morton, who would never tell, was that for eleven of the twelve months that she had been employed by Universal Talent Management, she and Gus Morton had been locked in an affair as overwhelming as anything she had ever experienced. Now, her good fortune in being alone with Gus in his office, able to feast her eyes on him with no danger of anyone observing, made her almost tremble with happiness. To add to it, she had something wonderful about the weekend to tell him.

Diana conscientiously drew out her notes on the contract, but Gus interrupted before she could begin. "Slide that stuff over here," he said. He picked up her notes, scanned them, and made three quick checkmarks. "That takes care of business."

"You don't want to hear Mr. Quincy's rationale for these?"

"No, I certainly do not. Quincy is too fond of protocol. He already knows I'll agree." Gus stood up and moved around the desk to Diana. He had broad shoulders and thick dark hair and exuded the kind of energy a person is born with or lacks forever.

"Oh, Gus," said Diana when he reached over and took her hand in his.

"Darling, I love you so much," he said.

"I love you too."

Their lips touched, lightly, but that was all that was necessary to suffuse Diana with yearning. She desperately wanted to hold him and make love to him, there on the gray tweed carpeting of his office. They could lock the door. Gus could tell his secretary he was napping.

As they pulled away from each other, Diana remembered what she had wanted to tell him. "My roommate called a little while ago," she said. "The bank's sending her to Chicago for a meeting. She was going to the apartment to pack. She'll be gone until Sunday. So . . ."

"We have your place to ourselves?"

"Yes, all weekend."

"Well, why didn't you say so earlier? That's wonderful."

"I know." Diana paused. "But what about . . . ?" What about Laura was what she wanted to ask, but she didn't dare. They never, ever spoke about Gus's wife.

"Don't worry," said Gus. He must have guessed what was on her mind. He was already back on the other side of his desk, looking at his appointment calendar. "I feel like celebrating, and I have a great idea. Why waste a beautiful day like this in the office? Let's play hooky. I don't have much on for this afternoon. The only thing that's important is Zanuck, and I can put him off until Monday. I want to take you to Trancas. Remember the house I told you I'm going to buy? I want to show it to you."

"I'd love that. What should I say to Mr. Quincy?"

"You tell *Mister* Quincy you're afraid *you're* coming down with the new flu bug now. You have to get home to bed. That's at least half-true, isn't it?" asked Gus with a teasing smile.

"If you say so," said Diana, laughing. "You're the boss." As she turned to leave, she watched Gus pick up the telephone to cancel his appointments. His face shone with pleasure as he cradled the phone under his chin and tilted his head to one side, just so.

Gus and Diana never got to the beach that day. They decided to stop first at Diana's apartment, in a block of flats below the Chateau Marmont, so she could pick up her bathing suit and some towels. It was a hot day, and when she emerged from the bathroom carrying the towels, Gus asked for something cool to drink. Diana poured them each a glass of wine from a bottle that she had opened the night before, then sat down on the couch next to Gus, leaving the smallest of spaces between them. They both realized, without saying anything, that their visit to Trancas was going to be put off to another day.

Gus took a swallow of wine, then pulled Diana close. "Let's make good on your promise to Quincy. About your going straight home to bed . . ."

"Mmmmm, we should," said Diana, into the hollow of Gus's neck where her face was pressed.

"Come on then," said Gus, trying to get up.

"I don't want to let you go," said Diana, hugging Gus tightly, before allowing herself to be pulled to her feet, where she swayed like a toddler who hasn't mastered the art of standing. She was so weak with desire now that she remained upright only long enough for Gus to open the couch into a bed, then she collapsed on it again. Gus helped her shimmy out of her ladylike linen dress and much less prim silk underwear—gifts from Gus. When they were both naked, they wrapped themselves around each other and then nothing could stop them from making shudderingly violent love of such acute intensity that it seemed like the first time all over again.

When Diana woke an hour later, she was alarmed to see Gus asleep beside her, but then she remembered the incredible gift of time and privacy that had been bestowed on them. This would be the first weekend they had ever spent together. Since the beginning, she had been forced to share him, but not with a woman she could do battle with. Instead, her rival was a person who had disappeared into a memory, with all the power of insubstantiality on her side. Laura, Gus's wife, had been in a coma at Cedars-Sinai for almost two years now, and because Gus thought himself responsible for her being there, he could not let her go. He could not acknowledge that she was no longer part of his life. He visited Laura at the hospital once a week. At Christmas, he set up a small tree in the hospital room and opened presents, taking turns, first one for Laura, then one for himself. He refused to bring Diana home with him to the house he believed he still shared with Laura, which made it difficult for Diana and him to be alone. He rarely mentioned Laura by name and never talked about her.

The little Diana knew about Laura came from office gossip, augmented by the barest of facts told her by Teddy, who was too kind not to tell her. Two years earlier, Diana had learned, Gus had insisted that Laura fly to Tahoe to meet him in spite of forecasts of a heavy storm approaching. The single-engine plane had crashed. The pilot had been killed, and Laura was comatose when they found her. She was not expected to regain consciousness. And she might live for years. Diana tried to feel sorry for Laura, but she couldn't. This vegetable, this nothing, this less than nothing, was stealing her future and she hated her for it.

Now Gus stirred. Diana laid her arm across his chest and kissed his neck.

"Don't. Tickles," mumbled Gus. Then he opened his eyes and drew Diana to him. "I've got pictures," he said, only half-awake.

"Pictures of what?"

"Of the house at the beach. What time is it?" he asked, propping himself up against the pillows.

"It's not even five, sweetie. You're not forgetting we have all weekend, are you? You must really love that house, to wake up thinking about it."

"I do," said Gus, lying down again. "It's the right place at the right time."

"I knew a girl in school named Jill who went to live in Paris after we graduated. Her idea was that you shouldn't wait for a right time to do anything. If you did, it might be too late. So she moved to Paris as soon as she could, even though she didn't have a job and she didn't know anyone, because she figured that whatever else happened in her life, good or bad, she'd be in a place that she really loved."

"How's it working out for her?"

"Maybe it's too early to say, but at least she has a plan. I admire her for that."

"You sound envious," said Gus, "but you shouldn't be. You planned to be a lawyer and you are."

"I mean an *emotional* plan."

"You're losing me a bit. But, you know, plans don't mean much. People do things the way they do because they have to. Usually, no matter what their plans, they don't have a choice. That little house at the beach isn't part of any grand scheme of mine. It's just that I need it. I need it to get the hell away from the craziness of the business and everything else. Just like I need you. Now, shut up and come here," he said, pulling her close again.

"I like to have you order me around," said Diana. She laid her body against his and slowly, tenderly this time, they made love again. Afterward it wasn't sleep Gus wanted, but something to eat.

Diana ticked off the possibilities: guacamole; cheese; Carr's water biscuits.

"That's all you have? No fruit?"

Diana shook her head.

"Darling, you run a skid row icebox. There's never anything in it."

"Whose fault is that, boss dear? Give me a raise and it'll be different," teased Diana.

"You make your demands so sweetly, who could turn you down? But in the meantime, make some guacamole. Nice and fiery. I'm going to take a shower."

The sound of the jet of water quickly drew Diana after Gus. When she opened the door, the steam enveloped her. Gus was standing in front of the mirror, watching as the reflection of his face disappeared in the moisture. His muscles had been brought to a pitch of perfection by a punishing routine of daily exercises. For her benefit, he punched a rolled-up fist against the hard surface of his chest, which was like hurling a handball against a wall.

Discarding her silk robe, Diana made a clearing in the glass with her hand, put an arm around Gus, and leaned her head against his, staring seriously at the mirror as if posing for a camera. "Do you like what you see?" she asked.

"I love what I see."

"So do I. We make a great-looking couple." When Gus did not respond, she went on, unable to stop herself. "Gus, I don't care if you're older than I am. What difference does it make? I mean, *really*."

"You want to know 'really'?" he said sharply. "Well, I'll tell you really, though I don't know why we need to talk about it, since it hasn't anything to do with us. Twenty years' difference doesn't matter now, you're right about that. But fifteen years from now, it would matter a lot. I'd be sixty, but you'd be just forty. In your prime. I'd be an old man, for God's sake. But, darling, we've gone over this too many times already. Why again? What's the point?"

"There isn't any point, I suppose," said Diana bleakly, though she knew better. The point was that she desperately wanted to marry Gus and have his child, and he knew it.

Gus smiled faintly and escaped into the shower. Diana silently followed him in. She positioned herself under the stream of hot water, and as it beat down on her she began to feel better. Nothing was changed, but nothing was lost either. She stood aside to let Gus have a turn. As he slid past her, she felt so much love for him that she reached over and kissed him on the lips, and then she became angry again. She couldn't help it. "Please make things change," she said, holding tight to him.

"What?" He blinked and rubbed water out of his eyes.

"Your . . . wife isn't going to get better. Why keep pretending? You've got to do something about us. I don't think I can stand this anymore."

The anger that sprang into Gus's face was so immediate and so fierce that Diana instinctively grabbed hold of the towel rack for security. She thought he might hit her.

"How can you bring her up now? Don't you know I'm on my way to see her?" he spat.

"You're going to the hospital? But you said earlier not to worry. I thought you meant—"

"You know I always go to the hospital on Fridays, and you thought I was actually going to *skip* it this time? Something I've never done . . . ever. You're so off base it's pathetic. And have I ever, ever given you any reason whatsoever to believe I would divorce her and marry you?"

"No," Diana answered softly.

"Well then!" Gus snapped, with triumphant nastiness.

"But, Gus, don't you see what it's like for me? I'm suspended. I'm trapped. I can't make a move in any direction. I don't know what's going to happen. I can't make plans."

"Plans," said Gus contemptuously. "So that's what was behind all that crap about your friend who went to Paris. Why can't you just come out and say what's on your mind? I can't stand deviousness. I'm getting out of here."

"Good idea," screamed Diana, as Gus got out of the shower. "Go away, and I don't want to see you again. Ever!" she managed to shout before he closed the bathroom door behind him. And then, under the roar of the shower, she began to cry.

She let five minutes pass, maybe ten, before she turned off the water and listened tentatively for sounds from the other side of the door. There was nothing. He must have left. At that moment she truly hated him. He'd be sorry for the way he had treated her. She would make him very sorry.

She had just begun to dry herself when the telephone rang. Gus! He was calling to apologize. He hadn't meant what he had said. She pulled the towel around her and raced for the phone.

"Diana? It's Teddy," said the voice on the other end.

"Oh, hi, Teddy." She couldn't keep the disappointment from her voice.

"Is Gus there? I hate to bother him, but I've got a problem. Something I have to settle now."

"He's not here. He left," she said in a monotone.

"Well, where'd he go?"

"Where do you think? It's Friday."

"Oh." Teddy knew Gus's habits by heart. He didn't know what else to say, and the silence grew awkward.

"I'm not going to see Gus anymore, Teddy," said Diana compulsively. "He's ruining my life. He'll never marry me. Things'll just drag on the way they are forever, I just know it."

"Diana, don't say that."

"It's ridiculous for me to keep on working at the agency. I'm going to quit. I'll go back East. That's where I really—"

"No, now you're being silly."

"No, I'm not."

"Diana, don't talk that way, please. You'll feel better in the morning. I know you will."

"Teddy, you're sweet, but you don't understand. . . ." And then

Diana couldn't hold back her emotions any longer. She began to cry again, quietly, but not so quietly that Teddy couldn't hear her.

"I'm coming over. You don't mean what you're saying. I'll be there in a few minutes."

"Don't, Teddy," she managed to say a few moments later, but he had already hung up.

"What a girl," said Gus, suddenly striding back to Diana from the golf cart, banishing all memories of the past. "Can you believe it, she thought of something I forgot to tell Murdoch this morning. She's going to be a wonder, just a wonder." He paused and shook his head with pride. "Now, whose shot is it?"

"Whose do you think?" said Diana dryly.

"Of course, darling. Take your time. Not another word from me, I mean it this time."

11

t was late Friday afternoon several weeks later when Gus walked into Allison's office. The office, or rather cubicle, was the smallest one in the television division, with a panoramic view of the parking lot. But to Allison the view was gorgeous. Because it was all hers. Hers alone. And she even had a secretary. Allison had asked for Neal Richmond, a bright, hardworking graduate of the USC film school whom she had gotten to know in the mailroom. It was doubly nice not only to extract herself from Mario's gang but to liberate a fellow galley mate, and Neal, of course, would now kill for Allison in gratitude for her freedom.

Allison, who was on the phone, saw her uncle signal her to finish her conversation by drawing his hand across his neck: cut it. She quickly hung up, but before she could ask him what was so important, he sat down on the edge of her desk, smiling conspiratorially.

"Busy?"

"Very. And I'm loving it," she answered.

"Too busy to take a little trip with me this weekend?"

"I don't think so, but what do you have in mind?"

"Give me your answer first, then I'll tell you," said Gus, enjoying himself.

"Okay, but I need a moment to think. I have a party tomorrow night that I was looking for an excuse to miss anyway. And a bunch of chores that I'd be delighted to put off. That's about it, so count me in. Where're we going?"

"Mazatlán"

"Hey, great! But you've always told me you don't like Mexico."

"I've resolved to become more open-minded as I enter my golden years," said Gus, his smile broadening.

"I'll believe that when I believe Boesky got his information out of fortune cookies. What are we going to do down there?"

"See the sights. Maybe a little fishing."

"You get seasick in the bathtub, Uncle Gus," Allison said laughingly.

"Can't let old habits run your life, my dear niece."

"If I may ask, when do we leave?"

"Now. Charlie's downstairs waiting for us. And don't worry about clothes. That's been taken care of already. I think this will be both a fun *and* an interesting weekend."

The Gulf Stream III leveled off at thirty-four thousand feet over Ocotillo Wells, the waters of the Salton Sea off to the left rippling like a party dress under the last light of day. Gus smiled. They were just where they were supposed to be. As soon as they had boarded and settled into their seats, the pilot had come out from the flight deck to review the flight plan. Though Gus gave no more thought to flying than to taking a morning shower, he wanted always to be in control, to know where the bad weather was or the high winds. Surprise was for farmers, he liked to say.

The body of the plane was sheathed in the same mirror-lacquer white as Gus's Rolls. Just as charcoal gray was the color of his business suits, all of which were identical so that Albert had to number the jackets and pants to ensure they received equal wear, all of his, or rather U.T.M.'s, means of transportation were in "Gus Morton White." He and the agency were interchangeable, or so his accountants maintained. So far they had labored successfully with the IRS to prove his every expense was a business expense.

The plane's interior was one of Angelo Donghia's last major assignments. The seats were soft glove leather, the color of a dove, except for a banquette upholstered in dark gray vicuña. The carpeting was a rich burgundy with the U.T.M. logo worked into the border in wavy chains. An Aubusson rug had been fitted over the bulkhead to conceal a specially designed TV screen. A table made of malachite that seated four occupied the middle of the cabin, with a map of the world inlayed on top in mother-of-pearl.

Allison, Gus, and Charlie were finishing off a platter of stone crabs and a salad of *mâche* and chanterelle mushrooms that the steward, Micky—who had been with Gus since the agency had acquired its first plane, a twin-engine Convair—had picked up at Chasen's just before takeoff. They washed the meal down with a blanc de blanc that came from a village just south of Grasse and was chilled to the temperature of water drawn from a deep well. Charlie, who never drank while on duty, was on his second bottle of Dr. Brown's celery tonic.

"I still smell business, Uncle Gus," said Allison, placing her glass on the table.

"That's funny. All I can smell is the ocean and maybe a little pompano grilled on the beach," said Gus. He was in his customary airborne attire—a burgundy silk smoking jacket and a pair of black slippers of nubby leather. An old Turkish shoemaker in Camden Passage outside central London made them for him. Luckily for Gus, the old man had two sons, so the slippers were in no danger of extinction. When Gus Morton found something he liked, he wanted that item and nothing else.

"You're not going to give me even a clue?"

"Allison, my dear," said Gus, leaning back in his lounge chair, "what type of business do you think we could conduct in Mazatlán? Book a rhumba band into a club? Can't an uncle get a little time alone with his niece? You're as suspicious as other people accuse me of being!"

"No way, boss," said Charlie, signaling Micky for another soda. "The guys in the mob are like blue-haired old dames compared to you. And by the way, I think the last time we were in Mexico was to visit Huston when he was directing that picture with Taylor and Burton."

"Can't we all just take it easy and enjoy a little time away from the office?" Gus asked, placing the backgammon board on the table. "I feel hot tonight. Who's the first victim?"

The next day went just as Gus had said it would. No business, just fun. With Charlie driving a hired stretch white Cadillac with fringed curtains draping the back windows, they shopped, took in the sights, and walked the beaches. It was good to see her uncle so relaxed, Allison thought, as she prepared for the evening. She loved his company, his stories, his sense of humor, and she realized that it had been a long time since the two of them had been together alone, without business or social demands. And, yes, without Diana, for that matter. Getting away to a new place was a wonderful idea. As she finished putting on her makeup, she eyed herself in the mirror. *From now on, dummy,* she thought, *take your uncle at his word instead of looking for something that's not there.*

Gus had heard of a seafood restaurant called Las Tres Marias that was located on the beach and reportedly served the best grilled lobster in town. They were led to a beautifully situated table, facing the ocean, by the owner, who greeted Gus as if he were royalty.

"It never hurts to have the right person make your reservations," he said, anticipating her question. "The ambassador said this place was terrific when I called to tell him we'd be down for a few days. He insisted on making the reservation for us."

Charlie, who had begged off dinner so he could catch the fights at the local *coliseo,* was not scheduled to pick them up for two hours, so they started with margaritas and settled in for a long, leisurely dinner. They had just ordered a second round when there was a sudden commotion across the room. Heads turned to see a large party enter the restaurant and approach the table next to the one where Gus and Allison were seated.

Leading the pack of beautiful women and large, menacing men was a figure as recognizable as any who appeared with regularity on the cover of *People* magazine. He stood six feet six in his bare feet, and the body that had made him NCAA heavyweight wrestling champion for all of his four years in college had not deserted him, though he had been out of school almost twenty years. He was dressed in a white linen suit over a black silk shirt, and by the unsteady way he walked it was clear that Rocco Rocallo was drunk. And he had reason to be. His new movie, *Midnight Time,* had opened two weeks earlier to scathing reviews. The second week's business was down by almost 75 percent and the first week hadn't been that hot to begin with. This was the third turkey in a row that he had starred in after making two of the biggest-grossing films of the last ten years, *Bomber* and *Bomber II.*

It wasn't until he sat down that Rocco noticed Gus Morton. He sprang up so suddenly that his bodyguards started to go for their holsters. Quieting them down, Rocco lurched over to Gus's side.

"Hi ya, Gus. What are you escaping from?" he asked as he shook the older man's hand.

"This is my niece, Rocco. Allison Morton. Allison, meet the famous Rocco Rocallo."

Rocco eyed Allison with the knowing look of someone experienced at buying both at Christie's, where he lately had taken a stab at the high end of the serious art market, and at much less formal auctions where other types of merchandise were offered. "Pleased to meet you, Allison," he said, putting on his best movie-star smile.

"Why don't you take a seat, Rocco. I haven't seen you in a long time," said Gus, who showed no surprise at encountering the actor in this unlikely spot.

"I'd love to, but I got my party with me and—"

"They're not going anywhere, Rocco. You still pick up the check, don't you?"

Rocco Rocallo tilted back his head and laughed mightily. Whatever few pairs of eyes had not been trained on him already were hooked now. "How long you down for, Gus?" he asked as he sat down.

"Just for the weekend, Rocco. You?"

"I've been here a week. I'll stick around for another. Maybe two. Maybe forever. Who knows."

"What have you lined up to do next?"

"Did you see my last picture, Gus?" Rocco asked, disregarding Gus's question. He shifted in his chair in such a way that his face was just inches from Gus's.

"I screened it last week, Rocco."

"And?"

"Unvarnished truth, Rocco?" asked Gus, looking directly at the star.

"Yes. They," he gestured over his shoulder at the table of his hangers-on, "certainly won't tell me."

"It was shit, Rocco. Pure shit."

"And my performance?"

"When you sleep with dogs you wake up with fleas. Even Olivier would look like a jackass in that role. Enough said?"

"You've always been a straight shooter, Gus. Remember that time after the first *Bomber* picture when you came to me for representation?"

"Sure. You turned me down," said Gus, sipping his drink.

"No one ever accused me of being a genius. What I need now is a drink," he said, signaling for a waiter.

"No, you don't, Rocco. What *you* need is a good script."

"You don't happen to have one with you, do you?" he asked with a grin that showed no humor at all.

"I might," said Gus matter-of-factly.

"Where is it?" asked Rocco excitedly. "I'd like to get my hands on it."

"Would you now? Well, maybe I can help you out, even though Mazatlán at nighttime isn't very conducive to reading. People have always told me I'm pretty good at telling a story, so I recorded a synopsis of the script on a cassette for you. I already asked the manager at your hotel to have it delivered to your suite, along with a tape deck in case you don't have one along with you."

"You're kidding, Gus."

"Not at all. And there's a second cassette, too. That one's an outline for *Bomber III,* which I've heard you've had problems getting off the ground. But bear in mind one thing, Rocco."

"What's that?"

"I haven't changed my occupation. I'm not interested in producing you. I still make my living representing people like yourself."

"So if I like the material, you get to represent me, is that it?"

"Exactly. But you know something? You need me, Rocco. You need me real bad."

"I think you might just be right," Rocco said after a moment.

"I want you to listen to both tapes tonight. If you like what's on them, I'll give you the scripts to read tomorrow."

"And I suppose you represent the writers, right?"

"Right. That's my business, isn't it? So, if you like what you hear on the cassettes, be at my suite at nine in the morning."

"You're some piece of work, Mr. Gus Morton. Just too much. But it's a deal. As soon as I've had dinner, I'll go back to the hotel and listen to the stuff."

"No, go back *now,* Rocco," said Gus firmly. "You've had enough booze already. I'll make sure a pot of hot coffee's waiting for you. And don't worry about your party. I'm a pretty good man at picking up a check, too. Remember, my place at nine."

"Where you staying, Gus?"

"Just look up, Rocco. That's all you have to do. Look up. I'm in the suite above you."

The next morning Gus signed Rocco Rocallo. He added a special clause to the contract specifying that if Rocco didn't get twice what he was receiving now per picture—which was just under four million—he could leave the agency at any time simply by giving written notice. In exchange, he extracted a promise from Rocco that he would never second-guess him. What Gus Morton told him to do, Rocco would do. No ifs, ands, or buts.

"I know your spies must have told you Rocco was going to be at the restaurant last night, but did they also say he'd be seated right next to us?" Allison asked Gus as they flew back to L.A. after the deal was completed.

"What do you think?"

"I'll bet you even knew he was going to be drunk," she said, smiling.

"I guessed that, which wasn't very hard, I'm afraid, but you noticed I wouldn't make a deal with him until today. When he was absolutely sober."

"Why didn't you wait until you both got back to town?"

"And go up against every other agent in town with the same idea? Remember, Allison, there's nothing wrong with approaching talent when their egos have suffered a contusion or two. A fragile ego is a wonderful thing to work with," he added with a smile. "Perfect for an agent who knows his craft. Highly malleable. If you need certain information to pull off a deal like this, by the way, it's okay to go after it in any way you can, including buying it, so long as you keep it legal and don't hurt anybody. Yes, I admit that I paid to find out where Rocco was staying, what his mood was, and what kind of daily routine he had. Fortunately, we're all creatures of habit. But I also gave Rocco something that's going to change his life."

"And what's that?"

"Me! He finally has an agent who can help him shape his career. He knows I'll always give him both sound counsel and straight answers. And best of all, I have his next two pictures worked out. I don't have a doubt in the world that he'll be earning at least twice what he's making within a year."

"But I was right, Uncle Gus, when I said that this would be a business trip."

"Did you have fun this weekend?" he asked Allison, looking closely at her.

"Well . . . yes. I had a great time."

"That's just it. Business is fun. It's always been that way for me. I love it. And I know you will also. You're just like me. But there's one little thing I promised Rocco that I think I may regret."

"What could that possibly be?"

"That I'd send the plane down to pick him up next week. Knowing Rocco Rocallo, it won't be the last time he'll use this G-Three."

12

---

llison Morton looked again at the note she had received from George Bellamy. It was written on a heavy piece of cream-colored stock with the initials G.B. engraved at the top.

In the six weeks she had been an agent, Allison had helped Gus renegotiate an incredible new deal with NBC for Eve and Alan Shore, a husband and wife writing and producing team whose show, *Pink Sands,* was one of the hits of the current season, and on her own had signed four promising young actors. One of them currently was up for a key supporting role in a movie that would star Charlie Sheen. She also had a big auction scheduled for the movie rights to Lavinia Tedesco's *The Question Is,* with at least two producers ready to do armed battle for it. Next to George Bellamy, however, Allison felt as if she were standing still. One rock group after another had flocked to him. He was suddenly the most talked about young agent in town. Some were calling him the next David Geffen. Allison knew for a fact that already Gus had had to sweeten George's deal, not once but twice. And not only had he been given a company Mercedes, but he had been granted one of the favored parking spots, a true indicator of status.

The torrid pace George was setting at the agency was more than matched by his social life. His name had begun to appear with the frequency of a star's in Army Archerd's column in *Daily Variety* and Hank Grant's in *The Hollywood Reporter*. And it didn't stop there. If a party was being covered by *Women's Wear Daily,* it was a sure bet George would be pictured in its pages the next day. Raw silk jacket over an open shirt. A few dark curling chest hairs visible, just enough to give the right virile signals. A pretty young thing on his arm. Often as not the pretty young thing had a glazed look in her eyes, and though this might be attributable to the pop of the camera, Allison doubted it.

Allison stood up at her desk and pulled on her jacket. She would be late for her lunch date if she didn't hurry. Irresistibly her eye was drawn once more to George's note.

I guess the only way I can get you to pay attention to me is to put a few words down on paper. You don't know how it makes me feel at meetings never to be able to catch your eye. Just give me a chance to explain. If we can't get back to where we were, at least we can learn to work together. And don't forget, I owe you a margarita.

The note, like everything else about George, was disarming. But Allison knew the truth: the only person who could trust George Bellamy was . . . George Bellamy. He didn't give a damn about her. He just liked the sound of her last name. Morton, as in Gus Morton.

When she thought about last fall and the great times they had had and how sexy he had seemed to her, it was laughable. The truth was that the great times wouldn't have lasted anyway, even if George hadn't stolen Felix Godwin from her. The other George, the real one, kept showing through, even then. The George who would do anything to get ahead. The worst of it was that he seemed to be succeeding at it. He had beaten her only by a month in being named an agent—February for him, March for her—but already he was making himself indispensable. He was the talk of the agency. George this, George that. It was disgusting. And where was she? Lost in the dust. Still Gus Morton's little niece. The heiress apparent. She despised the comparison. Who knew, maybe Gus even compared them privately—and found her wanting. The thought galled her, but what could she do? And then, in that moment, an idea occurred to her. If she put some distance between herself and George, she could be more her own person. She could transfer to New York for a while, where two important divisions of the agency, dramatic and literary, were headquartered. Gus had always told her he wanted her to have a taste of every side of the agency, those included. Well, now was the time. Her life in L.A.—the house, the car, the proximity to Gus—wouldn't disappear. It would still be here.

New York would be a perfect testing ground for her. The name Gus Morton was important there, but it did not have the same clout as in Los Angeles, a town obsessed with movies and television. Many other worlds intersected in New York. This would give her a chance to prove herself to Gus, show him she could measure up on her own, that she didn't need him beside her. The more she thought about New York, the better the idea of moving there seemed. In fact, it was a positively brilliant idea.

Allison didn't waste time raising the question with Gus. The opportunity came the following Saturday in Palm Springs. After a marathon backgammon contest between Gus and Charlie that lasted the better part of the afternoon, Charlie and Diana had driven into town to buy steaks for dinner. Although Gus always brought Albert and his wife, Maria, down for the weekend to run the household, there was nothing he enjoyed more than grilling thick steaks himself out by the pool.

The afternoon sun was beginning to sink behind the mountains. Gus and Allison sat side by side on the patio looking out over the golf course spread before them like a lush private park. The intensity of its greenness next to the surrounding desert always amazed Allison. It was like stepping into a walled oasis. A water hazard, masquerading as a small, charming pond complete with a family of ducks, nestled below them where the lawn sloped down to meet the fairway. The house was situated at the fourth tee, so the last golfers of the day had come and gone a good half hour earlier. Gus stood up to mix himself a gin and tonic and, after a nod from Allison, one for her as well.

"What's on your mind, Allie sweetheart?" he asked as he handed her the drink.

"What do you mean?"

"I wouldn't be much of an uncle," he said, smiling, "if I didn't have some notion what makes you tick. You've been much too quiet all afternoon. When I asked you about the Meyers deal earlier you actually had to go look up the answer in your briefcase. Not like you, Allie! Not at all. You were miles away."

Allison, who had been gazing idly over the pond, turned and looked directly at her uncle. "I want to move to New York."

"Why, for God's sake?"

"It makes perfect sense."

"Really? I may be slow, but I don't understand. You finally got what you wanted. You're an agent. You're doing what you've wanted to do all along. Why turn your back on it?"

"But I wouldn't be. I'm not suggesting I want to live there permanently. Just long enough to see how that part of the business works."

"But L.A. is the center of our operation, honey. Eighty percent of our revenue comes from here."

"Yes, I know, but lots of movie packages start out as books and plays, don't they? And that's in New York. Uncle Gus, you remember the fabulous time I had the summer I read for the literary department. I loved it, but it wasn't enough. I want to learn more. You know whatever I pick up will just make me all the more valuable to you. You've said so yourself."

"Are you giving me the real reason, Allie?"

"Yes, absolutely," she answered with what she hoped was conviction.

"You and George were pretty friendly once, weren't you?" said Gus, after taking a small sip from his drink.

"This has nothing to do with George."

"I don't think I completely believe you, but I'll let it slide. You know, George is a phenomenon. I haven't seen anybody with his drive, his savvy, his acute social instinct, since I don't know when. He reminds me of Charley Feldman, or even Leland a bit. Only not as polished, of course. He's just the right man for his generation. He seems to understand these weird rock musicians inside out. And they love him for it."

Allison said nothing. These were exactly the sort of comments she would no longer have to hear when she moved to New York.

"All right," said Gus, observing Allison's continuing silence. "You have my blessing. I won't stand in your way, though I hate to lose my new right hand as soon as I've acquired her. But so be it. Until you find a place of your own, I want you to stay in our apartment in the Olympic Tower. The location is perfect—only a few blocks from our offices. There's something else I must talk to you about now, though. If you're going East, I can't put it off any longer. I've made a change in my finances that affects you directly. And I'm not talking about my will." Gus paused, then continued, his voice softening. "You know, Allie honey, you're the most important thing in the world to me. Everything I have will go to you when I hang up my . . . What does an agent hang up?"

"The telephone?"

"Yes, something like that. I intend to live forever, naturally, but when I do go, you know my dream is for you to succeed me. Someday you'll run U.T.M. And it will be a very different U.T.M. than it is now. I'm on the verge of making some acquisitions that are going to change the entire scope of the company. Make it much more than just a talent agency. Since you'll be at the center of it, you have to start preparing."

"What are you talking about, Uncle Gus?"

"Money, Allie. Money. Something we haven't talked about much, but now we must. I've just transferred some investments into one of your accounts. It will generate ten thousand a month after taxes. I'm going to leave it entirely up to you what you do with it. Spend it, invest it, save it. Whatever you want. That's on top of your salary, of course."

Allison looked stunned. She started to say something, but Gus held up his hand.

"Hear me out, Allie. This is important. It's time you realized you're a wealthy young woman. I want you to have experience dealing with money. Money always complicates things. Here you are, beautiful, smart, funny, charming. Maybe I'm prejudiced, but I don't think so. You're everything some young guy could possibly want. But someday a man may come along who isn't interested in you because you're you, but because you have money. You have to learn how to deal with that kind of situation."

"Oh, Uncle Gus, this is beginning to sound like the start of a miniseries. But I've got to tell you, I'm a bit overwhelmed by all this."

"Well, don't be. It'll sort itself out, you'll see. We'll talk more about it later. Right now I have a couple of secrets to confess. I hope they won't make you mad. I may not be ready to write a script myself yet, but you'll see how well I can put my imagination to use when I'm inspired."

Allison looked questioningly at her uncle.

"You remember your first day in the mailroom?"

"How could I forget?" she said with a smile.

"Rob Loomis had you chase down a pair of sunglasses for him? Then he sent you in search of a particular carwash he insisted on using?"

"I remember."

"And then, what was it happened the next week? Jack Epstein made you go all the way out to Malibu twice a day to feed that stupid cat of his?" Gus paused, really grinning now. "Well, those were all my ideas. I told everybody to make it as tough for you as they could. To be as demanding and petty as they chose. I wanted to see if you could take it. And did you ever! With flying colors. You didn't let it rattle you one little bit."

Allison, who couldn't believe what she was hearing, felt a rush of irritation at the remembrance of those weeks. It already seemed so long ago, though, and her uncle was so evidently relishing his joke that it was impossible to stay angry for long.

"And what about Lee Simons's license plates?" Allison asked caustically.

"No, that one I can't take credit for. I never included Lee in my schemes. That was Lee's idea entirely. Lee's in a class of her own. She's a user. If she thought she could get away with it, she would have sent *me* to the motor vehicle bureau."

Allison laughed. "Does this mean you're going to conjure up more surprises for me in New York?"

"No, honey, I'm through with surprises, though I do wish one more on you. I wish you'd discover you didn't like New York so much after all and you'd come right back home. I'm going to miss you. Diana will too."

When Allison made no comment, Gus added, "She really will, you know. She cares a great deal for you, and why wouldn't she? The three of us have been together a long time. I've never talked about this to you, and now is not the time, but I should have married her after your aunt

Laura died. You were only three then. It's so long ago, it seems like another lifetime."

Allison and Gus met each other's eyes, and then as if a signal had passed between them, Gus fell silent and let the beauty of the sunset take over. As the last fingers of sunlight, like the points of a star, pushed out over the jagged mountains, the sense of peace became almost palpable. Without a word, they reached out and clasped hands. And there they sat as the sky shaded into darkness, just holding hands, for they didn't know how long, until suddenly Diana was asking when Charlie should light the coals for the steaks.

13

The man Gus Morton turned Allison over to in New York was Hal Gilliam, head of the agency's literary department.

"Show her the ropes, Hal," Gus had said. "She wants to find out how you book people run things. She's always had her nose in a book since she was a kid. How you fit her in is your business. Her law degree should turn out to be a real help to you, by the way. She's a hell of a negotiator. Figure she'll stay with you three months. Maybe. Certainly no more than six."

Sure thing, Hal had thought. Three months. No more than six. He'd believe it when he saw her go. With Allison's entire generation in love with movies, it was his luck that the boss's heir was a bookworm. He had no reason to distrust Gus. He had never played dirty with him. Even so, it smelled like a setup. Probably Allison wanted the book department for herself.

Lee Simons had given him an earful about Allison. The princess-in-waiting, Lee called her with a sneer. But that was typical Lee. Lee reserved nice remarks for people who were dead, socially advantageous to her, or clients. It must have been six or seven summers ago that Allison had worked in Hal's department. She was pretty, smart, and eager. And she reeked of privilege. She had not behaved like a spoiled brat, but she was one of those kids who had grown up with options. Every option. She could pick and choose what to do with her life, with no constraints, and the poor-boy sensibility that Hal had never completely shed was stung by the comparison with his own meager beginnings. Allison had performed beautifully that summer. Too beautifully, Hal now thought. In his mind's ear, he heard Gus reason: My darling Allison, why don't you take charge of a department of the agency so you really get a sense of bottom-line responsibility?

Hal knew he was being irrational, but since Allison had reported for work, he couldn't keep waves of paranoia from sweeping over him daily. He told himself over and over again that Gus wouldn't replace him, even with his niece. He had taken over a nonentity of a literary department and made it the best in town.

When Hal had joined the department, it had been a lackluster affair, with few bestselling or important writers. It seemed to function mainly as a service to the agency's big name performers who wanted fluff autobiographies churned out by the hacks who made up the bulk of the client list. During his apprenticeship, Hal honed his skills and read voraciously. He moved into the New York literary world and became known not just to writers and publishers but to critics and foundation heads. When the chance came to head the department, he was ready. In his first year, he managed to pull off enough coups to get the place noticed, something that had never happened before. He weeded the second-raters off the list and hired several bright, young agents. People in the industry started to notice. Within five years he had accomplished the unimaginable. He had made U.T.M. the premier book agency in town, with more major authors on its client list, both commercial and literary, than any other.

Gus Morton was gratified to see U.T.M.'s serious writers collecting awards, but he was ecstatic over the bestsellers generated by its substantial number of top authors. The possibilities for packaging these big hits was where U.T.M. really made its money. The television and movie divisions joyously competed for the spoils. Last year's Academy Award picture had been based on a novel written by a U.T.M. client. It was then adapted, directed, and produced for the screen by U.T.M. clients. Even one of its stars was from the U.T.M. roster. And Hal Gilliam deserved a large part of the credit for making it happen.

Now that he was a success, Hal had started to live that way. He dressed in Versaces, Armanis, and Missonis. More and more often he stayed in town overnight at the company's Olympic Tower apartment so he could attend functions he thought he ought to be seen at. When Gus installed Allison in what he had begun to think of as "his" apartment, it was a major struggle for Hal to get his petulance under control.

Before Allison had left for New York, Gus had told her a few things about Hal Gilliam.

"Hal might seem a little pretentious," he said, "but don't let that throw you. He's extremely knowledgeable. Very well-read. And that includes the classics. Doesn't hurt him, that. Just the opposite. As you know, creativity in this business often means creative copying, so that gives Hal the jump on a lot of people. He can go back a hundred years, two hundred years, instead of only half a dozen, to help writers find good plots. He's terribly clever at it. He can go into a story session with a writer and really wing it. The writer's grateful—at last, an idea!—and U.T.M. is sitting pretty on another big, filmable property."

When Allison tried to get to know Hal, she was disappointed. Though pleasant, he was remote. She felt she didn't know him any better than she had during those few summer months when she was screening over-the-transom submissions and running errands. He seemed to be holding back some important part of himself. She couldn't put her finger on the problem. His staff of some two dozen kept their distance, too. At loose ends, Allison studied the contract files, read through the manuscripts of the agency's upcoming big books, and sat in on every meeting she could.

At one of these meetings two weeks or so after she'd arrived, Allison came up with something that she instantly recognized as beginner's luck. They were discussing a major client with an overabundance of talent and a highly messy personal life. Hugo Perlstein was about to go through a fourth divorce, which he desperately required some cash to finance, yet he refused to sign a contract for another book even though publishers were lined up for him. During his last crisis he had overcommitted himself, he said, and it had nearly killed him. He had frozen up, with almost a terminal case of creative gridlock, and had been unable to write a coherent word for nearly a year.

"Well," said Allison after hearing about the impasse, "if Perlstein won't let us auction a new book, what about auctioning an *option* to a new book? One of these publishers who says they're dying to have him can buy the right to the first crack at the next book. On his terms, when he's ready."

"Dammit, that's a good idea," said Hal, who had been leaning back in his chair tugging distractedly on an earlobe. "The first good idea I've heard in days. About anything."

And that, thought Allison, *is the first enthusiasm you've shown me.* Almost, but not quite. He had been delighted when she told him she had decided to move out of the company apartment. That is, as soon as she could find an apartment of her own.

Cynthia, who lived on the Upper West Side, didn't have any leads, and the ads in *The Times* were equally unproductive, so after a week of frustration Allison called a real estate agent Gus had suggested. As she spoke to the agent from the U.T.M. apartment on the top floor of the Olympic Tower, she looked out at the view down Fifth Avenue. It was addictive. She could see over the spires of St. Patrick's, reduced from this lofty height to the delicate, twisted accretions of a sandcastle, down past the monolithic towers of Rockefeller Center shouldering their way into the sky, to the Empire State Building beyond, and finally to the elegant wedge of the Flatiron Building, which marked not just a turn in the avenue but the end of another era. It was a gorgeous early May morning. The sky was Tintoretto blue, and flags hanging from nearly every façade snapped in the wind. During a freak spring snowstorm that occurred shortly after she had arrived, the view had been completely obscured but in the most entrancing and magical way. With nothing to see but heavy white tumultuous flakes against the backdrop of a white sky, she felt as if she had been thrust into the middle of a child's whirling snow scene toy.

Even though it meant sacrificing this spectacular site, Allison wanted to be on her own.

In the first two days the agent showed her a dozen apartments on the Upper East Side. Money was no problem and several were charming and spacious. This was the part of town where Allison had grown up, but something had changed. Or rather, she had changed. It was so neat and tidy . . . and antiseptic. She immediately switched her search-and-buy mission to Lower Manhattan, and that weekend saw a huge loft in an exquisite cast-iron building on Chambers Street. Cynthia declared it a find. Three thousand square feet of raw space. Skylights. High, deep, sit-in windows. And best of all, a marvelous view of the Hudson, punctuated by water towers and roof gardens.

"TriBeCa! Where the devil is that? New Jersey?" joked Uncle Gus when Allison called to tell him she was buying a loft. "And a loft? I thought that's where people sewed shirts."

"I didn't say Trenton, Uncle Gus. And a loft gives me several times the space I would have in a regular apartment."

"Is it safe?"

"Yes, if you rule out being attacked by rich old men on their way from their limos to the hot new restaurants."

"Luckily, I'm not in that group. Can't remember the last time I was south of the Four Seasons. By the way, how are you and Hal Gilliam getting along? He told me you came up with a great scheme for solving Perlstein's money problems. Simon and Schuster snapped the deal up right away, he said."

"I was hoping it would work out that way."

"You mean you didn't know? What gives? You two don't talk to each other?"

"Of course we do. All the time," she said, scrambling. "I'm just a little out of touch with the day-to-day stuff, that's all. I think Hal's great, even if—"

"Even if nothing. I just talked with him. He thinks you're the bright-
est thing to come down the pike in years. And I know he wasn't buttering
me up either. He said that your idea was the most creative approach to
deal-making he's heard of since he got into the business."

In a flurry of activity, Allison hired a young woman architect to trans-
form the empty interior of her new loft into two enormous rooms, one for
entertaining and one for her bedroom and dressing room. During lunch
she shopped for furniture and fabrics in the Decoration & Design Building and along Madison Avenue. Sotheby's was holding an important
Continental furniture auction later in May, which she circled in her date-
book. She wanted at least one large Biedermeier piece to set the mood.
While she camped out in a corner of the loft behind a folding screen, the
construction work began around her. She extracted a promise from the
architect that the space would be in decent enough shape by mid-June so
that she could throw a party for everybody she had met in New York
before they scattered for the summer.

Although Allison knew relatively few people before she arrived in the
city and no one well except for Cynthia, her social calendar started filling
up. She had more invitations than she could handle, and why not? She
was smart and pretty, and being the heir to U.T.M. certainly did not
hurt. Her name began to appear in the columns, flitting from Suzy to
Liz. *Women's Wear Daily* dubbed her "the talent scionette." Hal, who had
finally decided that Allison had no designs on his job, became the biggest
tease of all, calling her "the semi-, demi-, and haute-monde's favorite
dinner guest."

Increasingly Hal drew Allison into the workings of the department.
She helped him negotiate new contracts for all the important authors and
began to develop her own list of writers. At the top of the list was Lavinia
Tedesco, whose big novel was due any day now.

Late one afternoon Hal asked her into his office and handed her three
heavy boxes bound together with thick rubber bands. It was an immense
novel by a writer who hadn't been heard from in almost ten years and in
fact had been dropped from the list of active clients. The author had
written a couple of novels in the late 1960s that had been well reviewed,
so attention had to be paid. Would Allison give Hal her opinion? That
night Allison took the manuscript home, settled down on her bed—the
one comfortable spot in the unfinished loft—and read until the lines began to blur and she could no longer hold her eyes open. The next morning she called in sick and delved back into the book. She was captivated.

The book was about a family of diamond merchants. The story began in Syria in the late 1800s, shifted to Antwerp, and then when the family split in two, moved to London and New York. The feuding American and English branches of the family set about sabotaging each other, almost, but not quite, destroying themselves and their fortune in the process. It was perfect for a miniseries. On a hunch Allison dug out the agency's file copies of the writer's earlier books, skimmed through them for early threads to the diamond saga, and quietly got back the author's rights to two essential titles whose publisher had long ago let them go out of print. Only when every detail was in place, and not a moment before, did Allison triumphantly give Hal the opinion he had casually requested barely a week earlier—and together they helped the West Coast TV department make a deal with ABC that set the book industry buzzing. The auction for the publication rights, though seemingly anticlimactic after the TV hubbub, proved anything but. And at the end of two days of fevered bidding, Hal and Allison closed a sale for just under two million dollars. The sweet note and case of champagne that Allison received the next day from the once-broke author was one of the best presents she had ever received.

After a score like that, Allison still didn't kid herself that the literary-agency business was easy. Even with the impressive client list that Hal Gilliam had put together, it was hard work. It hadn't been any fun, for instance, picking up the pieces of the career of a wildly successful writer of contemporary romantic novels named Sheila Lapham, a.k.a. Melody Trask, after she'd been busted for cocaine. The headlines were terrible, *Entertainment Tonight* gave Sheila's problems three nights' play, and worst of all, her publisher, a conservative, family-owned house, decided not to pick up her option. The department and the writer sweated it out until Hal and Allison hit upon the idea of Sheila reestablishing herself by writing a candid account of how drugs had taken over her life. The book proposal—and a multibook contract for three romances—sold overnight to a new publisher for the largest advance the author had ever received.

Juggling her work and her social life was a trick Allison had not quite mastered. One evening in early June, soaking in her brand new Jacuzzi while she studied the seating arrangement for the business party she was throwing the following week, it occurred to Allison that in the last month she had been out every single evening but one. There had been dinners for media and political guests of honor, larger gatherings at spots like Mortimer's, black-tie benefits for somebody's favorite charity. In between were concerts at Lincoln Center, dancing at Nell's, dinners at Le Bernardin or Elio's. Small wonder that she was exhausted, and here she was complicating her life further. But this party was important. It would be the first in her new loft.

Before the party she showed the guest list to Hal.

"Quite a line-up of authors. I'd call it literary A-prime. But you're going to put a lot of our colleagues in the business into a state."

"Look at the next page," answered Allison.

"You crafty devil," said Hal with a grin. "You've also invited their agents."

"Why deprive anyone of a good party," said Allison mischievously.

And from Asimov to Wolfe, they all came to Allison's loft. Most came because they wanted to meet Gus Morton's niece, others for the excitement of an important New York literary event. Allison added to the broth of writers, agents, and publishers by sprinkling in a few movie stars. Publishing folk, no matter how much they paraded a blasé attitude, loved being around stars. And the stars, for their part, relished the idea that someone might think they read books and were therefore "serious." The party was an unqualified success.

The one thing all this social activity did not produce was an interesting man. The charming ones were already spoken for. The others, the availables, were either wealthy, old, and randy, or wealthy, young, and undersexed. As unlikely as it seemed, these encounters made her wistful for the relationship she might have had with George Bellamy.

Although these social occasions seemed thoroughly innocuous, one of them was not. It was a dinner dance at the Met for cancer research, one of the last parties of the season, and, though Allison was unaware of it, forces were set in motion that would change her life significantly. The setting was romantic—the Temple of Dendur, masses of roses and peonies, a full moon shining down through the glass ceiling—but the company was distinctly unseductive. On Allison's left was a middle-aged senator from the West, on her right, a self-important, middle-aged philanthropist. She massaged their egos through the requisite number of courses and danced with them the requisite number of dances.

From a table across the dance floor a man who was not one of her partners that evening kept a close eye on her. He had striking blue eyes and thick dark hair that he kept brushing off his forehead. He had noticed Allison's photograph in a recent story in *Women's Wear,* and he found her even more enchanting in person. This was a woman he wanted to meet, but not here. He would prefer a situation more under his control. Setting up such an occasion was easy. It was only a matter of when.

As she was leaving on the arm of one of her older admirers, who had insisted on giving her a lift home in his limousine, Allison attracted the attention of a second man who also knew who she was but likewise chose not to speak. He was tall and thin, with jet-black hair and a small black pearl cross in one ear. He wore an odd, midnight-blue, tunic-jacketed suit with a black silk scarf at his throat. In his case there was no need to arrange a meeting, for he knew not only that they would meet but that they would find themselves on opposite sides of a battle—a battle that would begin very soon.

The first of these strangers was interested in her money. The other had a more ambitious goal. He wanted to take everything she had away from her, including her very soul.

14

The call usually came late in the evening. Sometimes midnight, New York time.

"How's my girl?" Gus said on this occasion. "Holding up under the heat? News out here said the humidity matched the temperature today. Ninety-five, wasn't it?"

"Ninety-seven in fact, Uncle Gus. Sixth day in a row in the nineties. But I'm holding up fine. What about you? I bet you're still at the office."

Allison could just see him. A pick-up supper from the deli on a tray next to his phone, around it a tide of cash flow charts, scripts, notes, and printouts. The incredible play of lights dancing up from the freeway through the wrap-around windows behind his desk, a giant pinball game pulsing with life. Diana, at one end of the sofa, earnestly studying contracts, Charlie in the outer office watching a baseball game on a portable TV, waiting to drive the two of them home. Allison had come to know that scene intimately.

"I'm just finishing up now, Allie. The reason I called so late is because . . . well, I need you."

"Another deal, Uncle Gus?" she asked with resignation.

"Not just 'another' deal. The best one yet. First Boston just brought it to me. Craig and Craig. The lecture-booking agency. Biggest in the business. A perfect fit for U.T.M."

"What's the price?"

"Forty-two. But we're not alone. There's another company after it. I have some ideas about how to handle that, though. With you here, I'll come up with even better ones."

"I'll catch the eight A.M. flight. I can be in the office before noon."

"I've already sent the G-Three for you. You can leave a little later if you want. Charlie will be waiting for you at Burbank. Have a good flight, and remember—"

"I love you, too," Allison responded before her uncle could complete his habitual goodbye line.

Though she knew the smart thing to do would be to go right to bed, Allison poured herself a large Marc de Champagne and sat watching a David Letterman rerun with the sound turned low. Her palm cradled the fine crystal goblet, almost parchment thin, so delicate that the heat from her hand warmed the golden liquid like a small flame.

—When's he going to call it quits? she asked herself. He's not happy these days unless he's writing out another check. The more zeros the better.

—So? What's so surprising? You heard what he said in Palm Springs. He wants to build up U.T.M. Make it a lot bigger and more exciting.

—Build it up! You make him sound like Arnold Schwarzenegger. I wish it were as simple as that.

—Well, what's so complicated?

—Uncle Gus is, that's who. He's been in a frenzy all summer.

—Wouldn't you be if you had to make up for so much lost time?

—But why now?

—Don't be dense. He's doing it for you. He must have woken up one morning and counted a few more gray hairs. He knows he's growing older.

—Who isn't. And I don't know if I want this . . . thing he's creating. It scares me. I like U.T.M. the way it is.

—You make it sound comfortable. Like an old shoe.

—I don't mean that at all.

—You didn't say boo about any of this in Palm Springs. What were you thinking about then?

—George, damn him—and how to get away from him.

—Maybe that's why Uncle Gus is who he is. He's got more than a one-track mind. But it isn't too late to speak up, chicken.

—I will. Just give me a little time. I need the right opportunity.

—Don't say any more, I think I can hum the rest.

The whole thing had started in Palm Springs the weekend she told him she wanted to move East, when he had mentioned that he was thinking of buying some other companies to flesh out U.T.M., as he put it. And then he had begun working at it like a man possessed, driving himself on in a furious way. She hadn't picked up on the strange urgency at first. She had been too preoccupied with getting clear of George Bellamy—and the comparisons she kept making between his meteoric rise and her own halting baby steps. But soon afterward, when the first acquisition—the largest outdoor billboard company in the country—was in final negotiations, Gus had brought Allison into the picture. He seemed consumed with the goal of taking the agency into a totally different realm. When she had asked him what his rationale was, his reaction had stopped her cold.

"So what if I'm personally worth eighty million if I sell the company," he demanded. "I don't want to sound boorish, but that's penny ante these days. Don't you see, U.T.M.'s a big success, it's really cooking, no one would say otherwise, but I realize now that that's not enough for me. I don't want to settle for that. Could Lew Wasserman have created MCA if he had been content to be just an agent? And what about Herb Siegel? The roots of his company were in a talent agency, but those roots are long gone. And what both of them have created has eclipsed by thousands what their ten percent commissions would have gotten them."

"I'm surprised, Uncle Gus. I didn't think you cared about playing that kind of game."

"Game, you say? Maybe. But it's the biggest game there is. That's kid talk anyway, Allie, nothing else. You give yourself away with that kind of line, and I know you're smarter than that even if you are still wet behind the ears." Gus smiled indulgently. "Next you'll say I'm making a bid to get my mug on the cover of *Fortune*."

"I'm not that foolish, Uncle Gus," protested Allison, blushing anyway.

"Look at it this way, honey. I'm in the agency business, yes, but I'm also in the communications business. What I'm doing now is getting out the word, loud and clear, so no one misses the point. If Warner's was able to parlay their way into a huge communications conglomerate from funeral parlors and parking lots, just think of the head start I have."

Earlier in the summer he had acquired two companies and just missed a third that insisted on an all-cash deal. After the outdoor billboard company there came, just two weeks later, the Jump Cut Catalog, a mail-order operation that specialized in videotapes. The one he missed, Just We Two, a video and computer dating service, was lost after thirty hours of nonstop negotiating in a hotel room at O'Hare Airport.

Though Gus had excellent outside counsel and first-class investment banking advice from several top firms on both coasts, as well as the in-house services of Diana and a crackerjack financial brain named Parker Welles, he wouldn't complete a deal without Allison at his side. She could not figure out why. Perhaps involving her in final negotiations was his way of trying to lure her back to Los Angeles and home base. Or maybe it was a "passing of the torch" kind of thing. The business was going to be hers someday, so she should be there to see it grow. Or maybe he simply viewed her as his lucky charm, the talisman that he always wanted near at hand.

Each deal was justifiable in one way or another, but Allison could not see where they were leading as a whole. Apart from this new lecture agency, the two acquisitions he had made already and the new ones he was looking at every day didn't match up with U.T.M. at all. And not only was he giving away significant pieces of his ownership of the company with each deal, but he was also allowing U.T.M.'s debt to rocket upward geometrically.

"What I'm doing, Allie, is building a modern company. And a very sexy one. A company that, if ever we decide to take it public, will be worth many times what it's worth now."

"But what about your control, Uncle Gus?" she had asked him before they closed on The Jump Cut Catalog.

"Don't worry about it, Allie. I still have effective control. And I always will. I don't intend to give that up."

"Effective control? Uncle Gus, you're the one who's always said U.T.M. might be run like a candy store, but it's your candy store! Effective control is like being a little bit pregnant."

"Hey," he had said, laughing. "You sound like you've been wrestling in the pits with Goldman, Sachs, and Shearson for the past twenty years. Is this really my niece Allison I'm talking to now?"

Yes, a little of that had been fun. And exciting. Zooming around the country in the G–III. Hush-hush talks with investment bankers and fund managers. Not that she herself had much to contribute at these meetings. But now it was beginning to taste like last night's champagne. Flat and a bit sour. Maybe this deal would be the last one for a while. God, she hoped so. Wasn't it time to take a breather and survey the latest wrinkles in their corporate landscape?

When she heard Gus hang up the phone, Diana looked up from her work. Though she had been in the office since eight that morning, she appeared as fresh as when the day had begun. If she was tired, it didn't show. Her blond hair was combed and arranged just so, her spectator pumps were dazzlingly white, not a smudge on them. Though she seemed to be in her middle to late thirties, Diana was a lot older. Nearer fifty. Luck played a little part in this—she had the kind of face that all her life had made her seem younger than she was—but mostly it was a matter of determination and fierce discipline. Golf and tennis, of course, plus a constant, unyielding regimen of diet and serious exercise—at least half an hour of abdominals six days a week—kept her figure taut and her energy at a high level.

"Allison's coming out tomorrow?" Diana asked now.

"She'll be here in the morning."

"It's tough on her, isn't it? All this traveling back and forth can't be easy." Diana stood up and reached for Gus's tray with its half-eaten sandwich. "You finished with this?"

Gus nodded impatiently. "She doesn't mind. She's young, and I need her. I did the same kind of thing when I was her age, and I didn't have the benefit of jets. It was three days to the coast on the Super Chief when I started. And then later, I can't remember how many twelve-hour flights I made. And those were not nonstops either. We always had to refuel at Midway Field in Chicago. Those DC–Sixes were real workhorses."

Diana placed the tray on the conference table next to hers for the cleaning woman to remove later and opened one of the cabinet doors in the bookcase. She took out a glass and some vintage Armagnac in a dark green bottle with a heavy red seal on its neck. "Tell me how much," she said, holding the bottle up like an auctioneer looking for an opening bid.

"I'll pass," Gus said, his head buried in yet another balance sheet.

"Oh? Well then, we can have a nightcap at home instead."

"Not tonight. It'll be too late," he said almost to himself, still without looking up.

Gus's response annoyed Diana, but before she could speak, he punched a button on his desk and immediately Charlie appeared in the doorway.

"Yes, boss?"

"Drive Diana home now, please. And come back for me in a couple of hours." Gus studied his watch for a moment. "Make it midnight."

"Sure thing."

As soon as Charlie disappeared, Diana strode over to the door and shut it with the exaggerated calm and purposefulness of a parent preparing to confront a wayward child. "What did you just say?" she asked.

Gus sighed, a fraction louder than he probably intended, and tossed his favorite gold Cartier pen down on top of the pile of papers in front of him. "I thought you'd prefer going home and getting comfortable to waiting around here for me. It's going to be a longer night than I anticipated. I want to look through the Craig material again."

"Why don't you let *me* decide what I'd prefer to do, all right? And what gives you the idea you can just dismiss me this way?"

"Dismiss you? Darling, you must be kidding," said Gus with a short laugh. "Forgive me if I was a little abrupt."

"Don't you 'darling' me," snapped Diana, anger hardening her features and making her look now as old as she really was. "I always used to fall for those lines of yours. You'd trample all over me, and I'd love you for it. But I don't know if I can take it anymore. I'm beginning to think I've had it. Do you know what time it is? Almost ten! Another night wasted. I don't know how many times it's happened this summer. I should have made other plans," she added bitterly.

"I wish you had," said Gus quietly.

"What does that mean?"

"We've talked about this before, darling," he continued in a reasonable tone that infuriated her. "It would do you wonders to take a break from me. Meet a girlfriend for dinner. See a movie. See someone else, for God's sake. Anyone other than me—or that family of yours. All those cousins and aunts and uncles. Don't you get tired of them? Don't you ever want a change of scenery?" He was beginning to get exasperated, so he stopped, took a breath, and then went on. "Well, look, this Craig and Craig business will be wrapped up soon. In a few days. Then you and I can take some time for ourselves."

"Oh, sure," said Diana, "just like all the other time we've had together lately. You know, what's the point, really, of my even staying in Bel-Air with you? The way it's been, I'm lucky if I get to see you shaving once in a while. When was the last time we had anybody over for dinner? Or even had a nice, simple dinner alone? Or what about the nights we used to spend in bed, watching television and . . . enjoying each other? What's happened to it all?"

"If you could just hear yourself, Diana. You're blowing everything out of proportion." Gus picked up his pen and drew a dark crosshatch across the top of the notepad in front of him as he spoke.

"Oh, is that right? So that's what I'm doing."

"Diana, I depend on you, you know. And I love you. Doesn't that make any difference to you?"

"Of course it does." She gave a brief, ironic laugh, her eyes tight with fury. "It'll sound great at my testimonial. 'The chief couldn't live without me. From nine to five, that is.'"

"Nine to ten is more like it," said Gus, trying to joke the moment away. "Correction," he added, looking at his watch. "Make that nine to ten-thirty. But I don't understand why you're so upset about the time we've been spending on acquisitions. We're in this together. I count on your opinion, both professional and personal. I had the impression you agreed that each one of these buys was good for U.T.M."

"What's 'good for U.T.M.,' as you put it, is only the half of it, though, isn't it?" Diana paused in an insinuating way. "I think you have the 'good' of something—or rather *someone*—else uppermost in your mind, don't you?"

"Careful," said Gus warningly, as they eyed each other. They had sailed these particular waters too many times already.

"Careful? Why do I have to be careful with you? It's not as if I would ever speak this way, this honestly, to anyone else. I'm smarter than that. So, Gus dear, I'll be as *un*careful as I please, and you'll just have to listen. Do you remember how it was—once? Way back then, I found myself playing third fiddle. The business, your wife . . . and me. Those were your priorities. Right? In that order. And you remember how I felt about it? I hated it. But I tolerated it because I knew it wouldn't last forever. I knew Laura would die eventually. That sounds heartless, doesn't it? Well, it's nothing worse than the way you've treated me."

"Don't say that, Diana. I've always loved you." Gus stood up and started around his desk toward her.

"Laura finally did die," continued Diana, ignoring him. "And, for a long time, things were much better. I think we were happy, don't you? I *know* we were happy! But then something happened, and guess what? Ever since a certain someone got out of law school, *surprise!* I'm third fiddle again. And I'm sick to death of it."

"Stop, Diana, please." Gus reached out to her.

"Call Charlie and tell him I'm coming downstairs, will you, Gus? I want to go home." She shook his arms away from her. "Home to my own place."

Without another word, she turned and left the office.

Later Gus's white Rolls again moved silently through the empty streets, this time toward his house in Bel-Air. From the cocoon of stillness inside the car, he stared absently through the windows at the dark outlines of houses looming above their small lawns like ships gone aground. He could tell from their size that he was close to home now. He knew few of his neighbors personally and wanted to keep it that way. Proximity was no excuse for familiarity. Yet show business was so public a business that if his neighbors were curious, they probably knew more about him than he would have liked. They certainly would have seen many dozens of photographs of him over the years with Diana on his arm. But they could not have guessed what she meant to him or what turns and twists their life together had taken.

The first terrible twist had occurred many years earlier, when Diana, so beautiful and young then, walked out on him after the night he insisted on visiting Laura's hospital room. Nobody had ever treated him that way. And it wasn't just his ego complaining. Diana had been at the heart of his life—he realized after she had left—and suddenly she was gone. By her own choice. Even now, twenty-five years later, the memory of her departure still hurt. He never thought of it unless he was surprised into it, as he had been this evening by Diana herself, for his memories of that quarrel and of what happened later were colored with shame, jealousy, and, most of all, anger.

It had taken Gus a few days to realize she actually was gone. He had telephoned her the next day to say he was sorry for being insensitive, but there was no answer at her apartment, then or on Sunday, Monday, or Tuesday. By Tuesday afternoon he was so frantic with worry that he contemplated calling the police. The hell with keeping their secret. And it was then that Teddy knocked on his office door. Diana had just called with a message she wished him to give to Gus. It was short and brutal. She never wanted to see him again. He was not to try to find out where she was. If he did, she would refuse to speak to him.

Gus wanted desperately to find her so that he could set things straight—he would divorce Laura, he would marry her, they would have a child—but he gave up the search almost before he began. He couldn't contact her parents. She had a sister she was close to, but the sister was married and Gus didn't know her name. Her roommate refused to talk to him. And that was it. Their relationship, which had seemed so full and alive, so hopeful and joyous, so important and even necessary, was shown up for what it was. Nothing.

Later it was the sister who contacted him, not the other way around, but only when he swore to keep his distance and to keep a promise that altered everything. He agreed because he had no choice. A year later, he learned that Diana had moved to New York to work for the William Morris Agency, but by then he had grown wary. It would be a mistake, he thought, to try to resurrect their past, and if they had not met each other by chance at a party, there things might have rested forever. Instead? Instead their lives had converged again, mysteriously, Gus felt, for the rupture between them was so deep it should have destroyed them.

Their life together was a fever chart of highs and lows. Beneath her facade of calmness, Diana was almost as quick-tempered and stubborn as Gus, and when they argued, their words were fierce and cutting and sometimes led to long periods of resentment and unhappiness. This had happened after it became obvious that they would never marry and again after Gus decided to make Allison his legal heir when Teddy died. The peace that would follow these standoffs was sweet, though, and often lengthy. But in the last few months . . . just the thought of his quarrels with Diana and their cause—Allison!—swept Gus into a cataract of depression.

"What did you say, boss?" asked Charlie from the front seat.

"Nothing, Charlie. Nothing." He must have groaned out loud, Gus realized.

What was he going to do? How could he make peace between these two women whom he loved more than anyone else in the world? The fault was more Diana's than Allison's, he thought, though he wasn't positive. He had seen his niece make overtures on several occasions and had seen Diana, politely but firmly, turn her away. Maybe everything was actually *his* fault, for shoving Allison onto center stage. Maybe he was the one who needed a good kick in the pants.

Gus suddenly heard Charlie speak again—and looked up and saw his house. Wearily he pulled himself out of the backseat of the car, said good night to Charlie, and, since it was Albert's night off, unlocked his front door. Inside, he started to call hello to Diana, then remembered she wasn't there. He poured himself a shot of an even mellower Armagnac than the one in his office and sank into a deep leather armchair in the library. With the first swallow, he sadly toasted Diana, then shut his eyes and tried to think of nothing.

The potent liquid traveled down his spine and along his legs to his toes, like the strong hand of a masseur, relaxing him, soothing him. He sat quietly for a few minutes, letting the drink do its work, then went upstairs. Before he had gone out, Albert had turned down the bed and laid out a freshly brushed suit for the next day. On Gus's bedside table was an advance copy of a new Latin American novel by a protegé of Gabriel García Márquez. No reading tonight, though. The scene with Diana had exhausted him, and he needed to replenish his energy. The famous Gus Morton energy, he thought with dry amusement. The envy of the industry. But it wasn't bestowed like magic. He needed his sleep as much as the next person.

He was bending down to take off his shoes when he felt a sudden, sharp needle of pain in his chest. He straightened up, pressing his hands hard against the spot that hurt, as if he were squashing the life out of an insect. The pain didn't go away, though. Was this a heart attack? He tried to breathe deeply while he thought about what he should do.

He would not panic. If the pain persisted, he would call Albert, who was probably in his quarters by now, on the intercom and Albert could drive him to the hospital. He recently had read that the first three hours after an attack were critical. If the victim postponed treatment, in the hope that the pain would go away, he was much more likely to die.

Gus started to reach for the intercom button, then hesitated. The pain seemed to be subsiding. Maybe it was only tension or something he'd eaten. That damned corned beef sandwich! The possibility made him smile, and he felt better immediately. He made a mental note to call his internist tomorrow, knowing that he wouldn't. Doctors always overreacted. They were like vice presidents of studios. All they knew how to do was say no. No booze. No late hours. No steaks. No fun. And Gus Morton never wanted to hear the word *no*.

He had been pushing himself for weeks . . . actually months. He was determined to do nothing less than take the talent agency and make it into—what was the right word?—an empire. Like a proud parent, he would have bristled at the suggestion that the company was not fabulous exactly as it was. True, it was hugely successful, but when it came down to it, U.T.M. was only a reflection of his own personality and talents. It was alarmingly fragile, a spider's web of relationships and connections that could dissolve as soon as he was no longer there to hold it together. Later he would slow down, if his doctor insisted, but not now. Now he was on an almost holy mission: to create for Allison, his heir, as large, powerful, and far-reaching a communications entity as he could. He wanted her to have everything possible to make up for the one thing she could never have.

Gus broke out of his reverie. He rubbed his chest. The pain was gone. He stood up, walked briskly around the room, sat down. Nothing. Suffused with relief, he lay back on his bed. He thought of Allison, then of Diana, then again of Allison, and fell quickly into a deep sleep where, once again, he was a little boy.

15

The day after their meeting with the lecture bureau—which went so well that Gus was sure the deal would go through, and on exactly his terms—Allison poked her head into her uncle's office on her way to lunch. He had talked her into staying in town for the week and then spending the weekend in Trancas.

"What are your plans this evening?" Gus asked.

"I'm not sure, but I thought I might drop in on my old aerobics class. Then maybe have dinner afterward with a couple of my pals. Why?"

"An early dinner?"

"I imagine. I think we'll all be bushed."

"Not too tired to do a little reading, I hope?"

"Of course not."

"Then I have something to add to your agenda. Come in and sit down. This will only take a second."

Gus folded his hands on his desk and leaned forward, motionless in the concentration of the moment, his eyes glittering. The sharpness of his gaze drove every particle of thought about anything else, including her lunch date, from Allison's head, and, like countless other people riveted by his single-mindedness, she almost held her breath in anticipation of what he was going to say. Rival agents scoffed at this intensity as a put-on, but they were wrong. There was nothing false or assumed about it. He always gave the subject at hand his total, undistracted attention, as if nothing else in the world was as important, and it was one of the reasons for his success.

"What does the name Stewart Gilles mean to you?" asked Gus.

"Wasn't he blacklisted? But later. Just after the Hollywood Ten."

"Precisely," said Gus, not needing this cue to continue. "He was only in his midtwenties then. He wrote a couple of early scripts, one of which was optioned. Then Preminger produced *Time Enough for Anger*. You ever see it? It was damned good, but the next script was fabulous. It was all set to go, but then the hearings started again and it got killed fast. No one would touch him. Hard to believe all that happened before you were born. Gilles went to Mexico to live. Wrote a couple of novels which didn't do well and, I guess, ran out of money. By then things had cooled enough for him to land a teaching job. He's been at Oberlin ever since, piddling his life away."

"*Piddling?* As a recent student, I object to your choice of words," interrupted Allison, laughing.

"I am being unfair, but you know what I mean. Teaching wasn't what he was meant to do. Still, Oberlin probably was the right place for him. I've stayed in touch with him. I call him once or twice a year, though in the middle of some of those conversations, I admit I've wondered why. He really and truly seemed to want to have nothing more to do with the movie business. I spoke to him again just a few days ago, and this time," Gus paused, savoring the moment, "this time, it was Gilles who placed the call. He told me he was coming into town. Here's the reason why."

Gus picked up a script bound between navy-blue covers and slid it toward Allison. Stamped in gold were the words THE MOON AT DAWN, by STEWART GILLES.

"Hey, terrific. How is it?" asked Allison, reaching for it.

"Take it home tonight, and you tell me," said Gus. Keeping his eyes on Allison, he stretched back in his chair, his arms behind his head. Allison knew what he was thinking without his needing to say it: The ball's in your court, honey. Show me some spin.

Over dinner at the Border Grill, Allison let her workout buddies give her a short course on the social etiquette of aerobics classes, just in case she ever found an interesting male specimen huffing and puffing next to her, and then after a cup of decaf espresso and a few more laughs, she bid the two good night. It wasn't even ten when she arrived home. She changed into sweatpants and a T-shirt and curled up on the sofa with *The Moon at Dawn*. When the phone rang a short while later, she was so caught up in the script and so annoyed by the interruption that she took the phone off the hook. She plunged back into the script, racing through the scenes, praying the momentum would not let up. And it did not. By the time she reached the final scene, tears were in her eyes. It was, quite simply, a wonderful story; strong, original, and moving.

It was a World War II picture set not in Europe or the Pacific but on an Air Force base in the California desert where a group of young fliers are in the last stages of training before being sent into combat. One afternoon, while driving into town, they see a figure lying on the ground a hundred feet off the road. It's a young Japanese-American girl who has escaped from a detention camp nearby. Although she is suffering from thirst and exposure, they can neither return her to the camp nor risk taking her to a doctor. Just before dark, they find an abandoned miner's shack, hide her there, and gradually nurse her back to health. One of the soldiers falls in love with her. As he sees men from other companies being sent to the front and knows it's only a matter of weeks before he's called also, he decides to flee with her to Mexico—deserting the Air Force, his family, his country, all for this girl.

Although Allison called her uncle's home as early as she dared the next morning, she had already missed him. It was not until the following day that she got to Gus, but when he saw the smile on her face, he laughed with pleasure.

"I knew you were going to love it," he said before she could speak. "Am I right?"

"You bet."

"You know, they say you never forget how to float in the water once you learn, so think what that says about storytelling. Gilles isn't as well known, for instance, as a Dalton Trumbo or an Alvah Bessie—he was too young—but he's every bit as good. Maybe better."

"I got hold of the Preminger movie yesterday. *Time Enough for Anger.* From a video freak I know. Tapes off his TV incessantly. He must have over two thousand movies by now. It was great, but not as good as this one."

"If you were handling this for us, who would you put on it as director?" asked Gus, toying with his gold pen.

"Funny you should ask," said Allison, unfolding a piece of paper with a list of names on it and handing it to Gus. "I put this together, just in case. Also some ideas for the two leads. Casting this is like eating pistachios. Hard to stop."

Gus smiled as he scanned the list. "I see you have an instinct for intelligent choices."

"Why do you say that?"

"These are all our clients."

"I am your niece, of course," Allison answered with a smile.

"And they're all good candidates. Who do you think is the best fit?"

"The one at the top of the list. Robby Bascombe. He'd be perfect."

"Tell me why," said Gus, letting the gold pen slide rhythmically back and forth between his fingers. He listened intently as Allison made her case for Bascombe. She pushed back a wave of dark hair that had fallen across her forehead, and her face grew serious as she spoke. Bascombe had two solid directorial credits, she said, both action pictures, and he'd written or collaborated on at least a half-dozen other scripts, one of which had been nominated for an Oscar. He knew how to keep his eye on a budget, had a reputation as an idea man, and, best of all, was supposed to have a real rapport with young actors, who apparently didn't resent the fact that he wasn't much older than they.

"He knows how young people think and behave, and that's crucial. We can't let this picture become a period piece. After all, it's about something that happened almost fifty years ago. Half a century ago. Have you thought of it that way?"

"Jesus, no, Allie, and I don't intend to start now," said Gus, with an exaggerated grimace. "You make this sound like *The Red Badge of Courage,* for God's sake, and I shudder to think how that dates me, a doddering old soldier who actually remembers fighting in this period piece, as you call it."

"Oh, Uncle Gus, you know I didn't mean it that way. But I do think, even though it's important to be true to the time when a story takes place, it's also important to make it translate, so that it means something to kids today. Bascombe can do that."

"Well, very possibly he can. He's loaded with talent. I tell you what, why don't you try to set up a meeting between Gilles and Bascombe if Bascombe likes the script?"

Now it was Allison's turn to smile again.

"I beat you to it, Uncle Gus," she said. "I already sent the script to Bascombe—I hope you don't mind—and, except for a few small changes he'd like to make, he absolutely loves it."

"Allie, you surprise me all the time."

"And," continued Allison, winding up with a flourish, "since we just last month finished negotiating a two-picture deal for Bascombe at Paramount, this should be a snap to get going."

"Okay," said Gus, all business once more. "Stewart's in town until tomorrow. Staying with friends in Encino. I have a lunch date with him, so why don't you see if you can arrange for him to meet with Bascombe here in the morning?"

Gilles arrived early for the meeting, and he, Allison, and Gus chatted together for a few minutes over coffee in the small conference room next to Gus's office before Gus excused himself. As soon as Robby Bascombe arrived a short while later and the two men began to sound each other out by comparing notes on earlier work, Allison started to feel a little uncomfortable. Bascombe was respectful about *Time Enough for Anger,* but not as admiring as he might have been. Gilles was interested in Bascombe's two earlier directorial assignments, particularly about how he had managed to cool off a widely publicized feud between the two leads, but he was a little condescending about the films as well. When the two men segued into a discussion of the moviemakers they most admired, Allison relaxed a bit until she noticed that the only people being mentioned either were dead or were icons of such unquestioned stature that there was no room for argument: Kurosawa, Hitchcock, Renoir. Sure enough, as soon as they got down to the specifics of this particular movie, the trouble began.

Bascombe, the idea man, now suddenly had lots of ideas about changing the script. He wanted to enlarge the character of the flier's commander, an abrasive stand-in for military inflexibility, add more action scenes, and, worst of all from the writer's point of view, Bascombe wanted the couple killed at the end in a crash of the plane that the flier had stolen from the base to take them to Mexico.

"Are you crazy? This is a love story. If you wipe out your lovers, the audience will kill you. And they should."

"Mr. Gilles, I thought you were interested in doing a war movie," said Bascombe coldly. "If I wanted a tearjerk romance, I'd just go to the first hack writer of soaps I could find and leave it at that. Besides, a crash would be a matter of justice, too."

"Justice? I don't know what the hell you mean. Hey, wait a minute, maybe I do," said Gilles, his face as well as the bald spot at the summit of his thinning salt-and-pepper hair flushing with anger. "Are you saying this guy and his girl *deserve* to die, because he went . . . AWOL, for God's sake? If that's what you're driving at, then you've really got your head up your ass."

"Mr. Gilles! Robby! Please," said Allison in a futile effort to restore some civility to the scene. Both men ignored her.

"I'll thank you not to question my patriotism, Gilles," Bascombe spat back.

"You self-righteous piece of shit," shouted Gilles. "You're talking to someone who fought in that war and is proud of it, so why don't you just shut the fuck up, you junior-grade John Wayne. You're nothing but a little kneejerk right-wing twerp who's fought all your wars in fucking screening rooms."

"Just a minute, Gilles—" began Bascombe, as the door that connected Gus's office to the conference room opened and Gus entered, smiling.

"Yes, gentlemen, just a minute," Gus said calmly. "I gather you two have reached a point of disagreement, so perhaps it's not too disruptive of me to spirit Stewart away to lunch now. Preliminary sessions of this kind can be a bit rocky, as I know you two professionals are both aware. Allison, wrap things up with Robby, will you, and thank you, Robby, for coming in." Gus shook Bascombe's hand quickly, then in one smooth operation that prevented either man from finding himself in the embarrassing position of having to acknowledge the other, put his arm around Gilles's shoulders, wheeled him around, and steered him out of the room.

It wasn't until almost the end of the day that Gus called Allison in to see him.

Earlier, "wrapping things up with Robby" had consisted of Allison's getting him to leave as fast as possible so she could retreat to the privacy of her office to try to figure out what had gone wrong. She couldn't understand how something that had seemed such a natural could take this kind of turn. As she had listened to the two men argue, she had begun to dislike them both, and so profound was her relief that the awful scene between them was finally over that at first she hadn't given any thought to the script itself. As soon as she remembered it, though, it was with the sinking certainty that the agency must have lost out on it, and in a dark and brooding funk, she could think of nothing else for the rest of the day.

"I'm really sorry, Uncle Gus. I feel like such an idiot," she began as soon as she sat down.

"It was pretty messy," agreed Gus almost cheerfully.

"After you worked so hard to get the script, I can't believe I screwed things up that way," continued Allison, oblivious to her uncle's mood.

"Hold up, Allie honey. No need to use the past tense. We still have the script. Gilles was pretty steamed up at Bascombe, it's true, but I was able to talk him into staying with us. I knew he and Bascombe would be an incendiary combination, but the second director on your list will do just fine. Would you still like to handle the project?"

"Would I ever!" Allison's impulse was to jump up and hug her uncle, but that would be too unprofessional, so she just sat tight and grinned. But almost immediately another thought occurred to her. "Isn't that going to be a little tough for me to do, from New York?"

"Indeed it would be. But there's a very easy solution."

"You mean move back to L.A.?"

Gus nodded, unable now to suppress a large smile.

"And skip theatrical? Oh, I can't, Uncle Gus. I'm sorry, but I'm just not ready to leave New York yet."

Allison frowned, pretending to give the idea more consideration. She and Gus sat in silence for a short while until Allison spoke again. "Did I hear you right a moment ago, Uncle Gus? Did you say that you *knew* all along that Bascombe and Gilles would not like each other?"

"Yes."

"How could you?" she almost shouted, as the anxiety of the afternoon crashed down around her. "How could you treat your friend Gilles that way? It's like cat and mouse. And what about me?"

"Allie, don't forget I've known Stewart Gilles for years. I've stood by him like nobody else, and he knows it. Sure, maybe this morning was a bit tough on him, but he's a big boy and I knew he could take it. And you . . ."

"Yes, what about me?" said Allison, biting her lip. "Why didn't you tell me it wouldn't work? The scene between the two of them was . . . well, it was horrible."

"Allie, if you can believe it, it was as hard for me not to warn you as for you to go through what you did. But I had to do it. You've learned something important, I hope. I understand why you thought of Bascombe, but if you'd done all your homework, you would have seen that his politics are dead wrong for an old antiwar activist like Stewart. Sort of like throwing the Mossad together with the P.L.O. There's never too much you can know about people before trying to put them together. Next time, don't forget that. By the way, how did you like the way I timed my entrance into the conference room?"

"It was impeccable. How did you manage it?"

Gus tried to remain serious and then almost immediately gave up and smiled again. "It's not too hard to do when you've bugged the room first."

16

ow did I get myself into this? Allison wondered as she waited in the green-room of *Arts Around Us* for the segment she was scheduled to appear on. The preceding week, she had moved from the literary to the theatrical division and, incidentally, observed an anniversary. It was September exactly a year ago that Mario Petrucelli had led her off to the mailroom on her first day working for U.T.M.

"They've been asking for you since you came to New York," Jackie Dillon, U.T.M.'s head of public relations for the New York office, had said. "It's just a five-minute segment and you'll be on with that yummy-looking Off-Broadway playwright, Sean Roberto Flores. Please do it," she pleaded. "It'll be good for the agency, and I'll have a lot easier time getting our clients on the show. So how about it?"

"But I don't know beans about the theatrical end of things. I'm brand new at it."

"They could care less. They've had their eye on you since you started showing up in *Women's Wear,* and they're very persistent."

So here she was, growing more nervous by the moment, as Jackie, who had insisted on accompanying her to the studio, chattered away about the new man she had just met who she *thought* was single.

"At least that's what he's told me. He has no mark of a wedding band, and he seems to be free most of the time. But I've been burned before and . . ."

God, her palms were actually sweaty! What a dummy she had been to give in to this. She'd only make a fool of herself. And why had she allowed the makeup man to slather all that pancake on her? Her image in the mirror across the room was such an exaggerated version of herself that she scarcely recognized her face. But Jackie Dillon had been right about Sean Flores, who sat opposite, calmly reading a copy of *The New York Review of Books*. He had smiled pleasantly and said hello when he came in, but any conversational overture that Allison thought of had been thwarted by Jackie's constant prattle.

Sean Flores was even better-looking than Jackie's description had led her to expect. He had been smart enough not to allow the makeup man even to powder his high, rugged cheekbones. A shock of hair, dark as a paintbrush, fell over his forehead and provided a startling contrast to his olive skin and slate-colored eyes. He was dressed in a blue chambray shirt and jeans that were almost the color of bone from many washings. His boots were old but polished and looked as if they had been used for things other than window shopping on Columbus Avenue. A soft brown leather jacket fit him loosely but still revealed his broad shoulders. Once or twice Allison thought that he was trying to glance at her, though when she turned toward him Sean Flores's eyes appeared glued to his journal.

"Time to take your places, people," said a young production assistant, holding the door open to the studio.

"Don't worry. You'll be great," said Jackie, as Allison walked into the studio, Sean Flores a few steps behind. Within moments they both had buttonhole mikes affixed to their clothing and voice levels taken. And then Allison was on the air.

"Good afternoon, Arts Fiends . . . I mean Friends," exclaimed Toby Bishop, a small round man whose large bow tie made his head seem an afterthought to the large present beneath. "Today we have two distinct sides of the contemporary theater scene. Allison Morton," the light on the camera pointing at Allison suddenly went on, "a lawyer by training, is an agent at Universal Talent Management, the largest talent agency in the country. Her uncle, Gus Morton, who heads the company, is, along with my friend Swifty Lazar, probably the most famous agent in the business. It's a pleasure having you here with us on *Arts Around Us,* Allison," said Toby Bishop, turning to face Allison with a huge toothy smile.

"It's good to be here, Toby," Allison answered, a rote response she realized came from watching so many shows like this. Her voice sounded thin and hopelessly scratchy to her ears.

"Also with us today is Sean Roberto Flores, a much talked about young playwright whose newest work, *Jake's Tale,* is about to open at The Combine, an experimental theater company on Great Jones Street. That's some distance from Broadway, isn't it, Sean?"

"You don't need a passport to get there, just a subway token," he said with a tight smile at the overly affable host.

"Allison, I have it on good authority that Sean here doesn't have an agent. What do you say about that?"

"Well, Toby," she replied too quickly, "there's an expression that people in the legal profession use that goes, a lawyer who represents himself has a fool for a client. I think Mr. Flores would only benefit from having representation."

"In what way?" asked Sean, looking past Toby, his mouth showing not a trace of a smile.

"Make it good, Allison, and maybe you'll pick up a client," said Bishop blithely, completely missing Sean's withering look.

"Well," answered Allison tensely, for she could see that Sean's question was a challenge, "a good agent might be able to find a wider audience for your work. An agent could—"

"By wider," Sean snapped back, "do you mean getting my work on Broadway, where the *wide*-ass expense-account set can talk and doze through a performance? Is that what you mean?"

"Of course not. I was referring to foreign productions, regional—"

"That doesn't sound like enough bread for a top agent like yourself," said Sean. "What about movie rights? Miniseries? Don't forget T-shirts."

"Whoooaaahh there, you two." Toby Bishop bounced right in on cue with his biggest grin yet, waving his hands incongruously as if he were about to jump up and do the Charleston. "Just because you're from different *sides* of the business doesn't mean you have to *sideswipe* each other, now does it?" Bishop chuckled at his little joke in case anybody had missed it. "We have to pause now for a short commercial message, but when we return, I'm going to ask you, Sean, to tell us all about your newest production," said Bishop, scrambling successfully to neutral ground. As the camera pulled away and the sound cut out, he nudged his two guests and the three of them looked up and smiled gamely at the home viewers.

After a commercial break that included plugs for dog food, panty hose, muffins, and nonalcoholic beer, Toby Bishop finished the segment by asking each of them who would they cast to play themselves and if there would ever be another Olivier. And then the show, mercifully, was over. Allison followed Sean Flores off the set, but before she could reach him and explain her remarks, Jackie Dillon pulled her aside to tell her how terrific she had been. The next show she must do, obviously, was Letterman. And, of course, by the time she freed herself of Jackie, Sean was gone.

17

B read, wine, and schmooze—a perfect combination, thought Allison. It was a Wednesday morning several weeks later and she had just asked Cynthia over for a pick-up supper that night at her loft.

Before she could get back to the papers on her desk, though, Gus called. He was in his plane on the way to New York for dinner at the Four Seasons with two BBC executives. Could Allison join them? Allison hesitated and then declined. She seldom turned down a chance to see Gus, but this dinner sounded too much like work, and besides, what about Cynthia? She would just have to miss him this visit—Diana was driving directly to Oyster Bay after dinner to spend a few days with an ailing aunt, and Gus was returning to California first thing next morning— but, if she knew her uncle, he'd be back in town within a few weeks. What she wanted tonight was exactly what she had arranged for herself: an easy dinner and good gossip. Nothing else.

"A pox on all the partners in my firm," Cynthia said as she stepped out of the elevator on Allison's floor. "If the lout who was directing us hadn't come down with the flu, I'd be at the office still. This is what they call an early night. Almost nine-thirty!"

"Doesn't bother me, Cyn. Dinner's simple. Did you get the bok choy?"

"Got it right here," said Cynthia, pointing at her briefcase. "By the way, your downstairs door was unlocked again."

"It's that damn kinetic sculptor again. He walks around in a fog most of the time. Sort of matches his work, I guess."

Cynthia had insisted on doing her bit for the evening by shopping in Chinatown, which was within walking distance of her office. "They said we could go home as soon as the switchboard closed. I shouldn't have believed them. They thought of something else for me and the other slaves to do. Tell me, did we joke about this kind of thing in law school?"

"Hate to say it, but we did," said Allison, handing her friend a glass of white wine.

"Well, 'out of the mouths of babes.' If I was so smart then, why the hell am I working like a prisoner in the Gulag now?"

"Cyn, you know why."

"Don't say it. I know the answer." Cynthia, who had short curly auburn hair and wore tortoiseshell glasses of the exact same shade, was laughing now. "The mantra goes, 'make partner and make money, make partner and make money.' But I've got to admit, I'm not so sure anymore. It may be another five years before I make partner. *If* I make partner, that is. I might as well have taken vows, I have such a social life. But that's probably the saving grace in all of this. If Tom lived here instead of L.A., we would both be so frustrated by these hours that it would be awful."

"How is Mr. District Attorney?" asked Allison. Cynthia had met and fallen in love with Tom Rosen shortly after she had started working in New York.

"He loves what he's doing. All of it. He's always been a Perry Mason junkie and a *Hill Street Blues* fanatic. Every day is like being in a crime-busters' theme park for him. He's a police groupie. He even goes out with the undercover detectives whenever he can. His whole circle of friends dress in blue. Excuse me," she added with a laugh. "That can't be, since they're all in plainclothes."

After Allison poured them another glass of wine and started setting things up for dinner, Cynthia began to tell a long story about a woman from her office who had entered strict Freudian therapy.

"She has to see the shrink *every* day. And because of her hours—"

"Damn! I think I'm out of garlic," said Allison, rummaging among the plastic bags in the vegetable bin of her refrigerator.

A sudden loud clap of thunder made her stop, and then she continued her search as the first drops of rain drummed against the window.

"Too bad. I could have picked up some."

"Oh, well, the scallops will just have to get along without it."

"Come on," said Cynthia. "What's life without garlic? I'll run out. It'll only take a minute. Isn't there a market nearby that's open?"

"Yes, but it's not important," said Allison, a lot less forcefully. "Well, all right. That would be great. It's right nearby, on Duane Street. Don't forget to take an umbrella. And for God's sake, put on my slicker. It's pouring."

They both looked out the window. It wasn't simply raining. TriBeCa looked like a scene from *Key Largo*. The rain, propelled now by whipsaw winds, seemed to be coming from every direction but up.

"Still want to go out?" Allison asked.

"Absolutely. Putting on a yellow slicker and going out in the pouring rain was a joy for me as a kid. Got a pair of sneakers I could wear?"

The slicker was a yellow that only school guards could appreciate. It was one of Allison's favorite pieces of clothing. Gus always kidded her about it when she donned it in an L.A. mist. It even amused Diana. As Allison repeated the directions, Cynthia hooked her way into the coat. When she finally flipped the hood over her head, the outfit made her look about ten years old.

After Cynthia left, Allison assembled the salad ingredients, dipping the tip of her finger into the vinaigrette for another quick taste. She wrinkled her nose at its acidity, stirred in a dollop more olive oil, and took a second taste. Much better. She put on a tape of an Erroll Garner session that her uncle always played in Palm Springs and, all at once very tired, dropped into the fattest of her cushiony chairs, glancing idly around the living room, thinking how perfect it looked except for one thing. No wonderful, sexy man sitting next to her. No wonderful, sexy man in her life.

Before George Bellamy, the last man whom Allison had been interested in was a guy at Harvard Law who wouldn't—or couldn't—break away from his family. He already, so she had heard, was busy following in his father's footsteps: living on Beacon Hill, working at the good gray law firm his grandfather had founded, and, to his parents' undisguised glee, seriously dating the "right" girl: St. Mark's, Wellesley, the Junior League. In New York, where that sort of behavior was so out of style no one considered it even an option, dues of another kind were exacted: the exercising of patience. All the best men either were married or gay. In four months she had gone out with exactly, and precisely, not one fascinating man. But surely this would change! As the sound of Garner's lovely, melodic piano filled the loft, she closed her eyes and tried to imagine who the future, fascinating man in her life would be.

Suddenly, above the music, Allison heard but didn't immediately comprehend a sharp, intrusive noise that snapped her back to the present. In an instant replay in her mind, she heard it again: the sound of someone slamming on the brakes of a car—hard. *Cynthia!* Allison jumped up and wrenched open one of her large windows, but the sill was too wide for her to see far enough into the street below. She shouted out Cynthia's name, but all she got in return was the echo of her own voice from the building across the street and the steady beat of the rain. She

turned and ran toward her front door, and it was only then that she noticed the revolving pattern of red and white lights from the street spinning across her ceiling like a crude light show.

More than anxious now at what she might discover outside, Allison
plunged down the stairs and into the street. In the dimness her eyes
darted toward the revolving light. It was a patrol car, not an ambulance.
Thank God! Then she saw Cynthia's yellow-slickered figure leaning
against the side of an automobile canted at an unnatural angle toward the
sidewalk. A short, dumpy, middle-aged man stood beside her, clutching
her hand in his.

"Cyn, what happened? Are you all right?" cried Allison, throwing
her arms around her friend's shoulders and hugging her.

"I—tripped and fell into the street. It was awful. I was so scared,
because I could see this car coming right at me. But at the last moment he
was able to veer away."

"Oh, you poor thing, you're shaking. Are you okay?" asked Allison.

"I think so," said Cynthia, attempting a bleak smile.

"Are you sure, miss?" asked the stricken-looking driver, still clutching her hand, though Allison was now standing between him and his
near-victim. "Maybe you should walk around and make sure nothing's
broken. Better yet, sit in my car until the ambulance arrives."

"I don't need an ambulance," said Cynthia, quickly moving away
from the car and spinning around on her toes. "I'm fine. Really. This is
the extent of my injuries," she added, holding out a scraped palm, "and a
little Mecurochrome will fix that up."

"If we stay out here talking in the rain," the young policeman said
with a smile, "we'll need that ambulance for a bunch of pneumonia
cases. Good night, folks."

Within moments both the squad car and the driver were gone, and
the small band of the New York curious who had suddenly appeared in
their wake, drawn like moths to a police car's revolving light, also disappeared.

Allison picked up the umbrella that she had given Cynthia, which
was leaning against a storefront, and, arm in arm, the two walked the few
doors back to her loft.

"I don't know why I'm holding this thing," Allison said with a nervous laugh. "I'm soaked to the bone. And by the way, remind me not to
send you on any more errands. Your service is not worth the rise in my
blood pressure."

Later, after they had both dried off, changed clothes, and were halfway through two big scotches, Cynthia said something that made Allison spill her drink onto the floor.

"What did you just say?"

"I didn't trip. Somebody pushed me."

"Are you joking?" Allison finally asked, knowing that Cynthia wasn't.

"Somebody followed me out of your hallway. I couldn't see who it was. I told you I noticed the light was out down there. Well, I just thought it was one of your neighbors. I didn't think anything of it until I left the grocery store. And then I realized that the person was still behind me as I walked back here."

"What did he look like?"

"He, she, it—I have no idea. I never really turned around. All I saw was a dark raincoat and a black umbrella. Remember, it was miserable out. And I didn't think I was being followed."

"And then what?"

"Not much. I stopped to check the traffic before crossing, just like the good little girl in me was taught to do, and *pow!* My friend from behind pushed me down. I was surprised as hell. Especially when I looked up and saw old man Buick making straight for me."

"Did he go for your purse?"

"What purse? Maybe the wacko was trying to jump in front of the car himself and was pissed that I was in the way. Who knows? Remember, we live in New York. There are eight million stories out there and eight million weirdos to tell them."

"You know," said Allison as she poured some more scotch into her glass, "a very scary shiver just passed through me. Thank God you're all right."

"But there is a tragedy here that you're missing," Cynthia remarked with a smile.

"What's that?"

"The garlic. That Buick mashed it better than a Cuisinart could."

18

For several days after Cynthia's accident, Allison was so rattled that she made sure she was inside her loft, with the door locked, before dark. But then, seeing nothing and no one out of the ordinary, she relaxed and went back to her nighttime schedule with a vengeance. The new theater season was in full swing. Every evening there was a play opening or some other event that at least someone in the department insisted was not to be missed.

On this particular evening she and another agent were scheduled to see the work-in-progress of a young playwright whose name she knew all too well. Sean Roberto Flores. *Jake's Tale* was being presented by The Combine, the performance group he worked with, in a downtown loft. She tried to convince herself that the whole affair was eminently skippable. Another angst-ridden young playwright and his playschool acting company searching for truth in an inadequately heated makeshift theater. If they were lucky there'd be some jug wine and crackers afterward. Madeleine Neuman, the other agent, would be annoyed, but Allison was determined to cancel.

—Why? she asked herself. And don't bring up this nonsense about being too tired to go out. Aren't you anxious as hell to meet Sean Roberto Flores again?

—Of course I am.

—What are you afraid of, then? That he'll cut you to pieces again?

—Maybe. But no—that's not it.

—Or are you afraid he won't even notice you this time? That would be much worse, wouldn't it? Maybe you haven't admitted it to yourself, but he's the first really attractive man you've flashed to in how long? Since George? But George isn't even in the same league as Sean Flores. Not in character or in looks or in talent. But you still don't have the courage to go tonight, do you?

—No, dammit, I don't.

—O gutless one.

—You're right. Spare me another rejection. I'd prefer a soft, warm scenario in which we meet someday in the misty future and that beautiful man falls head over heels for me. Okay? Enough? That's my decision. So leave me alone.

Allison threw a couple of scripts in her briefcase and, bolstered now by the belief that she was doing absolutely the right thing, stopped by Madeleine's office on the way to the elevator.

"You'll kick yourself if you miss this," said Madeleine. "I saw a couple of his one-acts last spring. They were very impressive. Every agent in town is trying to sign him up, including me. So far, he's playing hard to get. Agents are the lampreys of the theater, he says. All they do is suck out your vital juices and slow you down."

"I guess I should say good luck to you then. But count me out."

"Oh, come on, Allison. You know I don't make a pitch like this about just anyone. I'd really like your opinion."

"I wish I could help you out, but—"

"If you need an excuse, there's going to be a great party afterward."

"I'll bet. Gallo hearty burgundy and—"

"Nothing like that at all. This hot artist friend of his, Wilson Weybright, is throwing it. He owns a converted matzo factory on the Lower East Side. It might sound strange, but the place is terrific and there'll be a real lively crowd."

"I think I'll still take a pass."

"Is the reason you're refusing to go that . . . episode you had with Flores on *Arts Around Us?*" Madeleine asked benignly. "You should give him another chance. I know you'd like him. Lots of people think he's another Sam Shepard. He's just as sexy. If I weren't married, I'd really be interested. But I probably wouldn't have a chance anyway. Women swarm around him like piranhas near a Christmas ham. And if you want to avoid him, that'll be no problem. A Weybright party is generally like Times Square as the ball is falling. So, how about it?"

"Well . . ." As soon as she heard the hesitation in her own voice, Allison knew she was hooked. *What have you got to lose? So what if there's a man who doesn't think you're perfect? You have your own strong doubts about that.*

Madeleine was right about the play. It was set on an Indian reservation in New Mexico and pitted the young leaders of the tribe against the Bureau of Indian Affairs. It was impossible to dismiss the play as merely political. The characters were intensely alive—angry, tender, ironic. The first act was masterful, the second needed work, but, rough as it was, the promise was all there. And the language! Flores had an ear for common speech that still allowed the poetry that was inherent to come through. Allison had no doubt that he was a major talent.

Madeleine turned out to be right about the party, too. Wilson Wey-bright's matzo factory had been gutted and transformed into a glistening series of levels, all painted in high-gloss white, that were reached by a continuous ramp, much like a miniature Guggenheim. The crowd—actors, painters, fashion people, writers—talked and drank against back-ground music that sounded like the Talking Heads under torture. Though Allison looked for Sean Roberto Flores, he was nowhere in sight, until a tap on her back made her turn around, and there he was. Smiling!

"Could you possibly give a major-league schmuck a chance to say he's sorry?" he asked. He looked even better than he had in the TV studio, and his large gray eyes were irresistible.

"I'd love to say something witty, but would a simple 'sure' do?"

"It's more than I hoped for," he replied, his smile dazzling. "Wouldn't you like some explanation for my descent into cretinism?"

"Only if you get me a drink."

"That's not so easy, but let's give it a try. If we pull it off, we can take our drinks outside. There should be a little peace and quiet out back where they used to bake the stuff. So, make yourself real skinny and follow me through this madhouse."

When they reached the backyard, there were only a few other people leaning against a brick oven that resembled a huge igloo.

"Wil converted it into a sauna," Sean said, noticing Allison looking at the neat wooden door cut into the front of the oven. He led her off to one side of it where they sat down on an old park bench. They clicked glasses and talked about the play for a few minutes before Sean deter-minedly steered them back to what he had promised to tell her.

"Well, are you ready for my reason?" he asked.

"Positively. Not even the chance to sign you up would persuade me to let you off the witness stand," Allison answered, laughing.

"A low blow, but deserved. First of all, I was in a pissy mood for allowing myself to be dragged on the show against my better judgment. Three minutes devoted to the art of theater. What a joke."

"Well, at least our moods were in sync that day."

"That's reason number one, but there are others," he replied, click-ing his glass against hers again. "That fool with the bow tie and the teeth, for instance. But the clincher was, I was angry at you."

"What did I do?" she asked, perplexed.

"Nothing, of course. But I was immediately turned on to you and I knew you probably wouldn't give me the time of day. Therefore, I at-tacked. I told you I was a schmuck."

"But an honest one. Now I know this sounds corny, but would you tell me a little about—The Combine, isn't it?"

"Sure, and I'll start with the best, which is its total absence of bullshit," he said. "If something doesn't work, nobody's afraid of hurting feelings by saying so. Criticism can be rough to hear, but the openness works wonders. We also give each other all the moral support you could want. And we don't have to rely on anything or anyone. We've pared things down to the point where we're totally self-sufficient. I can't figure a better way to develop as a writer. It's a bit like that college workshop you always dreamed about and never got to attend."

"But you can't live on this."

"No, that I can't," said Sean, laughing. "We have lots of bartenders and waitresses in The Combine. Also a housepainter and a dog walker. I'm a carpenter. Bookshelves, repairs, stuff like that." He shrugged. "It pays the bills."

"Where did you go to school?" asked Allison.

"Berkeley, then Oxford. But before you get too impressed, I didn't graduate from either one. God knows, if I had gotten a degree it could have led to others. It's like a virus. It spreads. I might even have become a lawyer."

"Watch it now. You're speaking to a lawyer," said Allison, with a pretense of indignation.

"A sometimes worthy calling in spite of what people say," Sean answered with a playful bow toward Allison. "I once thought I would get a law degree and go back to New Mexico and fight the good fight in the courtrooms, but my heart was really in writing. I think, or rather I hope, I can accomplish the same things on stage. If I make it, of course."

"If you make it?" echoed a large, heavily made-up woman swooping down on them. Allison recognized her as a theatrical lawyer and producer. "There's no question you'll make it, Sean. Eventually, that is. If you want to hasten the process, though, you'll let me produce you and this darling young lady here represent you."

"That's what we were discussing right now, Harriet," Sean said as pleasantly as possible.

"Knowing you, I doubt it, but I really have to pull him away, Allison. I've been looking high and low for him. Horst Droemer, a client of mine, who's the best director in Germany, is dying to meet Sean, and I know you wouldn't want to stand in the way of a possible foreign production, would you?"

"Couldn't it wait, Harr—" Sean started to say.

But Harriet Riley already had Sean on his feet and was guiding him adroitly into the maelstrom inside.

"I've got to go out of town for a week, but would it be okay if I call you someday?" asked Sean quickly.

And then he was gone, but nothing could take the grin off Allison's face.

One week went by and then several and still Sean did not call. Then one Sunday afternoon when Allison wasn't expecting anybody, her front doorbell rang, and it was Sean.

"I was in your neighborhood, and I thought I'd see if you were in. If I'm interrupting anything—"

"You're not. I'm just reading."

"The competition?" asked Sean, laughing a bit awkwardly at the sight of a script lying open on a fat, overstuffed chair.

"You could say so," said Allison, smiling. "Why don't you sit down?"

"I've got a better idea. How about going for a walk? We can stop somewhere for a cup of coffee."

"I'd love it."

"This place of yours is terrific," said Sean, looking around for the first time.

"Want to see the rest?" asked Allison.

She was pleased with the way the loft had turned out. The palette was muted—creams, whites, and pale browns that showed off the spacious proportions of the rooms and the play of textures: the tin stamped ceilings, the wooden floors now bleached, the original iron strutwork on the gigantic window frames. The living room was furnished with large-scale, generously upholstered armchairs grouped around a fat sofa that looked as if it would be impossible to sit in it without falling asleep. A honey-colored Biedermeier dining table surrounded by eight curving matched chairs occupied one wall. Two other walls were given over to canvases, one figurative, the other abstract, that filled the space from floor to ceiling and shot bright volleys of color through the room. Sunlight flooded the bedroom and the adjoining dressing room, which was dominated by a tiled Jacuzzi set at precisely that point which allowed a person to float in it while looking out the window at the same time.

"Jesus," said Sean with a low whistle on seeing it. "We could finance The Combine for six months on what this tiling must have cost. Oh, damn," he added immediately, "I didn't mean that the way it sounded."

"That's okay," said Allison. "I'm a big girl. I can take it."

They walked up West Broadway, past the Odeon, and then into the

Village to avoid the crowds in SoHo. Sean knew an Italian café that left its customers alone.

"I've been thinking about what you said about the play the last time I saw you," said Sean as they each sat down with a cup of espresso. "You have a good eye. And a better bullshit detector."

"Why, thanks."

"You weren't too happy with the scene between the boy and his father, were you?"

Allison shook her head, but not too vehemently, and waited for Sean to continue.

"I think you might be right. Do you remember what you said? The father gets too angry. He probably should hold back more," said Sean. "The way I've written it, he puts too much on the kid, and it's not the kid's fault."

"The man's just looking for an excuse to blow up."

"Yeah, I think I've got to focus the whole thing better. What else doesn't work for you? You can tell me. I can take it, just like you," he added with a half-smile.

They talked more about the play and about the current theater season, which was fairly dismal, and then Sean asked Allison why she wanted to be an agent.

"A nice girl like you should be—"

"Doing something worthwhile? I think I am, actually. It's not as if I chose the profession out of the blue. I grew up with it."

Sean looked at Allison blankly.

"My uncle owns the agency. You know, Gus Morton. Same last name and all that. Just like the man with the bow tie said on the show that day."

"What a jerk I am," said Sean, shaking his head. "I guess I've been living south of Canal Street too long. I keep misplacing my field guide to the movers and shakers. I don't want to sound like that much of a hayseed, though. U.T.M. is a lot like the General Motors of the talent business, isn't it?"

Allison nodded.

"And what exactly do you do?"

"Well, I'm just starting off, trying a bit of everything. I'll probably end up in L.A. handling movies and television. It's the biggest part of the business. But theater's what I love. Do you think you can cope with a little soul-baring?"

"Of course, fraulein, but please to lie down on my couch first," Sean said, in the heavy Germanic accent of a stage psychiatrist.

"When I was growing up I wanted to be an actress. Correction. I was dying to be an actress. All my friends were horse-crazy, but my idea of heaven was getting up on the stage. I had more than the usual share of leading roles in grade school—they always try to divvy them up equally, you know—but by high school I was serious. I mean really serious."

"What stopped you?"

"Uncle Gus. As he should have," she added, seeing Sean's look of mild surprise. "Someone had to, because I wasn't very good. It took me forever to face up to the unfortunate truth. In fact, I still have trouble with it," she said with a laugh.

"Did you ever wonder whether your uncle had an ulterior motive? I mean, here you are working for him and all that."

"It never occurred to me, but it's the silliest idea I've heard of."

"Did it upset you?"

"Upset me? I was devastated. You have to picture the way it was for me. This grand passion of mine was what made me different from everyone else. It was my thing. Special. And then I lost it. But . . . I survived. I was beginning college, and other things took over."

The sun was starting to drop in the sky. Allison saw in her mind's eye the unread scripts waiting for her in her loft, but they didn't tempt her. She didn't want to do anything other than sit here and look at and listen to this man. She was disappointed when Sean noticed the time too and asked for the check.

Later, when they were near her loft, Sean abruptly stopped and turned to Allison. "How about dinner tonight?"

"I'm afraid I can't. I have to work. I'm going to Chicago tomorrow. Early."

As soon as she had spoken, Allison cursed herself. What a fool. The most exciting man she had met in a very, very long while wanted to take her to dinner and she had just turned him down. She could have figured out a way to finish her work!

"I'll be back in a couple of days," she said dispiritedly.

"Maybe I'll give you a call then."

"I'll give you my number. It's unlisted."

"Unlisted? Why? Do you get a lot of dirty calls?"

"The dirtiest call I've ever gotten was from Bloomingdale's credit department about my delinquent account. Unlisted numbers are just a . . ." Allison almost said, "just a habit in L.A.," but stopped herself.

Sean felt his jacket pockets for a pen, but couldn't find one. "I'll get the number from your office. I'll call them tomorrow."

■   ■   ■

When she returned to the city, Allison found a message from Sean on her answering machine. "I've got eggs. I've got chorizo. I've got beer. Pearl's, that is, my chiquita. Chilled *muy perfecto*. All that is missing is you. Let me know when you're back."

Allison immediately called him, and they made a date for the next evening.

"I'll make huevos rancheros. My grandmother's recipe. They're so good even I can't mess them up. Besides . . ." His voice trailed off.

"Besides what?"

"It'll give you a chance to see what a real loft looks like. There I go again. I hope that remark doesn't piss you off. Does it?"

"No, Sean, it doesn't piss me off. Unless the huevos rancheros are not up to snuff. I have been around, you know."

Sean lived at the top of a rundown former factory building in a neighborhood that was tilting toward gentrification since the old Beaux Arts police station on Centre Street had been turned into million-dollar condominiums. He came down to meet Allison in a rickety hand-operated freight elevator that bobbed and dipped at the ground-floor level like a boat coming into dock. The elevator was papered with vacate notices from the landlord. The inside of the loft itself was furnished frugally with straight-back chairs and simple tables that Sean described as "early Salvation Army." The furniture, floor, and walls were painted in high-gloss combinations of black, white, green, and royal blue.

"What you see is what you get," said Sean. "At least for six more months. I think I can keep the landlord at bay until then."

Sean's family recipe was terrific, but they only picked at the food. Allison couldn't think of anything but him.

After dinner, Sean punched up the pillows on his bed, the only comfortable place to sit in the loft, and they listened to a Keith Jarrett album while they drank poisonously strong coffee. When Sean stood up to change the record, their eyes caught and held, and he sat down again. He pulled Allison toward him. Slowly they undressed each other, and even more slowly made love into the night.

PART TWO

19

W hat about ModuleCon?" Hector Frame asked.

"Opened late. Up a quarter," answered his gaunt, dark-haired son, Adrian. Dressed in a gray, raw silk suit that he had had specially made in London, the tunic jacket so tightly fitted that it lacked pockets, he sat ramrod straight on a short metal stool at the foot of the surgical table where his father was "attended to" each day.

As Adrian watched, the old man was given a haircut, shave, manicure, pedicure, and massage, all the while lying supine. The milky color of his skin made the white cotton loincloth he wore almost undetectable. Earlier a dermatologist had completed his weekly examination of Frame and departed. On each visit he inspected every inch of Frame's body for skin changes no matter how innocuous, sending a biopsy of anything new to the lab for analysis. On Wednesdays, a dentist cleaned the old man's teeth, beginning with a thorough flossing since Frame found doing it himself distasteful, and an internist ran a series of heart and blood tests that most people received once a year, if at all.

For the past twenty years, except for traveling on rare occasions to an annual meeting of a company he was attempting to take over or appearing before a grand jury, Hector Frame had seldom left his Toronto stronghold, preferring instead to send Adrian out on forays on behalf of Frame Properties, Ltd. He lived surrounded by his personal staff, including never fewer than six bodyguards in attendance at all times, on four floors of a not very distinguished white brick apartment building that he owned on the lake. As leases expired, tenants were told they would not be renewed no matter how much money they offered to pay, so that now Frame resided virtually alone, except for his staff, in a twenty-four-story building. The few remaining tenants, all elderly, seemed like ghosts on the TV monitors in the security room, as they scuttled through the deserted lobby with the speed of children moving past a cemetery at night.

"You've met all the key U.T.M. people?" the old man asked suddenly, as the barber finished trimming his nasal hairs. Rarely did Hector

Frame address his son by his first name, and then only when they were alone or when Adrian had accomplished something either particularly brilliant or devious, qualities the old man prized in himself and was always genuinely surprised to see his son exhibit, since he thought of his only child and heir as incredibly "soft." He dismissed his physical pit crew with a nearly imperceptible wave of his fingers.

"I've seen almost everybody, or talked to them on the phone," Adrian answered promptly, knowing that his father viewed hesitancy as a precursor to failure.

" 'Almost,' my dear boy," he snapped, "is a word employed solely by losers. The important things that will happen to you will never be accompanied by an 'almost.' "

"The only person I haven't gotten to yet is Allison Morton. Though I've observed her closely on a recent occasion. She's beautiful. I could have an interesting time with her—"

"Get your mind back on business. I don't intend to rescue you from another criminal charge ever again. God knows how I kept your name out of the papers when that adolescent's body was discovered in Palm Beach."

"Things just got a little out of hand that time, Father," protested Adrian. "It was an accident."

"Do you realize you just interrupted me?"

"Yes, Father," Adrian answered automatically, suppressing a flash of anger.

" 'The only person I haven't gotten to yet is Allison Morton,' "said Hector Frame, mimicking his son with a withering look. "Just like you to spend your time taking every fucking piece on the board but the king, or should I say the queen," said Hector, his voice rising and ricocheting off the tiled walls of the large room. He nodded to the two bodyguards, like all the others in the cadre recruited exclusively from the ranks of cashiered Delta Force members and dressed identically in white jumpsuits. The two men silently left the room.

"Go on," he said to his son.

"You told me to stay away from Gus Morton. But I've had Reidy on him, and I have a complete rundown of his traveling schedule and appointments for the past month. It's in a folder on your desk," he said, looking up at his father. The old man's smile, as tight as a boxer's fist, cut across his mouth for an instant and then was gone. Adrian felt a surge of pleasure wash over him. His father approved of something he had done!

"Getting back to Allison Morton," he continued. "She's been travel-

ing with her uncle too much on his little buying sprees. And I didn't want
to tip anything until I'd gotten to the others." His tone had become apologetic. It was a tone he never used with anyone else, but frequently with
his father, and then as reflexively as waving a hand to brush away a fly.

"And the others?"

"In most cases, money or an enhanced title will do the job. I've got
Lee Simons in our pocket. She's the most important agent they've got.
She also occupies a dominant place in the social scene out there. She'll
help us a lot. Ben Wildman is a little tricky, but I'm confident he'll come
around."

"And that prig of a money man, Parker Welles?"

"I'm working on him too. There'll be no wholesale exodus of the
staff. That I guarantee you. But you haven't told me yet, Father, why you
want U.T.M. so much. From an earnings point of view, where can a
company like that go?"

"If you gave a fraction of the time you spend on your perversions to
studying the business before you, I could rest easy, my boy. You use your
intelligence like a nun uses her body. Sparingly.

"There are three things U.T.M. can do for us. First, Gus Morton sits
on a lot of real estate that is vastly undervalued. The land abutting his
office, where he has that stupid parking lot, is worth the company itself.
Morton has a poor-man's attitude toward property. He lets it become part
of him. Family. He doesn't realize you should treat it as dispassionately as
you do a woman you've grown tired of. But with real estate the deal is
infinitely better. You don't have to pay to be rid of it," he said with a
short, barking laugh that would have scared a child. "Instead you get
something in return, and that something is very nice indeed."

"What's the second thing, Father?" Adrian asked, as his father rose
off the table and waited for Adrian to help him on with his white silk robe.
He stood on a freshly laundered and starched strip of linen that the barber had unrolled like a royal carpet before leaving. He never placed his
bare feet on any floor where other people had walked.

"One of the big studios will come up for sale someday soon. And I
will want to buy it. You've heard me say that before, haven't you? Well,
to operate it, I'll need executives. The best I can find. What better pool
to draw from than the group that runs the top talent agency in the business? It's a business of deals and it's based on who controls the talent,
right? Steve Ross had the same idea years ago when he acquired Ted
Ashley's agency prior to buying Warner's. It was a good idea then and it's
a better one now."

"Who's going to present the StellarVue package to Morton?" asked Adrian, holding his arm out for support while his father stepped into his slippers.

"Winthrop in Chicago. Morton trusts him."

"And there's no way to trace our convertible position in StellarVue back to us?"

"I doubt it. The deal will look too good to him. He'll be too anxious to close on it. StellarVue's cash position will be enormously enticing. And besides, there are two dummy corporations in place before our hand would be revealed. Unless the interests are added together, there's no perceivable threat to him. Anyway, he's not going to dig that far."

Hector Frame stood in front of the door to his office, waiting for Adrian to open it. The old man's carefully combed long white hair fell to the collar of his robe.

"You mentioned three things, Father," said Adrian.

"Yes. The third is Gus Morton himself. He's treated me like scum whenever I've dealt with him. I've waited a long time to pay him in kind. For over forty years. But now, finally, the time is at hand." Frame's face lit up with a predatory smile. "Morton loves U.T.M., and that's what I'm going to take from him. Never forget that, Adrian. Always take what they love. That way they will always remember it."

Hector Frame left him standing alone in the white room. He didn't turn to look at his son, so he missed the incredibly pleased look on the young man's face. Adrian always felt good when his father called him by his first name.

20

H ello," said Felix Godwin, picking up the telephone on the first ring.
"Hi, Felix. It's—"

"Allison," he interrupted happily. "How are you? *Where* are you?"

"About three miles away and breathing the same noxious air you are,
but how'd you guess it was me?"

"I didn't guess. I knew," said Felix, laughing. "I'm an actor, remember? If I couldn't tell one voice from another I'd be in trouble. When can
I see you?" he asked.

"How about now?" Allison paused, then said, "I always seem to fall
back on clichés at times like this, Felix, but I'd like to bury the hatchet. I
want to be friends again."

"I'd like that."

"Are you free for lunch? I'll drive over to your place, and then we can
go out somewhere."

"Fabulous. I guess you heard that George and I parted company?"

"I don't think I'd be on the line if you two were still an item," she
said with a laugh.

"Well, I'll tell you all the gory details when you get here. Now, let me
give you directions. From the Beverly Hills office, right? Go south on
Wil—"

"Felix, I know where your house is. Remember?"

"Oh, yes, so you do, so you do," echoed Felix.

On the way to his house, Allison stopped at Williams-Sonoma to buy
a large, festive straw basket, then detoured from there to a local greengrocer and stuffed it full of every variety of fresh fruit the store had. Felix
was rumored to have shed most of his bad habits, and this was her way of
saying she was happy for him.

As soon as Allison pulled into Felix's driveway, the front door banged
open and he came bounding down the steps toward her. "God, it's great
to see you," he said, hugging her. "Come on inside."

"Okay, but first I need a hand," she said, opening the back door of the car.

Felix peered inside at the mound of fresh fruit and let out a snort of laughter. "You think I'm on a health kick, do you? That I'm ready to trade grams of coke for kiwi slices? Well, kiddo, think again."

Allison looked up quickly at Felix, more than a little aghast.

This time Felix really laughed. "If you could only have seen your face," he said. "But I'm just teasing. You heard right. I'm a reformed man. A new Felix. At least I'm trying to be. Honest."

"I've got another surprise for you, only this one we have to drive to. You game?" asked Allison.

Five minutes and a half-dozen turns later they pulled into a parking lot next to a modest one-story building. HEAVENLY BODIES read the sign above the door.

"You can't be serious," groaned Felix, seeing where they were. "I've been avoiding gyms for years. Please don't tell me you expect me to climb out of this nice, cozy BMW and start abusing my body?"

Allison nodded. "You look like you're up for it. Let's take a quick class, and then we can have lunch."

Felix was a good sport, and the two of them staggered through an hour of arm-, leg-, and gut-wrenching aerobics before rewarding themselves with a Japanese lunch. After the waitress had taken their order and poured them tea, Felix brought Allison up-to-date with what he was doing. He had recently completed a TV movie about corruption in the New York police force ("Nothing new. I did it for the old checking account, not for the resumé.") and was flying to New Delhi in two weeks for the lead role in a remake of *The River*.

"Colonial India is always a favorite with producers. Exotic—and safe. Too far removed from reality to ruffle anyone's feathers. But tell me," he said, eyeing Allison curiously, "what brings you to town?"

"You."

"Me? But I'm the chap who worked you over the last time we met. Treated you like shit. True to my reputation. I can't believe you're eager for more," Felix said with a roguish smile.

"Positively not. But I don't think there'll ever be a next time. You've mellowed, and I think you're beginning to like yourself."

"Let's just say that I've decided to stop trying to kill myself. I was beginning to get too good at it."

"Great. Are you ready to hear about a dynamite proposal that's got your name written all over it?"

"After that workout," he said, "you have my full attention. I'm too exhausted to move."

"About a month ago," said Allison, after a swallow of tea, "I went to New Haven for an opening of a play at the Long Wharf. At the request of one of our clients. She thought there was a perfect role for her in the play and wanted to see it moved to Broadway. In fact she was dead wrong, which is neither here nor there. On the train back to New York, I tried to nap—I was pretty wiped out—but I couldn't, so I started going through my mail. In the midst of the usual stuff was a long letter from Lavinia Tedesco. I'm sure you know who she is."

"Allison, you have finally hurt my feelings. Don't you remember that I played Granby in *The Dream Builders* in the West End. Got pretty good notices too," he said with a smile that tried valiantly to be modest.

"Of course! How could I forget. Please forgive me."

"Don't worry a bit, this ego is as strong as the Aswan Dam."

"Where was I?" she asked after a moment.

"Lavinia Tedesco's letter."

"Yes, the letter. It was a long letter. Since I started representing her we've gotten quite close. And about half the letter dealt with her late husband. You may or may not know but Christopher died in a car crash several years ago. He was quite a bit younger than Lavinia and their relationship was the most important thing in her life. She was also terribly injured in the accident. I read the letter four times, or rather, the part about Christopher, on the ride back to the city. When I got back to my place I fished out Lavinia's other letters. And I realized what she had done in those letters was to write the outline of a play. A beautiful and totally original take on that old chestnut, the love story between an older woman and a younger man."

"Sounds fabulous," Felix replied. "What's it all got to do with old Godwin, however?"

"I see you playing the Christopher part."

"I'm all for it. Send me the script when it's ready," Felix said blithely.

"It's not that easy. First, I have to persuade Lavinia to write the play."

"Well, go to it, lass. You're a very convincing young woman. I can vouch for that."

"This time I think I need help."

"Meaning?" he asked, taking another bite of the fruit.

"You're a charmer and I need all the charm I can get. Also, this could be a great role for you. Lavinia, I know, admires your work and the

fact that you've come with me will mean a lot. I've booked us on a six
P.M. flight to Carmel tomorrow. I'll pick you up. And I'll send copies of
the letters over this afternoon. Now I've got an office to get back to," she
said as she left, not even giving Felix time for a ta-ta.

The next evening Allison and Felix had drinks with Lavinia on her terrace before dinner. The setting sun, the color of an overripe mango,
balanced on the horizon like a conjurer's trick. The boom of the surf fifty
feet below sounded strangely comforting. In the more than half-year
since Allison had met Lavinia her condition had continued to improve.
She walked now with less of a limp, and the combination of a few added
pounds and a little sunshine had erased years from her face. Lavinia's
strong features had softened into a mature beauty that served as a frame
for distinctive black eyes that were at once intelligent and compassionate.

The talk through dinner moved from California politics and the staying power of short skirts, to the plays of Oscar Wilde. Through it all,
Felix was oddly quiet, sipping his wine and stealing glances at Lavinia.
Finally, back on the terrace for brandy, Allison got to the subject that had
brought them to the writer's home.

"You must do it, Lavinia," she said, and listened to the surf adding
dramatic punctuation to her words.

"I think I've wrestled with that beautiful ghost enough, Allison. Let
him rest," she answered, looking out at the dark, booming sea.

"Lavinia," Felix started slowly, "I want to confess that at first I
agreed to accompany Allison up here because I was curious. She said
there was a chance for a great role and by helping her persuade you to do
the play I'd get to act it, but I've heard that more times than I've heard
'happy birthday.' I've admired your work for a long time, and like a true
celebrity," he said with a shy smile, "I'm always interested in meeting
another. But then I read your letters, and I realized that here was a part
that I *had* to play and a play that you *had* to write." He stood up and
moved to the terrace railing, then quickly turned and talked to Lavinia in
a way that made Allison feel they had forgotten she was there. "I've lived
a life I'm sorry to say I'm not proud of. More bad scripts, booze, drugs,
and one-night stands than I care to remember. When I read about your
relationship with Christopher, I saw not just a star role for me, but a way
of life that was free of gameplaying and illusion, something I've never
had but still desperately want, even at this late date. So, as much as I
need for my own reasons to re-create a part of that life that you lived,

many others need to see it and learn from it. Lavinia," he moved over to her and took her hand in his, "please write this play. You must."

The next morning, before Allison left to pick up Felix for the drive to the airport, there was a knock at the door of her hotel room. When she answered it, a bellhop handed her a note.

Luv,
Please forgive me but I'm not returning with you. In a lifetime of countless girls, I found a woman last night. I have no idea if she shares my feelings, but I know that I have to lay siege here until I find out if I'm right or if it's hopeless. Of course, I would also like to persuade Mme. Tedesco to write the play. I promise to report in regularly and start getting in shape (our little trip to the gym was a gentle hint, was it not?) and to be an extremely good boy.
Piece of business: You do realize that I need an agent, don't you? Would you please accept this old boy as a client? If you do, please send to me at this hotel (for the time being only, I hope!) the appropriate papers marking my happy indenture. Another piece of business: After last night I realize that there is no way that I can do that Indian picture. Extricate me, I pray. If it's messy, so be it. But I've reached a time in my life when the things I do from now on will have to be important—at least to me.
I remain, your devoted client *and* friend,
Felix

21

"It could have been worse, I guess," said Madeleine Neuman over what must have been her sixth cup of coffee of the day.

"How?" asked Allison innocently.

"The theater could have burned down."

It was a Friday afternoon toward the end of October, and Allison and her colleagues in the U.T.M. theatrical department were dejectedly dragging themselves through the end of what had been a tough week. The highlight, or rather lowlight, had occurred the preceding night, when a new work by a playwright they had successfully represented for years had opened. The two leads also were U.T.M. clients, as were the set designer and the director. The play had been an unqualified disaster. The pain of making small talk with the playwright during intermission, while bored and disgruntled members of the audience milled around them in the lobby, was nothing compared with pretending that the opening night party that followed was anything but a deathwatch. The reviews in the late night editions of the papers and on the eleven o'clock news were even more savage than expected. At the party, everybody took the reviews philosophically, but the following morning it was a different matter. The playwright screamed at the head of the division, Bert Kipler, who screamed at Madeleine Neuman, the agent directly responsible.

"Why didn't you get him to shelve it, Maddy? The only people involved in this fucking play who are *not* our clients are the usherettes. And you know there's just one thing worse than getting the expected 'cool' call from Gus the day after. It's not getting it. This morning—*nada*. The aroma of this dog must already have hit the Coast. And that's going against the prevailing winds."

"Don't give me that crap, Bert. I won't let you drop all the blame for this production on me. You read the damn play, too. I think I remember you saying, 'This is a great vehicle for Terri Borden. It fits her perfectly.' So lay off me."

Madeleine had been in and out of Allison's office all day, alternately bitching about Kipler and berating herself. By the end of the afternoon Allison was so emotionally drained that she felt almost as if she had been responsible.

After one final therapy session with the still distraught Madeleine, Allison got ready to leave for the weekend. It wasn't even four yet, but she had had it. She fed the material she planned to read into her brief-case. The heftiest of the items was a long, sprawling comedy that was the season's biggest hit in Paris. A bedroom farce in extremis, it depicted a modern Don Juan who numbered his sexual conquests in four digits. A *thousand* lovers? What could it possibly say to the anxious modern sensi-bility, even if the author went for laughs? She wasn't certain why Bert wanted her instant opinion on it, but he did. Perhaps it was because Alli-son's French was excellent, though she knew that two other U.T.M. agents were also fluent. Next was a proposal for a biography of Tito by a friend of a friend from college. Being an agent meant receiving a steady stream of plays, scripts, novels, cookbooks, and what have you, theatri-cal or otherwise, from everyone from former lab partners to fellows she had dated once. Last of all was a slim manila folder that she slipped onto the top of the pile, icing on the cake. This was the first draft of the book for a musical about the Vietnam War that she and Oscar Buckman were developing. It was her reward for doing the rest of the reading, the one piece of material she couldn't wait to see. Oscar had just messengered it over. "Right on target," his note on the cover said, "has lots of great lead-ins for songs." If Allison thought as highly of it as he did, they could schedule a preliminary meeting next week with the composer.

Of all U.T.M.'s clients, Allison had learned, the only one Sean Flores was interested in meeting someday was Oscar Buckman.

"He's a genius," Sean had said to her just last week.

"A *successful* genius. Who has also reached, if I may be so bold to add, a large audience."

"I agree he's very successful, but probably not for your reasons. He has a brilliant imagination and he's never, never compromised it. That's what accounts for his success. So what that he's rich enough to fly to Paris for the weekend on the Concorde and never notice the difference. It doesn't affect his judgment. As far as reaching a large audience, I'm more interested in attracting the *right* audience."

"Maybe Oscar cares about that, too," said Allison with a little smile. "And give me a break. Don't you think I respect Oscar for exactly the same reasons you do?"

Sean laughed. "You're right. I was being unfair."

The fact that this hero of Sean's had an agent, her uncle Gus, who had been representing him for nearly thirty years, seemed to make no impression on him. Though Allison, because of their relationship, wouldn't have represented Sean in any case, she still thought he did himself a disservice by not having an agent. Connie, a cute but flaky assistant at The Combine, handled in a lackadaisical fashion everything from the requests of regional companies wanting to do a production by one of the members to copyright registrations. An agent, a real agent, like Madeleine for instance, could make all the difference between having a play talked about as "promising" and having it actually produced. Produced, that is, with a topflight cast, scenery, and direction. She had stopped within an inch of saying this half a dozen times, but it wasn't necessary to consult a tarot deck to know what Sean's response would be. Agents cared only about Broadway, and whatever it was that emerged from the Broadway gristmill, whether a hit or a flop or something in between, it no longer belonged to the playwright. Too many people would have "collaborated" on it, a polite way of saying co-opted it. He'd rather stay broke than parlay himself—and The Combine—away in that fashion, thank you.

There wasn't a moment when Allison wasn't thinking about Sean. The way he looked. His touch. His smell. She was in love with him, as simple as that. Truly in love. And it had never happened to her before, ever, in this way. Not even close. Allison realized that her affair with George was just that—an affair. Good for the body, but corrosive to the soul.

Since the night she and Sean had fallen into bed together, they had seen each other as much as possible. He had stayed at her loft for the last two weekends. When they weren't in bed, they were working. Allison staked out one of her soft, cushiony chairs, and Sean stretched out on the sofa, writing in longhand. He still was fiddling with *Jake's Tale,* but he was also well into a new play. Occasionally he read out bits of dialogue for her reaction, but since he never gave her the context of the passage, it was like walking into the middle of a movie. A good movie to be sure, she sensed.

He was just as close-mouthed, Allison discovered, about other parts of his life, though occasionally he surprised her with his openness. Several evenings earlier, as they waited for a table at Umberto's Clam House, he informed her that he had lived for a couple of years with an actress who had moved back to Chicago last year. He didn't say whether he cared about her still, but he didn't really need to. His expression told Allison all she wanted to know. She was the only one who counted now. And she felt deep down that it would be that way for a long time. How long? She was superstitious enough not to want to know the answer to that.

As soon as Allison stepped into the elevator, the woes of the day at the office slipped away. She felt terrific. Sean was coming for dinner, and on Saturday they were getting together with Cynthia and her boyfriend Tom, who was in town for the weekend. Though they hadn't talked about it, she knew they would spend the time in between together, too. Sean wasn't due at the loft until eight, so she had plenty of time to prepare dinner. Roasted peppers, grilled veal chops, a huge salad. She spun through the revolving door onto Fifth Avenue, still running over in her mind what she wanted to do before he arrived, when a short blast from a car horn made her look up. There was Sean, grinning at her from a shiny blue Volvo station wagon. He waved at her through the sunroof.

"What're you doing here?" asked Allison delightedly.

"Don't ask, just jump in," said Sean, leaning over and opening the door for her.

Sean drove toward the river and then onto the West Side Highway. Allison looked at him in surprise. He shook his head, refusing to say anything, until they reached the tollbooth at the northern end of Manhattan. As they eased to a stop, he leaned over and brushed his lips against Allison's. He was wearing a pale pink sweater that threw a flush of rose onto his cheeks the way a buttercup colors a chin.

"This trip wasn't on your agenda," he said, "but I think you're going to be pleased. Now don't try to worm anything out of me. I'm taking the fifth. No amount of torture, even the carnal variety, will make me tell you where we're going. I want it to be a surprise."

"But what about dinner?" asked Allison, thinking of the two fat, double-thick veal chops in her refrigerator.

"What about it?" teased Sean. "Listen, this little baby we're sitting in is ours until Sunday night, on loan from Wil Weybright, so just relax and enjoy it. And, by the way, before you bring it up, Cynthia and Tom aren't bothered about our not seeing them tomorrow night. When I spoke with Cynthia, I got the distinct impression of just the opposite. I think they're delighted to have more time alone. Next time he's in town, we'll see them. He sounds like a good guy, and I want to meet him."

As they left the city, heading north, the leaves on the trees began to change. Bright patches of orange and yellow flashed out at them like signals from the mass of green. The air grew cooler. Sean rolled the sunroof shut and, reaching around for a canvas bag on the backseat, pulled out a sweater and dropped it onto Allison's lap. After an hour and a half, they left the Taconic Parkway for a secondary road and soon after that turned onto a narrow, deserted road that wound in and out of stands of trees and past small farmhouses set in front of gentle meadows. Finally Sean told Allison where they were going: Ashbury, Massachusetts. Allison located it on a map of New England that was crushed into the back of the glove compartment. It was a tiny dot floating in a sea of green state parkland.

When they turned onto a dirt road some ten miles later, Allison knew they must be near. They climbed slowly up the rock-studded road beneath a canopy of pine boughs that arched over them, blocking out what was left of the daylight. Sean shifted into low gear and they continued upward, past an old cemetery and a rusted, abandoned hay wagon, until the road suddenly leveled off at the top of the mountain. They veered onto another road snaking away to the left, jounced through several long turns, then stopped. In front of them was a small cabin, perched at the far edge of a field with a backdrop of trees falling away behind it.

"You like it?" asked Sean.

"I love it. Whose is it?"

"Mine," he said proudly. "I finished building it this past summer. Come on, I'll show you around."

"I'm impressed, but why didn't you ever tell me about it?" asked Allison, allowing Sean to pull her out of the car and across the tall grass. As they drew near, she saw that all the corners of the structure were not simply notched but beautifully constructed in a perfectly matched tongue and groove pattern. The view from the deck on the far side of the cabin was magnificent. A narrow, deep gorge slashed through a range of hills, thickly forested in a mixed palette of colors, drawing the eye forward for what must be miles into the distance, past other hills overlapping each other like breaking waves. The mountain they were on, he told her, belonged to one of his best friends at college. Someday the friend would build a house a half-mile away. That would be it. Everything else she could see in all directions was part of a state preserve that would never be touched.

When the mosquitoes chased them indoors, Sean lit kerosene lamps and Allison changed into long pants and a flannel shirt Sean had packed for her. The cabin had only one room, simply furnished. A bunk bed, a desk, a few shelves of books, skis and a pair of snowshoes leaning together in one corner, a woodburning stove, and lots of odd-sized pillows and cushions scattered about the floor. He put a match to some logs stacked in the fireplace, sank down on the lower bunk, and drew Allison into his arms. Soon they were fast asleep, and it wasn't until almost midnight that they woke, made love again, and, dinner forgotten, slipped back to sleep.

The next morning they hiked up a neighboring peak to a fire tower, where they picnicked and watched hawks riding the thermals above the ridges. By the time they climbed down again, the warm temperature, one last snatch of Indian summer, had caught up with them, but they didn't have far to go to cool off. In a stream that ran down the hillside below the cabin, which Allison had heard whispering during the night, Sean had carved out a deep swimming hole, and there they dived and swam in the nude until they were shivering with cold. Later they drove to the nearest town, where Sean knew a farm family that had a magic touch with vegetables. For a friend like Sean, produce picked even just a few hours earlier to sell at the farm stand was not fresh enough. Instead, the farmer's wife, a genial woman with a sun-weathered face and dirt in the seams of her hands, invited them to walk out into the garden with her, where she picked perfect specimens of end-of-the-season beans, cukes, tomatoes, and cauliflower—all straight from the vine. When they went into her kitchen to pay for the vegetables, two fat, squirming, black-and-white puppies bounded toward them, frantic with pleasure.

That night, as they sat by the fire eating dinner, Sean talked for the first time about his family. He had grown up in New Mexico, one of five children. His mother's parents were second-generation Irish from Pawtucket, Rhode Island. Respectable, middle-class, lace-curtain, he described them. They had worked hard to achieve their comfortable life—and to shed their telltale old-country ways. They were as bland and as proper as their Congregational neighbors who still viewed them as immigrants. They were mildly disconcerted when their daughter, Sean's mother, insisted on getting away from home by traveling clear across the country to attend the University of Colorado. There she fell in love with a dirt-poor half-Mexican student attending college on the GI Bill who had more than a trickle of Navaho blood coursing through his veins. It was then that her parents showed just how important it was to them to belong to the new world they had edged their way into. They didn't disown their daughter or anything that melodramatic, but they gradually and almost imperceptibly shifted their attention to their other children, probably without even noticing it themselves. They continued to send presents at Christmas and on birthdays and made perfunctory visits after the births of each of their grandchildren, but they showed little enthusiasm for it. It wasn't until Sean's mother was dying of cancer that the love her parents had suppressed so long showed itself again.

Sean, who was five at the time, remembered only vaguely the two elderly strangers standing at his mother's bedside. Later, when he thought about that time, he wasn't certain whether their quietness was their genteel way of grieving or whether they had been stunned into silence by the boisterousness of his father's Mexican relatives, with their sobs, their exhortations, and their priests.

"And that was the last I saw of my grandparents. After Mama died, we really belonged to Dad." Sean laughed. "*And* to the rest of his family. His brothers and sisters and aunts and uncles and cousins. And friends of cousins and cousins of friends."

"Lucky you. When I was growing up, I was wildly jealous of people with big families. I was positive they were all happy families, too. It was no fun being an only kid. Did you have a great time together?"

"Mostly. Seems like every Flores who crossed the border settled in my hometown. That was our social life. The family."

"What does your dad do?"

"He runs a small herd of cattle. Enough to get by on. Some years he does okay, other years he's close to bankruptcy. He doesn't care enough about it to do well. What he does care about are 'his people.' Sounds corny, but that's what he calls them. There's a big reservation near him. Part of Dad's family's still there. He's stuck his neck out more than once for them."

"Like father, like son," said Allison.

"Oh, you mean *Jake's Tale*? The redskins versus the feds? Yeah, I guess I get a lot of that feeling from him. He should have been a union organizer. But that's city work, and there's no way he would ever leave the ranch."

"Is it really beautiful?"

"If you think this is pretty, you ought to see it," said Sean, his voice softening.

Allison watched the light from the open stove lick across his face.

"I miss it," he continued. "Two of my brothers are there still. I think they're trying to figure out a way to stay there forever. No one in my family likes cities much."

"Except for you."

"Yeah, except for me," said Sean without conviction.

"At least you've got this."

"True," said Sean, and then he fell silent. "You know when I like it best here?" he asked after a while. "In the winter. In New York, the only way you know the season's changed is that it's colder. And more miserable. But here, with the snow up to the window and nobody around, then you've only got yourself to count on. It's very elemental. And when it's like that, it is beautiful. Not just pretty. Beautiful."

"But how do you get in here? They don't clear this road, do they?"

"I have my ways," said Sean, nodding toward the corner of the room with a half-smile.

Allison looked at the snowshoes leaning there. She had snowshoed once when she was in boarding school—and hated it. It was much too much work.

"God, you're determined," she said after a moment.

"I know what I want, if that's what you mean," he said, drawing Allison into his arms. "What do you want, Allie?"

"I'm in its grip right now," she said before kissing him.

"No, I mean . . . you know, did you always think you'd be doing what you're doing now?"

"There was that brief period I told you about when I thought I'd be the next Geraldine Page. The only thing missing was the talent. But aside from that fantasy—a very young girl's fantasy—I guess I always assumed I'd join my uncle."

"Really? That surprises me."

"Why?"

"Well, you're so smart. A lot smarter than I am. You could do anything."

"Rather than being a talent agent? I'm fascinated by the way you avoid saying the words, as if they were unfit to speak. Sort of like curses in a confessional," she said, her voice unconsciously rising as she untangled herself from Sean and moved over to the stove.

"I didn't mean that at all, Allie. I'm just trying to understand you better, that's all."

"And the thing you can't understand," she continued, pouring herself two fingers of bourbon from a bottle on Sean's makeshift desk, "is how a smart girl like me, a lawyer no less, could be satisfied pursuing a career as a ten percent hustler for comedians and rock stars. Of course I shouldn't forget the occasional artist like Oscar Buckman, should I? That almost gives my profession a legitimacy. Why, I could be doing poverty law. Or how about the Peace Corps? A few years in Gabon could do wonders for our relationship."

"That's not what I meant," Sean said as he walked toward her.

"Did you know that my father was a talent agent? And Uncle Gus, whom I love and respect more than anyone else in the entire world, is the best in the business. And he's also perceptive and tasteful and fair and every other attribute that I'd wish for myself . . . and for you."

"You're getting yourself way off base," he said, reaching out to put his arms around her.

"I hate having to justify myself to you," she said, yanking herself away from him. "It's not what you say, it's the way you look at me. As if I had horns and cloven hooves. When are you going to grow up and realize that agents are just like other people? There are good ones and there are bad ones. Almost anybody from our office could be more genuine help to you than that . . . that space cadet from The Combine who subs as an agent, Connie Whatserface."

"Hey!" said Sean angrily.

"Oooops, I forgot, I mustn't say anything negative about the sacred group, must I? But I have to laugh. I think you would have been happier if I were a corporate lawyer, fattening myself up on the merging and acquisitioning of America."

"Well, speaking of acquisitions . . ." said Sean, with an edge to his voice.

"Is that a reference to Uncle Gus?" Allison almost shouted. "How dare you!" Her voice was so tight with anger that she couldn't speak for a moment. She was about to say something she knew she'd regret, but before she could, she wheeled around, slammed her glass down on a table, and rushed out of the cabin.

The moon, a knife peel away from full, shone in a cloudless sky. Stars pinwheeled above as Allison ran down from the cabin to a small meadow that hung above the stream like a shelf. She leaned against a tree and stared down into the dark water.

—What are you pissed at? she asked herself.

—Sean, of course.

—Really?

—Well, who the hell else was in that cabin just now?

—Another snappy answer from the fast-talking agent. But be fair. Mentioning The Combine was a real red flag. And you deliberately chose to make more of that last remark than he intended. He wasn't trying to tick you off. Isn't it more a matter of you being unhappy with your own response?

—What does that mean?

—Hasn't Uncle Gus called all the shots so far? They all feel right, but they're more his moves than yours.

—So what?

—Nothing. That's just the way it is. I don't think Sean was being critical, it was more . . . Jesus, can't you fill in my pauses?

—I *should* go back up there, shouldn't I?

—Go to the head of the class. Yes, dummy, get your tail back up there this very moment.

But as soon as Allison turned toward the cabin, she saw Sean walking through the field toward her.

"Allie," he said as he put his arms around her, "you're cold."

"Not any longer," she answered, moving deeper into his arms.

"There are a lot of differences between us and probably there always will be. I don't pretend to understand what you do or . . . maybe I should say, I miss the absolute necessity for some of what you do, just as you may not really appreciate what The Combine means to me, but that doesn't affect in any way what I feel about Allison Morton. You're the person I've always been waiting for. And that takes in lots and lots of long, lonely nights. Just have patience with me. I'll eventually understand, because I know I have to. Now, can I have a long and dirty kiss, because I need it? And, most of all, I need you."

On Sunday they left early so they could stop at Sean's favorite orchard to pick apples, but first, he said, he had a surprise for her. As soon as she saw they were detouring back to the farmer's, Allison started smiling with delight. Five minutes after Sean disappeared into the farmhouse, he emerged with a wiggling black-and-white bundle tucked into the crook of his arm.

"He's the runt, Edith says, but not for long. She says he does nothing but eat."

At the orchard, the pup, which had been lulled into sleep instantly by the motion of the car, woke up and scrambled down into the grass. The branches of the trees were so laden with fruit that they arched all the way down to the ground, and the fall breeze swirled them around the tree trunks like the ruffled skirts of flamenco dancers. The puppy raced under and around the trees, growling and pawing fiercely at the fallen apples, while Sean and Allison filled two bushel baskets with gleaming Macs.

They pulled up at Allison's loft just as it was growing dark.

"You want to come up for a bite of supper?" she asked, shifting the sleeping dog in her arms.

Sean nodded and started to get out of the car, then stopped abruptly. He put his hand on Allison's arm.

"No, I've changed my mind. I don't."

"What?" was all she could say.

"I want you to come home with me. What I really mean is, move in with me. Allie, I want to wake up in the morning and see your face. Every morning. Not just on weekends." He hesitated. "Is that what you want too?"

The only way she could answer was to put her arms around him and kiss him deeply.

"The pup, too," said Sean, laughing, as they both suddenly became aware of the little animal struggling desperately to extract itself from between them.

And so Allison and Sean started living together. His way—at his place.

22

You look like you could use a drink, Ben. If you moved in a faster crowd, I would recommend something in a powdery form. But for you, a drink would be fine," said Lee, as she breezed into Ben Wildman's office.

Ben looked up from his desk, its surface literally covered with papers. A cracker-sized piece of green blotter stuck out from under the papers like a park in the South Bronx.

"Sorry, but I got another hour here at least," he replied wearily. "I'm waiting to see Gus. I have a lot of things to review with him."

"You've been working too hard lately, Ben."

"It'll pass. I'm hoping to take a week in Acapulco over Thanksgiving."

"You've been saying that for the past two months. With Gus always off on buying sprees these days, you're like Haig just before Nixon resigned. You're running the whole damned company."

"I hope I'm not doing a bad job," Ben answered, smiling weakly.

"If you're fishing for a compliment, you got it. The place has been operating like a solar clock in July. How's that for gross flattery? Actually, I'd say the same thing even if you hadn't discovered me, Ben."

"I was just in the right place at the right time, Lee. And all I did was hire you. Nothing could have stopped you from becoming a star in this business."

"Well, I didn't think so at the time. You'd better believe that," Lee answered, as she searched her bag for a match. Ben reached over the desk and lit Lee's cigarette and then one of his own, a habit he hadn't kicked despite his obsession with fitness. "Aside from the fact that it would do you good," continued Lee, "there's another reason I want you to have a drink with me tonight. Do you know Adrian Frame?"

"Hector Frame's son?"

"The same. Adrian and I have become quite friendly in the past few months."

"Well, next time you shake hands with him, count your fingers. If he's anything like his father, that is."

"What's so awful about Hector Frame? Stories always circulate about people who have the kind of money and power he has. It's natural."

"Sure. It was natural for him to start out as a slumlord and still be one to this very day. The only difference between him and thousands of other swine like him is that he's bigger. Lots bigger. He should stay in Canada," Ben said, his voice rising.

"That might not suit Gus."

"What do you mean?" Ben asked quickly.

"Adrian told me his father's been interested in getting a piece of U.T.M. for years," Lee answered coolly. "He thinks Gus finally might be receptive because of all the companies he's been buying lately. A lot more money has been going out of U.T.M. lately than has been coming in."

"That's bullshit!" said Ben. "Gus wouldn't touch Hector Frame with a ten-foot pole. And the son is pure slime. He telephoned me recently for some obscure reason, and I'm happy to say I hung up on him. He's a criminal! You heard about the killing in Palm Beach he was implicated in. Of course, there wasn't even an indictment, much less a trial. Obviously Hector Frame paid off someone big. If Gus had diabetes and the Frames controlled the world's insulin supply, he would rather die than deal with those bastards. And besides, I'd know about it if he were even contemplating something like that."

"Take it easy, Ben," said Lee, her voice softening. "I'm not saying anything against Gus. He's like a father to me. But things change. And he isn't getting any younger. We all know who's going to run the company after Gus, don't we? And though I think Allison is as bright as anyone, who knows what she might do? We're just hired help. If, by some crazy chance, my information is right and the Frames do wind up with a piece of this company, it wouldn't hurt to be friendly with Adrian. That's not being disloyal. Just smart. Case closed," she concluded, throwing her hands up in a mock gesture of surrender.

"You're some piece of work, Lee," said Ben, relaxing a bit. "Even though you're wrong, your survival instincts are probably right."

"Well, whatever happens, Ben, my darling, we'll always be able to seek a safe harbor in each other's arms. Right?"

"You can bet that aerobically tortured tush of yours on that."

"See you tomorrow," Lee said, as she turned and started to walk out of Ben's office. "Oh, by the way, Adrian and I will be having a light supper after drinks, so you'll have plenty of time to drop by if you change your mind. We'll be at my place."

"Thanks again, but I think I'll take a raincheck."

Ben sat for a long time at his desk, staring out at the points of light just beginning to shine from the houses scattered in the hills, like glitter dust thrown by a careless hand, before the phone rang.

It was Gus's secretary, Lillian. "He's ready to see you now," she said. "I'll be right there."

Gus was on the phone when Lillian led Ben into the office. She made him a weak scotch, then went back to her office. Ben sat in a soft leather armchair next to the desk as he sipped his drink and listened to Gus's end of the phone call. After a few minutes it struck Ben that not only did he not have a clue to whom Gus was talking, but he had no idea what he was talking about. It hadn't been too long ago that he knew everything Gus was involved in. Everything.

"Who was that?" he asked casually when Gus finally hung up.

"Just a banker with Manny Hanny. It seems like I spend more time with bankers these days than I do with talent."

It's not even close, Ben thought, as he drained his glass and then placed it carefully on one of the coasters Lillian always kept ready to protect the delicate inlay of Gus's desk.

"I have an agenda worked up, Gus. You don't mind if I just plunge in, do you?" he asked as he opened his folder.

Gus nodded and leaned back in his chair.

At first Ben simply ran through the dozens of deals that had been completed or were about to be, to make sure Gus was up-to-date. A few times, Gus commented on a price that he had thought was going to be higher, or in one case lower, and Ben told him why it had turned out the way it had. Then followed a few personnel problems. After that, Ben reported on some client signings they were working on.

"I know how to sign Chantra," said Gus suddenly, after Ben told him of George Bellamy's efforts to persuade one of the hottest young female singing stars around to sign with U.T.M.

"We've tried everything, Gus. Her stupid manager has hinted that if we cut our commissions she'd come with us. But I told him we don't cut commissions for anyone. Not even the Pope."

"Right, but there's another way to get her. Tell Chantra that if she comes with us, I'll arrange it so she can buy that co-op on Central Park West that turned her down."

"That's a great idea, Gus, but can you do it?" Ben asked excitedly.

"I know half the board in that building and can get to the rest. It won't be a cakewalk, but I can do it. Just get her to sign our contract contingent on our lining up the co-op for her. And make sure she understands that once we get her in there, she's to act like a grown-up. No wild parties or weird scenes."

Ben talked for another few minutes before he closed his folder. "That's it for the week, Gus. All in all, things seem pretty good."

"*Pretty* good? You're running the place better than I ever did, Ben. How about another drink?"

Gus rose and walked to the bar that was set into the bookcase.

"That would be great, Gus."

"To you, Ben," said Gus, as he handed the other man his glass. "May our friendship in and out of business always continue."

"Amen," answered Ben, clinking his glass against Gus's. "You know, we haven't had a drink together like this in I don't know how long. You've been either heading into another meeting here or onto the plane for a meeting out of town."

"It's been a crazy, exciting time, my friend, but I've been able to do it only because I knew that with you sitting here, everything would be under control."

"Thank you. It's important for me to hear that from you, Gus. To tell you the truth, lately I've felt a little left out."

"What do you mean, 'left out'?" Gus asked, his voice rising slightly.

"I appreciate your letting me run the show here, but you've kept me completely on the outside on every one of your acquisitions. On all the recent financial dealings, I've felt like an outsider. It always used to be the two of us on anything major. Now it's just you . . . and Allison."

"But don't you see why I need Allison? She's a lawyer. You're an agent. She has skills that you don't have. But you're the heart and guts of this business. I need you now more than ever."

Ben took a long drink and then looked directly at Gus.

"Remember last year when I asked you to give me the title of chief operating officer?" he asked. "You told me to hold off awhile. Well, it's been more than a while now. Maybe you forgot that conversation, but I haven't. I need that title, Gus. You know how this town operates. People are starting to think I'm not as important to you anymore. But I helped you build this business. I deserve it."

"Relax, Ben. I'm going to take care of you. Your bonus last year is going to look like a maître d's tip compared to the one you're going to get this year. Don't get hung up on titles. That's for small-time schmucks. Not for a man like you."

"Then I'm a small-time schmuck, Gus. I need that title. People are beginning to think I'm slipping. How many times have I ever asked you for anything?"

"I told you your bonus will be fantastic. Isn't that enough? I just can't give you the title now."

"Why not? You think I don't deserve it?" Ben's voice was almost pleading.

"I haven't said a word about this to anyone here, Ben, but I'm going to take you into my confidence. I'm planning to take the company public. Not immediately, but soon. And, quite frankly, under the circumstances, the title you want is a little too out-front."

"What do you mean 'under the circumstances'?" asked Ben, his voice tense.

"Oh, Ben, you know what I'm talking about. Don't force me to give you chapter and verse." Gus's tone was gentle, his eyes focused on his old friend.

"I guess I do know what you're referring to," said Ben after a long, painful pause. "I can't help what I am, you know," he added in a choked voice.

"I know, Ben. I understand. I don't mean to hurt you." Gus walked around his desk and put his hand on the anguished man's shoulder.

"But, Gus, you of all people," said Ben, angrily shrugging the other man's hand away. "I never thought I'd hear you speak this way. You sound like a yahoo from the Moral Majority, afraid that I'll contaminate the next person I shake hands with or break out in a dress and a bobbed pageboy. What's happened to you?"

"It's not me, Ben, it's those people out there who I want to invest in us. It's going to be a different ball game. Things have happened to you, don't forget, and there is a record, a public record. We can't afford scandal. You do understand, don't you?"

Ben's shoulders had slumped and he did not answer.

"Oh, Ben, I'm sorry, I truly am. I'd give anything not to have had to have this conversation," he said, handing Ben his handkerchief. "Why don't you go back to your office and have another drink? Then join Diana and me for dinner. We're going out in about half an hour. How about it?"

"Thanks, but I have other plans."

Ben walked slowly to the door. He stopped there, drew a deep breath, and then opened it. He said good night to Lillian, nodded to Charlie, and went directly to his office. After pouring himself four fingers of Dewar's and downing it in two swallows, he reached for the phone.

"Hello," answered Lee Simons.

"It's me. Ben. About that drink you mentioned—"

23

The telephone on Adrian Frame's desk in the Los Angeles office of Frame Properties, Ltd., gave one short, sharp ring. There was only one person, anywhere, who knew this particular number.

"Yes, Father?" Adrian Frame said in a low voice into the receiver.

"Did you review our StellarVue strategy with the Tuckermans?" Hector Frame asked in a cold, impersonal tone.

"I flew to Orlando yesterday and briefed them fully."

"And Governor Gannon?"

"Tomorrow. I'm meeting him in Pebble Beach. He's playing in some pro-celebrity golf tournament up there."

There was a slight pause and, for one exhilarating moment, Adrian thought that his father actually was going to praise him for carrying out his duties exactly as he had been instructed; for as tough and as cruel as he could be with others, he still craved his father's approval and would do anything to win it.

"And Allison Morton?"

"I'm going to see her soon."

"Soon? That word is fit for children who have yet to be toilet trained. Not for Hector Frame," his father spat into the phone.

"What I meant to say, Father, is that I'm still working on it."

"That's what you told me last week. Do you know why it's important for you to get to her?"

"Well, I guess—"

"Guessing is what you do when you play roulette, idiot. I shouldn't have to explain this to you, but Gus Morton loves this girl. Loves her! She's his entire life. If you upset the girl and she tells her uncle, then he'll be upset too. *Very* upset. And perhaps he won't be able to think quite as clearly as he would otherwise. That's your assignment. Rough her head up a bit. Now do you understand?"

Before Adrian could answer in the affirmative, Hector Frame hung up the phone.

. . .

It was a magically bright November day at Santa Anita. The San Gabriel Mountains, as muscular as a weight lifter's body, were so clear they might be a painted backdrop, yet magnificent as the scenery was, it did not in the least interest Adrian Frame or his guest at the races, Lee Simons. Although Adrian had a horse running in the seventh race that had a good chance of winning, a two-year-old filly he had paid half a million for at the Keeneland auction the year before, the horse was not on his mind either. And though Lee, who sat next to him in his owner's box, seemed preoccupied with handicapping the next race, she too had other thoughts that were much more pressing.

"You still haven't answered me, Adrian," Lee said, staring down at the *Racing Form*.

"If you don't let up on me, I'll stuff that paper—"

"Easy, Adrian. The Firestones are two boxes away and the Chandlers are right behind us," she whispered.

"Then just use your imagination, dear, about what I might do to that sweet little body of yours if you don't shut up," he whispered back angrily. "Can't you get it through your head that your continual need for reassurance is not a priority item for me? What's important is your getting me together with Allison Morton. I want some time alone with her. The little bitch has refused to see me twice already. I want you to set it up for me. Now."

"I've tried, Adrian. Believe me, I've tried."

"Then try again. If you can't manage a simple thing like that, maybe I'll start wondering if you have the ability to run U.T.M."

"Okay, Adrian," said Lee, her face screwed tight by anxiety. "I'll come up with something. Just give me a little more time."

"Sure, Lee. Take all the time you need, so long as you get me together with little Allison this week. I hear she's coming into town tomorrow. Now, one good turn deserves another. That number-three horse you've circled in the next race has as much chance of winning as your boss has of holding on to U.T.M. If you had taken the time to notice, you'd have seen that it only runs well on an off-track. I'd lay my money on the six horse. But I'm not really a betting man. I much prefer sure things."

It was a typical night at DC3. All the power tables were occupied by the usual cadre of studio heads, top directors and producers, a sprinkling of big name actors and actresses who didn't have early morning calls, and a goodly number of the major agents in town who actually ran the whole game as coolly as croupiers at a casino. In between mouthfuls of unfashionable but delicious beef washed down by buckets of burgundy and beer, a constant stream of air-blown kisses and hand waves were semaphored from table to table. The noise in the room made conversation difficult at best, but nobody cared, since the players were there for the "action," the continual eye contact.

"We could have held this meeting in the office in half the time," Allison shouted to Lee, who sat across the table from her and whose head kept whipping from side to side, like the light atop a police cruiser, as she nodded and smiled to the other tables.

"I don't know how many times I've told you, Allison, that ninety percent of this business is socially derived. It's important to be seen. And, of course, at the *right* table. You've got to learn to loosen up a little. Just ask your uncle. His dinner parties are the most sought-after invitations in this town. And if Gus Morton goes to a restaurant regularly, that place is made. I'm surprised he's not here tonight."

"He had to go up to Seattle."

"Looking at another acquisition?"

"I don't know. Could be. You might not believe it, but he doesn't tell me everything. Lee, I'm worried about this option clause in Gary—"

"What's wrong with your steak?" Lee asked suddenly. "You haven't touched it."

"It's fine. I'm just not that hungry. Now about that option—"

A waiter appeared at Lee's side and whispered into her ear.

"I'll be right back, Allison. There's a phone call for me."

Allison picked at her food while she waited for Lee to return.

"It was Christa Galleon. I've got to go over to her place," said Lee. "She's had another fight with that psycho boyfriend of hers, you know, the linebacker. Boy, can she pick them. I've always told her that if you want to be roughed up, get a wimp to do it. Then you won't get really hurt. I just hope he hasn't worked her over too much. She starts a picture in a few days. It's our package."

"Want me to go with you?" asked Allison.

"Thanks, but I can handle it. Since we took my car over here, how are you going to get home?"

"That's no problem. I'll just have them call a taxi for me."

"If you could also get the check, that would be terrific. I really have to rush."

"No problem. I'll see you in the office tomorrow, Lee."

"Ciao," Lee replied, as she left the restaurant gymkhana-style, weaving past the key tables, kissing and hugging everyone in reach like someone running for office.

It took several minutes for Allison to get the waiter's attention.

"Yes, Miss Morton," he said. If your name was important, the waiters knew it.

"I'd like the check, please."

"But that's been taken care of," he said.

"What do you mean?"

"That gentleman over there paid it." The waiter pointed to the bar.

"That's funny, he was there a moment ago."

"But he's right here now," said the tall man with dark hair slicked down to a mirror finish who had appeared beside Allison's table. He wore a tunic-jacketed suit with a black silk scarf at his throat.

"Good evening," said Allison noncommittally. "Though we've spoken on the phone, we haven't met before. How do you do, Mr. Frame."

"There's a man with white hair living in Toronto who goes by that name. Mine is Adrian."

"So you've made clear on the telephone. I guess I should say thank you for picking up the check."

"Oh, there's no need to thank me yet. I'm going to drop you off at your house. Don't look so surprised. Lee told me as she was leaving that you were stranded. My chariot awaits you."

"That's very generous of you . . . Adrian. But it's easy enough to ask the restaurant to call a taxi for me."

"Though no doubt you know my reputation is less than unsullied, Hughes, my driver, has impeccable manners. What's more, if you accept a ride, I'll stop badgering you for a date. I can't believe you'll turn down that offer. What do you say?"

"All right, why not," she said, looking for a moment into Adrian Frame's eyes, which were as shiny and flat as the scales of a fish.

The conversation in Adrian Frame's Daimler, upholstered in python and carpeted in kilims, was innocuous until the car pulled up in front of a small, squat building on a quiet street. A discreet neon sign on the door gave its name: ORDERS.

"Just one, brief stop before I take you home," Adrian said, as his driver emerged from the car and opened the door on Allison's side.

"I really must get home now. I have an early meeting tomorrow."

"Indulge me, please. Only one drink," he said.

"I'm sorry, but I can't."

"Fifteen minutes. No more. Remember, I promised I'd stop pursuing you, and I will, but grant me this one favor. Hughes will be waiting right out here in front. Motor running. Anytime you want to leave, all you have to do is walk out the door. It's my last chance to get to know you," he pleaded.

The only way she would get home at this point was to have the drink with him, Allison thought angrily. Why hadn't she brought her own car? Hadn't Lee insisted they take her car? Had she set this up? Heaven help her if that was so, Allison swore to herself as she walked into the club.

Orders was a small, low-ceilinged cocktail lounge outfitted in a motif suited to a bat cave, all dark wood and thick carpeting in an arterial red that made Allison feel as if she were at the scene of an accident. The staff's effusive greeting left no doubt that Adrian was a regular. They took a table at the back, and Allison ordered a Diet Pepsi, Adrian a double Wild Turkey without ice.

"To the next Morton generation at U.T.M.," Adrian said as he touched his glass to Allison's. "My father has always felt that business is war. Do you think you're tough enough for it?" he asked after swigging down half his bourbon. "The decent people in the game are the losers with no power. The people at the top make killer sharks look like guppies," he added with a smile.

"I'm sure my uncle would be touched by your sentiments," said Allison, thinking, *you miserable, depraved lowlife.* In any random minute Gus Morton spent at work, he would exhibit more generosity than Adrian or Hector Frame had managed in a lifetime. "But the answer to your question is, yes," she continued. "I am tough enough for the business. *When* it's required."

"I'm glad to hear you say that, but I wonder if it's true. Are you really ready for the combat?"

"What I'm ready for," Allison said, placing her glass on the table, "is to go home. Thanks for the management advice, Adrian. If I find that my skills in brutality need some sharpening, I'll make sure to give you a call."

"That's quite cute. I think you have a lot of abilities, Allison Morton, though I think they'd probably be better utilized by a charity benefit committee. That might sound like a put-down, but it's just an assessment."

"Since it doesn't cost anything, I'll take it at its value."

"What you unquestionably are," Adrian said, placing his hand over hers, "is a very beautiful woman. I hope you take this as a compliment, but I bet you're a great fuck."

"I don't think a swine like yourself is capable of knowing what a compliment is," she said, pushing back her chair. "I'll take you up on having your chauffeur drive me home now. Alone, that is."

"By the way, you're passing up a very interesting experience by not going to bed with me."

"I'd rather couple with a diseased jackal, thank you."

As Allison started walking to the front door, Adrian grabbed her elbow. "Hughes is waiting in the back. This way is quicker," he said, pointing to a leather-padded door at the rear. An immense man with a shaved skull stood beside it. Without thinking, just wanting to get away from her odious companion, Allison walked toward the door. The guard, responding to a signal from Frame, opened it for her.

She entered a small, dark theater and for a moment couldn't see anything. But then she saw not only the heads of the audience but what they were watching. On a stage bathed in a purple light, a naked woman stood pinioned to a metal rack. A leather mask hid her features. Before Allison could turn and run out, Adrian was beside her, his hands gripping her elbows tightly.

"Watch carefully, Allison, and you'll see another kind of toughness. My favorite kind. The kind that leads to pure pleasure. I want you to see what you're missing by turning me down. Maybe it'll make you change your mind," he whispered in her ear, as another woman, dressed completely in black, appeared on stage and started to push a needle through the victim's nipple.

Allison turned away, but Adrian twisted her around so that she had to look.

"Get into it, dear. We all have a little bit of the slave in us. A good master like me understands—"

"You filthy scum!" Allison shouted, wheeling around and driving her knee, with all her power, into Frame's scrotum.

Adrian doubled over, his face contorted with rage and pain. He made a noise like wet laundry hitting the floor, as a couple standing nearby side-stepped away and glanced down indifferently to see what they had avoided sullying their feet with. A dark stain where Adrian had urinated spread out across his pants. "Nothing important. Only Frame," said the man.

As Adrian's eyes rolled up in his head and he lost consciousness, Allison rushed past him. Luckily the door was unlocked from the inside, and she quickly walked out of the club and into Frame's car.

"Mr. Frame is going to stay, Hughes," she said quietly. "He's having fun on the dance floor."

Hughes, ever the perfect chauffeur, put the car into gear and drove Allison home.

24

A young blond woman in a dark, tailored suit and Reeboks collided headlong into Gus Morton as he entered an office building on Park Avenue several weeks later.

"Excuse me," she said, looking up. The headset she wore, still fixed in place, was blasting a stream of words into her ears.

"That's perfectly all right, my dear," answered Gus loudly, patting her on the shoulder.

"You see," he said, turning to Allison, who was beside him, "that girl's a perfect example. It's just like I was saying to Parker Welles the other day. A lot of yuppies don't want to take time out to read, but they're eager to learn. Very eager. If we can buy this audio cassette firm we're going to see now, it'll be a winner for us. And a terrific match-up. After all, we have access to writers, don't we, and they're ready and willing to write about anything we ask them to, from sex tips to tax planning."

The negotiations with the cassette people broke briefly for dinner and then went on until almost two in the morning, but Allison was less perturbed by the late hours than by the way her uncle looked. As the discussions wore on, she couldn't take her eyes off him. Though she had seen him recently, his appearance had altered considerably—for the worse. His color was poor, his face drawn, and he seemed tense, a condition she had never before associated with him. It occurred to her, with a jolt of dismay, that this was the first time she had ever seen him looking old. But he wasn't old! He was sixty-eight (or was he sixty-nine?) and so vigorous and energetic that his age always had been irrelevant.

Later, in the cab to the U.T.M. apartment to drop off Gus, Allison won a concession. Gus would cancel a meeting the next morning and not come into the office until after lunchtime. Allison was surprised at how quickly he agreed to her suggestion that he sleep late. This too was unlike him.

The next morning, Allison woke up realizing that the only way she could find out what was bothering Gus was to talk with Diana. If she asked Gus himself, he would deny that anything was wrong. But it would be best if she and Diana spoke in person rather than over the phone. She lay in bed turning over the problem. Diana, she knew, had favorite stopping-off places in New York: Georgette Klinger for facials, Hisao for haircuts, Martha for dresses. Perhaps she could contrive to run into her in one of these spots, catch her off guard, maybe learn a little more than she would otherwise.

Allison got up and fed the puppy. They had named him Tonny, short for Tonnage, because, just as the farmer's wife had said, the little creature was always ravenous. While Sean was showering, she telephoned the Klinger salon on the hunch that it would be a logical first stop for an out-of-towner and discovered she had guessed right. Diana had an appointment at ten.

Calculating how much time Diana's facial would take, Allison arrived at the salon fifteen minutes before the other woman would be finished, ostensibly to select some new beauty products, but really to lie in wait for Diana. Fortunately the cosmetics counter was positioned so that no one could enter or leave the salon without passing by it. A short while later Diana emerged, and Allison, in a flutter of happy astonishment (after all, she knew something about acting), jumped up to greet her.

"What a wonderful surprise," she cried, hugging Diana and kissing her on both cheeks. "I was hoping I would see you on this visit."

"Why, Allison, I didn't know you ever came here," said Diana, blinking her pale lashes at Allison. "I thought it was just for women of . . . a certain age."

"You're joking. I've been a fan of this place since I first conned Uncle Gus into picking up the tab when I was starting college. How about having a cup of coffee with me?"

"Oh, I don't think I have the time. . . ."

"Come on. I know a quiet spot around the corner. We can make it a quick cup."

"Well, all right."

While they waited to be served, Allison worked at making small talk. When they were alone, she always felt awkward with Diana, as if they might run out of things to say and be left eyeing each other uncomfortably. As a teenager, she had tried to emulate Diana's sense of style, even though she was resentful of her closeness to Gus, and several times when she was thirteen or fourteen Diana had taken her shopping for party dresses. When she went off to boarding school and then to college and returned to Gus's on school breaks, she kept waiting for her relationship with Diana to move on to the next phase, but there turned out to be no next phase. Diana was always pleasant and cordial, but so reserved that it was hard to find common ground, something they both cared about and could discuss easily. "A very private person" was the way Gus liked to describe her, but whatever the words used, the distance between them was considerable and now made Allison nervous.

As soon as the waiter brought their coffee, Allison got to the point immediately. "I'm worried about Uncle Gus. Is he all right? Last night he looked simply wiped out."

"He *is* tired," conceded Diana.

"Well, what I really mean is, he looked *sick*. Is anything wrong?"

"I don't think so. He's been working very hard, as you know, but he takes care of himself. He sees his doctor regularly."

"Dr. Elliott, isn't it? Howard Elliott? Maybe I ought to call him," said Allison, half to herself.

"Why? Don't you think I know all that needs to be known about your uncle's health?" Diana asked a bit crisply.

"Yes, I'm sure you do," Allison said so quickly that her words came out louder than she had intended. "Since you see him all the time, though, maybe you haven't noticed how awful he's looking. If I were in California, maybe I could make him go see Dr. Elliott, but I can't do anything about it long distance. You could, though. You're right there."

"Are you suggesting I'm not on top of the situation?" asked Diana.

"No, of course not, it's just—"

"Because I want to tell you—and you listen closely—that what I feel for your uncle puts your puny emotions to shame. Of course you care about him, whatever you mean by that. He's your uncle. He's family. For me, though, it's very different. I *choose* to care. I long ago decided that he would be my life. He knows that, even if you don't." Diana's voice was low, but she spat the words out.

"I do understand how important he is to you, Diana."

"How dare you pretend to understand my feelings for your uncle!"

"Please, Diana. I didn't mean to offend you. I only want to help." Allison was shocked. The conversation was spinning out of control. She had never heard Diana speak this way.

"Help? Some help you are. Don't you see, he's doing all this for you. He's working like a slave. For you! Nobody else. Just for you. I think he's crazy, but try to tell him that! It's the way he wants it. Sometimes I think he *will* kill himself. And if he does—" Diana's voice dropped almost to a whisper, "if that should happen, remember who's to blame. You, Allison. No one else but you."

Allison stared at Diana in amazement, unable to say a word.

"I'm going now," said Diana, standing up and giving Allison the briefest of nods before she turned and walked out the door.

Allison sat totally still, too stunned to move. What had just happened? She tried for a minute to work her way back over the conversation to see what horrible, insensitive thing she might have said to unleash this torrent, but she couldn't get beyond Diana's last ghastly accusation and gave up the effort. It was almost as if Diana had been waiting for an excuse to say those things.

She paid the bill and walked blindly along Fifth Avenue, one moment furious with Diana, the next, embarrassed and ashamed by her own behavior. When she arrived at her office, she found a stack of messages waiting for her. The one on top was from Gus.

"The boss is at the airport," said Charlie, picking up Allison's return call. "I just got back from driving him there. He wanted me to tell you he's sorry he missed you. He'll call you as soon as he gets home."

"Why did he leave a day early?" asked Allison, suddenly panicky, remembering she hadn't found out a thing about how he really was.

"Oh, no big reason," said Charlie. "He told me he just decided he wanted some extra rest. I'm taking Diana out to Long Island this afternoon to see that aunt of hers—she's thinking of putting the old lady in a nursing home—but I'll be back by four or five if you want anything. The boss is sending the plane back for us in the morning. Take care."

Listening to Charlie's matter-of-fact voice, Allison thought to herself that she really had been an alarmist. She had stuck her neck way out. For nothing! Her uncle was fine. Just tired. No wonder Diana was outraged by her prying. But then she remembered Diana's ugly refrain: "He's working like a slave. For you. Just for you." Diana had touched her where it hurt. This was the very thing Allison was struggling with. Why *was* Gus so obsessed with changing the face of the company? And for her, undeniably for her. *Why?*

Exhausted by the questions racing through her mind, Allison suddenly felt so emotionally drained that she did something she hadn't done since her days in the mailroom: she made up an excuse and went home in the middle of the day. She pitched into bed and fell into a sleep so engulfing that she didn't wake until dark, when she heard Sean's key in the lock. As soon as he sat down on the edge of the bed, she clutched him to her tightly.

"Hey, what's wrong?" he asked, sensing her unhappiness and beginning to stroke her hair.

And then, without her intending to say so much, it all came out. Her worries about Gus's health; her disastrous talk with Diana; her questions and her confusion.

As he listened, Sean busied himself heating a bottle of sake. When it was warm, he poured some into two white porcelain cups, each almost eggshell thin, and brought them over to Allison on a small lacquered tray.

"I regard this," he said, taking a small sip, "as the Japanese version of chicken soup. Good for aches, particularly spiritual ones."

"I think I feel better already." She reached up to kiss him.

"Was there ever a time when you felt close to Diana?" Sean asked, after filling their cups again.

"I've always regarded her as . . . well, part of the family."

"That's not what I asked you."

"My uncle cares for her. He has for a long time. As long as I can remember. I can't think of a time when she wasn't around. Anyone he feels that way about, I have to care for also."

"Oh, come on, Allie. That sounds like a position paper, not a description of the way you feel. You don't have to watch what you say to *me*!"

"Okay, you're right," said Allison, looking somewhat chastened. "I have trouble admitting this even to myself, but I never have gotten close to her. I've wanted to, and I've tried, but she makes it tough."

"Yeah, that's kind of the impression I've always gotten from you. She's a pretty chilly number. Not like your uncle. From everything you've said about him, it's obvious your feelings for him, and his for you, are uncomplicated and strong. But Diana? That's a whole different piece of business." He took a sip of sake before continuing. "The reality is that the two of you have been competing for the same guy for quite a while."

"No wonder you became a playwright. You have an extremely fertile imagination."

"Just hear me out, because in this competition you've had a very unfair advantage. First of all, you're so damn cute," he said, bending to give her a little kiss on the nose.

"I certainly agree with you there."

"That actually wasn't as facetious as it sounded. The point is, you've grown up to be just the kind of person your uncle must have been hoping you would become, which has made it very easy for him to give you everything he always planned. And more! And you've never made any demands on him, either. Diana, though, has always been an outsider. First because of your uncle's sick wife. And then because of, well, because of you. Haven't you ever asked yourself why, when he was free to marry Diana, he didn't. More important, who do you think Diana might blame for that?"

"That's ridiculous," Allison interjected testily.

"Wait a minute. I didn't say that you *were* to blame. I just said that she might feel that way."

"Well, maybe," said Allison, sounding doubtful.

"Okay, that is conjecture, but what happened today doesn't require any fancy guesswork. You said she kept saying Gus was doing all this running around for you, right? She apparently doesn't think she figures into it at all, and she can't feel good about that."

"You're right, and I've got to do something about this whole thing, even though I don't know quite how we got here. I've got to do something to . . . make peace with her. Any ideas?" Allison looked searchingly at Sean.

"Well, keep showing her affection, if you can, and . . . wait it out. Give it time. Let her know you respect her place in your uncle's life. I can see why she was pissed when you started firing questions at her, can't you? Now that's it, Allie. End of analysis."

"You know something?" she said after a moment, wrapping her arms around him.

"Yes, and I love you, too."

25

W ho do we now have at table three, Kimberly?"

Lee Simons's New York secretary squinted at the large board that showed the seating arrangements for the dinner party the night following the screening of *Operation Cutlass,* a film that had been packaged by U.T.M. and included three of Lee's clients.

"The Pecks, Lazars, Murdochs, and Chip Masters and his date."

"That'll never work. Chances are, nine out of ten, that Chip will be coked out of his mind. He always needs a little extra when he goes to a screening of one of his own films. He'll be popping out of his seat so often to go to the can that the others will think he has the runs. Put him at table seven. That's where we have two of the Stones. They'll understand."

Lee spent the rest of the morning dealing with the details of the dinner: flowers, limos, music, and menu. Lee felt at her best when she was working on a party. It wasn't only that she had a talent for every aspect of it, or even that she liked doing it—no, it was the private joy she felt thinking back to all those years of being *Leah Simonson,* living with her father above the butcher shop in Hackensack. Fat Leah who never got invited anywhere, ever, now threw parties that people would do almost anything to attend. And it was the fat Leah part of her that enjoyed seating the most beautiful and desirable young starlet at a table in Outer Siberia or telling those born to looks and money that she was sorry, she'd love to invite them, but, after all, the guest list was out of her hands. She would make sure, of course, that the next time they would be included. Absolutely. And with the instinct of a brilliant maître d' at a chic restaurant, Lee knew that the rich and the beautiful deep down enjoyed being treated as social wetbacks.

It was just before noon when Lee suddenly got a terrific idea. She was having dinner that evening with Allison and that marvelous man of hers. Lee had thought of Sean frequently even though she had met him only once. She could feel the fire within him, and though Lee had worked him over with her eyes as thoroughly as possible, considering that Allison had been standing right next to her, she knew that Sean hadn't given her a second thought. What could he see in Allison? Lee wondered. She was so . . . demure. That couldn't be what a man like Sean needed. He needed someone who loved to do it with the lights on. All the lights on. Someone who was ready to try anything. Not a Miss Proper Behavior. A little time alone with him, Lee thought, should straighten him out on that score. And why not start tonight? All that was necessary was for Allison to be delayed a bit in meeting them. No more than an hour or so. She was smiling as she picked up the phone.

"Ben darling. How's the weather? But most important, how are you?" Lee asked gaily.

"Busy, what else. How's the dinner shaping up?"

"An A-list affair in A-one shape. What else do you expect when Lee Simons throws a little party? Suzy, Liz, and Eye are all coming. We're going to get a lot of coverage. I wish you were here, Ben."

"You're not calling just to schmooze, Lee. You want something," said Ben, laughing. "What's up?"

"A favor. Just a teensy one," Lee answered in her little-girl voice.

"What's it going to cost me? My corneas? You sound very devilish, my dear."

"Horny is closer to it. But it's only going to cost you a phone call."

"And who is the lucky recipient, may I ask?"

"Allison."

"I'm beginning to like this joke a lot less," said Ben, suddenly serious.

"Oh, stop it, Ben. I guarantee you the whole thing is harmless. And don't worry, there won't be any fallout in your direction. I just want you to call Allison at seven-thirty New York time. She'll be home. Not at her place, but at her boyfriend's. The number is five-five-five-eight-one-nine-six. You got that? I want you to review the Breslin-M.G.M. contract with her. It won't take more than an hour. And I want you to be sure it doesn't take *less* than an hour."

"But the contract is set. There are only a few minor points to iron out," Ben responded, his voice tight.

"I don't think Allison knows that. And you know how she cares about all our contracts. She *is* a lawyer, you know. Not just an agent like *tu et moi. N'est-ce pas?*" Lee said, a bubble of laughter in her voice.

"What are you up to, Lee? It's the boyfriend, isn't it? Tell me the truth. I'm right, aren't I."

"You can read me, Ben, like a gypsy palm reader. I just want a few minutes alone with that divine boy. After all, it's a very rare cat who will eat out of only one dish."

"You're terrible, Lee."

"Just the same little girl you've always loved, Ben. I appreciate this very much. And by the way, dear, keep one thing firmly in mind."

"What's that, Lee?" Ben asked with trepidation.

"Seven-thirty. That's all. I'll give you a full report tomorrow."

Lee purposely chose Felidia's for dinner. The food was excellent, the ambience lovely, the sound level conducive to intimate conversation, and it was close to the Sherry, where she always stayed. What counted most, though, was that Felidia's was uptown. A full fifteen-minute cab ride from that strange neighborhood where Allison lived with Sean. Lee wanted all the extra time she could get alone with him.

The reservation was for seven forty-five and Lee arrived early. Though she had been there only a few times before, Lee Simons was the kind of name that most restaurants recognized and wanted as a patron. Other celebrities generally trailed in her wake. Also, Lee tipped like a highroller on a winning streak. Therefore, she was warmly greeted by not only the maître d' but by the owner as well and led to a prime table at the back of the room. A bottle of Moët's Crème de Crémant rested in a silver ice bucket, its shiny metal surface ringed by a curtain of tiny chilled drops.

Sean walked into the restaurant just after eight. Alone. *You're a good reliable friend, Ben,* she thought. As Sean was escorted to the table, Lee looked him over carefully. He had the assured walk of an athlete. His complexion, the color of expensive, fine leather, seemed to glow under the restaurant's soft light. He had high cheekbones that provided a frame for an incredible pair of large, deep gray eyes, as unique in their hue as the fur of a Russian Blue cat. He stood just over six feet and Lee knew there wasn't an ounce of extra flesh on him. He wore a tweed sports jacket with patches on the elbows, which was old but fitted him perfectly, over a faded work shirt with a thin maroon tie—Sean's concession to uptown restaurant life.

"Hi, Lee," said Sean, reaching out to shake her hand. His grip was firm, his skin animal-warm. Lee would have liked a kiss on the cheek, but she knew Sean was the reserved type. But she would get him over that. And soon.

"Where's Allison?" she asked, keeping her smile under control.

"Ben called her just as we were leaving. I hope she won't be too late, but whenever I see her get out her lined pad, it's generally a long session."

"Your lady friend is a very serious and diligent worker. *And* a great colleague. I'm sure she won't rush Ben's call to get up here until all the business is concluded. She's just like her uncle. They're both perfectionists." She looked away from him just long enough to signal the sommelier. "I know Allison wouldn't want us just to wait and get thirsty," she went on, smiling. "You do like champagne?"

"I do, but frankly I don't drink it very often. I'm more of an Almadén Chablis man," he answered, returning her smile politely.

"Make that two Kir Royales, please," Lee said to the sommelier. "It's just a touch of cassis added to the champagne," she explained to Sean. "We've got to get you used to some new things. From what Allison has said, you deserve only the best. Now tell me all about yourself." Lee reached across the table and lightly put her hand over his.

"That's not fair," he answered. "You already know lots about me. Tell me about yourself." And he actually seemed to be interested, Lee thought.

She gave Sean a ten-minute version of the now standard, authorized Lee Simons bio: indulged, only child (true) of an upper middle class, cultured couple from Short Hills, New Jersey (the state was the only fact that was correct). Private schools followed by two years at Barnard, where she dropped out, determined to get into show business, one way or the other. (Lee had learned not to say she had graduated from Barnard. If someone ever bothered to check, there would be no problem. She never said she had earned a degree.)

Sean let Lee's hand rest on his for a polite few seconds during Lee's recitation, before he extracted it to light a cigarette.

"It's surprising that someone from as comfortable a background as yours has the desire to start out at the bottom and to continue to hustle. I'm very impressed," said Sean, with seemingly genuine admiration.

Could he know, Lee wondered, that all of it was a crock of shit? For a moment she was unnerved, but then she realized that he really meant what he had said.

"Allison told me you just finished a marvelous new play. What's it called?"

"Sandia Mountain Song."

"That's pretty. Tell me what it's about," Lee said, as their glasses were refilled.

"You know what Hemingway said, don't you, Lee? If you can talk it, you won't write it."

"That's not fair," said Lee, in poutish despair, now grabbing Sean's hands between her own and trying, just a bit, to pull them close to her breasts.

"I'm just a writer, Lee," he replied, quietly removing his hands from her grasp, ostensibly to straighten his tie. "I'm not a very good story-teller. I promise you that when the play gets staged, there'll be a seat with your name on it."

"I'm sure you've heard this before, Sean, but you're good-looking enough to be a movie star. And I bet you have more than enough talent, too. I'd love to be your agent if you ever decide to give it a try."

"That's very flattering, Lee," Sean said with a laugh, "but though I do a little acting sometimes, writing is what I care about. Anyway, I think the playwriting profession is already pretty well represented on screen by Sam Shepard. If I ever change my mind, though, I'll give you a call. Because of Allison, I've got the U.T.M. phone number memorized."

"The number that I'd like you to call is unlisted. It's mine. I would love you to have it," Lee said hoarsely, sliding her hand under the table onto Sean's thigh.

"I'm sure Allison has it already," he answered, moving his leg away. "If I ever need it, I'll ask *her* for it."

"I thought you were the kind of man who was interested in women," Lee said peevishly.

"I am. In fact, I'm very much in love with one now. I think you know her," Sean said. The smile was gone from his face.

"Don't you like an aggressive woman, Sean?"

"Just what do you mean, Lee?"

"I didn't think you were the coy type, dear. What I've been trying to get across to you is that I'd like very much to fuck you. I know we'd both love it. I'm a very different type of woman than Allison," she said, lowering her voice and leaning toward him.

"I can see that," he responded flatly.

"I love doing all sorts of things that most men only dream about. Plenty of men have told me I do them very well indeed."

"Is that all, Lee?"

"If you mean, would you like me to do something right here in this restaurant, why the answer is, yes. Of course. I'd like nothing better than to reprise Julie Christie's scene in *Shampoo* with you. Allison won't be here for at least another half hour. But if you'd rather have the services of my hand, that would be fine, too. I'm at your disposal, darling."

"How do you know Allison won't be here sooner?" Sean asked, his voice taut.

"I've been wanting to see you alone since the first time I met you. Let's just say that I'm getting a little help making that wish come true. I've always admired men who see a woman they want and pursue her until they get her. I'm like that, too. Someone once told me that I fuck like a man. I took it as a compliment."

"Listen carefully to me, Lee," Sean said, picking up her hand and squeezing it tightly.

"You're hurting me, Sean," Lee said, grimacing with pain.

"I'll do more than that if you ever try anything like this again. I find you a gross travesty of what a woman should be. I've never used this word in front of a woman, but since I don't consider you one, I have no trouble using it. You're a cunt," he said, his voice a harsh whisper, as he released Lee's hand. "I'll keep this obscene little episode between the two of us private, but I don't want to lay eyes on you again after tonight. Ever. You are the most foul, most repellent person, man or woman, that I've ever met. And to think that Allison considers you a friend! I'm going to order a double vodka now, and for the remainder of the time until Allison arrives, we're going to make inconsequential small talk," he said as he signaled the waiter.

Lee stared at Sean. Her mouth tasted bilious from the hatred boiling up inside her. *Who the fuck do you think you are?* she screamed inside. *You're nobody. I'm going to make you and your ice-virgin heiress wish the two of you had never met. I swear I will!*

When the waiter came for Sean's drink order, Lee couldn't help herself and asked for an entrée portion of carpaccio to fill the roiling void that she felt enveloping her. Sean watched in disgust as she ravenously wolfed it down, then rushed to the bathroom a moment later. When she returned, she saw Allison at the table, Sean lightly touching her hair. The two looked like a cameo of what lovers are supposed to be.

"Feeling better, Lee dear?" Sean asked solicitously. "I didn't mention it to you, darling, but Lee seems to have picked up the stomach virus that's going around. She didn't want to leave until you arrived. Now I think we shouldn't keep her here a moment longer."

"Oh, Lee, you shouldn't have waited for me. You should go to bed immediately. Sean, maybe you could help Lee get a cab."

"That's all right. I can walk to the Sherry easily enough," Lee said, a sick smile cutting into her face, the fury within her barely disguised. "You two enjoy your dinner. Good night."

Lee Simons turned quickly and left the restaurant, anger pulling her face as tight as a drum skin. As she walked back to her hotel, she was vaguely aware that people were staring at her. She was dressed fashionably and bore no resemblance to the usual New York street crazy, but what startled the people she passed on the street was the screamed invective that poured from her, like a spoken toxic waste. She finally was able to regain a semblance of composure a block from the hotel, but the pure anger remained.

I'll get you, Sean, she yelled to herself. *And that privileged bitch, too. I'll get you both. Oh, yes I will.*

26

Lee sat by her window, staring at but not seeing the lights of Central Park flickering like fireflies in the gentle movement of the trees. Periodically she poured more vodka into her tumbler, but her fury burned with such intensity that as the night wore on, she felt more sober and more in control. A few hours before dawn Lee decided what she would do. She left a wake-up call for five and immediately fell asleep.

She was in the office at six, perfectly turned out, her face a mask of composure as implacably serene as a Benin bronze. She walked the entire floor, looking in every office to make sure no one else was in yet. When she was satisfied that she was alone, Lee went into Allison's office, leaving the door open behind her. If anyone arrived early and stuck his head in, she would say she was just looking for a deal memo. An everyday occurrence. She moved quickly and efficiently, making certain that every drawer, surface, and file that she searched were left exactly as she had found them.

Allison kept a photograph of Sean and herself on the corner of her desk. Circled by a simple, narrow silver frame, the two of them stood arm in arm in front of what looked like a cabin. They were turned toward each other, laughing, but behind the laughter even Lee couldn't help seeing the affection . . . the love, as clear as a passage underlined in a book. It took all her willpower to stop from seizing the hateful object and heaving it down to the street below. She couldn't stop staring at the vile thing. Had she ever had a look on her face like Allison's? At that moment, Lee could have cried as easily as she could have laughed. Finally, almost willing her hands to move, she placed the picture face down on the desk. Twenty minutes later, she had completed her search of the office, but had found nothing. She heard voices from the reception area. Time to leave. She was almost out the door when she remembered the framed photograph. As she picked it up to put it back the way it had been, a rage of such intensity gripped her that before she could stop herself, she hit it against the corner of the desk. She looked down at it and smiled. The blow had landed precisely between the two heads, and a fan of jagged lines, like those caused by a footstep on thin ice, separated the two lovers. How appropriate, thought Lee. She set it down and walked out of the office. *It's awful,* she said silently to herself, *how careless the cleaning people are these days. Why, they're all thumbs.* And then she laughed out loud.

Lee knew later that morning what her next move would be. There was a meeting after lunch about the casting of a play that Allison had helped to arrange the financing for. It was the Off-Broadway hit of the season and had more than a six-month advance ticket sale. After the meeting, Lee waited for the others to leave.

"It's favor time," she said to Allison.

"As long as it's not illegal, you've got it," Allison answered with a smile. She didn't completely trust Lee, but she was fascinated by and, yes, even admiring of Lee's confidence and aggressiveness, and she tried her best to be friendly toward her.

"It's not for me actually," Lee said. "It's for Mona Lacey."

Mona was a fast-rising client of Lee's who was the star of the number-two rated sit-com. She was sexy and funny and had just been on the cover of *People.*

"Well, we are a full service agency. What can I do for Mona?"

"She's in town for my party tonight, and, I don't know if you know this, but she's been having a very hot thing with Quentin Frost. By some mix-up I put them both into the Sherry. These two can't keep away from each other. They almost fucked on the elevator the other night. But Quentin's married, and he thinks his wife might be tailing him. The important thing is to get them away from the hotel. So if I could put Mona in your loft downtown, where she'll have lots of privacy," said Lee, winking at Allison, "we'll have two very satisfied clients on our hands."

"Anything for the cause of love. But I don't see them as TriBeCa types, Lee. Wouldn't they be happier at some other hotel?"

"They'd be too easy to follow from the Sherry to another hotel. They need, as you lawyers would say, a change of venue."

"The idea of two of this country's biggest sex symbols spending the night in my loft is absolutely delicious," said Allison, as she dug into her purse for her keys. "Everything is ready for them, since I only go there to work these days."

"I'm not surprised that Gus Morton's niece is such a gracious hostess," said Lee. "Would it be too much of a problem to have your assistant send the keys to the Sherry? To Mona, of course." She stopped at the door and blew Allison a kiss. The castanet chatter of her high heels underlined the bounce of her step as she walked back to her office. Perfect, thought Lee. No need to have informed the little princess that she had arranged with the desk clerk, who after countless tips over the years was a great buddy of hers, to send all of Ms. Lacey's packages up to her room first. She was, after all, Mona's agent.

The party after the premiere that night was a smash. That's what Liz said in her column, as did Suzy. A battery of cameras greeted the celebrities both at the theater and at the party with a firefight of flashes. Lee arrived in a sequined purple silk Scaasi and received as much attention as most of the stars. Though few people outside the business recognized the name of a powerful agent like Ben Wildman, Lee Simons regularly appeared in the pages of *WWD* and *Vanity Fair,* and anyone who wanted a lively few words on any industry scandal could always count on Lee. She recently had been filmed dining poolside, attended by two servants in livery—their uniforms rented especially for the occasion—by *Lifestyles of the Rich and Famous,* and her house had been featured in both *Architectural Digest* and *Metropolitan Home* in the last year. But tonight Lee's mind was not on milking the last bit of publicity out of the party. Nor, as was her habit, did she cruise the guests for a partner to share her bed, though there were certainly enough candidates around. All she could think of was getting to Allison's loft and finding *his* play. Sean, of course, was at the party with Allison. Lee tried to keep as far away from him as possible, but she couldn't avoid running into him once. To anyone watching the encounter, Sean's smile would have seemed warm, but Lee knew that inside he was laughing at her. She barely nodded to him and then turned and scrambled away.

The limo dropped Lee off at Allison's loft a little past one. The driver was surprised when Lee told him she was through for the night. He had driven Lee many times before and had never ended a night as early as this. Lee always wanted him to stick around in case she felt like hitting a few clubs. Though she explained that she was scouting new talent, the man, or sometimes, men, whom she brought back to the stretch never looked like performers to him.

Lee found Allison's liquor cabinet and poured herself a large brandy. She took half of it in one swallow and started to walk slowly around the immense space. The room had a clean, understated look that bordered on sparseness. How could someone with Allison's money decorate a place this way? wondered Lee. It might belong to any girl whose folks had a bit of bread, but for Gus Morton's only niece it seemed ridiculous. There wasn't a single painting that she could identify. Probably a lot of new crap from the East Village. Here was a woman who could have a Matisse or a

Braque for the asking, or, if she wanted to be on the more modern side, a Kline or a Fischl. And why only one of each? That holier-than-thou attitude of not showing how much money you had made Lee uncomfortable.

Lee didn't have to search long to find what she was looking for. It was sitting right on top of a pile of magazines on a table next to the sofa. Lee swallowed the rest of her drink as she ran her hand over the red binder that contained the play. A feeling that was intensely warm and satisfying suffused her body. She took off her gown and just let it drop to the ground. She rolled the red binder into a tight tube and ran it over the prominent mound of her panties.

"Sean," Lee screamed aloud as she moved the hard cylinder against her groin, "I'm going to fuck you over, you bastard, like you could never imagine. You and your rich bitch girlfriend are going to wish you had never met."

She let the script fall to the floor as she reached down to pull off her underpants and brought herself to a climax that left her thrashing on the sofa like a fish flung to the bottom of a boat.

When she finally rose, it took Lee some time to realize where she was. Slowly she sat up and saw the script lying on top of her gown. The clock on the table read three-fourteen. Plenty of time. She went to the kitchen to boil some water for coffee, then went into the bathroom and took a long, icy shower. There was a fluffy terrycloth robe hanging behind the door, and she put it on. After a second cup of coffee, Lee settled down on Allison's bed and started to read the play. She finished it in an hour and a half, made herself another cup of coffee, then read the play again. The second time through, she took notes.

Sandia Mountain Song was rich in larger-than-life characters and emotional high points that carried the reader along on a river of whitewater intensity. The language was powerful in its raw description of the land and the plain poetry of the people who had lived and worked the land for generations. Lee felt what Allison had seen the first time she had read Sean's play. Here was an enormous talent just beginning to reach its first fruition. It was the kind of work that could win a Pulitzer, thought Lee, but it also had the kind of powerful storyline that made a perfect mini-series. And that was the direction that Lee intended to take *Sandia Mountain Song*.

When Sean found out that his beloved play had been co-opted into eight hours of overblown dialogue and attenuated suspense, would he be . . . hurt? shocked? enraged? Even though he probably had not copyrighted it yet, Lee knew he would have no trouble proving that the original material was his. He would surely try every legal means possible to stop the miniseries. But so what if it didn't get made? The important thing was to turn the lovers into haters. Although Allison could never hate Sean, the possibility of Sean's despising his little love object was very real, for he would have to ask himself how anyone could have seen the script without Allison's approval? Hadn't Allison told Lee that Sean was somewhat, let's say, dubious about the talent agenting profession? Well, Lee would show Sean that he had been right. Once an agent, always an agent.

It was almost dawn before Lee finally turned off the lights, but even though she was bone-tired, she could not wait to get to the office. She would set to work immediately commissioning a treatment of *Sandia Mountain Song*. That title would never do, of course. It needed something with a little more punch. She started pairing words in her mind that might create the right sound for the title. And then she had it. Yes! Perfect. *The Flame and The Mountain*. Now that had a ring to it.

As soon as Lee arrived in the office, she told her New York secretary to clear her appointments. Then she called Arnie Nelson into her office. Arnie was a hustler par excellence whom Ben had just lured away from I.C.M.'s TV department. He was just past thirty, socially still on Coney Island Avenue, and bald as an egg. Unfortunately, he didn't have anyone close to him to tell him that the toupee he wore would look more at home on a mannequin. Lee could see from the satisfied smile that was stuck like a decal on his face that this meeting was the high point of his brief tenure with U.T.M.

"I've been wanting to meet you for a long time, Arnie. I've heard only good things about you," said Lee.

"The same here, Lee. But we did meet once before," Arnie answered, reaching up for the fourth time in a minute to pat his hair, a gesture so regular as to be almost a tic. "At the B'nai B'rith dinner for Ben last May," he concluded, his smile never wavering.

"Of course. How could I forget," Lee answered automatically, remembering Arnie almost as well as the busboys who had worked the affair. "I'm told, Arnie, that you have quite a few writers who don't have big reputations but already are real pros."

"No big names, Lee, but steady producers. Regular workhorses."

"That's exactly what I'm looking for. A friend has given me a great idea and I need a solid professional to get it down in treatment form real fast."

"Comedy?"

"No. Miniseries. No less than six hours."

"How fast?"

"Yesterday would have been perfect. I need it by the end of the week. This is the kind of idea that someone else could be working on right now," Lee said with a small, tight smile.

"Wow, that's pretty quick. But I think I got the guy. He just finished his second episode for a new Aaron Spelling series."

"He's here?"

"Lives on First Avenue."

"Get him in to see me this afternoon."

"Who's paying for this, Lee?"

"Don't worry about that. If your writer gets it down the way I tell him to, I'll definitely sell it. Anyway, I will guarantee his fee. The idea is *that* good. And by the way, Arnie. This writer—"

"Plesser. Mike Plesser."

"I hope he's got a closed mouth. If anyone asks him down the road, I would want them to know that this idea was his. Understand?"

"Perfectly, Lee. Mike's your man."

Mike Plesser turned out to be exactly what Lee had in mind. An un-blocked journeyman who hadn't had an original idea in years but was more than appreciative of one when it was placed in front of him. He didn't raise an eyebrow when Lee insisted that he take no notes. She went through the story three times, each time adding more detail, until she was sure that he had it. Her insistence on secrecy had no doubt sug-gested to Plesser that this story might not be her own idea. But who cared? Lee was sure she had read him correctly: he knew this was terrific material that, if translated into a workable treatment, would grab any network executive's cojones after the first few pages.

And he delivered. Three days later Lee had a fifty-two page treat-ment that, though not prize quality like Sean's play, promised two things that to Lee were even better: a good deal could be made from it, and it was eminently packageable. When Lee asked Plesser to make a few changes, he simply went into a spare office down the hall and two hours later emerged with the work completed. Lee wondered whether Sean would appreciate the job that was being done. It was a little like sending a hand-built Ferrari to Chevrolet's Lordstown plant for an engine and paint job.

Lee flew back to L.A. the next day on the Gulfstream. Gus was stay-ing on in New York for a few days, so she shared the plane with just Mona Lacey. Two hours after taking off from the Marine Air Terminal, Lee casually brought up *The Flame and The Mountain*. Mona asked to read it.

"But it's just a treatment, Mona," Lee said, with the sugary tone of a molester luring a child into an alley.

"Yes, and by the time it's a script it will be fully cast. Now let me see it, please."

Before they started their descent over Big Bear Lake, Mona had committed herself to the project. Lee cautioned Mona on all the potential pitfalls that existed before *The Flame and The Mountain* could make it to production. But Mona was not to be dissuaded. Lee, with a small smile, gave in to the young star's pressure. The packaging had begun.

Within two days of her return to Los Angeles, Lee had secured the involvement, pending script approval, of Cheney Wyman and Tod Davenport, as bankable as any two actors on the tube. Skip Callan and Ira Flagler, who had produced over twenty hours of miniseries in the past two seasons, quickly signed on. The networks loved them because of the look they were able to achieve while still adhering scrupulously to the budget. And to cap off one of the most frantic periods in her professional life, Lee got a commitment from Mel Graves, the Emmy-winning director of the twelve-hour *Hannibal* and the scarcely shorter *Golden Spike,* which had traced, mile after mind-numbing mile, the building of the first transcontinental railroad.

Her phone was ringing even before the Xeroxes were messengered to the networks and the large independents. Bidding followed the day after the scripts reached the desks of the key executives. By Friday a deal memo had been prepared by CBS, which had just edged out David Wolper.

Because of the number of her own U.T.M. clients involved, Lee insisted on approval of the press release that went out. She also obtained permission to include, though CBS didn't like it, enough of the plot of *The Flame and The Mountain* to make sure that a certain person would not miss the parallels. Just to guarantee that the word reached the quarter it was intended for, Lee spent an entire afternoon on the phone with columnists at the trades and at every important newspaper. Lee had given Mike Plesser something that neither genes nor experience had ever done: an original, exciting premise. Now all Lee had to do was sit back and wait. She knew that it wouldn't be a long wait.

27

What are you doing in the office, Allie? I was sure you'd be home by now preparing dinner." Gus Morton's voice was faint, as if it were filtered through cloth, and his words were fragmented by bursts of scratchy static. "I thought I ought to warn you I missed lunch today, so you're going to face an uncle with a gargantuan appetite. I'm a two-legged version of that little dog of yours you've told me about," he said with a laugh. "What's his name? Pounds?"

"You were close. It's Tonny. Short for Tonnage. Where are you, Uncle Gus? You sound like you're calling from the Amazon."

"The plane. We just left Denver."

"Denver? I thought you were in Chicago today."

"Oh, something's come up that I think might be interesting."

"Don't tell me you're looking at something else to buy. Please don't tell me that."

"Relax, Allie. There's never any harm in looking, is there?" The reasonableness in his voice made Allison feel guilty for jumping on him so quickly.

"Of course, you're right, Uncle Gus," she said apologetically.

"I'm looking forward to finally meeting this playwright of yours, honey. I've met more of them than I can count, as you know, but never one who wasn't interested in an agent, a Broadway production, or money, though not necessarily in that order. You've got yourself a rare bird."

"You're going to love each other, Uncle Gus. I just know it."

"Well, hurry home now," said Gus. "That's an order."

"You're the boss. I have one foot out the door already. And remember, my place at eight."

"How could I forget? You've been reminding me of it for the past two weeks. See you soon, honey. Love you."

Allison looked down at her desk and knew that if she didn't take her uncle's advice to leave immediately, she'd be opening cans for dinner.

Her table desk was littered with contracts, scripts, deal memos, letters to be signed, and a dozen or so grab-bag folders of general office business. She was still shuttling back and forth between helping Gus with his unending string of acquisitions and doing business for U.T.M.'s dramatic division and sometimes the literary one as well. The result was that she found herself at the office most nights until nine, and many nights well past eleven. By necessity, she had become highly selective in going through the paper that flowed across her desk, putting aside until later what she could of the relentless stream of press releases and announcements that tumbled in front of her like ticker tape onto a parade. So, though she was aware of Lee's coup in packaging a miniseries called *The Flame and The Mountain*—it had been, after all, the main topic of conversation for the last week in their offices on both coasts—Allison had not yet read any of the coverage on it. No matter how preoccupied she was, though, Allison always squeezed in a minimum of two calls a day to Sean, who was rehearsing a new one-act play of his at The Combine and finishing yet another rewrite of *Sandia Mountain Song*. At night they both were so tired that the comfort they found in each other's bodies was generally restricted to intimately entwined sleeping positions.

One benefit of all this work was that it had kept Allison too involved to worry much about how her uncle and Sean would react to each other. It had been tough persuading Sean to meet Gus at all, and he also had balked at having the dinner at her loft instead of his.

"Why not ask him here? This is where we live, after all. Or are you worried that the great mogul will think he's on the set of an old Bowery Boys film?" Sean had asked a few nights earlier, with a laugh that didn't quite mask a nervousness that Allison had never seen in him before.

"Reason one is, it's a little difficult making a decent dinner with an oven that doesn't work. And by the way, Mr. Bocuse, all I've ever seen you make on the stove is chili. As for the second reason, yes, I've told my uncle that we're living together at your place, and without making it seem like Calcutta, I've made him understand it's not quite what he's used to. I've also told him how much I care for you and how very, very," Allison leaned over and kissed Sean, "*very* happy I am living with you. But it would still be easier for him to take all of this in at my place."

"Promise me, then, that our second dinner with the great Gus Morton will be at my, or should I say *our*, place," said Sean, really smiling now.

"That's easy. I promise. I've already told Uncle Gus, who I want you to know is a great afficionado of chili, about your powers in the fiery cuisine department. So, our next dinner is all set. Location: here. Bill of fare: Sean's Nine Alarm Original. Beverage: Pearl's beer. How does that sound?"

"It sounds like just what we're about to have tonight," Allison remembered Sean saying, as he picked her up and walked over to the bed. "But first a little R and R for the chef."

Allison stopped at Dean & DeLuca for salad greens and cheese—arugula and curly chicory, both glistening a bright jade green under a film of mist, and a chevre rolled in tiny balls the size of robin's eggs, each morsel outfitted with a stick like an exclamation point to hold it by. A pound of freshly ground Jamaican Blue coffee and a similar amount of kumquats completed her last-minute food list. Her other stop was at a wine shop on West Broadway, where she bought two bottles of Sancerre, Domaine de la Moussiere, Uncle Gus's favorite. Then, hailing a taxi, she detoured to Sean's loft to pick up Tonny, whom she wanted to show off to her uncle.

It was just past six o'clock when she reached her loft. Since she was making a roast veal with a sauce of wine and chanterelles, which was delicious and easy, she had plenty of time to shower and relax before Sean arrived. Her uncle would be there at the stroke of eight. She could depend on that.

The phone was ringing when Allison stepped out of the shower.

"I can't believe it," said the voice at the other end. It was Lee Simons. "Working only half a day?" she asked with a laugh. "Where will U.T.M. be when Allison Morton cannot be found at her desk until midnight?"

"Could you hold on a sec, Lee. I just stepped out of the shower."

"No problem. It can wait till tomorrow. But, by the way, why *are* you home so early?"

"I'm chef and hostess tonight. Uncle Gus is meeting Sean for the first time."

"Sean?"

"Well, if I've been living with someone else the last three months, I'd like to know who it is."

"Sorry, Allie. My mind was somewhere else. It's been one of those days. I'm going to want a full report on this tomorrow, though. Don't forget. Got to run now. I'm having my therapy group over for dinner. Linguini puttanesca, radicchio salad, and two divine hours to cut up the shrink. It ought to be good 'cause I think he's making it with two group members—one of each sex. But that's Hollywood, *n'est-ce pas?* Ciao."

It was only after Allison was dressed and had cleaned and dried the lettuce that she realized Sean was late. She didn't start getting nervous, though, until the news ended at seven-thirty. Then she picked up the phone and called the loft. No answer. She tried twice again at five-minute intervals. Still no answer. He must be at The Combine. She never felt comfortable calling there, but she punched out the number. Glancing at her watch, she saw that her uncle would be ringing her bell any minute.

"Combine. Jenny speaking."

Jenny Ryan was the group's resident set designer. She was short and lively and wore her bright blond hair like the kid on the Dutch Boy paint can. The two times Allison had met her she had been wearing bib overalls with building tools sprouting out of all the loops and pockets on her pants.

"Hi, Jenny. It's Allison. Could I speak to Sean, please?"

"He's not here," she answered coldly.

"Do you have any idea where he might be? You see, he's a little late—"

"I told you, he's not here."

And then Jenny hung up. Bang. Just like that. At that moment, Allison suddenly felt that something was wrong. Very wrong. *Wait a second, girl,* she told herself. Sean was just late. Nothing more than that. Jenny had never been very friendly toward her anyway. Allison had always suspected that maybe something had existed between Sean and Jenny at one time. That's probably why she had been so abrupt. Tea leaves were just tea leaves. Why look for a gallows in a soggy clump of Earl Grey?

She was trying Sean's number again when her doorbell rang. Sean! Allison started for the door. But Sean had a key. She opened the door and ran into her uncle's arms.

"That's what I call a greeting," Gus said, hugging Allison tightly and kissing both her cheeks. He walked into the loft, ostensibly taking in the furniture and pictures, but Allison knew he was looking for Sean. Since he had seen the loft once before, his present walking tour, with Allison following along behind him, Tonny tagging at her heels, was merely pro forma. He turned and faced his niece, an uncertain smile on his lips.

"Sean's late," Allison said. "He ought to be here any moment. But let's you and I have a drink. I've got something icy and potent just for you."

When Allison returned with a glass of wine for herself and vodka for Gus in a chilled glass with a frosty rime around its edge, like a window on a freezing winter morning, her uncle was already seated on the sofa.

"To my favorite colleague," Gus said, clicking his glass against Allison's. "You know I'm a conservative old guy—Bel-Air, the Upper East Side, places like that—but I want to tell you I think this area is terrific. If I were your age, Allie, I'd be living down here, too. Hey, that's some cute little fella," he added, switching his attention to the puppy who was stationed on the floor in front of him, tail wagging, eyes expectant.

"Uncle Gus, meet Tonny," said Allison, smiling for a moment.

"Come here, Tonny. Atta boy," said Gus, patting his knee, as the dog, needing only the hint of an invitation, bounded joyfully over to him.

"He's a real sweetie, isn't he? We think he's mostly springer spaniel and a little bit collie, his nose is so pointy. What do you think?"

"Maybe a touch of poodle?" Gus laughed as Allison did a mild double take. "I'm only kidding, honey. Here, come sit beside me." As she sank down next to him, he put his arm around her. "As much as we see each other, I still miss having you in California with me. Christmas wasn't the same without you. You know, I'm glad New York agrees with you, but you've been here almost a year."

"Three more months to go. It'll be a year in April."

"I said *almost* a year, but are you sure you're really coming home one of these days?"

"Yes, Uncle Gus. Promise," said Allison, trying to be cheerful.

Gus observed the extent of Allison's preoccupation and switched to gossip. "Did I tell you, by the way, that Chip Masters is determined to take on New York? He told Lee yesterday he's not interested in doing another movie until he's had a shot at Broadway. Just turned down two point five mil with Spielberg. Who would have guessed he took himself so seriously."

Gus kept the mood as buoyant as he could with all the juicy tidbits he'd picked up in the last few days about studio heads, stars, and political figures. Allison excused herself twice to try Sean's number. Still no answer. When she came back the second time, her uncle reached over and grasped her hands.

"There's nothing to worry about. I'm sure he'll be here very soon."

"But it's not like him, Uncle Gus. He's just like you about being on time. He's the one who's always waiting for me. He's never been late like this before. I'm really worried something's happened." Allison barely finished speaking before her throat closed up and tears began sliding down her cheeks.

"It's okay, hon," said Gus, squeezing her shoulder. "It's always all right to cry when you care for a person." He glanced at his watch. "It's almost nine. Hmm. He *is* a bit late. Where's the phone, Allie? I'll call him."

Allison gave him Sean's number and led him to the telephone in her bedroom. He quickly called, listened for a few moments, then tried another number.

"Charlie, could you come up here, please."

A minute later Charlie Horner was at the door. Gus asked Allison to give him the addresses of Sean's loft and The Combine. Twenty minutes later the phone rang. Allison rushed to answer it. It was Charlie; he asked to speak to Gus.

"Charlie says there's no sign of him at the theater or at the loft. His place was dark. Now let's just catch our breath for a moment about this whole thing. I'm sure your friend's fine. But I think we'll both feel better if we get something to eat. Are you still up to cooking, or should we go out? We could leave a message on the door saying where we are. What do you want to do?"

"I'd rather stay here, Uncle Gus. Everything's ready to go. It'll just take a few minutes."

"If you can find an apron for me, I'll show you how to make Morton's famous Garlic and the Kitchen Sink Salad Dressing. Paul Newman's been after me for the recipe for years," he said with a laugh. "And I could also use another drink, too. Wine this time."

As soon as Allison handed her uncle a glass of wine, Gus took a pill from his pocket and quickly swallowed it.

"What's that?" asked Allison. "Are you all right?"

"Just vitamin B, Allie. A pick-me-up. I'm feeling a little tired. Shouldn't have skipped lunch."

Allison regarded her uncle for a moment. She had not seen him since the night his sickly appearance had prompted her awful conversation with Diana, but they had spoken every day and he had repeatedly assured her that he was fine. Indeed he looked fine, even if he was tired. It had just been a silly scare. Her falling out with Diana, though, was not something she could dismiss as quickly. She was still trying to repair the damage, and at least they had progressed over the phone from arctic to cool, with warming trends.

Allison began to slice the roast veal and arrange it on a platter. "You should have told me you were starving, Uncle Gus. You make your dressing, and I'll get the other things on the table."

Before they sat down for dinner, Allison ducked into the bedroom to dial Sean's number again. Still there was no answer. During dinner, Gus tried valiantly to entertain Allison with another round of gossip and jokes, but soon the space between his quips lengthened and in time he too fell silent.

"You know, this once happened to me," he said finally, "or rather, it happened to Diana. I was so nervous about something that I just couldn't face seeing her . . . but that was a long time ago."

They drank their espresso in silence. Allison didn't try Sean's number again.

"I'm flying back to L.A. tomorrow morning, early. If you'd like, I can spend the night here with you, Allie. This sofa doesn't look too bad."

Allison, who desperately wanted to be alone, convinced him that she would be all right, and after a while he left. She went to the window and watched Charlie hold open the door of the white Rolls for him. Just before the door closed, Gus looked up and waved. Then the car rolled quietly away down the deserted street. Allison began to straighten up the kitchen, and then she started to cry again. With a weariness that made her feel as if she hadn't slept in days, she dragged herself to bed and fell immediately into a deep, dreamless sleep.

And then suddenly she was awake. The dog was barking. Allison looked at the clock on the night table. Three thirty-five. Then she heard another noise. It was Sean. He was home. She ran into the living room, and there he was, standing in front of the door, his eyes red, his face tight. Around his feet were piles of clothes. Her clothes! Before she could say anything, he wheeled around and ran down the stairs. In a moment he was back, his arms filled with more of her clothes.

"Sean, what are you doing?" she screamed. A part of her thought she was still sleeping, dreaming a terrible dream. In a moment she would wake. Sean would be lying beside her, and everything would be all right. He dropped the clothes on top of the others heaped messily on the floor. "Sean," she cried, "what's wrong?"

"This," he answered, roughly pulling a script out of his pocket and throwing it down. It skittered across the polished hardwood floor, stopping at Allison's feet. "And you."

She reached down and picked it up. THE FLAME AND THE MOUNTAIN was printed across the cover.

"One of our apprentices works as a reader for NBC. He thought that this *thing,*" he said, indicating the script at Allison's feet, "was kind of familiar. I think you'll feel that way too. But then, you already know exactly how familiar it is. It must be comforting to know that whenever an opportunity shows itself, your agenting instincts automatically kick in. Grab the commission! the voice screams out inside of you. After all, you were born into this life, weren't you?"

"I don't know what you're talking about, Sean. What have I done? Please tell me!"

He looked at her for a long moment, then ran down the stairs into the street.

Allison lay balled up on the sofa until the first fingers of morning light splayed across her face. She had tried again and again to reach Sean during the night, but all she got was a busy signal, as harsh and repetitive as the call of a crow. Finally pulling herself to her feet, Allison moved like a sleepwalker to the shower, but the needles of hot water did not revive her. She still felt numb inside and out. She put on a pair of old jeans and a sweatshirt and forced herself to walk over to the mound of clothes at the door. There on the floor next to them was the script.

After staring at it for what seemed hours, Allison opened the script and with galloping astonishment and then rage read through it without stopping. As soon as she had finished it, she got her copy of Sean's play and compared the two. Without thinking about the time in California, she picked up the phone and called Lee Simons.

"Hello," Lee answered, her voice cobwebbed with sleep.

"Lee, *The Flame and The Mountain* is a total plagiarization of Sean's play. I think you know something about it. A lot about it. I want answers and I want them fast," Allison shouted, as if the louder her voice became, the more chance there was that Sean might hear her. Might understand that she had nothing to do with this hideous business.

"Take it easy, Allie. It's five in the morning here, for Christ's sake. Give me a minute to wake up. I'm going to speak softly because I've got the loveliest young Mexican busboy in my bed right now. I found him late last night at Chianti. Let me tell you, he gave this old number quite a—"

"Lee, I'm not interested in your sex life, dammit. I want to know how Sean's play got into some hack plagiarist's hands. That's *all* I want to know."

"I've sort of woken up, but I still don't have any idea what you're talking about," Lee responded matter-of-factly.

"Don't give me that, Lee. I just read this piece of shit, this so-called *Flame and The Mountain,* and it's a complete steal from Sean's play. The only difference is that everything about this treatment by somebody named Plesser is totally banal. But it's exactly the same story, Lee."

"Allison," said Lee in her most professional, formal tone, "I never—I repeat, *never*—have read Sean's play, so if there's any talk of theft, I'd like to get to the bottom of it as much as you. I might not, like you, have a boyfriend involved, but I care about my reputation. I care about it very much. And I do not like being called at five in the goddamn fucking morning to be accused of being part of some cabal involving his play. Just who do you think you are, making accusations like that?" she said, raising her voice with the timing of a practiced performer. "I refuse to be yelled at by anyone. And I don't care if your uncle owns the business. I'd say the same thing to him."

"I'm sorry, Lee. I didn't mean it that way. It's just that—"

"Well, that's better," said Lee, sounding mollified. "Look, I don't know how Mike Plesser came up with his story, but I trust him. It's his idea. He's a pro, and I know enough about him to know he wouldn't crib someone else's idea. Sometimes this sort of thing happens, you know."

"I know, Lee . . . it's just that—" And then Allison started to cry.

"Allie, what's wrong? Take it easy and tell me."

"Something awful happened," she answered, and then, in spite of Lee's most soothing entreaties, she refused to say a word more, but neither could she stop weeping. As she listened to the sound of the other woman's anguish, Lee thought that the only thing lacking in her pleasure was a large box of Kron chocolates. Or better yet, she suddenly thought, her beautiful Mexican busboy. Wouldn't it be nice while listening to Allison to be screwed by . . . what was his name? Pablo? No. Paco. Yes, that was it—but that would be too risky. Allison might be able to hear her over the phone. But then again, Lee wouldn't be where she was now if she hadn't taken risks. She had to do it. It would be the perfect capper.

"You poor kid! Please tell me what's bothering you. Maybe I can help, just by being a listening post," Lee interjected softly, looking over at Paco. He was sleeping on his back, the sheet pulled just above his groin, his stomach a hard smooth delta between two ropy muscles that flared down from his rib cage. Holding the phone to her ear, Lee reached over and pulled the sheet down off the young Mexican's body with the slow movement of a skilled magician who has his audience in complete control. Skillfully and rapidly she brought him to full erection. He stirred only slightly, captured in a warm sensual dream. It was only when Lee lowered herself onto him that his eyes opened.

"That's a good boy," she said to him, smiling, her hand cupping the receiver. "But you must be quiet. The lady on the other end is very, you know, mucho unhappy. But that shouldn't stop us from having some more fun. Right, Paco?"

Lee rhythmically rode the dark, muscular man, whose only reaction was a white-toothed smile.

"Did something happen between you and Sean?" Lee asked with studied innocence, just before a rushing swell of pure heat overwhelmed her and she fell forward across Paco. Still holding the phone to her ear, she kissed the young man, who was already asleep. Lee sensed that Allison was winding down. "He's got to believe me, he's got to, he's got to," Allison was saying into the phone.

"Darling, he will believe you, I promise you," said Lee, taking up Allison's theme. "You'll be able to get to the bottom of things and explain it all to him." *Not if I can help it,* she thought. "But right now you've got to pull yourself together. You've probably been up all night. That's not good for anyone. Get some sleep and then call me. We'll be able to work this out."

"I guess you're right, Lee. You always know what to do. Thanks for listening. And I am sorry for what I said earlier. I didn't mean it, I promise."

"I believe you, Allie. Now get some rest. I'll talk to you later."

Lee replaced the phone in its cradle. For a moment she thought of waking Paco again, but there would be time for that later. What she had to do now was call Mike Plesser. Allison would be on to him before the day was out, and he had to be prepped again on what to say. He had served in the Air Force in New Mexico. Spent lots of time with the locals. The story had been kicking around inside his head for over ten years. That was the tale that Lee had strung together for him just last week. Now it was only a matter of rehearsing Plesser a bit. Lee was confident that he could handle his end like the professional he was. He had taken many, many meetings with agents, producers, directors, and God knows who else, so this one wouldn't throw him.

Lee instinctively knew that the more Allison tried to convince Sean that she'd had nothing to do with the theft of his story, the more he would believe that she had. He was very much his own man. Probably more so than any other man Lee had ever met. Imagine, not wanting fame or money. Or wanting to fuck her! But she had paid him back. Yes, she had. In spades. It was time to call Mike Plesser. And then she could get back to Paco. But business first, she thought, as she tapped out the phone number.

28

It had been almost seven years since Hector Frame had left his Toronto headquarters or, as the *Enquirer* called it, Fortress Frame, and on that occasion he had gone unwillingly. He had been subpoenaed by a federal grand jury in Florida that was investigating Governor Francis Gannon's role in winning approval for a group led by Frame that wished to build a large apartment complex on former state land. But this trip now was different. This trip was for pleasure, pure and simple, and he had waited forty years to make it. Hector Frame was flying to Los Angeles to get even with Gus Morton.

The Canadair ten-passenger executive jet, which was owned by Frame Properties, Ltd., and used almost exclusively by Adrian, would not do because Hector needed a plane with unusual facilities. To this end, a specially outfitted medical emergency jet was hired to make the round-trip flight. In addition to the standard luxury amenities, it had a self-contained operating room with all the necessary equipment for any medical emergency, a portable oxygen tent, and six pints of Hector Frame's rare B-positive blood. A duplicate of the custom-designed surgical table used in his headquarters for his various daily treatments had been bolted onto the floor of the plane, and it was from this odd vantage that Hector Frame looked down at the rolling, snow-covered prairie of Montana as the jet cruised at thirty-six thousand feet in a sky as clear as a fishbowl.

"You know, Father, I don't think there's a chance in hell that Gus Morton will go for your land proposal," said Adrian, as he finished off a plate of tea sandwiches with a glass of Bâtard Montrachet, '76. His black pearl earring in the shape of a cross glinted in the bright sunlight.

"Neither do I," answered his father, without turning his gaze from the white canvas below. "As always, your mind is as subtle as a truncheon. Before we see Morton this afternoon, what will he be doing?"

"Closing on the StellarVue deal," answered Adrian tentatively.

"Correct. And what will that give us?" the old man asked, in a tone of excruciating patience.

"Four seats on the board of U.T.M.," Adrian responded with more certainty.

"But Morton doesn't know that yet, isn't that correct?"

"No, he thinks Sabinson and three other executives from StellarVue will join the board."

"Exactly. But today I am going to have the distinct pleasure of telling him otherwise. That you and three of our close associates will be going on the board instead. And not only that, but as a sort of topping to this delicious concoction, I'm also informing him that if he can't exercise his option to buy the rest of StellarVue within nine months, or ten, if he uses the thirty-day extension—and I know he won't be able to since he's leveraged so tight he makes a piano wire look slack—we can add two more seats. And ergo . . . " Hector Frame looked significantly at his son, who instantly lowered his wineglass from his lips.

"We will have control!"

"And?" the old man demanded, continuing to play the exacting schoolmaster.

"Morton will be out on his ass," Adrian answered with a laugh.

"Precisely. Do you know how long I've waited for this, Adrian?" his father asked, smiling to himself.

"A long time, Father," he answered, basking in Hector's use of his first name and returning the smile he thought was directed at him.

"A long time?" Hector screamed. "You call forty years a long time? I'd hate to depend on you for directions if I were lost. You've always been sloppy. In thought and in deed." He turned to the now-empty cabin, the steward having discreetly fled at the outburst, as if he were addressing a jury seated before him. "This is my heir! This whelp is going to inherit an empire I've fought over fifty years to create. Stropped my soul against a whetstone of brutal work and risk for what, I ask you? For what? So that my prodigal son will live the life of a slack-spined degenerate?"

"Father, I only said—"

"What you said diminishes an event that I've anticipated for more years than you've seen on this earth. Do you know what Gus Morton did to me? He testified against me! And I had promised him as rich a deal as he had ever seen to keep his mouth shut. And I haven't been able to pay him back until now."

"You never told me exactly what happened, Father," Adrian ventured.

"It upsets me too much even now to talk about it. I'll tell you the entire story some other time. Maybe even tonight, when we fly back after reading Morton his eviction notice," said the old man with a laugh, which sounded more like a cough in a tuberculosis ward. "Suffice it to say that Morton took the high road and testified against me. If not for some fortuitous help from Governor Gannon, who was in a position to assist, then, your father might have spent some contemplative time at the expense of the hardworking American taxpayers. It was close, the closest I've ever come, and all because Gus Morton wore his conscience on his sleeve. Now I'm tired," he said with a sigh, pulling a vicuña comforter up to his chin. "I must take a small nap. Do not wake me for any reason until we're about to make our approach."

"Of course, Father. What if—"

But Hector Frame was already asleep.

"Hello, Frame," Gus Morton said as Lillian led the father and son into Gus's office. His voice, normally animated and warm, was flat and hard.

"The years have treated you well, Morton. You look ten years younger than you are. Unfortunately, my genes haven't dealt me quite so lucky a hand," said Hector Frame in his most ingratiating voice.

"You were always a hypochondriac, Frame," said Gus, standing in front of the black marble fireplace, where a small fire burned. Though the temperature outside was in the low seventies, Gus liked to keep the gas fire lit in the winter months. It reminded him of the changing seasons. "You'll probably outlive us all, but if you live to be two hundred, I doubt that you'll ever have an ordinary, happy day. I've never understood how someone could be born as miserable a creature as you. But I know you didn't come here to reminisce. What do you want?"

"My son," said the old man, his eyes averted from Gus to a distant point in the Hollywood Hills behind the smoked, floor-to-ceiling glass, "will present our proposal."

Adrian opened a folder and, as he had rehearsed a half-dozen times under his father's exacting scrutiny, offered their plan to buy the U.T.M. real estate holdings.

"Is that all?" Gus asked when Adrian had finished.

"Yes. I have a copy here for your perusal," said Adrian, handing an identical folder to Gus, who accepted it without opening it. He turned around and pitched the folder into the fireplace. The fire licked at the corners, as if tasting it, then consumed the papers in its fiery maw.

"Is that enough of an answer for you, Frame? I'd rather deal with the devil for a trinket than with you for the secret of eternal life. Now get out of here."

Frame rose slowly from his chair and started to walk out of the office.

"I advise you not to talk that way to me, Morton," he warned.

"Oh, excuse me. I'm not used to dealing with vermin."

Hector Frame waited until his hand was on the door, his son at his side, then turned and confronted Morton, a malicious leer contorting his face. "I didn't expect that reaction from you, Morton. You surprise me, but I welcome it. Now my victory will be all the sweeter." His smile widened as he started to pull out his trump card. "My son forgot to include one bit of very necessary information in our offer."

"You mean the business of your hidden interest in two companies? Sun Scan and Futurscope?" Gus asked nonchalantly.

Hector Frame felt a whiplash of hate charge through his body.

"I knew the StellarVue deal looked just a little too good, so I checked it quite closely, Frame. Rest assured that U.T.M. will be able to exercise its option in the time allotted us. Perhaps it won't be easy, but I know a way to do it. In the meantime, it will indeed be fun having you on our board. Even if your stay is a short one. Now, good day, and I hope you don't mind if I do not use the term *gentlemen*."

Frame tried to speak, but nothing came out. His face tightened as if pulled by a string from behind, and for a moment Gus thought the man would scream. Then he disappeared through the door, pulling his son after him.

Gus walked back to his desk and took a Davidoff cigar out of his humidor. He lit it and savored its aroma. He knew he shouldn't be smoking the cigar, but so what, he thought. If there ever was a time to celebrate, this was it. Not only had U.T.M. made a great deal on StellarVue, but in the process Gus had succeeded in uncovering Hector Frame's foolish efforts to deceive him. What could be more satisfying? He had kept the whole matter entirely to himself, involving neither Parker Welles nor, more important, Allison. It was the only one of his acquisitions that he had not brought her into, but it was better this way, for he knew that Frame's hidden interest would trouble her. In time he would tell her everything about it, including how they would extricate themselves from the Frames. But that could wait. The important thing now was to savor the moment. He sat back in his chair and blew a fat, lazy smoke ring. It held together almost to the ceiling. Gus smiled. That was a good omen, he thought.

29

George Bellamy stared at the dozen shirts he had spread out on his bed like large colorful pieces in a strange puzzle. In his hands were an equal number of ties, silk and knit, solid and patterned, which he held up first against one shirt, then against another. Suddenly he realized he had been playing this mixing and matching game for the better part of a half hour. Unless he made a decision now about what to wear, he ran the risk of being late for dinner, and this was one occasion when he wanted everything to go just right. He would push his charm, his wit, his attentiveness, everything he had learned in the last year, for all it was worth. This wasn't just another studio bash with a cast-of-hundreds guest list or another night out with a dope-smoking rock group. This was an infinitely more important event, an invitation to a Lee Simons dinner. Small, select, at her home. It was the crème de la crème of invitations. He had turned down three others to accept it. He would have turned down thirty.

George chose a dove-gray Turnbull & Asser shirt with pale cherry stripes the width of matchsticks. A dark blue Charvet silk tie complemented it perfectly. He rushed into the shower. The steam that quickly filled the bathroom didn't stop him from shaving while showering. The nonfogging mirror that he had had installed in the shower enabled him to save five minutes every day. And tonight he needed every extra minute he could get to prepare himself for the dinner party.

He had been living in this house for only three months, and the reality of it had yet to sink in. It was a perfect example of Neutra's architectural genius, perched at the very top of Benedict Canyon. Essentially all glass, it shone like a glistening jewel as the sun dissolved into the Pacific. A huge black-tiled deck hung off the back of the house, as if ready for a disabled fighter plane to make an emergency landing. He had an option to buy and was waiting for the right moment to speak to Gus Morton about a loan. A loan *and* another raise. Quagmire, the new heavy-metal band he had just signed, was on the way up the charts, and he knew if it hit number one there was no way Gus could turn him down on either request. And then George would own the house. "Stop smiling like an idiot," he said out loud. "You'll be late for dinner at Lee's." And then he laughed. He almost couldn't stop. He caught his image in the full-length mirror and winked. "You've come a long way, baby. Think of it. Dinner at Lee Simons's! Jesus, barely two years ago, you would have been lucky to have a job valet parking at her place."

Lee Simons's house sat on three acres at the top of Trousdale. The grounds were tended by a battery of Japanese gardeners who manicured every inch with exacting care. George pulled his new Porsche, leased by U.T.M., in between a silver Bentley and a black Aston-Martin. He put on his suit jacket, which he had carefully folded on the front seat so as not to wrinkle it, and walked to the front door.

"Good evening, sir," said a smiling, mocha-colored man in a crisp white linen jacket who held the door open for George. The servant motioned him to the rear of the house, where the soft murmur of voices and guitar music drifted easily into the large, airy Spanish interior. George followed the sound outside to a marble patio surrounding a large oval pool at the bottom of which was a vivid, anatomically precise painting of a nude man doing the backstroke.

"Like it?" asked Lee, as she moved next to George and kissed him lightly on the cheek. "Hockney. David just finished it for me last month. I think there's nothing so boring as a big, empty aqua-blue Esther Williams pool. Sort of like looking into the eye of an animal in a butcher shop window."

But before George could answer, Lee was leading him around the patio like a young corgi just out of obedience school, introducing him to the other guests. There were the requisite stars, one of each gender: Sybil Chandon, of uncertain English parentage and startlingly beautiful eyes, who had just come off an incredible international success co-starring with both Connery *and* Mastroianni, and Pack Jellicoe, tall and almost feline, who, though gay as Oscar Wilde, was teen America's favorite pinup thanks to his starring role in NBC's *Dirt Bike Blues*. Then came Dr. Irv Swift, the Beverly Hills shrink, who claimed he was running over half the movie studios in town by reason of having their operating heads supine on his couch Monday through Friday. Next to him, in a faded denim jacket and parchment-thin leather pants, was Rico Cartman, the new wunderkind director who had hit it big with a low-budget picture he had brought in for under a million that grossed nearly forty. Now all the majors were bidding for his services, and the next picture he was set to direct had a budget of twenty-five million. He, like Chandon and Jellicoe, were Lee Simons's clients.

Talking together under a dazzling white umbrella that was large enough to keep a pitcher's mound dry were the remaining two guests: Moira Lackenberg and Adrian Frame, both in their late-thirties and the products of huge inherited fortunes. Moira, the daughter of mall-builder extraordinaire, Moe Lackenberg, had gone through years of depression and plastic surgery in her quest to "find" herself. Now she had her niche. Moira ran L.A.'s hottest salon. Next to Lee's, of course. An invitation from her was a choice ticket; all that she presently lacked was a husband to round things out. Her last, number three, was the surgeon who had performed the herculean task of narrowing and raising Moira's futon-shaped bottom, a job that one of her friends had said made the raising of the *Titanic* seem like child's play. The man she was drinking in with her lachrymose, cowlike eyes was not interested in her at all. Adrian had more than enough money of his own and had heard from several backgammon-playing buddies that Moira was one of the town's worst lays. Dickie Weekes, one of the few heterosexual walkers in L.A., had told him that even with her recent derriere surgery, it would take a nine on the Richter scale to get Moira to move her booty.

Lee seated George to her left and Adrian on her other side. Of all the guests at the dinner, the only one who had ignored George was Adrian. He knew precisely who George was, of course, because of his researches into U.T.M. on his father's behalf, and though he could see that George was bright and aggressive, on his way up, and potentially of great value to the agency, he found him personally distasteful. Adrian, who lived in a world of snobs, was a veritable Everest among them, and, for him, George still carried about him a bit too much an air of the mailroom. Adrian wasn't interested in diamonds in the rough. Only those in fine settings.

To annoy Adrian, Lee played almost exclusively to George through-out the dinner. Though George had gotten to know Lee quite well in the office and even had collaborated with her on a film deal for Billy Trey, George's newest singing find, this was the first occasion he had ever spent time with her socially.

"I hope you like softshell crabs, George," Lee said to him softly. "They were flown in this morning from Chesapeake Bay."

"Oh, sure. I love them," George answered with a show of conviction. He stared down with revulsion at the creatures on his plate. They looked like props from a low-budget horror movie. Having frequented expensive restaurants as a customer only for the past year—he had worked as a busboy before landing the mailroom job at U.T.M.—he rarely ordered anything more daring than steak or veal.

"Well, since they're from the East, not everyone out here is familiar with them." Lee dropped her voice even lower. "In case you haven't had them in a while, you eat the whole thing. Just like a hamburger."

George braced himself as he cut into the softshell crab. The first bite was both an act of faith and a further rite of passage into the world that he had always dreamed of being a part of.

"They're good, aren't they?" asked Lee.

"Terrific," George answered, his mouth filled with crab, and he meant it. The weird little things were delicious.

After dinner, Lee led the guests into her screening room, which was housed in an ivy-covered building next to the poolhouse. Large, soft brown leather chairs with arms each the thickness of an elephant's leg were arranged in three rows facing a floor-to-ceiling screen thirty feet away. Small brass tables, positioned between chairs, held an assortment of gum balls, jelly beans, and cigarettes.

"Barry was a doll to send this over," Lee announced when everyone was seated, "but since the only U.T.M. client in it left us six months ago for an unnamed skid row agency, feel free to hiss, boo, or laugh in all the wrong places."

Passion Alley starred two of the most bankable young actors of the moment, neither of them yet twenty-three. The story, which concerned two rock musicians whose careers head in opposite directions, was subordinate to the music, which made heavy-metal rock seem like a string quartet.

"I defy anyone to walk out humming this score," shouted Rico Cartman.

"Screaming it would be more like it," Dr. Irv Swift yelled back.

"George," Lee said, leaning so close to him that her lips lightly touched his ear, "when this piece of indescribable shit is over, I think it would be nice if you left shortly thereafter. That will help me get the rest of the guests on their way. They should clear out in no more than forty minutes. Then you come back, and the two of us can have a drink and some nice quiet conversation. We have *lots* to discuss. It's important for us to really get to know each other. And by the way," she added, inserting the tip of her tongue into his ear, "I just got some great dope today. I think we'll have some real fun. How does that sound?"

George nodded, as Lee sat back in her armchair, though not before nipping his earlobe.

. . .

"You want to hear something really weird?" Lee rhetorically asked the group, as the screening room lights came on. "I think this cacophonous dog is going to make a lot of money."

"I hope so," countered Adrian Frame in a half-serious tone. "My father and I, not to mention a couple of thousand worthy dentists from the Midwest that we lured into the deal, have financed this turd. We're not interested in bankrolling art, Lee. As the queen once said, 'Let them see shit.' With luck, your commercial judgment will be shared by the box office God in the sky," he concluded with a laugh.

"I have an eight o'clock meeting tomorrow, but I'm still game for a brandy. Any takers?" asked Lee.

George was ready to signal his acceptance when he caught Lee's look.

"Sorry, Lee," he said quickly. "Unfortunately I have a meeting at seven. I had a great time," he continued, smiling. "I actually found the movie fun, maybe because it's closer to my end of the business. But the entire evening was even better. Much better," he concluded, kissing Lee on both cheeks.

"You're in the wrong game, George," she whispered back. "A line like that is worthy of a four-picture deal at any studio in this town. See you in a little bit."

George's goodbyes were pleasant and perfunctory until he reached Adrian Frame. Adrian wouldn't deign to look directly at him and insisted on calling him Joe.

George drove down the long driveway that doglegged both left and right before spilling out onto quiet darkness. He considered for a moment pulling his car off on the next side street and just waiting out the half hour with a cigarette and the images that were tumbling across his mind like an erotic fever dream, but immediately he realized how stupid that would be. Within minutes of parking in front of a modest two-mil bungalow, puffing contentedly on his Marlboro, he'd be surrounded by a squad of Trousdale's finest, their Dirty Harry guns the size of howitzers tickling his nose. They'd have him across the hood of his car, reading him the Miranda in four languages before he could exhale. That wouldn't do at all. Not with Lee up there waiting for him. Of course! Why hadn't he thought of it already? The Bel-Air Hotel was only a few miles away. That would be the perfect spot to kill time.

As he walked across the narrow bridge arching gracefully over the pond by the hotel entrance, George thought for a moment of Allison.

About the night they came to the hotel bar and swore they weren't going to stop until they became agents. Well, they both had made it, though George had never had any doubt that Allison would. Why couldn't she understand that he'd had to do it that way? He hadn't been born with a golden spoon in his mouth the way she had. He couldn't let an opportunity like that pass by him. She had been the first woman he had ever really felt anything for, though, and now she wouldn't even give him the time of day. When a business matter arose, she showed him as much warmth as he got from a toll collector. Luckily he wasn't sentimental— and he knew he had been right. Look where he had gotten. And what lay ahead would be even better. George smiled as he watched the bartender pour him the brandy he had passed up at Lee's. He didn't need Allison. He didn't need anybody. *Here's to you, Allie,* he thought as he raised the snifter to his lips. *You don't know what you're missing.*

An hour later he was at Lee's door. He purposely arrived a little late. It wouldn't do to seem too eager.

"I was beginning to wonder, Georgie, if maybe you weren't going to show up. I thought I might have scared you off. Or pegged you wrong. You know, that maybe you preferred boys."

"We all have our hangups, Lee, but that isn't one of mine," George answered as he walked past her into the darkened hallway.

"Adrian would be sorry to hear that, sweetie."

"Oh, is Mr. Charm of that persuasion?"

"He's a real shithead, I agree, but he swings in *many* directions. He wanted to stay here tonight. I made my excuses, but I bet he'd really be killing himself if he knew you were here, too."

"I got to tell you something else about me, Lee. I don't like sharing."

"We'll deal with that little matter some other night, dear. Come on, take my hand. My bedroom is at the back of the house. I don't want you bumping into my new Nevelson."

Lee led George down the hallway. Her hand was dry and warm and she gripped his the way a man would.

"Here we are," she said, opening the door to the bedroom.

The room was lit by two silk-shaded lamps on either side of an enormous bed covered with pale blue satin sheets.

"I turned on the hot tub. We can have a nice soak later. Here, have a hit on this," Lee said in a choked voice as she passed George a lighted joint. "Not too much, honey. Don't want you going to sleep on me. I have plans for the two of us."

After George took his fourth puff, any hope he had of staying in command of events slipped away completely. Only later did he realize that

Lee was a force that would be hard to handle even if he were stone cold sober. When he awoke the next morning, all he could remember of that long night were fractured scenes. Images of a pornographic movie on the huge screen that rose from the foot of the bed at the touch of a button; of the sexual accessories—creams and vibrators, whips and handcuffs— that Lee kept arrayed on her night table like objets d'art, ready for use; of the tastes of champagne, coke, and sex; and, most of all, of the sensation of being totally controlled by a woman. Treated like a . . . he didn't want to admit it, but yes, like a slave. He had done everything Lee ordered him to do, and he had liked it. No, he had loved it.

George heard the door to the bedroom open, and before he could cover himself with the sheet, in walked the servant who had opened the front door the preceding night. He pushed a large trolley before him and smiled generously at George.

"Morning, sir. Lovely day, too. No smog," he said as he arranged what appeared to be a breakfast for four on a table that looked out over the pool.

As soon as the servant left, Lee walked out of the bathroom, naked save for a small towel wrapped around her hair.

"Good morning, George," she said as she knelt on the bed and kissed him lightly. "I hope Manolo didn't surprise you too much when he came in. Don't worry about him, though. He's the soul of discretion. And he's seen *everything*. If Manolo wasn't so loyal and close-mouthed, there'd be a bidding war between the *Enquirer* and the *Star* that would make the pro basketball draft look like a Girl Scout cookie sale. By the way, you were marvelous last night, dear. I hope you enjoyed it as much as I did. You seem to be not quite awake yet. A little too much drink? Or maybe the dope was too strong?"

"I'm fine. Really." George answered groggily.

Later, when George finished showering, he found Lee at the table, finishing what had been a huge stack of pancakes. She then started to devour a breakfast steak the size of the plate.

"Looks like you really have an appetite," George said as he sat down.

"After a night like the one we just had, I got a lot of energy to re-place."

Lee immediately switched the conversation to business and for the next half hour she questioned George closely about his present and pro-spective clients. It was as if they were having a meeting in the office, except for the rhythm of Lee's almost manic chewing.

The only breaks came when twice Lee suddenly excused herself and went into the bathroom. It sounded to George as if she was having a choking fit, or maybe even throwing up, but it only lasted a few moments. When she came back to the table after her first absence, she rang for Manolo and ordered a three-egg omelet and a plate of hash. When Lee returned to the table after disappearing the second time, George asked her if anything was wrong.

"I guess my eyes are just a little bigger than my tummy," she said.

As George dressed, Lee brought him a cup of coffee.

"You remind me of myself when I first got started in the business, but you're moving even faster. Only thing is, though, you don't cover your tracks very well, Georgie."

"Tracks? I don't know what you're talking about," said George, the uneasiness surfacing in his voice.

"Let me tell you what I mean. I've been very impressed with how much air time Quagmire is getting, even though they suck. The real top-forty treatment."

"What are you trying to say?" demanded George in as firm a tone as he could muster.

"Lee Simons doesn't *try* to do anything. And don't ever raise your voice to me."

George nodded obediently. He suddenly felt flushed all over. Was everything he had fought for going to be taken away from him?

"I felt we were going to be friends," said Lee, "and I wanted to know a little more about you, so I did a little digging. Funny what turns up, isn't it? What I found out was that the big five disc jockeys in town have been getting a little extra consideration for playing Quagmire. Sound familiar? I must say, George, I'm really surprised at you. That's the oldest game there is."

It took George a while before he was able to speak.

"Who else knows about this, Lee?" he finally asked.

"Not Gus Morton, if that's who you mean."

George Bellamy looked as if it were his turn to go into the bathroom and get sick. He had begun to perspire and couldn't seem to figure out what question he dared to ask next.

"Oh, relax, George. I'm not going to tell on you, and the only other person who knows won't either. He doesn't care enough about you to waste his breath. Don't ever forget, however, what I know. And I can guess at some other things. Understand? But I'm glad we finally got together, George. It's important that we get to know—and trust—each other as much as we can. Things are changing at U.T.M. We're going to have to look after ourselves, because no one else is going to." She paused to light a cigarette. "I seem to recall that you and Allison once had a little fling." She inhaled and blew a column of smoke into the air. "She's coming back to L.A., you know."

"No, I didn't know. Why?" George felt a jolt of interest that he was careful to hide from Lee. Jesus, he'd just written her off. He shouldn't be reacting this way!

"Her boyfriend walked out on her," Lee said, smiling. "But the point is, she's going to be a very important part of our lives someday. Now that she's going to be around here again, I need to know a lot more about her. I want you to tell me everything you can. And don't rush it. I called the office and cleared both our calendars for the morning. We have plenty of time."

30

’ve got a little surprise for you, Uncle Gus,” said Allison, as the two of
them rode through the inky February night toward Palm Springs, “but
you have to shut your eyes.” She reached into the front seat of the Rolls,
next to Charlie, and picked up a gaily wrapped package the size of a hat
box and handed it to her uncle.

“Why, Allie honey, what’s the occasion?”

“No occasion really.”

“You know how much I love presents,” Gus said, already tearing off
the paper. “Your father and I never got enough of them when we were
kids, or thought we didn’t,” he added, laughing at himself.

When he looked inside the box, the smile on his face turned to puz-
zlement, for he found himself staring down at his own briefcase. He
opened it and peered in.

“There’s nothing in here.”

“That’s part of your surprise. I took out all your work before we left.
This weekend is for fun and rest only. When you canceled the retreat, I
decided you owed it to yourself.”

This was supposed to have been one of Gus’s business retreat weekends, which he staged several times a year with different combinations of
executives. Sometimes he invited these groups to the house in Trancas,
but more often to Palm Springs, where everybody was delighted to get
out on the beautifully groomed golf course in between brainstorming
sessions. This weekend was to have included Ben Wildman, Diana, and
Lee, but on Tuesday Ben had pulled his back badly while exercising. On
this occasion, more than others, his presence was essential, since he had
been virtually running U.T.M. while Gus was busy acquiring. When
Ben still wasn’t better by Thursday and it seemed almost certain Gus
would postpone the retreat, Lee jumped the gun and reneged, claiming
the press of work (though confiding to Allison that her real reason for
wanting to stay in town was a new young stud she had just met at a

screening), and Diana, following suit, grabbed the free weekend to visit a niece who had just had a baby.

"All right. You win," Gus now said genially. "I'll go along with your no-work, all-play scheme."

"You have no choice anyway," said Allison, smiling. "All we're going to do for the next couple of days is talk, eat, lie in the sun, and watch some old movies that I know you love. That's it."

"Sounds like what the doctor ordered, Doctor."

'Well, now that you mention M.D.'s, maybe you need an eye doctor, too," Allison said with a laugh. "You didn't search your briefcase very thoroughly. The other part of your present is still in there."

Gus reached in again and pulled out a small, flat envelope. Inside he found a card that read: "Redeemable for one pretty terrific Jean Dunand vase." Before Gus could say anything, Charlie handed back another wrapped box. The big man, driving steadily at exactly the speed limit, smiled conspiratorially in the rearview mirror.

"How did you know I wanted this?" asked Gus as he unwrapped a sensational black and gold enameled vase.

"I saw you looking at it in Christie's catalog a couple of months ago, and since you've had more on your mind lately than buying beautiful objects, it wasn't very tough for me to go over to Park Avenue on the sly and bid on it. It was one of the pieces Dunand did for the Exposition in twenty-five. And I happen to know the perfect place for it."

"Let me guess. On the shelf next to my Giacometti dog?"

"Close. Above it, by that photo of you and Dad and Grandma and Grandpa."

"You're absolutely right. It goes there Monday morning. But it's not going to stay in the box all weekend. I want to look at it, so we'll put it on the mantel in the study. Then if we play a game of Scrabble—and by the way you owe me a return match—I can look up to it for inspiration."

"Well, you're going to need it, Uncle Gus. I'm out to prove that my win last time was no fluke."

"Did you hear that, Charlie? A challenge! Now, I don't know if you're aware that your uncle has earned a pretty formidable reputation as a Scrabble player over the years. Isn't that right, Charlie?"

"What was that, boss?" asked Charlie innocently.

"Don't play the hard-of-hearing game with me. You know what I'm talking about. That game I played at Hotel du Cap with Tennessee Williams and Harry Kurnitz."

"Oh, that night! Sure I remember," answered Charlie. "I kept score. You won by a mile. Absolutely creamed them."

"See!" said Gus to Allison. "And that was against two writers. Men who made a living from words. You just caught me on an off night."

"But as I recall," Charlie continued, almost to himself, "both Mr. Williams and Mr. Kurnitz were feeling no pain."

"Stop exaggerating, Charlie."

"I don't want to disagree with you, boss, but I was bartending that night. I used that cocktail shaker so much that when I woke up the next morning my hands were still trembling. I thought I had the palsy."

"You must be thinking of another game, Uncle Gus," said Allison, laughing so hard that tears rolled down her cheeks. She looked over at her uncle, who was trying unsuccessfully to keep a straight face. God, it was good to be laughing again, thought Allison, but then another thought stopped her short.

"What's wrong, hon?" asked her uncle.

"Nothing, Uncle Gus. I was just thinking about . . . us. And my father. You know, sometimes I have to get out his picture to remember his face."

"You were pretty young when he died. But there's something else on your mind. It's that playwright, isn't it?"

Allison looked out the window on her side. Hills like dark knuckles were backlighted by a full moon as round as a plate.

"Yes," she answered.

"Want to talk about it?" he asked after a while.

Allison shook her head.

"Charlie," said Gus spiritedly after a few moments of silence, "I have a question of some delicacy to pose to you."

"Boss, you know I'm strongest on baseball, World War Two, and Broadway musicals, but go ahead anyway."

"How upset would Maria be if we grab a bite at La Paloma and skip dinner at home? Tell me honestly."

"If we call right away, only mildly pissed. If we don't call at all, the cossacks will seem like the Four-H Club compared to her."

"Do me a favor then, Charlie, and pull over at the next gas station and give her a call. Tell her we broke down. If you call from the car she won't believe that line."

"Ah, please, boss. Why can't *you* make the call? If I do, she'll think it's my idea. She'll give me grief for months. You know how she is. She'll throw too much chili powder in my eggs tomorrow morning. She's done it before."

"I'll call, Charlie. Maria will go easier on me," Allison said.

"Thanks a lot, Allison," Charlie answered, genuinely relieved. "That's a big one I owe you."

La Paloma was located in a former grocery store sandwiched between a Pentecostal church and a Midas Muffler shop. It was in the town of Banning, just off the highway, and all that Gus knew about the place was that some of the best Tex-Mex food he had ever eaten was cooked there on an ancient six-burner stove by a stooped man of indeterminate age who went by the name of Zapata. When Gus first discovered the restaurant in the early 1950s, Zapata seemed an old man even then. The only visible sign of the progression of time was the rest of his family, who spanned at least three generations and had grown numerous enough to fill all the other positions in the restaurant. Gus's entrance into the restaurant was greeted with hugs and cries of welcome, and within moments old man Zapata emerged from his kitchen to embrace one of his oldest customers. After a new baby was presented to Gus for a kiss and a trio of frosty margaritas placed before them, Zapata returned to his stove to cook an array of specialties for his good friend. Gus hadn't consulted a menu in the restaurant in twenty-five years.

"This food gets better and better, Uncle Gus," said Allison between mouthfuls of a ceviche that contained fresh, chilled pieces of octopus, abalone, and sea scallops, all drenched in a bath of lime juice. In the middle of the table were a half-dozen other dishes.

"There are two things you must not forget, Allie," said Gus, after he drained his bottle of Carta Blanca. "Number one, never tell Maria we stopped here. La Paloma is a real red flag to her. Like the Red Sox to the Yankees. And secondly, don't ever tell a soul about this place. And I mean nobody."

As Allison jokingly raised her hand in an oath, Gus's face suddenly turned pale. He took a small silver cylinder out of his pocket and tapped out of it a white pill. He swallowed it and closed his eyes for a few moments. When he opened them again, the color was returning to his face.

"You okay, boss?" asked Charlie, a look of concern pulling his broad features down like a window shade being lowered.

"Are you all right?" Allison echoed.

"I'm fine. Really I am."

"What was that, Uncle Gus? It looks like the same thing you took that night you had dinner in my loft. You said it was some kind of vitamin."

"I guess I didn't tell you the truth that night. Probably because it sounds more formidable than it is. This little dynamo," he shook the container so that another pill rolled out onto the table, "is nitroglycerine. Like the stuff they trucked in *Wages of Fear*. Ever see that movie, Allie? Directed by Clouzot. It's a fabulous film. He also directed *Diabo*—"

"I'll say it sounds formidable. Don't people take that for heart trouble?" Allison asked urgently. She had been right all along to be concerned about his health.

"It's just a little angina," Gus was explaining in a reasonable voice. "It's a minor heart problem. *The* most minor. Doc Elliott has me watching my diet and my drinking, which I have been doing faithfully, haven't I, Charlie? And when I get one of these pains, which is seldom, these little babies," said Gus as he rolled two of the pills in his palm like dice, "take care of it just like that."

"Those pains must be pretty strong, Uncle Gus. You should have seen your face."

"Now that's enough about my little problem, Allison. Let's not make it into something more than it is. It's absolutely nothing to worry about. It's getting late now. Let's finish up and hit the road."

It was almost midnight when they reached Palm Springs, but Gus was full of energy.

"Did I ever show you the first house I owned here, Allie?" he asked as they passed the old estate section. Before she could answer, he told Charlie to turn off the highway onto a quiet road that looked as if it ran clear into the hills. From this angle the hills jutted abruptly up from the desert floor like pieces of furniture.

"Remember when we first came out here, Charlie?"

"It was right after the war, boss."

"What a place it was then. All you heard at night was the breeze fanning the date palms and an occasional coyote. And the air! It was sweet and soft like a baby's skin. It was God's country, Allie."

"It's not too bad now, Uncle Gus."

"Oh, sure. I know I'm sounding like an old man reminiscing about the good old days. But this place really was something. All the big stars spent time here either winding down or drying out. Now the place is wall-to-wall tax shelter promoters, shopping-mall developers, and deal-makers. There's hardly any talk of scripts and productions. It's all leveraged buyouts and tender offers."

"You haven't exactly been a purist yourself lately, with all your acquisitions. In fact, I'd say you've picked up more corporate and tax law since all this started than I learned in three years of law school."

"But the situation for our company is different," protested Gus. "I'm not in this for green mail or some other quick profit. I'm not interested in doing unfriendly deals. I'm just trying to make U.T.M. into something bigger and broader. Something more than just personal services. That's all the talent agency business is, after all. The so-called assets feel free to call you up anytime day or night to say they're moving on when their contract term is up."

A fire engine roared past them, its siren screaming and its flashing lights spinning and blinking like an amusement park ride gone berserk. Within moments, another engine and several police cars sped by.

"Looks like a bad fire," said Gus almost to himself.

"We'll see for ourselves," said Charlie. "We're headed the same way."

In a matter of moments they saw an eerie orange glow lighting up the sky ahead of them. Of course it can't be our house, Allison and Gus both thought, without saying a word. They could see flames now, reaching into the night sky like supplicants at a bizarre altar.

"Jesus," said Charlie as they drew close. "It's our place."

"Oh my God!" Gus shouted, throwing open the door as soon as Charlie brought the car to a shuddering stop.

Allison ran after him. "Be careful, Uncle Gus!" she cried, knowing there was no way he could hear her above the roar of the disaster. She caught up with him near a pumper truck, frantically questioning one of the firemen.

"The chief said it started with an explosion in a small building out back, Mr. Morton. By the time we got here, the main house was engaged."

"I employ a couple who live in the house. Do you know where they are?" Gus asked, his voice rasping.

"We're treating a Mexican male who's about fifty for shock and minor burns. He's in that ambulance next to the cruiser."

Albert Salazar lay on a gurney, his hands swathed in gauze, his head twisting from side to side as if trying to shake off an invisible hand. An attendant sat on a seat next to him.

"Albert! Albert! It's me," shouted Gus, climbing into the ambulance and leaning over him. "You're going to be all right. Where's Maria?"

At the name Maria, Albert's head stopped moving and he stared at Gus. "Oh, Señor Morton," he cried. "My Maria. My beautiful Maria."

"It's all right, Albert. Just tell me where she is," Gus said urgently.

Tears poured down Albert's cheeks as he gripped Gus's shoulders and pulled himself up until their faces almost touched.

"She's there. In the guest house, Señor Morton. My Maria! I couldn't get her out." He stopped as if he couldn't go on, his face contorted. "She was turning down Miss Allison's bed," he continued, shuddering. "I went to help her. There was a big explosion. Fire. Fire everywhere. And Maria! Maria screaming. Screaming for me! I couldn't help her. My Maria! Oh, my poor Maria!" Albert collapsed back onto the gurney.

"You have to leave, mister," the attendant said to Gus. "We got to get this man to the hospital."

"Come on, boss," said Charlie, who was at Gus's side as soon as he stepped out of the ambulance. "You got to take it easy. Everybody's doing all they can."

"You look so pale, Uncle Gus," said Allison. "Why don't you sit down?"

Gus reached into his pocket for his silver pill case. As he started to shake out a pill, the case slipped from his hand. Allison watched in horror as he clutched his chest, as if he had been struck by a fist, and fell to the ground. Within moments, ambulance attendants and highway patrolmen surrounded him, struggling to revive him. The next thing Allison knew, she was in an ambulance, kneeling next to him. Gus was conscious now, shuddering and sweating, his head rolling from side to side, sounds of agony welling up from his throat. As they raced toward town, Gus clung to Allison's hand. She was his lifeline. He seemed to be trying to speak. Allison bent over him, straining to hear. His speech was distorted and it was difficult to understand him, but in the slow march of seconds that seemed like hours, she began to piece together his words. "I have to tell you . . . what happened. I promised. Secret. I have to tell you. You were so small. I dreamed."

"What is it, Uncle Gus? Tell me!" cried Allison. "I'm right here."

Gus's lips started to move again, but before he could say another word, his hand tightened in hers. As certainly as if a bell had tolled, Allison knew then that she had lost him and that she was alone.

31

The only light in Gus Morton's library came from the fireplace, where the wood was now reduced to a few red embers, and from a small desk lamp on the other side of the room. It was late. Diana, Ben, and Charlie had all gone home and Allison had talked with Cynthia for the last time that day, once more insisting that her friend not fly out for Gus's funeral. The service would be held the following afternoon on a bluff overlooking his beach house at Trancas. He had left explicit instructions on how he wanted the service to be: who was to be invited (fewer than a hundred close friends, clients, and associates), who should speak (Oscar Buckman, Ben Wildman, and Allison, if she wanted to), and who should be excluded (the press). A year later, on the first anniversary of his death, he wanted a big bash. A party at Spago for three hundred, rival agents included. Champagne, dinner, and dancing. A remembrance—and a celebration of the business. A real party.

From her vantage point in the huge, overstuffed chair that had been her uncle's favorite, Allison stared at the fireplace, taking long swallows of scotch from a glass that was now almost empty. Was this her third drink? Or her fourth? It didn't matter. She had been drinking compulsively all evening, even through dinner, in an effort to blunt the rawness of her feelings. It hadn't worked. Not one bit. She still felt as empty as an airplane hangar, and the ache that pressed in on her from all sides as if she were being squeezed by some huge, malevolent hand had grown so familiar that it seemed as if she had borne it all her life. And yet, the time that had elapsed since Gus had died was not a matter of weeks or days but of hours, for at this time not quite forty-eight hours earlier they had been at La Paloma, drinking, eating, and joking. She winced as she thought of it and without realizing what she was doing slid her right hand over the face of her watch to keep herself from observing, morbidly, the precise minute in time that he had died two days ago. So many painful landmarks of this kind were yet to come. This time last week, this time last month, this time last year . . .

The tall man who sat opposite her in the room stubbed out a cigarette and lit another. Allison looked toward him at the sound his lighter made as he clicked it shut.

"I thought you gave up cigarettes, Parker. Smoking out here is crazy. Everybody coughs just from the air, even on a good day," she said, getting up to pour another shot of whiskey into her glass.

"I did quit," said Parker Welles, then he gave a short laugh. "But here I am, at it again. Did Gus ever tell you about the time he left me behind in Tahoe? We were standing on the tarmac waiting for the plane to taxi over, when he asked me to go inside and call the office, and then as I walked back outside I saw the plane taking off. Whoosh! Just like that. I couldn't believe it. I was still standing there, my mouth hanging open, when it came around again and landed. And you know what Gus said to me? 'Parker,' he said, 'I've warned you for the last time to stop smoking. I've got enough to take care of without adding your family to my responsibilities. And you know too damn many of my secrets for me to start telling them to someone else. So, the next time you decide to take up smoking again, I'll leave you watching our contrail with your ass on the ground in some place like Timbuktu. And I'm not kidding.' "

"He cared a lot for you, Parker," said Allison. Just as she too had begun to care for him. Though Parker had worked for her uncle for nearly twenty years as his chief financial officer, Allison had never known him well because he always worked behind the scenes, as he had on Gus's acquisitions. In the last few days, his kindness and decency had made all the difference. He listened when she had a question or when she simply wanted to talk about Gus, and he knew how to get things done. He was co-executor of the estate with her, and in choosing him Gus had shown how well he understood the quality of the man.

Allison and Parker both fell silent. The pile of embers gave a soft shudder and collapsed in upon itself.

"I still find it hard to believe it was arson," said Allison, half to herself.

"I know."

"Usually when you hear about arson, it's a disgruntled employee trying to get even. But this time there were no disgruntled employees, only loyal ones, and one of them died. Who would want to do such a thing?"

"Obviously somebody sick. But the police will find whoever did it, that I'm sure of."

"Right now, I almost don't care. Next to losing Uncle Gus, what does the house mean? Except that it killed him. If it hadn't been for the shock of that fire . . ."

"Oh, Allison," said Parker, his voice warm with sympathy, "you know that if it hadn't been the fire, it would have been something else. Gus wasn't taking care of himself."

Slumped in the chair across from her, his long legs extending lankily in front of him like a pair of oars that someone had forgotten to put away, Parker looked exhausted. Allison took another swallow of her drink and peered again into the fireplace. She thought again, as she had over and over, of what Gus had been struggling to say just before he died. There was some secret he had promised not to reveal. About something that had happened a long time ago. To her? "You were so small," he had said. What did that mean? Would she ever find out?

"There's never a right time to bring up something like this, Allison," said Parker, suddenly intruding, "but we have to talk about exactly what is in Gus's will. I've been putting this discussion off, but I can't any longer."

"That's all right, Parker," she answered, looking at him curiously. The urgency in his voice surprised her. "I don't give a damn about the money."

"Listen to me, Allie. There's an emergency board meeting set for two weeks from now, and as Gus's heir and the new head of U.T.M., you have to be prepared—"

"I told you. I don't care about the money. Being rich means nothing to me."

"That's just it, Allison. You're not rich. Far from it."

"What?" Allison managed to say after a moment.

"You heard me right, unfortunately. Everything you've inherited from Gus, literally everything, is tied into U.T.M., and Gus leveraged the company out of sight in the past year. There's an annuity set aside for Diana and a smaller one for Charlie, but your inheritance is U.T.M. *and* its debt. One misstep, maybe even one bad break, and it'll all be gone. Even your BMW is leased by the company. You're going to need every bit of ingenuity you can muster, all the luck in the world, and all the help you can get from me and from the others to hang on to the company. Specifically, to keep it out of the hands of the Frames."

"Parker, what on earth are you talking about? Do you mean Adrian Frame? That disgusting animal?"

"He's just the front man for his father. If you think the son is bad, wait until you meet the genes in an undiluted form."

"What have the Frames got to do with U.T.M.?"

Parker stood up, walked over to the chair where Allison sat and reached down and took her hand in his. "You really don't know, do you?" he asked in a gentle voice.

Allison shook her head.

"You're not going to like this, and I'm sorry to be the one to have to tell you about it," said Parker, pulling over a footstool and sitting down again. "I believe what you say, that you're the kind of woman who doesn't care much about money, and even if you did, you're smart enough to earn a handsome living on your own with no help from anyone. But you do care about the company, don't you? Because Gus cared so much for it, well, it's as if it's his legacy. A living legacy. He cared for all the people in the company in a very special way. Sort of an extended family. Well, for his own reasons—he didn't discuss this one at all with me—he allowed the Frames to buy into U.T.M. In a big, big way. They came in through StellarVue."

"Oh, my God, and he seemed so happy about that one going through," said Allison, suddenly feeling weak.

"It might make you feel a little better to hear that he knew they were behind StellarVue. It looks like they tried to hide their ownership, but they didn't fool him. It's absolutely clear from his notes that he saw through their maneuvers. I'm afraid it isn't at all clear what he intended to do about them, though. He's too smart not to have had some plan, but until we discover it or figure out something else ourselves, we're awfully vulnerable." Parker's voice trailed into silence.

"Meaning what?" asked Allison.

"Meaning they have a big position already, but, much worse, they have the option to increase it to the point of controlling the company. We've got to stop this from happening, and we don't have a lot of time to do it. If we can't pull it off, you end up with zilch and—"

"And U.T.M. goes to the Frames."

"Allie, do you have the energy to talk about this now?" asked Parker, his pale blue eyes earnestly holding her gaze. "Because if you don't, it can wait a little longer. The ice is broken, and that's what was important. I felt I had to say something."

"No, I want to talk about it now. I'm fine."

"Okay, in that case I'll heat up some water for coffee," said Parker. "It's a long story, but I promise you, I won't keep you up too late. You'll be home by eleven."

Home. Allison turned the word over in her mind as she watched Parker disappear in the direction of the kitchen. What did that word mean? Certainly it didn't have much to do with the pink Spanish house over on Creston Drive that she was living in once more. She had been back there now for almost two weeks, but it still had the air of a hotel suite. Her adorable Tonny was the only thing that gave the place any life. What was missing was Sean. Allison had been trying not to think about him, and bleak as the circumstances were, Gus's death had distracted her, but not entirely. She could not believe Sean had not called since the night he walked out. But he hadn't. There had been nothing. Just silence.

As Parker, balancing two cups of coffee, stepped through the door, Allison looked up. "Where do we begin?" she asked.

Later, much later, Allison drove slowly along Sunset toward her house. The problems that Parker had presented her with were ricocheting around in strange ways in her head, making her feel almost sick. The discovery that Adrian Frame was entangled in her life made the future even darker and more unsettling. She was too tired now, though, to sort any of it out and pushed it out of her mind.

When she arrived home and stepped through the front door, she sensed immediately that someone else was in the house. Sean! She ran into the living room and abruptly stopped.

There, ensconced in the middle of the sofa, was a woman with a mass of dyed red hair and a heavily powdered face bisected by a wet slash of vermilion lipstick.

"Mother!" Allison blurted.

The former Françoise Morton stood up unsteadily, a large tumbler of vodka in her hand.

"Come into the comfort of these arms, Allison, my precious darling. This is a time when a little girl needs her mother."

32

llison's first impulse on finding Françoise in her living room was to turn around and walk back out the front door. Her mother was not someone she needed in her life again, now or maybe ever.

"What are you doing here, Mother?" Allison finally asked.

"I'm here to take care of you, of course. It's a mother's instinct. When I heard the news I caught the very first plane I could. Come here, darling. Put your head on my shoulder and have a good cry."

"I'm pretty much cried out, Mother," said Allison dryly, nonetheless letting Françoise clasp her briefly to her sagging bosom in order to keep the peace. As soon as she could, Allison stepped back from Françoise, who made another grab for her, lost her balance, and fell back heavily onto the sofa. When she realized that the transition from standing to sitting had made her spill her drink onto the upholstery, the expression on her face collapsed as well. She looked so worn down, her features almost blending into each other like some old stuffed animal, that Allison in spite of herself felt a stirring of pity. Françoise once had been so shamelessly vain about her looks. What had happened?

"Allison dear, where are your manners?"

"What do you mean?"

"Haven't you noticed my glass? It's quite empty. I'd love a touch more." Françoise looked down at the empty glass in her hand.

"I think you've had enough," Allison answered coldly.

"Allison, I'm surprised at you. That's certainly not the way I taught you to act. Remember, I am your mother. I have also had a long, tiring flight."

"What will it be . . . Mother?"

"A double vodka on the rocks, with a splash of tonic, would be perfection. Just the tiniest of splashes," she added with a giggle. "Then again, forget the tonic. It's loaded with sugar anyway."

After she had made the drink, Allison went to the kitchen to feed

Tonny. When she returned, she poured herself a light scotch and sat down in a chair opposite Françoise.

"Thank God you got that awful dog of yours out of my sight," said Françoise. "He wouldn't leave me alone. He kept wanting to be petted."

"But he's just a puppy—" Allison began, then stopped. Why should she make excuses for the one warm, undemanding, and totally lovable creature in her life to someone who had turned her back on her years ago? Instead, she asked, with an acid edge to her voice, "How did you hear about Uncle Gus?"

"Oh, the marvelous Parker Welles telephoned me. Efficient as ever. What a pain in the ass that man always was. At all times knew where every cent of Gus's money had gone. Guarded it like he was protecting a piece of the true cross. The man's part bookkeeper and part concierge. Devoted to your uncle. And tight! Almost as bad as dear, departed Gus."

"Don't you dare speak about Uncle Gus that way," said Allison.

"Oh, pardon me, Miss Morton. Perhaps you don't recall how your beloved uncle Gus treated me all these years. He never gave me the time of day. Ever! He effectively killed my acting career. In spite of all I did for your father. Some gratitude. Frankly, I can't imagine what Teddy would have done without me. A sweet man, but weak. I don't know what possessed me to marry him, I really don't," she said, taking another swallow of her drink, a rivulet of vodka trickling down the corner of her mouth like runoff from a rain gutter.

"You damned well do know, and so do I. He was your ticket out," said Allison. "Poor Daddy." Whenever she thought of him, one scene predominated: her father doing his morning stretches—doctor's orders after his first heart attack—with herself, age six or seven, standing alongside copying his movements. And, always, one certainty about him prevailed: He had loved her, just as her mother had not. "I have trouble now remembering exactly what he looked like," said Allison, half to herself.

"Me too," said Françoise, this time taking such a deep gulp of vodka that the ice cubes in her glass clicked like castanets against her teeth.

"Well, of course," said Allison sarcastically. "He was only husband number one. The first of three that you buried."

"That's not nice, Allison. Besides, you would have liked Alain. And Rene too. Especially Rene. I can't believe it's already four months since he died."

"I'm sorry I never had the pleasure of meeting them," said Allison in a flat voice.

In fact, she wasn't the least bit sorry. When her mother had married

an elderly Swiss and moved to Geneva, Allison moved in with Uncle
Gus. She was at boarding school then and away most of the time, but it
was wonderful coming home for weekends and vacations, knowing he
would be there. He made them a real family. It took her years to come to
terms with Françoise's laissez-faire style of mothering, but her physical
absence helped. Probably the event that finally finished them off as
mother and daughter, at least in Allison's view, was Françoise's failure to
show up for her college graduation. She later explained that an appointment for a face and derriere lift with the famed "miracle fanny" doctor of
Rio had opened up at the last moment and, of course, as Allison surely
understood, she couldn't pass that up. Within a few years Françoise's
husband died and she quickly acquired another, a *pied noir* who had managed to get most of his money out of Algeria before the roof fell in.

"Are you going to Uncle Gus's service?" asked Allison.

"No, I wasn't invited."

"How did you get into the house?"

"Your cleaning woman. I met her as she was leaving. She showed me
where you hide the key. In case I ever need it again, she said. Very ac-
commodating. I'm sure she's a wonderful daughter to *her* mother. But
what I can't understand is why you don't have full-time help. I would if I
were you. At least two maids. Plus a cook. And a gardener."

"Mother, why are you here?" Allison asked.

"I told you. I was worried about you."

"No, I don't think so. What's the real reason?"

Françoise stalled, by taking one last swallow of her drink. She
seemed to be having trouble focusing. "Parker told me Gus didn't leave
me anything in his will," she said. "He sounded so pleased, the bastard.
Couldn't wait to give me the news. Not that I was surprised, but I am
worried about my checks."

"What checks?"

"Oh, didn't you know? Gus sent me a little contribution the first of
every month. When Teddy died, he made a deathbed promise to look
after me. Believe me, he wouldn't have thought of it all by himself."

"How much did he send you?"

"Five thousand. Well, don't look so shocked," said Françoise at Allison's expression of disbelief. "It's not as if that's enough for a person to
live on decently."

"I wouldn't call sixty thousand a year pin money. You truly disgust
me, Mother. Letting Uncle Gus support you even after you remarried.
What was wrong with your two husbands? Couldn't they have footed
your bills?"

"It wasn't their fault they weren't rich."

"Rich like me, you mean?"

"Yes, exactly," said Françoise, her voice slurring.

"Look at you, Mother," said Allison, jumping up in irritation. "You're in no shape to discuss anything. You should be in bed." Allison reached down to give Françoise a hand up, but she was dead weight.

"No, no, let's talk."

"Not now, Mother, but rest assured you've made yourself perfectly clear. You want me to take over from Uncle Gus, don't you?" Allison stared at her mother, who had shut her eyes. "Don't you?" she demanded a second time. But Françoise, her mission accomplished, had passed out. Allison maneuvered her into a sleeping position, threw a blanket over her, and retreated upstairs to her bedroom.

Early the next morning, while Françoise slept, Allison escaped from the house back to the peace of her uncle's, where she sat in the library, writing notes and answering condolence calls, keeping busy until Parker arrived. The service for Gus later in the afternoon was all that he could have wished for and, to Allison's gratitude, blessedly brief. Afterward she let Charlie drive her from Trancas back to Creston Drive to finish the conversation with Françoise that had begun the night before. The sooner she got it over with, the better.

In between swallows of inky black coffee and long, deep drags on her Gauloise cigarettes, Françoise tearfully explained why she needed Allison's help. She had gone into debt gambling in Evian-les-Bains and was afraid she would lose her house in Lausanne.

"After Rene died, I was so lonely I started going to the casinos for company. Everybody there was so friendly."

"I bet. So friendly you couldn't live without them."

"Yes, that's exactly it," said Françoise, not catching the irony in Allison's voice. "Only the chemin-de-fer table wasn't very nice."

"All right, Mother. I'll bail you out, but only this once. After that, you're on your own. How much is this 'problem'?"

"Just forty thousand. Dollars, that is."

"I'll try to get the money for you before you leave," said Allison. She had money left over from what her uncle had given her to buy and furnish her loft. She would manage.

"But what about my checks?"

"What about them? When I'm ready to put someone on a monthly retainer, I'll look elsewhere, thank you very much."

"Well, thank *you,*" said Françoise nastily. "At least I know where I stand with my daughter now."

"What can I say, Mother? You're a fine one to talk. Have you forgotten the disappearing act you played with me? Disappearing from my life, if you need it spelled out. But," she said when there was no flicker of response in Françoise's eyes, "don't strain yourself to remember. Let's get back to more important things. I'm obviously not going to let you starve. Tell me what your needs are and I'll work out some kind of budget for you, though you can forget about playing at the tables. It turns out I'm not so rich after all, certainly not rich enough to pick up any more gambling tabs."

"Allison, darling, I'm through with casinos, I promise," said Françoise, assuming a sweetly contrite expression now that she had been offered at least some of what she had come for. "But do you think you could make me one small, tiny loan right now? I've always heard how marvelous La Costa is. I'd love to spend a few days there. It would be an awful waste not to, being just up the road from it, so to speak."

It took Allison no time at all to say yes. Getting Françoise out of the way and out of her hair was the best gift she could make to herself.

The next day, Allison's first as chairman and chief executive officer of Universal Talent Management, she felt as if she were walking on the moon. The familiar was now so bizarrely unfamiliar that it was as if she had never been there before. Though Gus had talked to her many times about how one day she would inherit and run the agency herself, it had been fantasy talk. Now that she actually was in his office, sitting in his leather chair—she had moved into the office immediately as a morale booster for the staff, though it nearly did her in emotionally—she felt so unprepared for the job that she was queasy and light-headed from tension.

Everyone was being terribly helpful, even Lee Simons. After Allison had approved a release announcing the change at the top and spoken briefly and, she hoped, reassuringly to the entire staff (it was to be business as usual, and she and Gus—in spirit—were counting on them), the department heads came in one by one to report on the agency's major clients and their projects. A few of them, like Lavinia Tedesco and Felix Godwin, now living together in Carmel and collaborating on the play about her marriage, had been tracked by Allison herself, but many others were little more than names to her. How was she going to catch up? All those months spent in New York and then accompanying Gus on buying trips had kept her away from the heart of the agency, and now, for a while anyway, she wouldn't be able to afford the time to get much closer. Staving off a Frame takeover had top priority. Otherwise there wouldn't be anything to catch up on.

After a quick lunch at her desk and time out to look over Ben's shoulder at the latest rushes from a Chip Taylor movie that the agency had packaged and that had about it the feel of a mega hit, Allison sat down to finish her most important calls to the East Coast. Then she would have to tackle the financial profiles Parker had drawn up for her on the new companies. She had been pushing these papers around on her desk all day, but she could not postpone looking at them any longer. Tomorrow morning they were having their first meeting on which of these companies were the easiest sell. They had no choice but to sell, so Parker said.

She was about to ask Neal to dial Hal Gilliam in the New York office when Lee Simons leaned into the office.

"There's something else I wanted to tell you about Mona Lacey and the Hauser deal," said Lee. "Got a moment?"

"Oh, sure," said Allison reluctantly. "Come on in and sit down." Not that Lee needed an invitation. She already had settled herself on the sofa.

As she listened to Lee, Allison wondered if it was really necessary for her to hear these details now. She looked deliberately at her watch and then back at Lee.

"That's it," said Lee. She started to stand up, but then she paused. "Do you miss him?" she asked after a beat.

Allison, aghast, stared at Lee, unable to respond. She had just buried her uncle. What did Lee think? "Of course," she finally said. "Terribly."

"Well, you know, sometimes these things are for the best. If he hadn't left, you wouldn't have wanted to come to L.A., and the whole transition would have been so much tougher for you. And cheer up, darling. I'll find you a new man. I promise."

The bitch, thought Allison, watching Lee's back until she turned a corner and disappeared. The perfect bitch. Today was the first day she had spent any time alone with Lee since Sean had walked out that night, and she should have guessed Lee couldn't leave it alone. She didn't care what kind of job Allison was doing. Not at all. Whenever she thought about their telephone conversation that night, Allison felt embarrassed, humiliated, and just plain angry. Lee wasn't a friend. How could she have poured out her soul to her that way? She needed a real friend to talk to. Somebody like Cynthia. Why was she still sticking it out in New York when Tom Rosen was here? Maybe, just maybe, she could be persuaded to move here herself.

Allison sighed, leaned back in the chair, and ran her fingers through her hair. She had to get back to work. She had meant what she had said to the group she had gathered together that morning. Gus was counting on them, just as he was counting on *her*. She had to make it work. She had to succeed.

Shortly after lunch on her fourth day as head of the agency, Allison held a meeting in her office with Ben, Sam Fine, a senior agent in the television department, and a client he was desperately wooing, the Reverend C. J. Horace.

The reverend, a telegenic Fundamentalist, was the host of the year's most popular syndicated talk show, *God Knows!*, which had recently eclipsed both Donahue and Oprah. Though the show's daily topics were mirror images of his competitors'—Fetishes in the Suburbs, Women Who Submit, Couch or Confession?—his frequent references to "the Lord" and "the American spirit" made the show's content seem racy by comparison. The minister, who knew Nielsen ratings and audience demographics as well as Leviticus and Deuteronomy, was interviewing U.T.M. for possible representation. He had been at both William Morris and I.C.M. for short intervals and was now seeking a new agency that combined both sharp show-business heads (read: Jewish) and unassailable moral rectitude (read: no substance abuse or excessive jewelry). To sign him would show the rest of the business that U.T.M. could still attract important clients, get the agency into an area of representation they hadn't been in before, and, most important, show that Allison was in control and leading the company.

The meeting started out well, with the reverend asking a series of pointed questions about the agency's expertise in syndication sales, which Allison and Ben answered with authority and succinctness, having prepared themselves fully the day before in a session that lasted more than an hour.

"I have some ideas for other shows, Miss Morton. All, of course, with a strong Christian sensibility. What are your strengths in packaging such programming?"

"I don't want to be boastful, Reverend Horace, but I think—" The intercom buzzed jarringly on Allison's desk. "Excuse me," she said as she picked up the receiver. "I said no interruptions, Neal."

"It's your mother," said her secretary. "She's out here and insists on coming in—"

"Tell her to wait," Allison said in an even tone that belied her anger.

"You were asking about our ability to package new programming in your area," she said, turning her attention back to the minister. "I'm glad you raised that question. Ben and I have worked up a client list of writers, directors—"

The heavy oak door leading to the outer office opened and in reeled Françoise Morton Bernard Bissette.

"It's not nice to keep a mother waiting, my dear daughter," she slurred, leaning, or more accurately bracing herself, against Allison's desk. "La Costa was . . . too exhausting. They want you to be doing something all the time. Can you imagine me playing volleyball!"

"Mother," said Allison, as she clasped Françoise by the elbow and started to lead her to the door, "I'll see you in a few minutes."

"Don't you say hello anymore, Ben?" she asked, spinning away from Allison's grasp. "If I was a little younger and of a different sex I'm sure you'd be more attentive."

A look of horror swept across Ben's face.

"I think," said the Reverend C. J. Horace, rising from his chair, "that it would be better for you, Miss Morton, to straighten out your domestic difficulties before we talk again. No need to call me. I'll call you. Thank you," he reached out to shake hands with the two men and with Allison, "for giving me your time. Perhaps someday we'll do something together. And, madam," he addressed Françoise, "there is great comfort to be had in the arms of Christ."

"Thanks for the advice, Padre. But that's not the set of arms I'm looking for right now."

One of the ways to dull the pain and to get back to something resembling normal sleep, Allison realized almost as soon as she got back to work, was to start exercising again. So she had Charlie take her each morning at six-thirty to an advanced aerobics class. And then, because it was on the way to the office, he would drive her to Duke's, where Allison had an extra-large orange juice and french toast. She had been following this routine for almost a week when she ran into Diana.

"Do you mind if I join you?" asked Diana, as she walked up to Allison's table, carrying her breakfast.

"Of course not. Please do."

For a minute the two sat in silence, studiously eating their food, not knowing what to say.

"Do you come here often?" Allison finally asked.

"About as often as you go to Georgette Klinger when you're in New York," Diana answered with a sad smile. "I hope you'll give me more of a chance to talk than I gave you that day. I was awful to you then."

All Allison could do was reach across the table and take hold of Diana's hand. This was the woman her uncle had loved. The thought of him cracked open her feelings again.

"I miss Uncle Gus so much," Allison said with a wrench of pain.

"The thing I wasn't able to accept was that we *both* loved him so much," continued Diana. "I've wanted to talk to you ever since that conversation of ours. I rehearsed what I was going to say to you again and again and now it all seems so false. Just believe me when I say I'm sorry for everything I've said and everything that I haven't said all these years. I've lost the man I loved. And so have you. But we can't lose each other. Do you think we can be friends?"

"There's nothing I want more, Diana."

"I haven't been in the office since . . . What I mean is, I'd like to continue. Maybe not full-time and not for that long. Gus left me some money, and I think I'd like to travel. But I believe I can help you right now."

"You have no idea how much I would like that."

"Actually," Diana said with a small laugh, "I brought my briefcase with me. I thought I might as well start today."

"If you didn't drive yourself here, we could ride together to the office with Charlie. There's so much I want to ask you."

"Well, in fact I did take a taxi here and was hoping you'd say that."

"Come on then," said Allison.

"There's one more thing I wanted to say."

"What's that?" Allison asked.

"If you need any help with Françoise, feel free to come to me. She's come by to see me a couple of times, and frankly I'm worried about her. She's drinking more than ever and her mood swings seem to be getting more severe all the time. I don't know if I can help much, but I want you to know I'm here if you need me."

A few minutes later, arm in arm, the two women walked out of the restaurant and, as Charlie held open the door, into the white Rolls.

·　■　·

The following Monday, after the gossips in the business had finally finished dishing the scene at U.T.M. with Reverend C. J. Horace—it had to be her own agent, Sam Fine, who had leaked the story, and she would wait for the right time to deal with him—Allison had a business lunch at Le Dome with Parker Welles and three bankers. The selloffs aside, U.T.M. was going to need some additional financing soon, and Parker decided it wouldn't hurt to have Allison meet (and impress) the bankers in the area who didn't have any prejudice about dealing with a talent agency. The three men ranged in age from forty to sixty. They all looked as if they had surfed at one time and all of them lived in or near Pasadena. Their questions were not as pointed as she had expected; they seemed intended simply to assess whether this young woman had what it took to run a business like U.T.M. They were just finishing their first course—chicken croquettes for the bankers, salads for Allison and Parker—and everything was going perfectly when the waiter came by with a bottle of champagne.

"We didn't order that," Parker told the waiter.

"I know, sir," the waiter answered. "It's from that lady over there." He nodded in the direction of a table in the corner. Allison turned and saw Françoise waving at them. But that wasn't what chilled her to the bone. What caused that feeling was the sight of her mother's lunch companion, Adrian Frame.

"Excuse me, gentlemen. I'll be right back," said Allison, as she stood up and walked quickly to the table across the room.

"What a nice surprise," said Adrian Frame when Allison reached the table. "I hope you'll share a libation with us. Your mother was just telling me what a charmer you were as a child. Of course, that comes as no surprise."

"Mother, what are you doing here?" asked Allison, ignoring Frame. The last time she had seen him, she had left him lying on the floor of the disgusting club he had taken her to.

"Just having lunch with a friend. Is there something wrong with that, Allison?"

"Yes. In this case there's a lot wrong with that. Don't you have any idea what he and his father are trying to do to the company?"

"All I know is that Adrian was good enough to send me an airline ticket to the States. Not economy, but first-class. And that when he and his father have some say in it, there will be acting roles waiting for me at U.T.M. It'll be quite a change from what my brother-in-law did for me . . . and my daughter."

"I want you out of my house by tomorrow," Allison said in a hoarse whisper. "I'm sure you'll have no problem finding accommodations with such good friends as this. Goodbye."

"It's a pity that a woman so attractive as you can also be so uncivil," said Adrian Frame. "You'd have much more fun here with us, I assure you. Those gentlemen you're dining with have already—how should I say it?—committed themselves to our side. So enjoy your lunch, but don't pick up the check. It's the least they can do for you." Adrian concluded with a loud laugh that made everyone in the restaurant turn, and Françoise laughed along with him.

The first bills arrived a week later. A hat from Giorgio's for $387 and two pair of boots from Gucci for over $1,100. The next day brought bills from Robinson's and Saks that totalled almost $3,000. They were all for items that had been delivered to the Beverly Hills Hotel. All had been signed for by Françoise and charged to Allison's accounts. So furious that she thought she'd have difficulty speaking, Allison dialed the hotel herself and asked for Françoise.

"Madame Bissette is at her cabana. She's not taking any calls right now," said the operator.

That does it! Allison thought, slamming down the phone. Although she had a staff meeting in an hour, she left the office immediately and, telling Charlie to step on it, arrived at the hotel in under ten minutes.

The pool at the Beverly Hills Hotel was set below the main building. Flanking its outer edge was a row of tall, regal palms that stood like a praetorian guard, their tops showing only the merest suggestion of a breeze. Allison headed straight for the cabanas that faced the hotel. The pool area was populated by a battalion of middle-aged, overweight executives, oiled like Channel swimmers and bejeweled like Vegas lounge acts, all talking on telephones stationed by their chaises. Françoise, wearing a bikini that Allison might have worn while sunning alone on her deck, was stretched out in one of the cabanas, nose slathered with white zinc ointment, eyes protected by a white plastic guard. A bottle of Moët in an ice bucket stood next to her. Allison noticed an empty bottle inside the cabana.

"Mother, you're out of your mind if you think I'm going to pay those bills. I don't care if the stores take the clothes off your back. You're not going to take advantage of me that way."

"Why, hello, Allison," said Françoise, slowly removing her eye guard and squinting up at her daughter. "What a lovely greeting to receive from one's only child."

"Don't try too hard for a put-down, Mother, because it just won't wash. These bills of yours are the first I've heard of you since you left my house. The only reason I know anything about what you've been doing is because I read the columns. You and Adrian Frame out together, first a premiere, then some party. Don't you realize that he and his father are trying to steal U.T.M. away from me? That's right, *steal* it. It took Uncle Gus a lifetime to build the company."

"What I realize is that Adrian is a delightful *and* generous man. If you had any sense at all, you'd be interested in him. If there was any part of me in you, you'd understand what I'm saying."

"What do you mean by that?"

"You're just like your father. Idealistic, head in the clouds. Sit down with Adrian. He'll make a deal with you. You'll be able to keep some of the money that's tied up in the company. You have the chance of living a comfortable life. You don't need the frustrations and tensions of running a business."

"You still can memorize lines, Mother. Is there anything else Adrian told you to tell me?"

"Yes. If you persist in fighting for the company, he'll wipe you out. It seems a rather simple decision to me."

"To you it would be."

"What's your answer?"

"Oh, so you're the messenger, too. Adrian wants you to report back to him, does he?"

"You sound just like Gus. He never thought much of me either."

"My uncle was the finest person I've ever known. And he was loved, too! By lots of people."

"Every other word out of your mouth is Gus!" Françoise sneered. "Get it into your head that he's dead. You can't run that company the way he did. And who are you to think you can do a better job of it than Adrian? And he's a much better person than you think he is. He's treated me with more kindness than either Gus or you ever did. Who do you think is paying for all this?" She waved a slack, fleshy arm around the cabana and then toward the hotel. "I never thought you'd begrudge me a few things for my wardrobe, but age can still bring surprises."

"There's a saying, Mother, that you're going to force me to use," said Allison, the anger in her voice barely under control.

"And what's that, dear," Françoise responded.

Allison paused just long enough to get her mother's full attention, then she spoke. "The friends of my enemy are my enemy."

33

François unexpectedly appeared in Allison's life again the following week, heralded by the buzz of the office intercom. Allison was annoyed to hear it. She had asked Neal not to disturb her unless it was something very important. She, Parker Welles, and the other top financial people at the agency were discussing strategies to use against the Frames at the board meeting, now only a week away. The "important" telephone call turned out to be from Françoise.

"How are you, Allison?"

"I'm fine, Mother. Just a little busy, that's all."

"Thanks for taking my call," Françoise said without a trace of sarcasm. "I'm phoning to ask a favor."

"Adrian stop paying the bills?" Allison asked flippantly, then immediately regretted saying it.

"As a matter of fact he has," Françoise answered with a sniffle. "I was told by the manager of the Beverly Hills that I have to be out by tomorrow. Luckily, I have my return ticket to Lausanne. I'm leaving tonight."

"Can I see you before you leave?" Allison asked, surprising herself with the question. She hadn't intended for things to turn out so badly between herself and Françoise and had been thinking about making a peace overture. This might be her only chance.

"All right, Allison," said Françoise after a moment. "There are some things I need to talk to you about. I've been meaning to for a while."

"When would you like to meet?"

"How about six o'clock. My flight's at ten."

"Shall I come to the hotel?"

"That sort of brings me back to the favor. . . . Could we meet at your place?"

"Of course."

"Would it be okay if I went over a bit earlier? I want to look for an earring I think I dropped somewhere in your house. It was an anniversary gift from your father."

"Sure. Go over anytime you like. The key's in—"

"I know where it is," said Françoise with a laugh.

Allison planned to leave the office at five, but a series of phone calls from investment bankers in New York delayed her departure by half an hour. Since she kept her car at the office, she decided to drive herself home. Then, if things went well between them, she could drive Françoise to the airport. It would give them more time to talk. Though Charlie looked absolutely forlorn when she told him she would not need him that evening, she promised he could pick her up the next morning.

As Allison pulled up in her driveway, she reached up to the visor and pressed the electronic garage-door opener. Nothing happened. She hit the switch again. Still nothing. She had never had trouble with the mechanism before. She took out her house keys and walked up the path to the front door.

"Mother, it's me," she called out, spotting Françoise's jacket and handbag on the chair in the hall next to her suitcases.

There was no answer. She stepped into the living room, reaching down to pet Tonny, who was jumping up on her skirt and shaking all over with the pleasure of seeing her. A copy of *Vogue* lay folded open on the coffee table next to a tall, half-empty glass. "Mother?" Allison called again, puzzled. Then she heard a sound that had not registered on her at first, a sound that was alien to the house. She stood still, frowning in concentration. It seemed to be coming from somewhere beyond the kitchen. And then she knew what it was.

"Oh, my God," she said to herself. As Tonny scrambled out of her way, Allison ran, moving as fast as she could to keep one step ahead of the panic building wildly within her. It was the sound of a car engine. It had to be the little blue Jeep she had bought to use at the beach. It could only mean . . . *No!* she thought, refusing to carry the idea any further.

She yanked open the door that led from the pantry to the garage. A wave of carbon monoxide so powerful that it almost knocked her down poured out. She gasped for breath. There didn't seem to be anyone slumped inside the Jeep, thank God, but she had to cut the engine off fast.

Holding her hand over her mouth, she reached into the car and turned off the ignition, but the poisoned air, like some hellish fog, still swirled around her. Coughing and gagging, she edged past the Jeep to the front of the garage to pull open the door. She grabbed the handle, but before she could do anything, she froze. Something on the floor pressed against her leg. She forced herself to look down. On the floor, wedged between the front of the Jeep and the garage door, was a body lying face down.

Allison jerked the door upward and sun flooded the gloomy interior. The noxious air spilled out and instantly dissipated into the peerless blue sky. Allison breathed deeply to clear her head, and then, as if another person were willing her movements, knelt down and looked at Françoise. She turned the body over and stared into her mother's lifeless eyes, as dull as coins that have been handled too much. Allison was still screaming when the first police car arrived.

"Do you think you can take a few more questions?" asked Tom Rosen, steepling his hands thoughtfully as he returned to the living room with the two detectives.

Allison looked up at him. His large face was pulled down with concern and his soft brown eyes showed compassion. After the police had arrived and she had pointed them toward the body, she had had the presence of mind to telephone Cynthia, and it was Cynthia who sent Tom racing over to her house only half an hour behind the two homicide detectives. As luck had it, Tom knew them both, and it was his presence at her side that was enabling her to help the detectives piece together the sequence of events that had caused Françoise to take her life, for it was, the detectives assured her, a clear case of suicide.

The detectives had questioned her earlier about Françoise's activities in Los Angeles, whom she had seen and what her state of mind had been. The short one was dark and named Damico. His heavyset partner, who sweated constantly, was Emerson.

"We've rounded the clubhouse turn, Miss Morton. Just want to go over a few more things, and it's a wrap," said Damico. Emerson eased himself into an armchair and wiped his brow with an already damp handkerchief.

"The lab boys will be finished pretty soon, too. It's standard stuff. There's no question what happened," continued Damico. "Will you be staying—"

"Ms. Morton will be staying in Bel-Air tonight, Vinnie. I gave Chick the address and phone number. I'll be staying there too," said Tom, who stood in a corner.

"Sure, Tom."

"The key, Vinnie?" asked Emerson, as he ran his handkerchief down inside his shirt.

"Yeah. The key," said Damico almost to himself. "Where do you generally keep the key to the Jeep?"

"One was on the ring with the emergency house keys and the other was in an ashtray on the desk in my bedroom."

"Your mother knew where you kept them?"

"No. I mean, yes. She knew where I kept the house keys."

"Did she give you any indication when you spoke to her this afternoon that she was . . . in this depressed a state?" asked Emerson.

"No. What I mean is, she wasn't exactly happy, but I never would have thought she would do this."

"We haven't been able to find a note," Damico said almost as an afterthought.

"That's not unusual, Ms. Morton," Emerson quickly added. "There's an outside possibility that your mother might have mailed one to you. Or maybe she hid it here somewhere. What I'm saying is, if you find one, please give us a call. Police work is eighty percent keeping tidy folders, and it would be important for us to have a copy. Only a copy."

The questions, which had seemed to have as much pattern as a Jackson Pollock canvas, continued for another few minutes before the two detectives quietly said good night. Tom walked them out to their car, a beat-up gray Oldsmobile, its floor carpeted with junk-food wrappers. "Still feel comfortable with your first call?" he asked.

Damico looked at Emerson, who nodded.

"It's as straightforward as a piece of toast," said Damico. "It's just your friend's tough luck that the old girl decided to take the carbon mono trip instead of touring Knott's Berry Farm or some other sightseeing spot. It's another *Appointment in Samarra* number. Most everything is."

"Jesus," said Emerson loudly, "ever since you started going to night school, I can't understand a fucking word you say."

"Fate, Chick. Fate. It crawls up everyone's ass sooner or later."

"What about the bruise on her head, Vinnie?" Tom asked.

"The booze probably had her a little shaky to begin with. She decided a little too far into it that it might be a bad idea. Went to open the garage door and did a half-gainer to the cement. This thing is pretty open-and-shut. Like painting by the numbers. We see a lot of them."

Tom nodded.

"I'll check out the names the young lady gave me, the people her mother saw here. Any surprises and I'll be back to you. We'll have the results on the blood tests tomorrow. I'm betting they'll be eighty—no, ninety proof."

Emerson started the car.

"I want to thank you guys for the way you handled Allison," said Tom. "She's my girl's best friend. Really a great kid."

"Easy to see," said Emerson.

"She the agent's daughter, Tom? You know, the famous one that died recently."

"Niece. She runs the thing now. It's a big business."

"My wife's father bought it last month," said Emerson, as he put the car into gear, "and all she got was a sixth of a share in a Carvel ice cream stand. Would you call that *Appointment in . . .* What the hell was it, Vinnie?"

"*Samarra,* Chick. Maybe. But I don't think O'Hara had your father-in-law buying it from a bad ticker in mind. The kind of fate he was—"

"Here we go, Tom. Another session in Lit. 203 with Professor Damico. Vinnie, our next appointment is with something called Burger King. Now give me a break for a while. Okay?"

The car backed out of the driveway.

"See what I have to put up with, Tom," said Damico, leaning out the car window. "Chick's a philistine. Throw away the law degree, counselor. You'd pass the cop exam in a walk. The two of us would make a beautiful team."

That night, lying in bed in her old bedroom at Gus's house, Allison couldn't stop going over the circumstances of Françoise's death. She literally could not believe she was dead. Françoise just did not seem like the type who would kill herself. But this kind of reasoning was probably fatuous. Who could speak confidently of "types"? Besides, what did she know about Françoise's real life? Only the couple of things Françoise had told her, and maybe those things had not been so much true as calculated to play on her heartstrings, or, more accurately, loosen her purse strings. Françoise certainly had been scrappy enough since she had arrived in L.A. (God knows she had caused enough trouble for Allison!), but maybe that had been only bravado. Drunken bravado. The drinking was a wild card, which made everything hard to read.

The one question about Françoise's suicide that made Allison acutely uncomfortable was whether she had played a part in causing it. Maybe she had helped tip Françoise into it. That last time she had seen her mother, she had called her an enemy. How could she have?

"Be fair to yourself, Allie," Cynthia had said to her on the phone. "Maybe you *were* too uptight about her. Maybe you overreacted, but that doesn't mean you had anything to do with what happened. Remember that. Please. Don't punish yourself. It wasn't your fault." But no matter what Cynthia said, the idea still haunted her.

Allison wasn't sure what time it was when she drifted into sleep, but the next morning came too quickly. She had decided to move into her uncle's house immediately, even though it would be painful at first. Charlie would drive her over to her house to pick up enough clothes for the next few days. Later, when she was less upset about Françoise's death, she would go back and collect more of her belongings. Albert had gone to Mexico for Maria's burial and was not going to return, so she would hire her housekeeper, Ernestine, to clean for her at Gus's house and walk the dog. Before long, she supposed, she would put her own house on the market.

After she had assured Tom Rosen that she was okay and he had left for his office, Allison sadly contemplated the small, poignant pile of personal papers she had removed from Françoise's purse the night before. Passport, driver's license, two credit cards, three or four worn-looking cards from Lausanne shops, and a single photograph—a creased snapshot of Françoise arm in arm with a small, bearded man wearing an overcoat that was too long on him. Rene Bissette? There was no plane ticket to Lausanne. Had she been planning to pick it up at the airport? Or could it be that there had been no ticket at all, no intention to return?

When the doorbell rang shortly after nine, Allison knew it would either be Charlie, with the car, or Parker, who had volunteered to make the necessary calls to Switzerland to settle Françoise's affairs. It was Charlie.

"Do you mind if I come in for a moment, Allison?" he asked in a serious voice.

"Of course not," she said, holding the door open. "Do you want a cup of coffee?"

Charlie shook his head, and after Allison sank down into her uncle's armchair he took a seat opposite her. "I haven't talked with you about the boss since he died. I don't know how to begin to say—"

"I know how you felt about Uncle Gus," said Allison gently.

"He was the most decent human being I've ever known. From the day I met him until the day he died, he always looked out for me. Did you ever hear how he saved my life?"

"Yes, Charlie."

"Well, I've thought a lot about that over the years, and the way I like to put it to myself is that the boss didn't just save my life. He *gave* me a life. And I don't mean a job. He gave me his friendship. The best thing that ever happened to me was meeting him. If we hadn't've been assigned to the same army unit, I never would have." Charlie looked at Allison with an expression of disbelief. "Wouldn't that have been something?"

"I know what you mean," said Allison. She knew Charlie had to let out his feelings about Gus, but it hurt her to listen.

"You know the boss left me something in his will, don't you? I knew he would remember me, but I still can't get used to the idea of being well-off. I don't ever have to work again—I could live comfortably for the rest of my life—but, Allison, I'd still like to work for you. Would that be all right?"

"Of course, Charlie. I was hoping you'd want to. I need you." She was touched by his wish, or maybe *honored* was a better way of putting it, since it was another form of tribute to Gus. "We'll work out something. Don't worry."

"Thanks. This has been some awful time for you, hasn't it?" He leaned back for a moment and shut his eyes, then sat up again. "You know, I knew your mother for a long time."

"Why, yes, I know," said Allison. She knew he had disliked Françoise, quietly but intensely, and was surprised that he seemed to want to talk about her.

"There's something I have to tell you. Something that may make you feel better." He stopped suddenly, reluctant to go on.

"Yes, Charlie. What is it?" asked Allison. She sensed that whatever it was Charlie was about to say was the real reason he had come to speak with her.

"It's something they always kept from you. I don't know why. But . . . but I think you should know it now."

"What, Charlie?"

"You shouldn't feel so bad about Françoise. You see, she wasn't your real mother. You were adopted."

34

You know how people sometimes say, 'I remember it as if it was yesterday'? Well, that's the way I feel about the day I drove the boss and Teddy out to the airport to pick you up. Teddy and Françoise had just lost a baby. A boy. It was born with some kind of heart problem. They never even got to bring it home from the hospital. I didn't see much of Françoise then so I don't know how she took it, but your dad was wiped out. He wanted that baby so much, and then when it died, I almost thought he wasn't going to make it. I've never seen anyone so depressed, but the boss came to the rescue. He always knew what strings to pull, and he sure did that time. He found you.

"When he called me that morning and told me to pick him up at ten, he didn't tell me why or where we were going. Afterward I thought it was because he was superstitious. He didn't want to blow the deal by talking about it. I was doing a lot of odds and ends for the boss then, so I didn't ask questions.

"I arrived in front of the office on the dot of ten, and the two of them jumped into the backseat before I had a chance to get out and open the door for them. This was before the boss got our first Rolls, by the way. The car was a Cadillac Eldorado. Big maroon job. Lots of chrome. Fins that stood up so high you could hang your wash out to dry on them.

"The boss told me to head out to LaGuardia. It was a cold, nasty day, and almost as soon as we got over the Triboro, it started raining. I was thinking about the races at Aqueduct that afternoon. I had placed a pretty heavy bet with my bookie on a horse that didn't like a sloppy track. I couldn't decide whether to cancel or not. I wanted to get my mind off it, so I started listening to the conversation in the backseat. The boss and Teddy were talking about some piece of business, but it was obvious something else was on their minds. You could feel it. It was like they were going off to make the biggest deal of their lives. They were all keyed up.

"The boss told me to turn off before LaGuardia. At the Marine Air

Terminal. You know the place. Where we keep the company plane. But there were no corporate planes in those days. Or hardly any. The place still looks like it belongs in a small town, not New York. The boss said we were meeting someone, but there was plenty of time for me to go get a cup of coffee. I bought the *Mirror* and chatted up the gal at the counter, who was a ringer for Jane Wyman. I mean it. I would have hung around there a lot longer, but she got busy, so I went back to check in with the boss.

"They were just where I left them, looking through one of the big windows at the action on the field. The place was busy as the devil. Small planes landing every few minutes. Just as I came up behind them, I heard the boss say to your father, 'There's the plane.'

"A Piper Cub had just taxied up. The door opened. One of the ground crew rolled some steps over and a tall man in a dark suit appeared. He was holding something all wrapped up in a yellow blanket. A gust of wind whipped a corner of it up so that it partly hid his face, but when he turned I could see he had a short, dark mustache, just like Governor Dewey. The boss and Teddy ran out to the chain link fence, which was as close as they let you get to the planes. They didn't seem to notice the rain. I followed right along behind them. I was getting excited myself, since I had a pretty good idea by then what was in the yellow blanket.

"You know that I never got married. I don't have any kids. Now I wish I did, but back then it was the last thing on my mind. After all, I was a young buck. I got to tell you, though, looking down at you that day, at your tiny face with the cutest little button eyes and a headful of coal-black hair, the idea of having a family got to me for the first time. Almost made me want to go out and grab the first decent-looking dame I saw and get going.

"The man with the mustache introduced himself. He had one of those very common names. Jones, maybe. Johnson? Standing there, a big tall guy with a tiny baby in his arms, he looked like a cover from the old *Saturday Evening Post*. He handed you to Teddy, then pulled a bunch of papers out of his pocket and gave them to the boss. I figured he was a lawyer, and these were the documents that made everything okay. The boss asked him if he wanted to come into the city with us and have some lunch, but he said no. As soon as his pilot refueled, he was flying back home. You were taking the whole thing in, as sweet and quiet as can be, and you couldn't have been more than a week or so old. I'm no expert in that kind of thing, but you were about as brand new as a baby can be.

"Driving back to New York they were like a couple of guys who'd just won the Irish Sweepstakes. They had those big funny lopsided smiles on their faces that you get when you've been to the dentist and had a shot of Novocain.

"I think they couldn't believe how lucky they were. I kept watching them in the rearview mirror. They were taking turns holding you. Once I looked back and I saw the boss giving you a bottle. They'd thought of everything! I felt sorry for the boss. He was probably thinking of his wife, who was in the hospital and looked like she'd never get out. They'd never get to have a kid. He wasn't the one that was going to take you home. Teddy was. He couldn't stop touching your face. Rubbing his hand along your cheek. Even then he was nuts about you. . . ."

Charlie's voice trailed off. For a long time neither of them spoke.

"This is so hard to believe, so strange. Nobody ever said anything—nothing at all," Allison finally said in a low, tight voice.

"I knew it. I shouldn't have opened my big mouth," groaned Charlie. He stared at the floor, unable to meet Allison's eyes.

"No, Charlie, I'm glad you did. You've done me a great favor. Really you have." Allison stood up, touched Charlie's shoulder to reassure him, and walked over to one of the tall windows that faced Gus's manicured lawn with its lush borders of foliage and flowers. It was still winter, only March, but in this climate things always seemed to be growing. A gardener was at work on one of the beds, watering, clipping, weeding, as if the house and its grounds had a life of their own independent of the owner of the property. It didn't seem to matter that Gus Morton was no longer in residence.

Allison leaned her head against the window glass, gripping the mullions for support, and tried to marshal her feelings. Too much was happening. She had buried her uncle less than two weeks ago. Tomorrow she was going to bury her mother. And now this. What she had just learned didn't alter what had happened, but it did affect her perception of these grim events and of herself.

—Uncle Gus was not my uncle. Françoise was not my mother. They aren't my people, a shocked voice inside her whispered.

—Aren't "your" people? Don't be theatrical. Of course they are. They brought you up, didn't they, they and your dad? They're your family, Allison. *Family*.

—But I feel like an impostor. Not like a real Morton.

—You mean because you don't have Morton blood coursing through your veins? Isn't that being just a bit technical?

—No, it isn't. It's what Uncle Gus always used to say about my running the company. "It's in your blood." Those were his words exactly.

—Oh, please, spare me.

—Just listen. Thousands of kids are adopted every year, right? And nobody makes a big secret about it. Not unless there's some reason to be secretive.

—You're wrong. Lots of people didn't talk about such things then. They didn't want their little tots to have nightmares about being left in a basket on somebody's doorstep or being found under a cabbage leaf.

—I suppose so.

—I know so. You've got reasons to be unhappy, but that isn't one of them.

—But I feel so strange. Nothing is the way it seemed.

—You can handle it. I know you can.

Allison looked at her watch and turned back to Charlie. "It's getting late," she said. "We've got to go get that stuff of mine."

"Sure."

"Charlie, what do you think?" she asked, as she watched him straighten his cap, which he hadn't removed, and stand up. "Why didn't Uncle Gus ever tell me I was adopted?"

"Well, you've got to remember, things were different back then. I'm sure they believed they were doing what was best for you."

Allison nodded. If Charlie didn't think it was odd, why should she? But she was not convinced.

As they drove from Gus's house to hers, more and more questions wheeled and swooped inside her head like a flock of sparrows frightened out of the branches of a tree. Had her uncle been trying to tell her something about the adoption when he died? Although she had thought she would remember forever what he had said, already it was hazy. Even so, she was positive he had mentioned a secret. Did the secret have something to do with her? Or was it the seed in a pod of other secrets? And what about Françoise? She had said to her on the phone there was something special she wanted to discuss. Was it this? But that would have been too coincidental, as if an emotional statute of limitations had run out for everyone at the same time. Was all of life a series of trades? If she was adopted, then Françoise was not her mother, and that was a relief of sorts, but then, who were her real parents? Were they alive? Not that she wanted to meet them—God no—but if she knew who they were, then she would know more about her background. Everything she had always been so certain about was now a matter of uncertainty.

"Charlie," she said after a while, "what did you say was the name of the lawyer on the plane?"

"I think it was Jones, or Johnson, but it could have even been Smith.

It was one of those names that's more American than apple pie. And I'm just guessing he was a lawyer."

"Did you get a first name?"

"No."

"Well, what about the plane, then? Do you know where it came from?"

Charlie shook his head again. "Nobody said."

"But if it was going to turn around and fly right home . . ."

"You mean, it had to be coming from somewhere nearby?" asked Charlie, picking up on Allison's thought. "That doesn't follow. You can get pretty far in a small plane in no time. I have a cousin in Pittsburgh who owns a share in a Cessna. He thinks nothing of flying to Boston to eat lunch at Durgin-Park."

"So . . . so already this is beginning to seem pretty impossible. But, Charlie," she added, thinking of something else, "did you hear them say anything in the car about an adoption agency?"

"They didn't say a word. Then, or ever. In my hearing, that is," said Charlie quietly. "You know how the boss was. He could get anything done he wanted. He had to have been the one that made the arrangements. He knew everybody. You got to remember, he was invited to the White House by every president since Eisenhower, though how he found someone as pretty and sweet as you, Allison, I'll never know."

"I wonder if they said anything about it to anyone else. I mean, there are other people still around who were around then. Ben. Diana. Parker. Maybe some others."

"Mr. Welles didn't come until later and Diana wasn't working for the boss then. But Mr. Wildman, he was there."

"Well, maybe I'll talk to him, then," said Allison, though the idea did not seem promising. She sighed and shut her eyes, and they rode in silence the rest of the way to her house.

Later, Allison wrote down everything Charlie had said. The list was short: a lawyer whose name could be Jones or Johnson and who might or might not actually be a lawyer; bad weather; Piper Cub; Marine Air Terminal; legal documents—if there were any papers still existing, Uncle Gus had not put them away for safekeeping in any of the normal places. As she stared at the list, she realized that if she were setting off on a trip and these were the directions, she would have found herself right back where she started.

PART THREE

35

Would you please just give me a chance to describe him?" Lee asked in her most pleading tone.

"Lee, I've already told you twice that I'm too busy. I've got a pile of work to get through, and I can tell I'm going to be here late tonight. Very late. There's no way I can have dinner at your place, no matter how irresistible this man is." Allison's amused tone of voice was stretched thin by Lee's persistence.

"Forget his looks, even though he's a mensch version of Richard Gere. More important, he's smart. And well-read. And best of all, he's straight. You know as well as I do that in this town that's as rare as a white rhino in a Bijan suit."

"I know you have my best interests at heart, Lee, but I still can't make it. I have a meeting now in Ben's office, which I'm already late for, so—"

"I'm not giving up that easily, Allison. As soon as I hang up this phone, I'm going to camp in your office until your meeting's over so I can convince you this is a man you definitely have to meet."

"Fine. I look forward to seeing you give your pitch in person. But right now I have to go."

Lee dictated two letters and then instructed her secretary to book a table at La Scala for lunch before heading down the corridor to Allison's office to wait for her. She nodded imperiously at Allison's secretary, Neal, and walked right into the office. It was strange—and wonderful—not to have to wait outside Gus's office until he was notified on the intercom. For all of Gus's warmth, he had been very formal about access to his office. That was where the power resided at U.T.M. And everyone knew it. But things were different now. And in time, who knew? Perhaps little Lee Simons, the girl who once lived over the butcher store in Hackensack, might just find her own tight tush in this office. *Stranger things have happened,* she thought with a smile. *Far, far stranger things.* The Frames knew she could do the job. Ben was no competition. He was steady and knowledgeable, but he was not a leader. He was just Gus's acolyte. He was lost without Gus around to tell him what to do and when to do it. There was no doubt about it—only Lee Simons could handle the job.

The thought of Allison filling in for Gus was only a joke. Sure, she was smart and hardworking. Lee would even give her points for being a lawyer. But she didn't have a feel for business. Why, she would just as soon have dinner with one of her nonentity friends from college as with a major star. Incredible! She'd probably be as happy with two bratty kids and a house in the suburbs as she was living in Gus's mansion, one of the truly major houses in Bel-Air.

Ronald Altman would be the perfect man to help Allison achieve that lifestyle. Yes, he was handsome. And bright and well-read. Lee wasn't lying about any of that. But he was also a total square who liked nothing better than staying home and curling up in front of old Alistair Cookie to catch the latest intellect-enriching goodie from PBS. If they fell for each other, there would be no question that Allison would quit the business. When Lee had hired Ronald to redesign her screening room, she never thought she would invite him over for a social evening. But now that the idea of getting Allison out of the business had begun to race constantly around in her head, she had become a full-time matchmaker.

Lee settled into a comfortable wing chair covered in a nubbly plaid and reached for a copy of *Daily Variety* that she saw lying folded on top of Allison's desk. As she picked up the paper, she noticed a neat stack of letters next to it. She glanced back at the door to make sure no one was watching her, then snatched up the envelopes. There were ten letters, and none of them had been opened. Neal probably had placed them there in Allison's absence. Lee scanned the return address on each before placing it back behind the others, as if she were studying for an exam with flashcards. Aside from a bill from Bullock's, they all seemed, from the look of the envelopes, to be condolence notes. Lee was about to return the stack to the desk without bothering to look through them all, when she suddenly stopped. The word *personal* was written on the bottom of the one she was staring at. But it was the name in the upper left corner that held her frozen. *S. Flores.* Lee folded the letter into a tight square that easily fitted into her palm and stood up.

"Tell Allison that something came up," she said to Neal as she left the office. "I'll see her after lunch."

She told her own secretary she didn't want to take any calls, then went into her office and locked the door behind her. She walked to the window before she opened the letter. Sean's handwriting was strong and even.

Dear Allie,

I just got back to the city from my place in Massachusetts, working on a new piece, and heard about your uncle. I know what he meant to you, so I can only guess what you're going through now.

I started this out as a short note just to let you know I was thinking about you at a tough time. But I also have to tell you you've been on my mind almost every minute of every day since I did what I did. I know that I was wrong. You couldn't have done what I accused you of. My stupid pride, or whatever you want to call it, has stopped me from picking up the phone or, better yet, getting on a plane and telling you how much I still love you. How much I always will love you. Maybe this is the wrong time to say this, but there it is. If you don't want to see me again, I'll understand. If you do, whenever and wherever, I'll be there. Just give me the word.

Stay strong and stay you.

All my love,
Sean

Lee read the letter three times. For a moment she thought she was going to cry. What would it be like to get a letter like this? To have someone like Sean Flores love you with every ounce of his being? But then the splintered memories of that hideous night exploded inside her like so many cutting shards. The rage she had felt surged through her again, as elemental and pure in its viciousness as the hunger of a predator.

She started to rip up the letter, then just as suddenly, she stopped. There was no need to destroy it. It would be far better to keep it, so she could look at it from time to time to remind herself that, thanks to her, Allison had no idea Sean still cared. That would be fun. She carefully smoothed out the letter and placed it back in its envelope. She dropped it into her purse and clicked it shut. The sound was satisfying, like getting attention with the snap of her fingers. Then Lee thought of something. What if she pulled the letter out of her purse by mistake and the wrong person caught sight of it? She opened her bag once more, took out the letter, and stuffed it deep into the phone directory on the bottom shelf of her bookcase. Nobody ever consulted the phonebook. If they needed a number, they called information. This was a far safer hiding place and a handy spot besides to keep something she would want to savor. She studied the directory. No telltale bulges. No one could possibly guess that something was stuck inside it.

Lee glanced at her watch and saw that it was nearing twelve-thirty. She had to hurry. It was bad form to be too late for lunch—bad for business—and no one could accuse Lee Simons of being inattentive to business.

36

It was five minutes to nine. The first board of directors meeting since Gus Morton's death was about to begin. It was Allison's opening round with the Frames. She had worked out a tentative plan for a short-term loan to meet the first of the interest-payment deadlines from the Stellar-Vue purchase. This, with the sale of some of the company's most disposable assets such as the G-III, should stave off a Frame takeover for at least a while, but she needed the board's approval.

Allison arrived at the office early that morning to go over once more what she was going to say. For the last half hour she had been watching the minute hand inch its way around the clock, apprehensive yet impatient to start. Now that the time had finally come, she forced herself to sit still for a few more minutes, leaning into the softness of Gus's moroccan leather chair, imagining he was holding her, comforting her, advising her. She would need all the strength and resolve she could draw from his memory.

The night before she had slept poorly, as she had for a number of nights. Françoise's death had depressed her more than she had anticipated, mainly because it seemed so unnecessary. The medical examiner's finding had confirmed the high level of alcohol in Françoise's blood at the time of death and thus the likelihood of suicide, but that seemed more a rebuke than a source of comfort. She felt uncertain and lonely, nearly bereft of comfort of any kind. If Cynthia lived here, she could have gone out with her to a movie or for dinner. It would have relaxed her. Instead, she stayed home, reviewing the agenda she and Parker Welles had spent the last week devising and perfecting. She had reread the dossiers on the new board members and again rehearsed her opening remarks. Striking exactly the right tone at the start of the meeting would set the mood for the presentation of her loan plan. She must not be apologetic ("I'm sorry I'm not Gus Morton—"), girlish ("—but I'll do my best, I promise, and if we all pull together, I'm sure everything will work out—"), or intimidated ("—that is, if you don't desert me . . ."). When she finally had climbed into bed, she couldn't stop playing out in her mind different scenarios for the meeting. She kept switching on the light by her bed, jotting down notes on options and nuances until she grew panicky at the thought that she would be too exhausted to function the next day. It wasn't until the first gray of dawn filtered around the corners of her drawn curtains that she had uneasily drifted off to sleep.

A few minutes after nine, Allison rose from her chair, collected her notes, and walked down the hall to the boardroom. As she had hoped, she had delayed her entrance long enough for all the others to assemble ahead of her. Adrian Frame and the three new board members were seated together. Allison circled her way around the vast table and introduced herself to the three Frame allies—former Governor Gannon of Florida, whose flowing gray mustache cascaded over a set of teeth as large and as white as Styrofoam packing chips, and the albino twins, Gene and Galen Tuckerman, their starkly pallid skin the color of a frog's belly accentuated by large inky-black aviator glasses that bounced Allison's image back at her.

While a waitress from the company dining room served the group coffee and croissants, Allison took her place at the head of the table. The highly polished satinwood oval was so immense that it made those who were seated at it look like passengers tossed overboard from a sunken ship, clinging to the gunwales of an oversized lifeboat. Gus had hired a decorator from San Francisco to design the room and instructed him to steer clear of "the Hollywood look." The result, perversely, was pure Beverly Hills glitz, from the overly elaborate marquetry of the table, to the sleek telephone and computer consoles that sprang up at each place with the push of a button, to the large club chairs so stuffed with pillows that the people seated in them had to battle down and feathers merely to get comfortable. It was hard to believe that someone with the refined and understated taste of Gus Morton could have had a hand in the decorating of this room. And, truth be known, he hadn't. Because of all the demands on his time, he had assigned one of his associates to oversee the project. That person had been Lee Simons.

Allison had asked Parker to sit on her right, and on her left, balancing a friend with someone she strongly suspected was a foe, Lee Simons. As she made small talk with Parker she noticed that Ben, seated one place over, on Lee's left, seemed tense and preoccupied. She continued to look slowly around the table at the rest of the board members. Which ones could she count on?

On Ben's other side was Diana. The two of them had fought each other for so long for Gus's attention that the pretense of casual conversation was an effort, but they were going through the motions. Next were her uncle's two oldest business associates, whom Allison knew she could rely on in any crisis. Randolph Gleason, who was Gus's age exactly, had been her uncle's personal banker and one of his closest friends for as long as Allison could remember. Although he had known Allison since she had been a little girl and had seen her grow up, he had the tact and good grace not to figuratively chuck her under the chin anymore. He was from old California money, beautifully tailored, and so handsome he could have launched a film career in the days when classic good looks were what mattered. Leon Frayer, the investment banker with whom he was chatting, was his opposite—a rumpled and neurotic genius with figures. His quick, inventive mind was the envy of other investment bankers and deal-makers from coast to coast.

The only people at the table who were silent were Adrian and his three men, and the sight of their expressionless faces sent a shiver through Allison. She looked quickly at Adrian, masking the loathing she felt for him. He was dressed as usual in one of the bizarre tunic suits that made him look like a sinister extra from *Star Trek*. This one was steel gray, which Allison guessed he thought complemented his black hair. Unnaturally black hair, she thought with satisfaction. One hot day several weeks earlier she had seen him in a restaurant and noticed small dark streaks on his collar—dye seeping out of his hair. Although Adrian always operated in the shadow of his father, he was reputed to be highly intelligent in business matters—he was one of the youngest graduates in the history of the London School of Economics—and equally ruthless. Whatever hand he intended to play would be at his father's direction, but he would know how to execute it expertly.

Allison's eye moved on to Gene and Galen Tuckerman. Their father, a farmer who had discovered that his alfalfa fields sat astride the third largest oil field in Texas, had died at a conveniently young age. Though he had left behind eight children to divvy up the largesse, the wunderkind twins, then only in high school, had bought out their siblings from the colossal money pot and promptly made the fortune even bigger. Much bigger. Before they graduated from Baylor, in two years rather than four, Hector Frame had persuaded them to join him as financial consultants and investors—and together, the Frames and the Tuckermans, like having gravitated to like, had prospered mightily. In matters of money, the two were brilliant. In all other areas, they showed as much human feeling as automatons. Now in their midforties and dressed identically in cheap black suits, they looked so much alike that Allison couldn't tell them apart. In comparison, the Frames' third board member, the former governor, was only a fool, though the dangerous kind, one who would do anything that his patrons requested. Together, these three sat on all the boards that the Frames either controlled or had positions on. Allison didn't need a George Gallup to tell her how they would vote.

When the waitress left the room, Allison tapped a spoon against her coffee cup. "I would like to call the meeting to order, please. I want to tell you about my hopes for our future, but first, Parker, would you please read the minutes from the last board meeting?"

"I move that the minutes be accepted," interrupted Adrian Frame from the other side of the table.

"I second the motion," said one of the Tuckermans.

"What did you say, Mr. Frame?" asked Parker, after a moment of stunned silence.

"I further move that we add an urgent item to the agenda and that we take it up forthwith," said Adrian, ignoring Parker.

"Seconded," said the other Tuckerman.

"One moment please, gentlemen," Parker answered angrily. "I am amazed at the necessity of having to do this, but may I remind you that Miss Morton is chairing this meeting. Surely it would be in the best interests of us all if we proceeded in an orderly manner."

"Thank you, Parker. But I'd like to hear what concerns Adrian Frame," said Allison. "Please continue . . . Mr. Frame."

"Thank you, Miss Morton," said Frame, pronouncing Allison's name with nasty facetiousness. "Everyone has been impressed with your quick grasp of the inner workings of U.T.M., especially under the difficult circumstances of your double tragedy. Clearly you are to be commended. Equally clearly, however, you are patently not qualified to handle the job of chief executive of this business on anything other than an ad hoc basis. I move therefore that we create a tripartite office of the president, to consist of you, Ben Wildman, and Lee Simons. Your collective responsibilities will be to attend to the day-to-day operation of U.T.M. under the guidance of the chairman of the company, who, of course, will also assume the additional role of setting company policy for the present as well as for the future."

"And who might that chairman be?" asked Allison coldly.

"You're looking at him."

"How dare you!" said Parker Welles. "In all my years as a board member here and at a number of other major corporations, I have never,

never heard a proposal of such presumptuousness. Allison Morton is Gus Morton's duly appointed successor. To question her right to assume this position represents a total breach of trust. I suggest, Mr. Frame, that you withdraw your remarks immediately so that we may continue with the business before us."

"Is that a threat, Welles?"

"No, it is not a threat. I am not in the habit of making threats, Mr. Frame. It is an option. Your other option should be obvious, even to you."

" 'Option'! Don't be fatuous, Welles. It doesn't become you."

"See here, Frame, either conduct yourself in a civil fashion or you'll have *no* options. I, for one, will demand that you leave this room instantly," Randolph Gleason interrupted angrily.

"Gentlemen, please. One at a time," said Allison. She was in shock. Adrian Frame's attack went so far beyond her worst imaginings that it was like being thrust on stage without knowing the name of the play, much less the lines. It had not occurred to her that the Frames would try to oust her now. Later, in all probability, but not at the first board meeting. She should have known better. They all should have known better. The Frames didn't play by commonly accepted rules.

"What you fail to appreciate, all of you, is that Miss Morton has no more 'right' to head Universal Talent than my houseboy," Adrian Frame said, coolly looking around the table. "So what that Gus Morton designated her. He's dead and so will this company be if this . . . young lady is allowed to run it. My father and I are major stockholders in U.T.M. and as such we have the right and the obligation to safeguard our investment. We have no intention whatsoever of doing otherwise. Therefore, we are wasting our time in any debate to the contrary. If the rest of you insist on continuing this . . . thumbsucking," he sneered, "I can wait you out. My lunch date isn't until twelve-thirty. But why wait until then to deal with reality. The new reality."

"My dear Mr. Frame," said Randolph Gleason in a more conciliatory tone, "have you fully considered the implications of what you're proposing?"

"Such as?"

"Miss Morton is young in a business dedicated to capturing the attention of the young. She is a first-rate lawyer, more than prepared to confront the legal ramifications unique to this business. The uninsured risks, the rampant suits, the freewheeling copyright challenges, on which millions of dollars often as not depend. And . . ." the banker paused for a moment, then continued a bit gruffly, "and Allison *is* Gus Morton's choice. Gus Morton was a true giant in this industry. Respected by all who knew him. He wouldn't put this company—his creation and love—into the hands of anyone who he didn't think could do the job. Relative or no relative. Not giving her a chance to shepherd this company is beyond consideration."

Frame gave no response, but it was obvious from his expression that he dismissed Gleason as a sentimental old man.

"Thanks, Randolph," Allison said to the banker, then directed her gaze to Frame, furiously debating what her next move should be. She knew she had to face him down now or everything might slip out of control. Before she could say a word, however, Diana unexpectedly broke the silence.

"May I say something?" she asked Allison.

"Of course, Diana."

"Mr. Frame," she said, nearly spitting the name out, "you and your colleagues may choose to view me simply as Gus Morton's lady friend. His *girl*friend. There've been occasions in the past when I've been described that way and bitterly resented it. But not today. Because in that role I came to know Gus Morton personally as well as anybody did. Professionally I worked with him for more than twenty years, closer to twenty-five, which gives me an intimate knowledge of this company as well, a knowledge that you will never have. I've watched Allison grow up and I've watched U.T.M. grow up. They are beautifully matched. Gus knew exactly what he was doing when he decided that Allison should succeed him. And it wasn't the indulgence of an adoring uncle. It was a wise business decision made by a supremely shrewd judge of character and ability. For you people who joined this company literally moments ago to think you know anything about it or about Allison's ability to take charge is . . . is . . . absurd! She is the perfect choice, and I want you—and her—to know I stand by her. Completely."

"Are you quite through, Miss Paget?" asked Frame.

"Yes," said Diana, her voice still shaking.

Allison wanted to hug her.

"I'm touched by your womanly concern for Miss Morton. It is very moving, I assure you. But now I suggest we get back to the matter I have raised about this enterprise, which you tell me I have no prayer of ever understanding."

"Yes, let's get back to it, I agree," said Allison, surprising Frame and the rest of the people in the room. "Let's put Mr. Frame's proposal to the board for a vote. Will you please put it in the form of a motion, Mr. Frame?''

As she listened to him formally state what was in effect a motion for her removal, Allison felt a wave of fear. Wasn't he too smart to put her to this test unless he believed he had the votes locked up?

"Now let's have a show of hands," said Frame, after one of the Tuckermans seconded his motion.

"No. That's not the way we'll handle this," said Allison. "As you know, Mr. Frame, the chairman designates the form of voting. I say we will vote one by one in the order in which we are seated, starting with me and then proceeding on to Parker Welles."

This, Allison thought, was her only chance of winning. If the vote was by a show of hands, it would be too easy for individuals to be swayed by the majority. It was too risky. She had quickly calculated her chances of winning. She knew she had four votes in addition to her own. But what about Lee? Most of all, what about Ben? Had the Frames gotten to them? Allison led off the voting, then turned to Parker Welles.

"I vote no to any change in the leadership of U.T.M.," said Parker briskly.

"A simple yes or no is all we need," said Adrian Frame.

As the vote moved to the Frame contingent, the affirmatives took over, but then Gleason, Frayer, and Diana cast their votes for Allison, putting her in the lead. The tally was four in favor of removing Allison as chief executive to five against.

All eyes turned to Ben. It was his turn. Allison held her breath. Lee Simons stared at him, trying to catch his attention.

Come on, Ben, just say yes, thought Lee. *It's such a nice, easy word to say. Then this little rich bitch will be gone and we, or rather I, will run this company. Don't forget what Adrian told you. You can have that title you crave if you vote the right way. It's all you have to do. Such a little thing. Nothing else. I promised him I could deliver your vote. Be a good boy now.*

Ben gave Adrian a long, unfathomable look, then faced Allison. Still he did not say a word. Lee thought she would burst with impatience.

"Gus Morton was not the easiest man in the world to get along with," Ben finally began. "He was tough. He was demanding. He gave his best, and he expected the same of the people who worked for him. Never anything less."

Come on, Ben, Lee silently screamed. *Get to the point.*

"At times Gus was egotistical. He could be as self-centered as a baby. But . . ." Ben paused, "but he was always fair. Unlike some other people seated at this table. Yes, Frame, I'm talking about you. You sicken me. You tried to buy my allegiance and I'm disgusted with myself for even listening to you. I will never do anything to demean the memory of Gus Morton or what he represented. I cast my vote—proudly—against the proposal. I vote no."

The vote was now six to four. Allison had won. There was one remaining vote to be cast. Lee Simons. A formality.

Lee felt as if a huge flame had sucked the breath out of her body. She stole a look at Adrian Frame.

If looks could kill, she thought, *I'd be dead. Think fast. You have to be cool. They're all looking at you. If you vote against Allison she'll know you sided with the Frames. You've got to vote against the proposal. You can explain it to Adrian later. He'll understand. He has to.*

"I wouldn't be here," Lee said, rising from her chair, "if it weren't for Gus Morton. I didn't start off life in Bel-Air. The early part of my life, the part I like to forget, was spent in the wrong part of the wrong city in New Jersey. It was Gus who got me to where I am now."

Lay it on, baby. What was it Gus liked to say? A good actor works the camera, a good agent works the emotions. That's it. Look at Allison. She's buying it. Give her some more.

"Though it was Ben who first spotted me, it was Gus who nurtured me. As he did countless others in this business. He had a great eye for talent. The best. And if he thought Allison could cut it, then so do I. I, too, vote no."

After the minutes from the previous meeting had been read, Allison had addressed the board, and her loan proposal had been raised, debated, and approved, again by a seven-to-four margin, her first board meeting came to an end. She was limp with exhaustion. As she gathered up her papers and notes while the others began to disperse, Parker waited in the doorway for her. Before she reached him, Adrian Frame suddenly appeared at her side. He gripped her elbow with his hand, forcing her to stop and look at him.

"You won this time, but all I have to say is, enjoy it while you can." His voice was low and insinuating, intended for her only, and he laughed in a cold, unpleasant way. "We can easily queer your loan with the banks by not cooperating, and we will. You're going to have to come up with some other scheme, and fast, to stop us from increasing our ownership of this company. And you can bet that delightful little bottom of yours, we're not waiting a moment longer than necessary to do exactly that. In case you have trouble with the arithmetic, that means you'll be outnumbered on the board. It won't be your candy store any longer. The only part of U.T.M. you'll be in charge of will be Gus Morton's ashes. Ciao."

37

Bricks of Blood, the rags-to-riches-to-rags-to-riches story of a woman entrepreneur who conquers New York, Paris, and London by developing the choicest real estate in each city, had already made a lot of money for U.T.M. It dominated *The New York Times* fiction bestseller list for over a year. It was translated into seventeen languages, including Tagalog and Serbo-Croatian. Now it was a movie. Though Allison had seen some of the rushes, she was not prepared for the sheer awfulness of the finished product.

As she suffered through the black-tie premiere, seated between Ben Wildman and Lee Simons—solely to promote the illusion of peace and harmony at the agency—Allison decided that the blame for this misbegotten project should be assigned to the Serbo-Croatian translator. If he had not been so skillful, the book would not have become a hit in Yugoslavia and never would have attracted the attention of the movie's producers, the Melicz brothers. They had made a fortune catering to the American sweet tooth with wines blended from fruity Dalmatian Coast grapes, and as avid converts to the American way of life, they wanted to make an American movie. A teen movie, naturally. The wonder of it was that the brothers had persuaded U.T.M. to sell them the rights to such a prime property as *Bricks of Blood*. The agency, of course, had packaged it and made a bundle doing so, but the result was a mess. The bomb contained two of U.T.M.'s hottest young stars, a bankable director and writer, and a cinematographer who unfortunately managed to shoot the thing gloriously, which only underlined the movie's emptiness. The real estate angle had been shifted from high rises to rock clubs, the storyline gussied up with music, booze, coke, and worn-out post–*Breakfast Club* dialogue, and the producers had allowed the budget to float upward like currency seeking its level, but it was all a waste. Even kids who were willing to see anything would boycott this one.

The reception following the premiere was at Citrus. Champagne and caviar were flowing, as were the adjectives. The crowded room was abuzz with "compelling," "marvelous," and "authentic" as once again members of the industry rose effortlessly to the challenge of total insincerity. After all, the Melicz brothers were purportedly worth north of two hundred million, and perhaps this turkey would not slake their thirst for the movie business. Always be nice, the rule went, to the people who might be able to finance your next picture. U.T.M. agents were out in full force, soothing the egos of agency clients unfortunate enough to be involved with this one.

The phoniness of the occasion depressed Allison, who was preoccupied with a meeting scheduled early the next morning with Adrian Frame—a command performance. She had prepared thoroughly, but now she wished she could reread her notes on the points she intended to make. They were sitting in a file folder on her desk. The more she thought about it, the more certain she became that she must read them over again even though it was almost midnight. As soon as she had spoken with all the necessary people and kissed all the requisite cheeks, she slipped out through a side door of the restaurant and drove to the U.T.M. Building.

Allison had just arrived when her telephone gave a sharp ring.

"Hi. It's a blast from the past. Does the name George Bellamy strike a bell? Remember, your fellow galley slave from the mailroom?" said the voice on the other end.

"George! Why are you calling? Is anything wrong? It's past midnight."

"Everybody knows the hours you keep, darling."

"Oh, really?"

"You don't buy that? All right, I admit it. I saw you leave the party, and I followed you here."

"Should I be flattered?"

"That's up to you, boss lady, but while you're puzzling over it, there are three things I want to tell you. Number one, I just signed Hawk City, and I know I don't have to tell you what happened to their last album. It went platinum a week after it was released. Number two, just today, I turned down another job at almost twice what you're paying me. And three, I'm in my office. Only one floor below yours, in case you've forgotten. How about a nightcap?"

"Another time, George."

"Oh, Allie Cat, be a sport. For old time's sake. We haven't spoken more than two words to each other in months. Except about business, of course."

Allison hesitated, then agreed. It wasn't what George said so much as hearing that silly nickname again. After she hung up the phone, she opened her compact and ran a comb through her hair. She had not been alone once with George socially since that night on the lawn in front of Felix Godwin's house. But maybe this wasn't a social call. Maybe he was trying to catch her off guard for some reason of his own. With George it was always important to read both between the lines and what was written on the back of the page. She hadn't needed his reminder that other agencies were courting him, for the truth was, she knew U.T.M. could not afford to lose him. Especially now. It would be further confirmation of the Frames' contention that she couldn't hold things together. Maybe he wanted to make a pitch for a raise, though it was a peculiar hour to do so. She was sorry now that she had told him he could come up.

"Hi," said George, just then appearing in her doorway. "May I enter the sanctum sanctorum?"

Allison's heart lurched unexpectedly. In that one half second, he seemed like the old George, the man she had been so crazy about when she first came to the agency. She blushed and turned to hide the color in her face by busying herself at her uncle's liquor cabinet. She handed George a snifter of Hennessey, which she remembered was his favorite after-dinner drink, and poured half as much for herself.

George sat down and stared silently into the rounded contours of the glass like a seer consulting a crystal ball. "I was a real shithead," he said finally. "I don't know how I could have behaved that way over Felix Godwin. You still haven't forgiven me, have you?"

Allison didn't answer him, but she didn't need to.

"I don't blame you," said George, "which makes it more important than ever that you believe me now. I'm truly sorry for the whole business. I can't tell you how sorry. I want you to know I think you're terrific. You're running this place like a real pro. Your uncle would have been so proud."

"Cut the bullshit, George. What do you want?"

"I mean it. Gus would have loved the way you—"

"Stop right there. Leave my uncle out of it. You stung me once. Badly. I'm not going to forget it, but that's all right. I can live with it. But why are you really here? You can afford a brandy on your own now. I don't believe that you just dropped by to tell me what a wonderful job I'm doing."

"Always the cross-examiner, Allie. But you're right. I came here for a reason I'm sure you won't believe. Friendship. You looked so forlorn at the premiere, I almost came over to hug you. I guess this is the next best thing." George put his glass down and looked for a moment as if he wanted to embrace her now.

"*Forlorn* isn't the word I'd use to describe the way I was feeling," said Allison quickly, still ill at ease. "How about . . . *pensive?*"

"That's what Jane Austen might have said." George laughed. "I see you're surprised I know that name. There are some things rattling around in me that have nothing to do with heavy-metal or rap music. You might enjoy getting to know that side of me again. But maybe you need time to consider the invitation. Can we level with each other on another matter, though? *Bricks of Blood.* The movie's an unbelievable dog, isn't it?"

They caught each other's eyes and began to giggle uncontrollably.

"Seriously, Allie," George began as soon as they were able to stop laughing, "I hope I'm pulling my weight here, but it's not just for the money. It's because I want to be part of your team. I also hope someday to be your friend again."

"Why wait for that day? I declare a truce, friend."

"I accept, since you're the boss. Come on now, let's celebrate. I can finally afford to buy you champagne and not worry that my car will be repossessed."

"Is this another car-tampering routine?" Allison asked with a smile.

George grinned broadly and shook his head. "My motto is: Never use the same shtick twice. Now what do you say to that drink?"

Allison almost said yes. What would it be like to be in his arms again? Maybe they could get back together. Sean was gone from her life. She was about to agree to a drink, when the image of herself running across Felix's lawn made her choke down the words. She knew she could never really know this man. Never really trust him. Not the way she had known and trusted Sean. It would be a mistake to become involved with George again.

"Let me take a raincheck," Allison finally said. "Right now I have to get back to this material. I have an early meeting tomorrow, and I really must spend some more time here."

"Are you sure?"

"Yes, I'm sure."

George took the stairs to his office and quickly dialed a phone number on his console. He was calling earlier than planned.

"Lee?"

"How'd it go?"

"Perfect. You read her like an eye chart."

"I can't believe you scored so fast."

"I didn't. But next time I will."

"That's what you call 'perfect,' you fool?" Lee Simons shouted angrily. "I wanted you to make her. I need a hook into that bitch."

"It'll happen, Lee. Soon. I promise."

"Listen closely, Georgie. Those things that I told you would come your way will only happen when the Frames—and I—take over. She won't do diddly-squat for you compared to what I'll do."

"I know that, Lee."

"Well, you'd better. Now, since you're not doing what you were supposed to be doing with our new CEO, I have something you can do for me. Get your tail over here right now, before I get angrier and," Lee's voice suddenly lowered, "hornier." Then she slammed down the phone.

George would have been surprised to hear one additional click after he hung up the telephone to head to Lee's house. It was something Allison had never done before, and she didn't know why she had chosen this time to listen in on a phone call from the receptionist's switchboard. It chilled her to have finally caught Lee in an act of treachery, but George, too? His duplicity truly shocked her. From now on, she would have to think like the Frames, if she was going to defeat them . . . and their allies. But thinking like them would not be enough. She would have to act like them, too.

38

W hat's up?" asked Ben Wildman as he walked into Allison's office. "Neal said you wanted to see me."

"You're a man of good taste, Ben. What do you think of this?" Allison asked, sliding a piece of the agency's stationery across the desk to him.

"It's fine. I mean, why wouldn't it be? It's our regular letterhead and stock," he answered, holding the paper up to the light.

"You're not looking at it very carefully. If I were you, I'd take a closer look at the upper left-hand corner."

"Allison!" Ben exclaimed after a moment. "What can I say?"

There in the top left-hand corner of the letterhead was his name, with the title "chief operating officer" right below.

" 'Thank you' will do, but even that's not necessary. In fact, I'm the one who should be thanking you. You've more than earned that title. Your expertise, counsel, and . . . loyalty have made an impossible job almost possible."

"Did you know that I asked Gus for this title and he turned me down?"

"No, but I'm sure he would have come through with it in time. He knew how important you are to this company. He always said that this was a business where the assets go home at five o'clock. And I don't think there's any greater asset than you. You know I mean that."

"Allison," said Ben, reaching across the desk for her hand, "all I felt for Gus, I feel for you."

"I know that, Ben. And I'm going to be needing your help more and more. We've got the Frames on one side and a business requiring open heart surgery on the other."

"I'm ready to do anything I can."

"How are you as an editor?" she asked suddenly, passing another sheet of paper across the desk to him.

"What's this?"

"The press release I propose to send out announcing your promotion. And while you're looking it over, give some thought to where you'd like to have your party. We haven't had anything to celebrate around here in a long time. I think that's finally beginning to change."

39

Some months before Gus Morton died, the Cannes Film Festival informed the agency that they planned to honor one of its major clients with a retrospective showing of his films at the next festival. Generally Cannes wasn't an important event for the firm. If an agent wanted to use it as an excuse to travel to Europe during the month of May, Gus, being a generous man, usually gave the go-ahead. Otherwise they let the thousands of producers, exhibitors, and distributors who shoehorned their way into the small city for those two frantic weeks fight it out among themselves. This time would be different, and the agency duly reserved five large oceanfront suites at the Carleton.

When Gus died, the Cannes equation changed too. Their star, Jake Gillette, was a cross between Sean Connery and Harrison Ford, equally appealing to men and to women and even a favorite with teenagers, who seemed to view him as Tom Cruise's tough and/or sexy older brother, depending on the gender of the beholder. The fact that Gillette happened also to be enormously talented was typically overlooked by his fans. But not by other agents, who had begun jockeying for position around him almost as soon as Gus had been lowered into the ground. Not even at the peak of his career yet, he would be the choicest of plums to acquire, and for any agent seriously trying to woo him away, signing him at a time and place like Cannes would be a delicious publicity coup. Accordingly, Allison quadrupled the agency's representation at the festival.

She decided to spend the weekend before Cannes alone in London. She badly needed a respite both from her emotions and from the daily crises at the office. Occasionally in the past she had tried to anticipate what it would be like when Gus died, but the pain of the loss was far beyond her imaginings. Then had come the shock of learning that she was adopted. If she wasn't a Morton, who was she? And without Sean in her life, where was she going? On top of this was the really big question: Could she run the company—and keep it from falling into the hands of the Frames? If she had to give herself a grade at this point it would be, "the jury is still out."

The weekend in London was exactly the antidote she needed. After the perpetual sunniness of California, the gray, drizzly weather was a relief, and the mindlessness of playing tourist kept her too busy to brood. One evening she saw a Sheridan revival at the Barbican and on another had dinner with a college friend at Le Souquet. She went to the Tate to see the Turners and to St. John's Wood to look at the Saatchi collection, spent an afternoon in Pimlico browsing in antique stores, and everywhere walked and walked, finishing up each day with a different route back to her cozy hotel in Cadogan Gardens.

By Tuesday morning, Allison was ready to take on Cannes. Eager to, though not because of Jake Gillette. She had another, secret motive for wanting to be there. Shortly before she left, she had heard that Sean had completed a low-budget movie with The Combine that was a last-minute entry to the list of films being shown out of competition. There was no confirmation of the screening in *Variety* or *The Hollywood Reporter,* but that was preferable to the comments a press announcement would have provoked from Lee Simons. One thing was certain, however: if the movie was being shown anywhere in Cannes, Sean would be there.

As her train slid south through the French countryside toward Nice, Allison couldn't stop thinking about him. She still had not heard from him. Every morning in the weeks immediately after he had left her, she woke up thinking that this would be the day when everything would be all right again. Today he would call and tell her he had made a terrible mistake. He understood now that she had nothing to do with the theft of *Sandia Mountain Song.* Could she forgive him? But that, she thought with a rueful smile, was the kind of storybook ending she helped sell to television. In real life it didn't happen that way.

The question of who had stolen Sean's play was still unanswered. Though the finger pointed toward Lee, Allison had no proof. It was like trying to draw a picture by connecting the dots, only to discover that certain critical numbers were missing. The pieces simply would not fit together. If Lee rather than her client, Mona Lacey, had borrowed Allison's loft, it would have been open-and-shut. But Mona, with a lewd laugh and a matching wink, confirmed that it was she and her boyfriend who had stayed there—and no one else. They were not so bored with each other yet that they had to turn to threesomes, and when and if they did, Lee would not be their choice. The man who had written the television script was just as adamant: the story was his and his alone. Short of calling them liars, there was nothing more Allison could do to clear up the mess. She promptly quashed the miniseries, and the project disappeared as rapidly as yesterday's disaster from the headlines. Everything returned to normal except for her relationship with Sean, and that was in ruins.

She now believed that if she and Sean ever were going to get back together, she would have to take the initiative.

Allison arrived in Cannes late in the afternoon. The others from U.T.M. were on a polar flight via Paris, due to land in Nice a few hours later. Lee Simons was part of the group only because she was Jake Gillette's agent and therefore was essential, but Parker and Ben would be there too, inadvertently acting as buffers between her and Lee, and a half-dozen junior agents as well. During the past week, Lee had made so many bad jokes about flying TWA instead of the G-III, now that the company plane was on the sales block, that Allison had almost bumped her down into tourist.

Allison chose one of the suites they had reserved and stepped out onto the balcony. The view was as contrived as a Hallmark card—blue water, white yachts, green palm trees—but it wasn't until she descended into the hotel lobby at cocktail time to meet her colleagues that she began to appreciate just how truly make-believe the scene was. In the next few days there were scores of screenings to choose from. Parties on boats, at villas in the mountains, and in every corner of every major hotel on the Croisette at any time of the day or evening. Banners, signs, stunts, press conferences, starlets, giveaways—every gimmick was employed to attract attention. The deals made here were real deals, and for small producers, crucial deals, but the atmosphere seemed to be derived from a script parodying the whole event. Movies and deals were the sole topic of interest and conversation, and the mood was contagious: everybody up and down the totem pole began to think of themselves as performers—as stars.

Lee Simons and the coterie of younger agents took charge of Jake Gillette, leaving Allison free to move among the buyers and sellers. Though Ben ran interference for her—it was Allison's first time at Cannes—she couldn't help feeling that Universal Talent Management without Gus Morton seemed to some of the people she was meeting like just another player, and not necessarily a very important one. Gus had been a truly international figure in the business. He had been on a first-name basis with creators such as Bergman and Fellini, as well as entrepreneurs like Ponti and Grade. It was more than a tough act to follow. As she scrambled to try to fill his place, at least one small corner of it, no one could have guessed that the real focus of her attention was not the agency and its reputation, but the film Sean had written.

On Saturday, the day it was being screened, she slipped away to the small theater where the movie was being shown, and took a seat at the back just as the lights were dimming. She thought she spotted Sean up front, but she couldn't be sure. In a few minutes, though, there he was on the screen. The sight of him magnified many times over shocked her and made her weak. What she felt was a dizzying farrago of sorrow, love, and . . . desire. Fortunately, the role he played was minor and he quickly disappeared from the story. Somewhere around the midway point she forgot about who had written the film and started to enjoy it. When the movie ended, she realized the audience shared her opinion. They clapped, cheered, and stomped their feet like fans at a soccer match.

Allison wanted to run down the aisle to Sean and throw her arms around him. She looked out from around two tall Swedes whom she was hiding behind—and her heart fell. As Sean and the others from The Combine were mobbed by well-wishers, a slender girl with long auburn hair clung possessively to his arm. Allison recognized Jodie Ballard, an actress in The Combine, who played one of the leads in the movie. As Allison wavered, Jodie and Sean smiled at each other in a way that seemed so intimate that without consciously making a decision to leave, Allison found herself outside, walking rapidly away from the theater. Sean must never know she had been there.

That evening the agency had a reservation for dinner at Moulin de Mougins, and as miserable as she felt, there was no way Allison could bow out. As the dinner proceeded, though, ceremoniously and elegantly, from fish mousse to mounds of langoustine, breast of duck, miniature vegetables, cheeses and exotic sorbets, with Jake Gillette on one side of her, Ben on the other, and Lee as far away from her as possible, with the wine, the lights shimmering against the restaurant's glass walls, and Roger Verge in his tall chef's hat moving through the dining room greeting his guests, Allison's depression gradually, imperceptibly lifted. They talked about skiing in Aspen, memorable meals, traveling by train in India, and big killings in real estate, about everything except the movie business for once, and as the conversation flowed around the table, Allison began to see the events of the afternoon in another perspective. She had overreacted. She had jumped to conclusions about Sean and the woman in the movie. Jodie Ballard, like everyone in The Combine, was simply Sean's friend. Of course he cared for them all, and of course he showed it.

As they drove back to Cannes later, Allison decided to try to see him again. Not the next day, but now. It was not yet midnight when they arrived back at the hotel and the Croisette was still crowded, so when Allison announced that she was going for a walk rather than joining the others for a drink, no one thought anything of it. If Sean wasn't at his hotel, she planned to walk along the Croisette to see if he was sitting in one of the cafés. Maybe his feelings for her really had changed, but she and Sean had mattered too much to each other for him not to feel at least . . . something.

When she saw his hotel ahead, Allison crossed to the other side of the street to gather her courage. Just then, Sean and four friends burst through the front door, laughing and joking. Jodie Ballard was still beside him. Allison froze, then pulled back into the shadows. As soon as Sean disappeared from view, she hurried off in the opposite direction, then traced her way back to the Carleton. She wanted to let go and cry, but she wouldn't, she swore she wouldn't, not until she had reached the privacy of her room.

At the front desk, there were a dozen telephone messages, including one that particularly pleased her from a young American director living in Paris whose work had impressed her, and a large envelope addressed to her in handwriting that looked familiar. She waved good night to a few rival agents whom she saw huddling with a hot American producer around a small table at the far end of the lounge, then entered the waiting elevator. Once in her room, she slit open the envelope with her fingernail. As she pulled out the script, a note fluttered to the floor. It was from Oscar Buckman.

> Can you meet me for a drink tomorrow? Six o'clock at the Majes-
> tic?
>   Uncle O.
> P.S. Read the script first!

Allison smiled. Oscar sounded just like Gus. The script was titled *Eagle on High*. The name of the writer was missing from the title page. She flipped it open and scanned the first page, read two or three more pages perched on the arm of a chair just inside the front door of her room, then reached for the telephone and ordered a large pot of coffee and some Perrier from room service. She read the script through to the end without moving once from the sofa where she lay. It was wonderful, and she had not a doubt in her mind that the name of the screenwriter was Sean Roberto Flores.

The next day, at six o'clock sharp, Allison arrived at the entrance to the bar in the Majestic. A plume of cigar smoke signaled Oscar's presence at a table in the back.

"Why didn't you tell me you were in Cannes?" asked Allison, kissing him on the cheek.

"I just arrived yesterday. You were the first person I called. It does my soul good to see you."

"Me too, Oscar," said Allison. She put the script down on the table between them. "But no more secrets, please. Who wrote this?"

"I thought you might be interested. Let's get you a drink, and we'll chat about it." He held up his hand for the waiter. "What'll it be?"

"A Negroni, please. On the rocks with a twist. But don't be coy. Sean Flores wrote this, didn't he?"

Oscar studied Allison for a moment. "Yes, though he might not be pleased if he knew I was showing it to you. What's happened to the two of you?"

"Don't play Dr. Joyce Brothers, Oscar. It won't work. Anyway, I think he's found somebody new. Let's talk about the screenplay instead. I love it."

"It's a wonderful piece of work, isn't it," said Oscar. "I'm just crazy about it. It's the most exciting piece of writing I've seen in years." Oscar smiled. "This is the next film I want to direct. I was in Paris on business, so I thought, why not come down here and try to wrap up the financing. You heard about the screening yesterday of the little movie Sean did with The Combine?"

"Yes," said Allison.

"Well, I was there. The audience went wild. It was done very inexpensively. Just under four hundred thousand. That's less than some commercials cost. They shot it in sixteen millimeter and blew it up. Yet, the amazing thing is, it's got some real box office potential. It might hit it big, like *Strangers in Paradise* several years ago. A lot of people are talking about Sean. You would think all this would play right into my hands with the new script, wouldn't you? It's so much bigger. So much more ambitious. But nothing of the kind has happened. I had a couple of very disappointing meetings today." Oscar shook his head and drew deeply on his cigar.

"What's the budget?"

"A million three. Take-home pay these days for seventeen-year-old stars, for God's sake! I'm astounded by the trouble I'm having getting someone to commit to it. Even at that price."

"I wonder why."

"I wish I knew. All I get from the studios are excuses. Too artsy. No stars. A Western. Another *Heaven's Gate.* Jesus! What this picture will cost wouldn't have covered the bar bill on that film."

Allison listened quietly to Oscar's litany of the difficulties he was having and then surprised herself and certainly Oscar.

"I'll raise the money for you," she said.

"What did you say?" asked Oscar after a moment of silence.

"I'll see you get the financing. I'd be thrilled to be part of getting it made. Anyway, it's a great investment. The videocassette rights will go for more than the negative cost."

"Where will you get the money?"

"You forget," Allison said with a laugh, "that I'm an heiress. Your job from now on, Uncle O., is to concentrate on our 'Eagle.' The money's my worry. Deal?"

"This deal we seal with a hug," said the director, reaching across the table and pulling Allison against his chest. "I'd like to start shooting by early fall," Oscar continued, smiling and puffing on his cigar, a cloud of white smoke drifting above his head.

"I have just two conditions," said Allison. "First, I want a big piece of it—"

"Now you sound like Gus," said Oscar, chuckling.

"But just as important, I don't want Sean to know I'm involved. My name can't appear on any document that he might see. I'll set up a new corporation to handle it. There mustn't be any sign of me, or U.T.M., in the deal. Promise?"

"You got it, Allie. But I have one question."

"Yes?"

"I'm going to call Sean a little later on. He'll be ecstatic about my news. What about my suggesting the three of us get together for a drink? You know, just as old friends? I'll tell him I ran into you. He won't see a link between you and the financing."

"Oscar, I'd love to. But now's not the right time," Allison said. She wished he would talk her into it anyway, but she could see, as he contentedly puffed away on his cigar, that in his mind he was already beginning to direct the movie.

. . .

Much later that night Allison sat on her terrace sipping a glass of champagne. First she silently toasted Gus, Teddy . . . and Françoise, too. Then, with more than a little trepidation, she began to confront what she had gotten herself into.

—Okay, Miss Shoot from the Lip, where the hell are you going to raise one million three hundred thousand dollars?

—I'll figure out a way. Oscar doesn't need it tomorrow.

—How about a week from tomorrow?

—Oscar has a very bankable name.

—True, but with Sean's script, it's like a bank that's had a run on it. The only studio he wasn't turned down by was Biograph. But there is an easy way to get the cash. Fast.

—What way is that?

—Talk to Adrian Frame. Like Françoise said, you'll walk away with money. Lots of it.

—Never!

—Come on, don't be so noble. You've thought of doing that, haven't you? If things got really bad . . .

—Not for real. It's just a depressing mind game, no more. Like picking at a scab. I'll never deal with Frame.

—All right, Miss Heiress. Pick up the phone. Call Oscar. Concoct some story about your inheritance being tied up in the courts longer than you figured. In other words, back out gracefully.

—You know I can't do that. Not to my uncle's best friend. Anyway, did you see the expression on his face when he realized he would get to direct the film? Absolutely beatific.

—Beatific? That's an idea. How about praying for the money?

—Or praying for Sean to come back.

—Now, now, don't be bitter.

—Well, much as I love Oscar, Sean's the real reason I stuck my neck out on this.

—You think you're telling me something I don't already know?

—Very funny. But I have an idea.

—Well, that's one very big secret you've kept from me. What is it?

—Do you think I have a bankable name too?

—It isn't deserved, but I guess so.

—I also had the advantage of going to the very best schools, didn't I?

—What has that to do with the price of tomatoes?

—Just that I got to know lots of people with *lots* of money. Why can't I—quietly, you understand—go to them to raise the money?

—I think you finally *do* have an idea.

—Thank you. And, you know, that gives me another. What about going to these same people to help fight off the Frames? I mean, seriously.

—Seriously, that's a lousy idea. You should know better. These young fat cats of yours aren't so fat they want to blow their money on that kind of maneuver. It won't make them fatter, and, worse, they won't have any fun. Or maybe it's the other way around. Remember, the movie business is sexy. The agency business is . . . well, a business.

—I see what you mean, but it was only a thought.

—Okay, but now you've got to get out your pad and pencil and start working.

—What on?

—Putting that "fat cat" list of yours together. We've got some money to raise.

40

D o you realize, Allie, that there's a vast, untapped resource out there in overfunded pension plans? We've only just begun to scratch the surface. You're going to see acquisitions that might initially seem . . ."

Had Harvey Black always been this boring? wondered Allison, trying to keep a modicum of interest in her expression as she listened to him drone on about corporate takeover financing and debt restructuring, which was both his job and, unfortunately, his passion. He was a vice president at Drexel, making, so he had informed Allison several times already that evening, "way north of three hundred K," and he had been pestering her to go out for dinner with him since she had moved back to Los Angeles. If *Eagle on High,* or anything else, was ever to bring Sean and her together again, it looked as if it would not happen for a long while, and in the meantime she was not signing off from male company. Still, there were limits, and a windbag like Harvey was one. No matter how lonely she was, she would not let herself fall into this kind of trap again. What had she ever seen in him? She had dated him three or four times when she was a freshman in college and Harvey a worldly senior at Brown. The thought pulled her up short. Harvey must have been in the same class as George Bellamy.

"Excuse me, Harvey."

"Was I going too fast, Allie?"

"No, it's something else."

"Yes?" asked Harvey, catching the hint of urgency in Allison's voice and flushing, as if he thought he had finally piqued her interest.

"Do you remember someone named George Bellamy in your class?"

"Andover, Brown, or Harvard B School?"

"Brown. George Bellamy. He graduated in your class."

"Bellamy. That does sound familiar. Did he have dark hair?"

"Yes."

"Went on to Yale Drama School?"

"That's George."

"Real shame about him. Where'd you know him?"

"What are you talking about, Harvey?"

"Actually, we weren't very close at all. We just took a couple of classes together."

"What do you mean a real shame?"

"I hope he wasn't too good a friend of yours because I read in the alumni magazine a couple of years ago that he had . . . well, died."

"That's impossible," Allison almost shouted.

"I'm sorry, but it's true. The reason I remember is that he got killed together with another classmate, who was a pretty good buddy of mine. Clay Lipton. They fell while climbing in the Cascades. I must say, the allure of mountain climbing really escapes me. The idea of risking total destruction for a sport seems like one of the crazier—"

But Allison was no longer pretending to listen to Harvey. She was remembering that night so long ago when she had casually asked George about his time at Brown and how for a few unsettling moments she thought he was lying about it. But then she had dismissed the idea as ridiculous. Now she wondered if maybe there had been two George Bellamys at Brown. Possibly, but what were the odds that both had gone on to Yale Drama? Pretty slim indeed. And if George Bellamy was not who he portrayed himself to be, then who was he?

"How about that raincheck you promised me the other day?" Allison asked George Bellamy as she walked into his office a week later. It was a large one with two windows, a huge, comfortable leather sofa, and an elaborate Mitsubishi sound system.

"Absolutely, Allie, anytime. Just name a date." He was wearing a pale green linen shirt with a silk regimental tie. His suit jacket, thrown over a chair in the corner, was a chestnut brown and unquestionably hand-tailored. Clearly, George was not holding back from pampering himself.

"What I'd really like to do is cook you dinner to celebrate our being friends again."

"That's great, but why don't you let me take you out instead? Anywhere you like. Primi? Chinois? I've gotten to know Wolf a bit, so I'll have no trouble getting a prime table."

"Is this a comment on my culinary abilities?"

"God, no. What I meant to say is . . . yes, I accept with pleasure. I'd love to have you cook dinner for me."

"How about tomorrow evening at your place. My kitchen is being painted. I'll bring all the ingredients."

"Can't we make it the next night? You see, I have—"

"George, do you really want to bury the hatchet?" Allison asked in a half-accusatory way.

"Of course, I do. Okay, dammit. I'll cancel my date. You're much more important. You always have been."

"Now, that's more like it. I'll be at your house at six. And, yes, I know the address. One more question, however."

"What's that?"

"Do you have any pots and pans?"

"That's an awful lot of food you're cooking, Allie," George said, as he sat on a stool next to the sink, obediently mixing the salad dressing.

"Haven't you heard of something called leftovers? This meal will taste even better tomorrow. By the way, do you ever use this kitchen?"

"If you mean pouring juice and making instant coffee, then yes, I use it all the time. I'm sort of the Julia Child of the boiling-water set. But after watching you in action tonight, I was hoping you'd become a regular feature here."

"We'll see," she answered as she tasted the sauce for the lamb, then added a pinch more rosemary to it.

"Isn't there anything else I can do? You've kept me cooped up in this kitchen so long, I'm beginning to think I belong here. Why don't I set the table?"

"It's already done. And don't go out there. I want it to be a . . . surprise. By the way, what time is it?"

"Almost eight, and I'm getting hungry," said George, moving off the stool so that he was now behind Allison. He put his hands on her shoulders, but she slid away to check something on the stove.

"No touching the chef until after dessert. And that's one of the surprises I have for you tonight, George. You're going to get a special, imported dessert."

"Sounds mysterious," he said with a leer.

"Can I get a truly honest answer out of you, George?" asked Allison in a serious tone.

"Try me."

"The night you went to Felix's house to sign him, did you think at all about how I'd feel? I thought you cared about me."

"Of course I thought about you, but I couldn't stand being stuck in that mailroom any longer. And unlike you, I had no guarantee I'd get out. Try putting yourself in my shoes. It was just too strong a temptation."

"Sort of like a bankrobber who finds a gun," said Allison, not bothering to look at George.

"That's unfair. I knew you'd be hurt, but I felt I could make it up to you. And I will if you give me half a chance."

"I don't believe that, George. But who knows? Maybe you can change."

"I know I can, Allie. Just give me one more shot. I'll show you how—"

The front doorbell rang loudly in the kitchen, interrupting them.

"I wonder who that is," said George, with a puzzled look. "I'll go see."

"Why don't we both go," said Allison, taking off her apron and following George into the dining room.

"Hey, why did you set all these places?" George asked, as he noticed not two place settings at the table but six.

"Just answer the door, George. You'll understand."

George opened the door and saw a heavyset man and woman, both in their late fifties. Behind them stood two teenagers, a boy and a girl, both dark-haired and dressed for an important occasion. The four newcomers smiled nervously. George leaned back against the door, limp as a banner on a still day, his face ashen.

"George! Are you just going to stand there or are you going to invite your parents inside? Come on in, Mr. and Mrs. Bellassarian. You too, Ina and Joey. You're right on time. Were my directions clear?"

"They were perfect, Miss Morton," George's father began. "But—"

"It's Allison, please."

"It was just . . ."

"Georgie," crooned his mother, stepping in front of her husband and stretching her arms open wide as she advanced on her firstborn with the unstoppable determination of a female bear retrieving an errant cub. "Let me get a good look at you."

"It was just I was nervous driving your car, Allison," George's father continued. "Such an expensive car. I was afraid I might do something to it. I kept asking everybody, you know how many suits I'd have to press to buy a car like this? Isn't that so, Joey? I couldn't get my mind off it."

"There wasn't a car around that didn't pass us," Joey said to Allison.

"It was really a scream," added Ina. "A kid on a bike almost beat us out at a red light. Luckily, Daddy started out half an hour early."

"But I got here on time," said George's father proudly. "And your car is in perfect shape."

"I'm sure it is, Mr. Bellassarian. Now, George, why don't you give everybody a kiss and then come help me in the kitchen for a moment."

George, looking dazed, allowed himself to be embraced by each member of his family in turn, like a birthday present being passed around at a party.

"Here, Georgie," said his mother, taking a large bakery box from Ina and pressing it into his hands. "I brought this all the way from Dearborn. Baklava just the way you like it. It was Allison's idea. She said that she would make the meal, but that I could bring the dessert. Right, Allison?"

"That's absolutely correct, Mrs. Bellassarian. And, George, I had a little bite of it last night, and it's the best I've ever tasted. If your mother lived around here, I'd gain twenty pounds in a weekend. Now if you'll excuse us for a moment, gang, George and I have a few last-minute things to do. Why don't you make yourselves comfortable and we'll be right back. There's some wine and soft drinks on that table by the door to the terrace, so help yourselves. See you in a few minutes. Come on, George."

As soon as the kitchen door closed, George stiffened, wheeled around, and grabbed Allison by the arm.

"You bitch!" he spat out.

"Watch your language, pal, and get your hands off me fast," Allison shot back, looking as if she were going to slap him.

"What right have you got to poke around in my personal life?" said George, letting go of Allison. "Looks like you've got some bug up your ass about my changing my name. What's the big deal? Everybody used to do that out here! I'd have told you all about it if you'd asked. Gladly."

"Oh, sure, George, but frankly I don't care what you call yourself. The name change isn't what's important, it's that you've been hiding behind it. And since you asked what the big deal is, I'll tell you. The big deal is you're a liar and a cheat. You've misrepresented yourself from the beginning. You pretended to be someone you aren't. When I think of that cozy, all-American, growing-up-in-the-suburbs story you fed me, complete with all the right degrees from all the right schools, it makes me want to puke. It says everything anybody needs to know about the kind of person you are. Of course, you were clever enough to assume the name and background of a real person, some poor soul who fell off a mountain and died, just in case anyone decided to check you out."

"Allison, you have no idea what I went through just to get *into* that fucking mailroom. Every decent talent agency in L.A. turned me down as George Bellassarian. Becoming George Bellamy was the only way I could do it."

"Horseshit. You were ashamed of who you were and where you came from, so don't give me any more stupid lies. Listen to me closely. As you see, I know a lot about you. If you don't want the rest of the business to know this stuff too, you'd better do as I say. Your family spent last night with me and they'll spend tonight with me also. You have a marvelous family, you bastard. Maybe a little humble for your tastes, but we all know where your head and heart reside. They've been worried sick about you. Not even a goddamn postcard in the past six months!"

Allison watched George as she spoke, but he was playing mute. His face was a study in blankness.

"I told them you've been traveling all over the Far East booking acts, that's why you haven't been in touch," continued Allison. "They'd love to believe that, and a bullshit artist like yourself shouldn't find it too tough to convince them. I've cleared your schedule for the next three days, so you can take them around and show them the sights. I flew them out here from Dearborn first class and that's the way they'll return. You'll have my bill for the tickets on your desk tomorrow. I'm going to make a point of keeping in touch with them, George, so I advise you not to suffer any more amnesia attacks on their behalf. They deserve a little attention from you. Also, since you're now in the chips, I expect you to send them at least two thousand a month to help out. If you don't, you'll regret it. Those agencies who've been wooing you won't be quite so hot for you if they hear how cavalier you are with the truth. How could they trust you with their own secrets? Think about it, George. I'd say you'd be lucky to get back your old valet-parking job."

George did not respond, but there was nothing in his expression or his manner that hinted of humility. As she looked at him, Allison felt a flush of satisfaction. *This is one for you, dear Mr. Bellassarian,* she thought, remembering his complicity with Lee. As for Lee, her turn was coming. When Allison was good and ready.

"You're a very capable agent, George, and you're going to get better," she continued, taking advantage of his silence. "The agency needs you. So as long as you hold up your end with your family and don't ever pull any more stuff like you did on me or on anyone else in the company, you'll be okay. Now put on your best party face, Georgie, and let's have a fun dinner with your family. They've earned it."

41

Allison flew into New York on a Thursday afternoon several weeks later. The next day she had meetings scheduled with the literary and drama divisions and then with Oscar Buckman to finalize the budget for *Eagle on High*. Her idea of asking friends from school and college to invest in the film was working, at least for the initial financing. She kept the amounts of money she requested small enough to make it easy for people to say yes, which many were inclined to do for the same reason they would consider backing a Broadway show: the show business connection flattered their egos.

Allison intended to stay in New York over the weekend, though she had no plans apart from seeing Cynthia Traynor for lunch or dinner. She would play it as it came, doing as much or as little as she chose, whatever struck her fancy. She knew Sean was still in Europe with The Combine, so she had no fear of turning a corner and running into him, and though the associations of the city were still painful, just being there would make her slow down for a few days.

On Saturdays and Sundays in Los Angeles she merely moved her office from U.T.M. to Gus's library, and on most weekends, paperwork, telephone calls, and conferences kept her as busy as she was during the week. She and Parker Welles were still searching for new sources of money to replace the original set of bankers the Frames had blown out from under them, just as Adrian had warned they would at the board meeting. They had managed to sell the billboard business, though at a loss, in time to meet the first round of interest payments, but this was only a stopgap measure. With each week that passed, the likelihood of the Frames making their final move against them became more acute.

The day-to-day business of the agency was a headache also. The competition continued its guerrilla attacks on their client list, and the clients themselves seemed more demanding than ever. Lee Simons was involved at the moment in an imbroglio with C.A.A. over an actor who was threatening to defect, and the truth was that if Lee, Ben, and the other key agents, among whom the newly compliant George became more important every day, could not keep the list from dissolving, where would any of them be?

Saturday morning Allison rose late, lingered over coffee and a French novel she had begun on the flight to New York, and left her loft around noon. She walked over to SoHo and wandered in and out of shops and galleries until they became too crowded, then taxied uptown. On Fifty-seventh Street, she stopped at Bergdorf's long enough to buy a Chloe cocktail dress that she didn't need but which looked terrific on her, and then, because it was a beautiful day for walking, she cut through the park to Columbus Avenue to see what new stores had opened.

One of her favorites was a bookstore behind the Museum of Natural History in an elegantly restored building. Just inside the door was a large library table with stacks of newly published books, layered end to end like the pieces of a well-crafted stone wall. She stopped to look at the cover designs, the descriptive copy, and, when her interest was piqued, the authors' first paragraphs. She found a promising short novel by a woman writer she had never heard of and picked it up. Book in hand, she turned toward the next table, as pleased by the prospect as a chocolate addict sighting the dessert trolley.

It was then that she had a small accident. A man carrying an enormous bouquet of flowers somehow stumbled against her, and the next thing she knew, flowers were flying through the air and she was on the floor. Surprised but not hurt, she started to get up, when suddenly she was pulled vigorously to her feet by the man who had just collided with her.

"I'm so sorry," he said with a look of concern. "I wasn't watching where I was going. Are you all right?"

"I think so," said Allison. "But what about your flowers?"

What seemed like dozens of flowers were scattered around them on the floor, transforming the hardwood surface into a raffish variation on an Aubusson rug. There were lilies, freesias, anemones, peonies, roses, and exotic blooms that Allison couldn't identify by name. The man bent down, gathering them back into a bouquet, and Allison kneeled down to help him. "This is a first for me, being knocked down by something so beautiful," she said, scooping up the flowers nearest her.

"They are beautiful, aren't they," said the man, smiling at Allison. He had a shock of dark hair and brilliant blue eyes of the same intensity as a boat pennant and they crinkled charmingly when he smiled. "And I want you to have them." He scooped up the last of the flowers and held the bouquet out to Allison.

"You can't be serious," she said, shaking her head.

"I might be smiling like an idiot, but I couldn't be more serious."

"It's a delightful thought and I appreciate it, but, no, I couldn't accept them."

"I insist," said the man, thrusting the flowers toward Allison before she could protest further. Her arms opened to receive them as unhesitatingly as if she were being handed a baby to hold.

"Well, the next line belongs to me, doesn't it? Thank you very much," said Allison. She was flattered by the attentions of this attractive man, but also embarrassed. Several other customers in the store were openly enjoying the little drama.

"My pleasure. And I assure you, there are hardly any strings attached."

"Thank you again, and goodbye," said Allison, saluting her benefactor with the bouquet. "I've got to go now."

"I did say '*hardly* any strings.' The one I was thinking of involves a glass of wine," said the man, following her to the cash register. "I know a very nice small establishment near here that serves a reasonable Chardonnay. I vouch for the libation since it comes from the vineyard of a friend in Napa. Please say yes."

Allison started to say no, then hesitated. He was sweet and earnest, and there was something about him she liked.

"A quick drink, that's all," he said, sensing her indecision. "We can discuss . . . books. That would make it all right, wouldn't it?"

Allison laughed and agreed. As he led the way, the man introduced himself as Lucian Hewitt. He had a long stride, and Allison had to quicken her pace to keep up with him. The extravagant bunch of flowers she was carrying made her feel special, like a ballerina who had just danced a premiere, or maybe it was the small tickle of interest and curiosity she felt about this stranger.

When they were seated in the restaurant, Lucian called for an ice bucket to put the flowers in to keep them fresh and ordered them each a glass of wine. They talked about reading and about gardening and about summertime in New York versus L.A., the opening conversational gambits of two people who don't yet know each other.

"I have a confession to make," said Lucian unexpectedly. "I knew your name before you told me. In fact, I've known who you are for months. I've wanted to meet you since I saw you at a benefit last spring."

"You're joking," said Allison, too surprised to say more.

"The gods were smiling on me today."

"You have an interesting way of introducing yourself."

"Divine intervention, I'd call it. I certainly didn't mean to bump into you, but it worked, didn't it? I should tell you that two of my trademarks are serendipity and heavy-duty klutziness."

"Do you make a habit of carrying half a florist shop with you all the time?"

"Only when my grandmother checks into Lenox Hill for a new model hip. I was just on my way across town."

"Well, hip-hip-hooray," said Allison, with a laugh. "But this whole episode makes me think I've been in California too long. It would never happen there. With everybody in cars, it's impossible to talk to somebody you don't know unless you're sweating together at an aerobics class or walking across hot coals in the same group. It's not easy starting conversations at red lights."

Allison and Lucian chatted awhile longer and then she said goodbye, a bit regretfully, and didn't think of him again until Monday. When she arrived in her office that morning, straight from the airport, a large bouquet of flowers waited for her on her desk. She didn't need to read the card to know who had sent them. They were the same combination of flowers that had fallen onto the floor of the bookstore two days ago. Later in the day, Lucian telephoned from New York to say hello, and the rest of the week brought more flowers and more calls. He made her feel that someone cared about her again, and the sensation was wonderful.

When she had first heard the name Hewitt, her ears had perked up. The name didn't have the singularity or weight of Astor or Rockefeller, but to most people, Allison included, it meant Hewitt Aircraft. She was too polite to ask, but in the course of one of their coast-to-coast calls she learned that he was indeed a member of *the* Hewitt family, though not involved with the family business. He was a broker, he told her, concentrating on managing his own investments.

"Don't look to me for investment advice," he said. "I have a rule never to touch friends' money. Makes for better friendships, don't you agree?"

Allison wasn't sure where her relationship with Lucian was going, but it definitely was in motion. Two weekends after they met, she put together enough business appointments to give her an excuse to return to New York, and did the same the following weekend. She wasn't serious about Lucian. How could she be, after Sean? But as unconcerned as Lucian was about the things that mattered most to Allison (she had seen at once, for instance, that books were unimportant to him and his presence in the bookstore was a rarity), he was attentive, spontaneous, and, most of all, fun. At another time in her life, Allison might have dismissed him as frivolous. His "work" seemed mainly a backdrop for squash at the Racquet Club, backgammon and bridge at the Regency, drinks at the Knickerbocker, and weekends houseguesting in the Hamptons or Connecticut. He appeared more than happy, however, to stay behind in the city if it meant seeing Allison, and she, for her part, escaped from her problems at the agency by making the cross-country trip more and more frequently. They used the city, half-deserted on these summer weekends, for long lunches, double-bills at movie revival houses, and evening strolls. Some weekends they stayed at her loft, others at his brownstone in the East Seventies, and on several occasions he flew to California. He was a gentle yet passionate lover, which added more than a soupçon of a reason for spending time with him.

One evening, a couple of months after they had met, Allison flew into New York and joined Lucian for dinner at one of their favorite Italian restaurants in the Eighties. Often he picked her up at the airport, but this time she had taken a later plane than usual. Almost as soon as she sat down at the table, a waiter appeared with Bellinis the color of a sunset. Lucian laid his hand over hers. As she listened to him tell her about what he had been doing in the last few weeks, her thoughts drifted to Sean, and it was only when Lucian pulled his hand away from hers that she stopped daydreaming. He was staring at her intently.

"I was just saying, there's a favor I have to ask you," he repeated, "but I don't know how to begin. I feel a little awkward."

"You shouldn't. After all, we know each other pretty well. What is it?"

Lucian still hesitated.

"Please tell me."

"All right. I'm in a small jam. My own money's tied up, and I need . . . ten thousand. Just for a week, no more. It goes against all my principles to ask you, but could you help me out?"

Lucian didn't explain why he needed the money, and Allison didn't ask.

"It's done," said Allison without a pause. She had learned from her uncle to be decisive, to go with her instincts, never to look back or second guess. She knew she could trust Lucian. "Don't think another minute about it. Now let's order. I'm starving."

The next morning, Allison had the ten thousand wired into Lucian's account, and precisely one week later, just as he had promised and she had expected, he returned the money.

That afternoon the flowers arrived. They were the same enchanting combination he had sent her before, that he had thrust into her arms that first day. How like Lucian, she thought. She pulled the cellophane away from them, smiling to herself, then buzzed Neal to come in and find a vase for them.

"Your secret admirer again?" asked Neal with a grin.

"Yes, my secret admirer," said Allison, turning her face away as a sudden feeling of sadness swept over her that had nothing to do with Lucian Hewitt and everything to do with Sean Roberto Flores.

42

Allison swiveled her chair around from the window and back to her desk, studied her appointment calendar for one moment more, then resolutely picked up the phone. Apologizing effusively, she canceled a meeting with the production head of Disney that was scheduled for two hours later. If she could complete a couple of important telephone calls and, to play it safe, postpone an early drink date she had with an English producer, she could put together the free time she had been half looking for, half avoiding for the past several weeks.

"Neal," she said to her secretary, "leave a message for Roland Tidmarsh at the Beverly Wilshire. I can't make drinks today, but see if Thursday's okay instead. But first try to get Gleason, Rosie Munroe, and Ryman on the line. In that order, please. And no other calls."

It was one of those times when everything that needed doing got done. She was able to reach all three people and quickly dispatch the business at hand. Then she dictated a half-dozen memos and letters that had to get out that day. Finally she placed one more telephone call herself, then met briefly with Lee Simons, always a distasteful chore, to recap the current status of a two-picture deal they were putting together for Jake Gillette and to commiserate with her on a client casualty. Lee had held on to the screenwriter C.A.A. had been courting, but they had just lost a sixteen-year-old actor who was the latest teenage heart throb. Luckily, he had not gone to any of their competitors, but to the inept hands of his father, an unsuccessful producer now turned agent-manager.

"The kid's old man will save the commission and ruin the career. You just watch," said Lee. Lee was right, of course, but that wouldn't stop Adrian Frame from using the defection as another example of Allison's ineptitude.

Then Allison was out of the office and, barely twenty minutes later, parking beneath the building near the Civic Center that was her destination. The person she was going to see, Guy Barnes, had been recommended to her by Tom Rosen. His firm, Barnes & Mitchell, Investigative Services, was on the eighth floor, which they had entirely to themselves, judging from the legend in the elevator.

"I'm here to see Mr. Barnes," Allison told the young receptionist. On the wall behind the girl's head was the name of the company, lettered in gold, and beneath it a list of their other office locations: Chicago, Houston, New York, Miami.

"Do you have an appointment?"

"Yes, I called a short while ago. It's Miss Traynor. Cynthia Traynor."

Allison sat down on a couch, picked up a magazine, and stared blankly at it. She felt absurd impersonating Cynthia, but it was the only way she could force herself to confront the issue of her adoption. She needed emotional distance from it, and pretending to be someone else helped. The only people she had felt comfortable speaking to about it were Ben Wildman and Parker Welles, but they knew nothing. And Cynthia, of course. Finally Cynthia suggested she ask Tom for the name of a private investigator who could help. She was afraid of what she might find out, but lately she had begun to be just as afraid of never finding out anything. The three people who knew best what had happened—Françoise, Teddy, and Gus—were dead.

". . . Well, Miss Traynor, that's not very much information to go on," said Guy Barnes, pulling a pair of rimless glasses down his nose and looking over the tops of them at Allison.

"I know, but it's terribly important to Miss Morton to find out who her parents are . . . or were. Is there a chance of it?"

"Chance is for fortune-tellers. It has as much to do with our line of business as throwing the I Ching." Mr. Barnes was very serious, as if he were instructing a bunch of rookie Sam Spades. He was tall and thin, and in his conservative gray suit he bore as much resemblance to Humphrey Bogart as a Bible Belt minister might. "We'll do our best, though, and, in all modesty, our 'best' is the best in the field."

"That's why I'm here," said Allison. "My friend is very aware of how little information she has, and, under the circumstances, she wanted me to make you a special offer."

"Yes?"

"If you're successful, she wants to give you a bonus. She was thinking of five thousand dollars."

"That's a handsome offer, Miss Traynor. And I won't refuse it," he added quickly. "The first thing we'll do is liaison with our New York office. I have a key man in the field there named Rubino, who I'll put in

charge of your friend's case. We'll see what we come up with in, say, two
weeks. I'll telephone you as soon as I know anything, but before you leave
I have a couple of other questions."

"Yes?"

"Did Miss Morton talk to anyone who worked with her father and
uncle at the time the adoption occurred?"

"Yes, she did," said Allison. A nervous smile punctuated the affirma-
tion. "She said she spoke to two of Gus Morton's closest aides, Ben Wildman and Parker Welles, but neither one could add anything."

"What about," Barnes looked down at his notes, "this Diana Paget?
You said she worked for Mr. Morton and was personally involved with
him for many years, isn't that correct?"

"Yes, that's true."

"Could she have any knowledge of the adoption?"

"I don't think so. She wasn't working for Mr. Morton at the time."

"I must say, I think that's an avenue that should be followed up,
though who knows if it will yield anything. Please tell Miss Morton that
everything has to be checked." Barnes pushed back his glasses with his
middle finger and closed his notebook. "I notice you didn't write down
Miss Morton's telephone number, though."

"Oh, there's no need for that. I'll call *you,* on her behalf."

"Really? That's fairly irregular, Miss Traynor," said Barnes, with a
hint of disapproval.

Allison opened her handbag and pulled out a soft leather purse. She
counted out ten hundred-dollar bills. "Is this irregular also?" she asked,
holding the money out to him.

"What's this?"

"A deposit, Mr. Barnes. A sign of Miss Morton's faith in you."

"If you insist . . . Miss Morton," said Barnes.

Allison looked up in surprise.

"Miss Morton, I knew who you were as soon as you walked into my
office. This sort of thing happens all the time. We expect it. Part of being
a detective is being informed. One has to keep up with a bit more than
the *Police Gazette* to get ahead in this business. I'm an avid reader of
Women's Wear Daily and both *The Hollywood Reporter* and *Variety*. Please be
assured, though, that as far as I'm concerned, and everyone else in my
organization, you'll be Cynthia Traynor as long as you want it that way."

"I appreciate that, Mr. Barnes," said Allison, shaking the detective's
hand.

"Save that for when I give you the information you came here for.

And believe me, this firm is going to do everything possible to see that you get it."

Allison drove slowly up the narrow canyon road that snaked to the crest. It was only a few hours after her meeting with Guy Barnes. Finally she pulled into a palm-lined driveway and parked next to a cobalt-blue Jaguar. She had arrived five minutes early.

—This is not a good idea, she told herself again.

—Don't be such a coward. You're only meeting her for a drink.

—Yes, but she probably knows nothing. She wasn't even working at U.T.M. then.

—She shared your uncle's bed for years, though, and, I'll bet you, most of his secrets too. She's got to have some idea.

—But Barnes thought she was a probable dead end, didn't he?

—What he said was, she should be questioned. Would you rather have him do it? You want everyone to know you've hired a private detective?

Allison got out of her car and, stalling for time, walked over to a low wall to look at the view. The land plunged down to another, secret canyon, secret because there was no road to it on the other side, and Diana and the few scattered neighbors nearby had it to themselves. It was overgrown with wild grasses and studded here and there, like a rich Christmas fruitcake, with tufted palms. A soft breeze blew up the canyon onto her face, giving her the illusion for a moment of standing at the railing of an ocean liner.

"Allison dear, come on in," called Diana, waving to her from a deck near the back of the house. "The front door's open."

As she walked through the living room, Allison could see Diana on the deck, backlighted against the darkening sky. Her silhouetted figure and the graceful way she held herself made her appear so youthful that the sight of her tired face startled Allison. The months since Gus's death had exacted their toll. After exchanging hugs and a few words, the two women fell silent as they gazed out over the canyon, a silence invoked by the beauty of the landscape but just as certainly by thoughts that must be similar: how strange it was not to have Gus there with them.

When Diana went to the kitchen to pour them some wine, Allison followed her back into the house. She moved around the living room, looking at the objects and framed photographs that crowded every table. Though most were of Diana and Gus, others were of Diana's family.

One, on the mantel, caught her eye. It was an old photograph of a much younger Diana standing beside a woman who bore a strong resemblance to her. Behind them was a stone clock tower surrounded by flowers.

"Is that one of your sisters?" asked Allison, as Diana returned with another glass of wine.

"Yes, that's Betsy. It was taken near her house."

"Oh, where's that?"

"In Connecticut," she said, reaching to straighten the frame. "Lyme."

Diana led the way back to the deck. A lattice trellis laden with bougainvillea covered the wall of the house and arched over their heads like a canopy. The breeze picked up, filling the air with the perfume of the flowers.

"It was nice of you to change your plans at the last minute," said Allison. "I really wanted to see you."

"It was only a bridge game. They'll have no problem finding a fourth with my level of skill. But you didn't come to hear about bridge, did you? You have something on your mind."

"Did you know I was adopted, Diana?"

Diana took a swallow of her wine, then turned to Allison.

"Of course."

"Do you know anything more? Like where I came from or who my parents were? Anything at all?"

"Gus never told me more than just the fact that you were adopted, and I never felt I wanted to ask Françoise."

"When did you find out?"

"It seems as if I always knew. When I went back to work for Gus you were already on the scene. But you were still an infant. And," she continued, now looking out into the darkness, "your uncle already loved you very much."

"I was lucky, wasn't I?"

"You're so right, Allison. And I'm not talking about money or anything like that. What Gus gave you was so pure and selfless that sometimes not even a real father is capable of that kind of love."

"Diana," said Allison, her throat tightening, "a crazy idea occurred to me today."

"What's that?" Diana asked.

Allison watched Diana closely. *This is it,* she thought. She wasn't sure she could get the words out. "That maybe Gus *was* my father," she finally said.

Diana seemed stunned for a moment, then reached over and pulled Allison to her.

"Oh, if only he could have been, my dear. He would have loved nothing better. But that would have been impossible." Allison started to interrupt but changed her mind. "We tried for a long, long time to have a baby. It was futile. Absolutely futile. After a while Gus decided to have some tests. He found out he was sterile. It nearly broke my heart. His too."

"Oh, Diana, I'm sorry. I never knew," said Allison, relief surging through her.

"Well, it's not the sort of thing a person likes to talk about, is it?" said Diana with a caustic laugh.

No, thought Allison, no it wasn't, any more than she would like to own up to the contradictory feelings she was experiencing. She was not the child of Gus and Diana, as she had begun to think in the last few hours. The enormity of the idea, unwittingly planted in her mind by Guy Barnes had taken her breath away. She had been obsessed by it and afraid, for if it had been so, how would she have dealt with the awfulness of Gus and Diana's never telling her? Everything she thought about herself and believed about them would have been utterly changed. But it was not true. That was not the way it had happened. The mystery of her birth remained and for now it was a strange source of comfort.

43

When Mr. Barnes arrives, Neal, show him in," said Allison, returning to her office after a long lunch with Parker Welles.

"I was just going to tell you he called while you were out. He can't make it, but he sent this over." Neal handed Allison an envelope marked Confidential.

"I see," said Allison, suppressing her disappointment. "Well, in that case, call Ben and ask him if he can come see me now."

In the privacy of her office, Allison opened the envelope. Inside was a handwritten note:

> Dear Miss Morton:
>   Sorry to break our appointment, but I have nothing to tell you yet. My office in New York thinks they may have turned up something, however, so I may have good news soon. Don't be discouraged. This type of investigation into the past takes time to produce results. I will be in touch, in the not too distant future, I hope.
>   Regards,
>   Guy Barnes

At the sound of the intercom, Allison looked up from the note, expecting word that Ben was on his way. "It's Mr. Hewitt," said Neal instead. "Do you want to take it or shall I tell him you'll call back?"

"Put him through, Neal," she said. Her plans for the coming weekend were still uncertain, depending on a family obligation of Lucian's. She would fly East if he either canceled his visit to an aunt and uncle in Dutchess County—a rather social pair, from the sound of it—or arranged for her to be included.

"Hi, Lucian."

"Hi, Al. I talked to Aunt Emily, and she and Uncle Oggie would like to have you come to Millbrook too. What do you say?"

"I'd love it."

"The Jack Russell trials are Saturday morning, so we should drive up Friday evening. Friday afternoon would be even better. Think you can make it that early?"

"I think so. Are you sure it's all right with your aunt, though?"

"Positive. I'm afraid I've made Aunt Emily out to be a real social dragon, which isn't fair. She's my favorite relative, and I know she'll adore you. And I guarantee you'll develop a real crush on Uncle Oggie. He's sort of a Yankee version of George Burns. Old, cute, and slightly lecherous. Be sure to bring your riding gear, by the way."

"Sounds great, Lucian, but I've got to run now."

"Sweets, there is one more thing," he said.

"What's that?"

"I've got a fantastic opportunity, Al, but I need your help."

"What kind of help?" asked Allison uneasily.

"I need twenty-five thousand. Just for two days. Forty-eight little hours."

"Oh, Lucian, I don't like this kind of thing."

"Don't be upset, please. I know it's a nuisance, but this is too good a thing to pass up. I'll tell you all about it when I see you."

"It's more than a nuisance, Lucian."

"You know you can trust me. You'll have the money back in two days. Promise."

"All right," said Allison unhappily. After meeting with Ben, she telephoned her bank and transferred the money, then called Diana to switch their lunch date on Friday to a later date.

"Of course I understand, Allison dear," said Diana, after Allison explained where she was going. "I hope I'll get to meet this new man of yours soon. He sounds thoroughly charming."

Before the afternoon was over Allison had to answer similar questions about the upcoming weekend from both Ben and Lee.

"Sounds more and more like a dish," said Lee, following her usual line of response to any information she was able to glean from Allison about Lucian. "A Waspy dish, but I sometimes think they're the best."

Then came a call from Adrian Frame.

"What can I do for you, Mr. Frame?" she asked in her coolest tone.

"I thought we were on a first-name basis, Allison."

"I'm busy, Frame. What's on your mind?"

"You. I still believe that we can work out this impasse and also become friends if only you'd stop being such a tight-ass. I'm saying that, I hope you understand, in the friendliest manner."

"Is that all?"

"Not quite. I'm going to New York this weekend and I thought you might like a ride. Now that the old Gus Morton G-Three is flying under another corporate banner."

"Who told you I'm going to New York?" Allison asked hotly, knowing at once that it had to be Lee.

"Lots of people tell me lots of things. You seem to be the only one who doesn't want to be civil. Maybe we'll cross paths in—"

Allison slammed down the phone.

Mrs. Ogden Longwood, Aunt Emily to Lucian, was every bit as stuffy as Lucian had hinted. She was tall and thin, with an unyieldingly straight carriage and the coarse, ruddy skin of someone who spends a lot of time outdoors. She was as haughty as royalty with Allison, immediately establishing that though Allison had gone to the right schools she was definitely in the wrong business. On the drive from New York, Lucian described her as one of the leading horsewomen of a very horsey county, one of whose two great passions was the local hunt, a subject that Lucian warned Allison not to raise. It appeared that Aunt Emily was in a snit about the hunt club's new egalitarian stance. Just this year it had relaxed its membership rules and invited a local housepainter to join. In this context, Allison imagined that her own show business association would seem to Lucian's aunt like just another arriviste trait.

Emily Longwood's other passion was her Jack Russell terriers, which she entered in a special competition held every fall to show off the feisty little breed's hunting skills. They were compact, utterly fearless dogs, first bred by a Reverend Jack Russell, a man of both the cloth and the hunt, to carry in his saddlebags. The last of the preliminary trials were to be held early the next morning, and Emily Longwood was convinced that only Lucian could handle her temperamental bitch, Pansy. Pansy had taken two firsts the preceding year, but lately she had been misbehaving. At a competition earlier in the summer, the dog had even taken a nip out of one of several pups Emily Longwood had begun to show successfully.

"Pansy's jealous, of course," said Emily Longwood at dinner. "She needs a man's touch. I can't persuade Oggie to help, so thank goodness for Lucian. He's volunteered to take her on."

"Since my aunt pinned me down by the neck with her riding crop . . ." Lucian added later with a laugh as he and Allison sat out on the terrace with brandy and coffee. The Longwoods had already retired in preparation for the next day. "You *are* going to come and see me work my charms on the good Pansy, are you not?"

"I wouldn't miss it for the world."

"Your reward will be a nice long ride. I'm lousy on a horse myself, but even I can appreciate how fabulous the riding country is here." It was now too dark to see anything more than the outlines of the hills surrounding them. Allison stared up at the stars, flung like a jewel-encrusted cape across the sky, and found herself wondering how soon Guy Barnes would get back to her.

"You're a good sport, Allison," Lucian continued after a while.

"Oh, you mean about your aunt? I'll bet she has a heart of gold," said Allison, cutting back to the present and picking up on what she supposed was Lucian's allusion. The brandy had relaxed her. She couldn't work up any emotion about Mrs. Longwood's unpleasantness.

"Aunt Emily? Oh, I wasn't talking about her, sweets. I was referring to the money you lent me. What I've been doing is shorting platinum. It's a way to really break the jackpot, but you've got to be ready to move. Fast. You ought to give it a try yourself."

"No, thanks. I'm not interested, really. . . ." She let her voice trail off. She never liked discussing money.

"You're too nice to say it, but what you're thinking is you've got all the money you need, right? Well, I'm not exactly hurting either. Don't think I'm in this game because I have to be. I'm in it for the fun. I get a bang out of it, and I have a hunch you would too. Does the thought tempt you?"

"I don't know. Maybe," said Allison noncommittally.

"I tell you what, I'll let you know the next time another deal like this turns up, okay? And now, if you're as sleepy as I am, let's go upstairs." He put his arm around Allison and pulled her close. "Aunt Emily is old-fashioned enough to put us in different bedrooms, but we can solve that problem, don't you think?"

The terrier trials were held in a large, well-mowed field stuck halfway up a high hillside like a patch on a pair of jeans. Though it wasn't yet nine and the grass was still wet from the night before, the parking field was already filled with vans and station wagons showing license plates from as far away as Maryland. Women in Bermudas and cable-knit cardigans were setting up luncheon tables under a blue-and-white-striped tent, and scores of serious-faced owners were leading their yapping, squirming charges over the courses they would run and putting them through their test paces. Lucian, with Allison tagging behind, set off in one direction to work Pansy, while his aunt took the pup who had been nipped and two other young dogs to the opposite end of the course.

At ten o'clock the meet began. Allison joined Ogden Longwood, who viewed his wife's obsession with laconic amusement, outside the enclosure fence for the first event, going-to-ground. The little dogs were renowned for their courage in chasing down quarry, even if it meant following the animal down its hole, and in this simulation they were tested for their speed in crawling on their bellies through an underground tunnel toward a "quarry," represented by a frantically squealing rat inside a cage.

Pansy's turn came at the midway point. Some dogs took so much time going through the tunnel that it seemed as if they had fallen through to some other world. Other dogs began the course, then panicked and backed out. Pansy, the former champ, however, distinguished herself by being the one dog to refuse even to give it a try. As they watched first Lucian and then Emily Longwood herself attempt to persuade the recalcitrant dog to perform, Ogden Longwood muttered under his breath, just loud enough for Allison's ears, "Poor Pansy." Then, a moment later, "Poor us."

And trouble there was. Though the only outward sign of Emily Longwood's extreme displeasure was a stiffer back and a tighter cast to her mouth, the anger her husband recognized spread like a virus to the dogs, causing a nervousness that rendered them incapable of following a command. The other events—the hurdles, which were a kind of steeplechase in miniature, and the flat races—were washouts not only for Pansy but for the three other dogs as well.

As Allison worked her way through knots of spectators, looking for Lucian, she felt a tap on her shoulder. She turned to face Adrian Frame.

"Fancy meeting you here, Miss Morton," he said, bowing extravagantly from the waist. For once he was dressed normally, in a tweed sports coat rather than in his signature tunic jacket. His dark, oiled hair glinted unpleasantly in the sunlight.

Allison was so taken aback that for a moment she could neither speak nor turn away.

"I've always liked this little breed. Love to inflict pain and don't mind taking a little in return to get what they want. They attract a fine crowd. Proper people with proper money. Perhaps you and your friend can join me for a drink?"

"I'd rather drink from a ditch. Good day," she said, wheeling around and walking away.

Later, as they waited in their car in the parking field for the traffic to clear, Mrs. Longwood announced that she was "not in the mood" for riding.

"I'll stay home and keep you company, Aunt Emily. Anything that's higher off the ground than a barstool makes me dizzy anyway," said Lucian, trying to gloss over his aunt's ill temper. "My uncle will do the honors, Allie. You don't have to worry about her, Uncle Oggie. She's a terrific rider."

After she had changed into jodhpurs and boots, Allison went to the stable to meet Ogden. There she found the Longwoods arguing about whether she could handle the high-spirited bay, Capitan, that Aunt Emily customarily rode and that Ogden had asked to have saddled for Allison. At his suggestion, she mounted the horse and walked and trotted it around the open yard until she had won Mrs. Longwood's grudging agreement.

"All right, Emily, now that that's settled, this young lady and I will be on our way," said Ogden. "I see Ed and Dickie waiting for us. Neighbors of ours we ride with every Saturday," he explained, turning back to Allison. "You'll enjoy them. Now this is what we're going to do. We'll ride straight ahead through a couple of fields until we get past the fruit trees, then we'll cut in—you'll see where when we get there. You're going to love this. Best riding in the East."

They started off at a trot across a long, narrow field that was bordered by a road on one side and an orchard on the other, then moved into a slow canter. Feeling exhilarated, Allison began to pull away from the others. She looked back at Ogden, who nodded and waved his hand forward in the direction she was going, and galloped the length of the field. There, she bent down to open a gate in front of her without dismounting, glanced up at a few cars passing by on the road, and continued ahead.

Once on the other side of the fence, she urged Capitan to pick up the pace again. As Allison leaned forward over the horse, she saw out of the corner of her eye a car parked on the edge of the road several hundred yards in front of her and a man standing beside it with a rifle pointed toward the sky. Something was odd about his stance, but before she could figure it out, there was a loud report from the gun and Capitan reared, throwing Allison backward through the air. Bruised and shaken, but all in one piece, she looked up and saw the man still standing there. Though he was too far away for her to make out his features, she could see he was staring at her. He gave no sign of being concerned for her welfare—in fact, she could swear she heard him laugh. By the time Ogden and the others reached her side, the man had climbed into his car and driven away.

"Damnation to hell," shouted Ogden. "We've been having trouble with people stopping their cars and shooting birds from the road. It's amazing nothing like this has happened before. Thank God you're all right. Lucian will forgive me for your bruises, but I would have disillusioned him forever if I had returned with a seriously hurt girl. Now, my dear, why don't you ride behind me on my horse? We'll go nice and easy."

"Oh, I can manage on Capitan, Mr. Longwood. Don't worry."

As they retraced their way to the house, Allison thought again about the man with the gun. She was sure now that she had heard him laugh. It was a dark, harsh sound, and the more she thought about it the more certain she was that she had heard it before. Of course, she realized after another few moments. It was Adrian Frame's laugh. And that explained the strange angle of his gun. He had not been shooting at a bird. He had been trying to spook her horse, and he had succeeded brilliantly.

"Do you remember our conversation at Aunt Emily's?" Lucian asked Allison on the telephone a few days later.

This was the first time they had spoken since she had returned to L.A. The weekend in Millbrook had ended on an unexpectedly convivial note, with Emily Longwood heaping praise on Allison for her spunky recovery from her fall. Allison had not mentioned her suspicions about Adrian Frame—why upset everyone?—but in the few days since then she had grown even more angry about the incident. Obviously Adrian had appeared at the dog trials only to irritate her, and then, by chance, he must have caught sight of them in the crush of cars leaving the parking lot and been able to follow them. But why had he gone to all that trouble? She considered calling him and demanding an explanation but rejected the idea. The explanation, in a way, was self-evident. He got a kick out of humiliating and unnerving people. It was his brand of good, clean fun.

"What conversation are you talking about?" Allison now asked Lucian.

"You know, when I said I'd tell you about the next good investment deal I heard of. So you could make a killing, too. Well, it's here."

"And?"

"And how about it? You seemed interested in it before. Listen, for just a hundred thou in we can triple that, and there's virtually no risk. We can go halves on the take this time, so all you have to put in is fifty. I'll have your half of the investment plus your share of the profits back to you by Friday. Remember, I haven't missed a deadline with you yet. Now what do you say?"

To her surprise, Allison said yes.

Though her flight to New York had been smooth, Allison arrived at JFK full of tension. The reason was simple: money. The money that she had given Lucian. Every day of the past week he had telephoned to say he was sorry it was late but that it was on its way. Nothing came. Now he was fully a week overdue. He was supposed to pick her up, but after all the other passengers on the flight had collected their luggage and gone, Lucian still had not appeared. Allison called the agency's theatrical of-fice, which she worked out of when she was in the city, and left a message for Lucian that she would be at her loft. He should meet her there.

As the dinner hour came and went and still there was no word from him, and no answer when she called his apartment, Allison grew increas-ingly puzzled and a little worried. The next day, she telephoned Lucian's home and his office, but there was again no answer at home and only a recorded message on the office phone. She had a break in her schedule at ten-thirty and, anxious to see if she could find out what had happened, she took a taxi to Lucian's apartment.

The door to the apartment was opened by a pretty, deeply tanned woman in her early thirties. "Yes?" she asked, smiling.

"Hello," said Allison, surprised. Who was this? "Is Lucian home? Lucian Hewitt?"

"I'm sorry, but he's not here. He left Wednesday when I got back from Sagaponack. He's been apartment-sitting for me."

"What?" said Allison in a voice like that of an amnesiac waking up. "I'm sorry, but I don't understand. Isn't this Lucian's apartment?"

"Well, no, it isn't, but come on in," the woman said, seeing how nonplussed Allison was. They walked into the kitchen, where the woman made them each a cup of coffee.

"Do you mind if I ask you something personal?" asked the woman, who had introduced herself as Maisie Boland.

"No," said Allison. "Go ahead."

"You haven't by any chance given Lucian money, have you?"

"Why do you ask?"

"You don't have to answer if you don't want to."

"Yes . . . yes, I did."

"Oh, you poor thing," said Maisie. "Lucian's a wonderful person. The nicest man in the world. I've known him all my life, and I just adore him. But he's absolutely hopeless with money. As his family and all his friends painfully discovered a long time ago."

"What do you mean?" asked Allison, realizing that she had been taken.

"You don't really know anything about him, do you? You poor dear. His father threw him out of the family business years ago. Since then he's been playing at being a broker. He inherited some money from his grandfather. Fortunately, he can't touch the principal. He just gets by somehow on the interest. And some of us help out by letting him look after our houses and apartments when we're away. He's also got a battle-ax of an aunt in Millbrook who watches out for him. But why am I telling you this? More gory details than you probably want to hear, right?"

"It's okay," said Allison. What a laugh—on her. Despite his illustrious name, Lucian obviously was one of those fortune hunters Gus had worried about. He had had his eye on her, too—wasn't that what he had said the day they met? The thought made her skin crawl. Funny that someone should come after her now, when she had no fortune to chase. "At least I understand now what happened," she added. "He said he needed the money for a market play."

"Market! I wouldn't trust him at Dean and DeLuca's with a shopping list. What a story! Lucian's only business is at the Regency playing backgammon. Or at Belmont, betting. If you don't mind my asking, how much does he owe you?"

"Fifty thousand," said Allison, choking slightly on the words.

"Oh!" said Maisie, in an appalled voice. "But I hope you realize he isn't a crook. He wouldn't intend to keep the money. He'll do his best to pay you back, I'm sure of it. Though it might take a while," she added, her voice trailing off as her supply of conviction seemed to run out.

There wasn't much more to say, so Allison rose and thanked Maisie Boland for the coffee. It crossed her mind that she might send Guy Barnes after Lucian, but she knew she wouldn't.

"By the way," said Maisie, as she opened the front door for Allison, "he didn't pull the flower trick on you, did he?"

"What?"

"They call him 'the florist' at The Brook. I shouldn't give away his secrets, but I will," said Maisie. "He told me once that it's the best technique, bar none, to meet a woman. He goes out and spends a hundred dollars on a beautiful bouquet of flowers and then figures out an excuse to present them to the woman he's interested in. She's flabbergasted and flattered. He strikes up a conversation, and the next thing you know, they're having a drink. He says it never fails. He *is* a charmer, too. Makes it hard to get too mad at him, doesn't it?"

44

don't like to have to use this word, but I think I must."

Craig Cutler paused long enough for Allison to ask, "And what word is that, Craig?"

"Disappointment. There's no other way to say it. That's what I feel, pure and simple. And I also feel as if I've been taken for granted way too long. Excuse me, Allison, but lately I've been thinking of myself as the good wife of many years, still holding on to the beachfront of being passably good-looking, a pretty fair cook, and a decent hump, but just not exciting anymore. That's the way U.T.M. regards me. And, take my word for it, the other agents who are constantly cruising me see Craig Cutler in a whole different way. To them I look like Madonna, cook like Bocuse, and fuck like the Happy Hooker. You both wanted to know what was on my mind, and that's it," Cutler concluded, finally looking directly at Hal Gilliam and Allison, after delivering his *cri de coeur* to a clothesline of clouds hanging above Central Park in an incredibly blue September sky.

"I don't really know where to begin, Craig," said Allison, after a long enough pause for the three of them to become aware of the distant insectlike drone of traffic thirty-two stories below. "All of us at U.T.M., and I mean *all* of us, both here and on the Coast, regard you as our most important literary client." Allison hit every syllable of *literary*, knowing that Craig Cutler dearly loved the word, though the closest his work came to that definition was as near as airline food came to quality French cooking.

"We also feel that we've handled our end well," she went on. "Exceptionally well. Hal is devoted to you, and you know it. I can't think of another literary agent who takes telephone calls almost every weekend or at one in the morning, as he frequently does from you, and who furthermore actually enjoys it. I am pretty certain he can't say that about many of his other clients, if any. That, by the way, should not leave this room,

Craig," Allison said, nodding significantly. "Our track record speaks for itself. Each book deal, both here and worldwide, has been substantially better than the one before it. We've sold every title of yours as a miniseries since *Dark and Deadly Land*. Not one of them for less than eight hours! So when you say you're disappointed, I'm frankly baffled. We believe we've performed. Performed damn well."

Craig Cutler slowly crossed and uncrossed his legs, clad in fine suede trousers, and twisted his gold I.D. bracelet so that the nameplate faced forward, catching the late afternoon sun like a downed pilot signaling for rescue, then he leaned forward, his face no more than a foot from Allison's.

"Your uncle would have known what's bothering me. He made a point of following my career closely. As well as those of my competitors."

"Craig, I can only agree with you that my uncle was an exceptional person. But please believe me that we care as much as he did about you *and* your career. Now what's the problem?"

Craig Cutler reached into his jacket pocket and tossed a folded newspaper clipping onto the small table beside Allison's chair. Craig had a propensity for dramatic gestures, probably a carryover from his years of writing scores of "bodice rippers" under as many aliases as a major Mafia family. But then, twelve years ago, he had broken out with his first multigenerational saga, nine hundred pages about a violent and incredibly successful family of lumber barons. Every eighteen months since then, another Cutler tome that stretched over a minimum of three generations, to his last book's amazing eleven, came out and went right to the top of the bestseller list. The reviews were uniformly terrible—one was headlined, GENERATION PAP—but his audience just kept growing.

Allison unfolded the newspaper article and read it quickly. It was an account of Stephen King's record-breaking new contract. It also listed the purported advances he had received from his foreign publishers.

"Well?" asked Craig, rolling out the word like a delicate but lethal weapon.

"I remember reading this," she answered after handing the article to Hal, who of course had seen it before.

"I'm glad you keep up with current events, Allison," Craig said snidely, "but I'm more interested in what you think about it."

"What I think? That's easy. I think we're going to do much better than that. In fact, I know we are. We'll better King's deal by twenty-five percent."

"That's very encouraging," said Craig with a smile he usually re-served for inept coatroom attendants, "but I'm not signing on again with U.T.M. unless you guarantee it."

"I have no problem with that. This is your best book by far. We'll make it," answered Allison.

"I knew you'd say . . . What was that?"

"I said, U.T.M. will guarantee that we'll beat King's deal by twenty-five percent."

"And if you don't?"

"Then we'll waive our entire commission on all book sales."

"But, Allison," Hal Gilliam interjected, "that will cost us—"

"I know, Hal. Easily over half a million dollars. What do you say, Craig? Do you accept my proposal?"

"Accept? I'll go you one better. If you put that in writing, I'll give the agency not just this book but my next three. How about that?"

"That's fine, Craig. Let's shake on it," said Allison, extending her hand. "Of course, the lawyer in me should also say, let's sign on it. But that will follow."

"You know something, Allison? There's a lot more of your uncle Gus in you than I realized," he said as he gripped her hand. "But tell me, how're you going to pull this off?"

"We'll tell you afterward how we did it, but I already know where we'll start."

"Where?" Craig Cutler asked excitedly.

"The Frankfurt Book Fair."

"I'd love to know what your strategy there is going to be."

"Hal will fill you in on every step *after* we've completed negotiations. For the time being, though, all you should concern yourself with is put-ting the finishing touches to *Storm of the Heart*. We'll need a clean manu-script for Frankfurt. Lots of them," she said with a confident laugh.

Later, when Hal returned from escorting Craig Cutler to the elevator, he went to the bar built into the bookcase and poured himself a large Chivas, neat.

"Want one, Allie?" he asked.

"Of course. This calls for a celebration."

"Celebration? Great idea. While we're at it, why don't we also cele-brate the anniversary of the Tet offensive! Allison, I think you've painted us into a corner that Houdini couldn't get out of. I hope you realize that my bottom line won't look too good this year when we lose Cutler's half a million in commissions."

"Don't worry, Hal. You're not going to lose a penny. There's even a chance you and I might have some fun with this. We'll pull it off. I should say, we have to pull it off! If we do, we'll buy some breathing room with the Frames, and that we could really use. This is the kind of big, innovative deal that will make U.T.M. look good."

"That's if we can do it," said Hal glumly.

"Come on, Hal, try to relax a little. This one rests on my shoulders. And just remember three things. No, make it four. First, is this the most commercial book you've seen in years?"

"Without question."

"Second, both Ben and Lee agree with us. They think we can sell one of the networks on twelve hours prime time, no problem. That will give us a packaging commission that's more than the half-million figure you just mentioned. Remember, I told Craig we'd forgo commissions on *book* sales. I never mentioned performance rights. Third, we're getting Cutler to sign for three books instead of one. And fourth, the deal's going to work. I think I have a pretty good plan."

"Jesus, I sure hope so," said Hal, numbing his anxieties with another large swallow of scotch.

The flight to Frankfurt three weeks later for the international book fair held there every October was uneventful except for the last-minute presence of Lee Simons. Allison was surprised that Lee wanted to join them, but she claimed she had always wanted to check out the land of tall, blond Aryan men, and besides, she had a client shooting a movie in Munich at the same time. How could Allison say no?

Just after the seatbelt sign was switched off, Lee crossed the aisle and headed toward Allison. Seeing her approach out of the corner of her eye, Allison quickly started poring over a contract that was on her lap.

"You know, Allie," said Lee, looking down at her, "we haven't had a glass of champagne and a chin-wag in such a long time. I'm sure Hal wouldn't mind switching seats with me for a bit."

"I'm sorry, Lee," answered Allison. It was harder every day for her to mask her feelings toward Lee, but she forced herself to be pleasant. "Hal and I have at least two flights' worth of work ahead of us. You and I'll get together soon."

When Lee had finally returned to her seat, Allison continued reviewing plans with Hal for the dinner they were throwing for Craig Cutler's foreign publishers.

"Don't you think they'll be surprised Craig isn't there?" asked Hal.

"That's the fourth time in the last four days that you've asked that.

And the answer is still no. Compared to the other surprise we have in store for them, Craig's absence will have as much impact as the last visitation of Haley's Comet. Are all the Xeroxes taken care of?"

"And you've asked me that question three times," answered Hal, laughing.

"Touché," said Allison. "Tell you what. Let's take a break. I'm just going to run through things one more time to make sure we didn't miss anything."

"You should try to grab a few winks, Allison. This is your first fair, and believe me, it's hectic. It has the pace of Cannes matched with the glamour of a Ford plant. Standing around all day on cocoa matting on top of a cement floor makes you feel like you've run in a marathon by the end of the afternoon."

But there was no chance she could sleep, Allison knew. As crucial as pulling off the Cutler deal would be to the future of U.T.M.—*her* future at U.T.M., to be more accurate—her head was crowded with other thoughts. A few days ago, Guy Barnes had called to say his New York office was making progress. The flight plans into the Marine Air Terminal for 1962 were surprisingly intact. He was almost certain now, by a process of elimination, that the plane that brought her to New York as an infant had been chartered out of Great Barrington, Massachusetts. By an E. Hanson, the record showed. There were no Hansons now in the area who fit the profile, and the name Hanson meant nothing to Allison, but Barnes was not discouraged. They were still searching for the lawyer and sifting through adoption papers in county seats within a sixty-mile radius of Great Barrington. "We're hanging in there, don't you worry," Barnes had said.

As she thought about Barnes and idly stared at Lee Simons's sleeping form several rows ahead of her, she had an idea. She took a small notepad out of her handbag and jotted down a few words. Why not ask Barnes if his man in New York could take on one small extra job? Getting the goods on the so-called screenwriter for *The Flame and The Mountain*. Allison remained convinced that Lee had had a big part in trashing Sean's script, and the feeling still gnawed at her. Even if she and Sean never got back together again, Allison wanted to know what had happened.

Sean . . . It was he who dominated her thoughts, for, unknown to the others, every mile they traveled over the black canvas of the North Atlantic brought her closer to him. Though she had not breathed a word to Oscar Buckman since Cannes about her feelings for Sean, Oscar, bless his heart, must have guessed anyway, for he had made it his business to keep Allison aware of Sean's whereabouts. Several weeks after Cannes, Sean and The Combine had received a grant to perform at a dozen universities in England and on the Continent, and it happened that while she was going to be in Frankfurt, he would be at one of the last universities on the tour, the University of Heidelberg, hardly more than an hour's drive from Frankfurt. This time, Allison determined, was not going to be like Cannes. This time, somehow, some way, she was going to see him.

When they arrived in Frankfurt it was not quite seven in the morning, and raining. Allison, who was unsure whether she had slept, felt a rush of excitement that wiped away her tiredness. A limousine took them in the opposite direction from the city, toward the Taunus mountains. They would be staying at the Schlosshotel in Kronberg.

Hal had raved about the Schloss, but nothing he had told her prepared Allison for her first sight of it. They rounded a turn, and there it was at the end of a sweeping driveway, a fairy-tale castle set among tall trees planted by the royalty of Europe. Its gray stones gleamed in the rain. Its roofline was so crowded with many-leveled gables and towers in so many different architectural styles that it seemed for a moment like an entire village rolled into a single building. It had been commissioned at the end of the nineteenth century by the eldest daughter of Queen Victoria, who had married the heir to the Prussian throne. The castle was for her to live in, with her own large family, a little bit of England in the middle of Germany, a reminder of houses she had loved as a girl.

After checking in, Allison placed a call to Sean's hotel in the hope that she just might catch him there. She didn't want to waste any time reaching him. When she found she had missed him, she left a message for him to call her at the Schloss and drove with Hal to the fair. They wandered together through the maze of booths on the three floors of the main international hall. Allison knew just a few of the publishers, so it was Hal who led the way, making introductions, renewing friendships, here and there describing new projects by their clients that various publishers might want to acquire.

Later that afternoon, they touched base with their guests for the dinner party that evening—Cutler's foreign publishers, from the largest to the smallest. As part of Allison's master plan, the American publisher Henry Spalding was not invited, even though he was in Frankfurt. To pique his interest, Allison had slipped him an early copy of the manuscript in New York. His response was all she could have wished. He thought the novel was Cutler's best. He wanted to buy it right then. He was prepared to sweeten his offer, over and above his advance for Cutler's last book. "Substantially sweeten it" were his words, but Allison was not prepared to accept an offer from him. Not yet. Not until after the Frankfurt dinner.

The party at the Schloss was to begin at seven, with drinks in the library. As Allison descended the broad, red-carpeted staircase at six-thirty, she glanced appreciatively around her. The expansive rooms downstairs were not as idiosyncratic as the facade, but they were just as personal. The paintings on the walls, the porcelains, the *objets,* the furnishings were part of the collection of a real person, rather than the assemblage of a hotel developer with a generous budget.

The publishers arrived promptly at the appointed time. Although most managed to suppress their curiosity about the new novel, of which so far they had been told almost nothing, the Japanese and Swedish publishers were bluntly inquisitive. The only aperitif offered was sherry, and though the cocktail hour lasted considerably less than an hour, it was long enough to give Allison the chance to slip away to the dining room to change the seating so that the insistent questioners were out of reach of both Hal and herself. She had her own delicate timetable for the unfolding of that evening's drama. No one would be allowed to disrupt it.

After everybody was seated at a long table in the adjoining private dining room and the first course had been served, the waiters moved down the table filling glasses. They were offering Evian, apple cider, and a nonalcoholic Swiss beer that Allison had asked the Schloss's somewhat startled sommelier to put on ice earlier in the day. Many of the guests declined all three choices, waiting for the wine to be poured. When it did not appear, they looked in confusion at Allison.

Allison had been waiting for just this moment. She tapped her glass for attention and rose to her feet.

"Ladies and gentlemen, Hal and I wish to extend a warm welcome to you on behalf of Craig Cutler and the rest of our colleagues at Universal Talent Management. We are honored to have you as our guests this evening, but even more honored by the seriousness, the dedication, and the brilliance with which you have published Craig Cutler in your own countries." Allison looked slowly around the table, locking eyes with every person seated there. "Although I am meeting most of you for the first time, I already think of you as . . . family, and as family members, I must ask you to bear with me, your American cousin. Our bond is strong and it is deep, and I am certain it can more than survive this one small experiment in abstinence. I will explain everything to you later, but for now, let us enjoy our dinner—without wine."

As Allison sat down, there were a few murmurs of discontent. One word, *idiotique,* voiced by the French publisher, floated up and over the others, like a soap bubble.

"Ah, Monsieur Carrier," said Allison lightly, "that is a word which does not need translation. In fact, I concur with your judgment."

"*Mais oui,* a marvelous cut of venison such as this," the Frenchman gestured at the serving in front of him, "should be accompanied by a nice Burgundy or perhaps a Beaujolais, but—"

"But, in any case, by some kind of wine. Especially a French wine," said Allison good-humoredly.

"Bring on the Coca-Cola. Or better yet, the Dr. Salt—I mean Pepper. Let's have a real Yank drink with a Yank dinner," interrupted the Australian publisher in a boisterous, amused tone.

The little frisson of tension burst in the laughter that followed and the dinner proceeded pleasantly. A few guests even took up the Australian's facetious suggestion and ordered Coca-Cola. By unspoken agreement, no one mentioned Craig Cutler. The arrival of coffee was another private signal for Allison, who rose from her chair.

"You've been very patient, all of you, and Hal and I deeply appreciate it," she said, "but now the time has come for you to see why we did not offer you any wine with dinner. We wanted you to conserve your energies and senses for the main event."

With perfect synchronization, the door to the dining room swung open and a stream of waiters entered, each holding aloft, like a precious Sèvres platter, a red manuscript box tied with a black ribbon. They set one down in front of each publisher. *Storm of the Heart* was inscribed on top of each box. Several recipients, as impatient as children around a Christmas tree, started at once to loosen the ribbons and open the boxes. Allison watched without a word until she had everybody's attention.

"You have in front of you what I believe is Craig Cutler's biggest, most important book to date. We are extremely excited about it. Its potential for success is, quite simply, astonishing, and I do not say that casually. Let me share with you, confidentially, the information that right now, the three major networks in the U.S. are locked in battle for the miniseries rights to the book. I expect a record-setting sale to result. We are gratified by this eagerness, *thrilled* really, but it advances our timetable substantially and puts us in an unusual position. And you as well, for we are going to propose a very unorthodox thing. We are going to ask you to go home tonight—and read."

The room was dead silent now. A teaspoon clattered against a cup, bringing a few nervous laughs.

"We have concluded that we have no alternative but to break with past precedents and sell foreign rights to *Storm of the Heart* right here in Frankfurt. You'll see when you open the manuscript—and please don't do so for one more moment," said Allison, looking directly at the over-zealous Spaniard who was about to open an envelope he had extracted from his box, "you'll see that we've indicated to each of you the figure we are looking for. If any of you think the price is out of line, feel free to withdraw. There'll be no hard feelings. I should warn you, though, that there are other publishers in every country who are prepared to pay what we want for the book. Sight unseen." Allison held up a thick bunch of envelopes and fanned the air with them. "These are their offers. Please don't make me turn to them. We want to keep all of you in the Cutler family, a sentiment that Craig himself sincerely shares. We are accepting bids tomorrow afternoon between twelve and two—"

"Tomorrow!" exclaimed the Portuguese publisher.

"The Schloss is providing us with three open telephone lines during that time to enable you to reach us without difficulty," Allison continued, unperturbed. "Limousines are waiting outside now to take you back to your hotels. Until tomorrow, good luck. And by the way, champagne is on us tomorrow. A case of Piper-Heidsieck 'seventy-six—for each of you who renews your family ties."

At the stroke of noon the following day, the first telephone rang in Allison's suite, where she and Hal had set up headquarters. From then on, the phones did not stop. With the exception of the Spanish publisher, whose firm was near collapse under the weight of a disastrous foray into the book-club business, every single one of the dinner guests met the agency's terms. The Japanese insisted on negotiating the terms upward, an almost unheard of circumstance, in exchange for a firm option on Cutler's next book.

Half an hour before the deadline, they had heard from every publisher but two. Allison and Hal could not stop grinning at each other. The grand total in foreign sales already was close to three million—40 percent more than Cutler had received for his last book. Hal took the next call and Allison the last, only minutes under the wire. Both of the last two callers accepted.

As soon as Allison put down the phone, she jumped up and hugged Hal. "We did it!" she shouted.

"I'm amazed," said Hal, shaking his head. "I didn't think it would work."

"Ye of little faith," she said, laughing.

"But I didn't. Just look at it from their point of view. Those poor schmucks—"

"Wait a minute. Why 'poor schmucks'? They should be overjoyed."

"Maybe. When they come out of shock. After all, they figure they've earned the right to Cutler. They know they're lucky to have him, but at the same time, they've done their jobs well. Then along we come. We invite them to a swell dinner. They think they're going to get patted on the backs. Celebrate. Hear about what Cutler's cooking up for them next and when to expect it. Instead we hit up on them then and there. *And* without any wine to drown their sorrows in. Raise the ante by a hefty sum. And inform them they only have overnight to answer."

"But that was the idea. Put them on a hot spot and see if they would jump."

"It was *your* idea, Allie, all yours, and I hand it to you. Just remind me to insist you come to Frankfurt next year," said Hal with a big grin. "Should we call Craig?"

"Absolutely. You make the call, and I'll order the champagne. I think we deserve some ourselves, don't you?"

While Hal called Craig Cutler, Allison stood at the window, staring down at the green vista. The park surrounding the Schloss had been turned into a golf course, the skyscrapers of the city off in the distance, like a mirage. It seemed incongruous that so much money had just changed hands in a setting so idyllic that it could pass for the kind of luxurious country estate one retreated to in order to escape the business world. After the waiter brought the champagne and poured it, they raised their glasses in a toast.

"Good old Craig took the news like the pro he is," said Hal dryly. 'Nice work; but I expected as much. The book really is good.'"

"You know, I've been thinking about Henry Spalding. Why keep him hanging until we get back to New York? Let's see if we can also make that deal now. What do you think?"

"If it feels good to you, let's do it. I'd be happy to take your instincts to the race track any day."

"Let's ask him to raise his offer by twenty percent, in view of what's happened just now. . . ."

Hal nodded.

"And tell him to give us an answer by tonight."

"Okay," said Hal finally. His hesitation, however, made it sound almost like a question.

"Henry's read the material," said Allison. "And had more than enough time to talk about it with his people. What I'd like to do is this: ask him to have dinner with us here tonight, with the understanding that he be prepared to wrap things up. If he doesn't accept, it'll be like saying no to the whole proposition."

"Are you prepared to give a little?"

"Yeah, I think so, don't you? But I'm not going to let him know that beforehand. Should we give it a try?"

Hal nodded, and Allison telephoned the American publisher at his booth in the convention hall. He wasn't there, but five minutes later he returned her call. While she spoke to Spalding, Allison watched Hal studying her to see if he could tell how the conversation was going.

"He said we're crazy to be asking what we are for it," she told Hal as she hung up, "but he didn't say no . . . yet."

That afternoon at the fair, Allison felt as high-spirited as she had early in her deal-making days with Uncle Gus. If Cutler's foreign publishers were in shock, they did not look or behave that way. There were handshakes and congratulations all around, and even a hug or two.

When they returned to the Schloss at the end of the day, Allison jogged for half an hour on the path around the perimeter of the golf course, then stopped at the front desk to check for messages. No, Mr. Spalding had not called. That was good. He intended to keep their dinner date. No, Miss Simons hadn't returned to the hotel yet. That was frustrating. Lee didn't need to know at this stage how well things had gone, but Allison had decided to tell her anyway, for the satisfaction of showing Lee that she wasn't the only one capable of pulling off a deal like this. No, still no word from Sean.

Allison showered and began to dress. She and Hal were meeting Henry Spalding in the bar in half an hour. She had decided that before she went downstairs she would try to reach Sean one more time, but then she suddenly lost her nerve. She started putting on her makeup in front of the bathroom mirror, and then all at once, before she could postpone the call a moment further, she ran into the bedroom, snatched up the phone, and asked the operator to dial Sean's hotel in Heidelberg.

Lee Simons had just arrived outside the door to Allison's suite. She was in a foul mood. An English director she had been courting for months had told her over lunch that he was going to sign with another agency. Her actor client in Munich, who had been telephoning all day to complain about his producer, finally had provoked her into losing her temper, and now she would have to patch things up with him. Ordinarily she would have ignored this summons from her highness. No doubt the princess wanted to share her cleverness over the Cutler property. Big deal. But, on the other hand, it would be Lee's first chance to satisfy her curiosity about Allison's frame of mind. Maybe Lee would be able to tell if things were going according to plan, and if they were, well then, little Lee Simons wouldn't be in such a bad mood after all.

Lee was about to knock when she caught the sound of Allison's voice. She must be on the phone. Lee strained against the door, but Allison's voice was muffled, indistinct. Then, realizing that Allison must be calling from the bedroom, from which she probably could not see the front door, Lee had an inspiration. She pushed down gently on the handle and the door gave. She eased it open a crack and was instantly rewarded.

"Is this the Atlas Hotel?" she heard Allison ask. "Could you please tell me if Mr. Flores is still registered there? Yes, F-l-o-r-e-s. Mr. Sean Flores."

Lee's heart began to pound. She held herself very still in order not to miss even one word of what Allison had to say. She wouldn't move now if a truck were bearing down on her.

"Oh, he *is* there?" said Allison, in an uncertain tone. "Well . . . I left a message for him yesterday, and—all right. If you think I should. This is Allison Morton. I'm at the Schlosshotel in Kronberg. Please ask Mr. Flores to call as soon as he can. It's very important."

Lee eased herself back out of the room and closed the door behind her. This was perfect. Lee had guessed exactly right. Allison *had* been trying to reach Sean, and it sounded as if Sean was avoiding her. God, what a genius she was, Lee thought. She wanted to shout her own praises to the heavens, but that would not do. She mustn't blow it now, after all her patience.

Last spring in Cannes, she had been furious when she discovered, at the very last moment, when it was too late to do anything but hope for the best, that the artsy playwright also was in town for the film festival. This was a real slip-up, the kind of thing Lee Simons usually managed to prevent. When she decreed the end of something, anything—a project, a career, a relationship—it stayed dead as a dog, but instead here were these two insufferable creeps, booked into hotels almost next door to each other and no doubt aching to make things up. Lee feared the worst, and when it didn't happen, she swore to make sure that there were no more close calls. She would see to it the two lovers stayed apart. Forever.

As soon as she had returned to L.A., she secretly put herself on The Combine's mailing list by making a modest donation to them in her housekeeper's name. She began to track their engagements, and when she noticed the converging dates in Germany, she called a friend at Oscar Buckman's office for the name of their hotel in Heidelberg. She explained that she wanted to send Sean a script, but actually she had something infinitely more special in mind.

On the day they were flying to Frankfurt, she shut the door to her office, reached into the phonebook where she had hidden Sean's condolence letter to Allison, and pulled it out. Working fast, she tore it into neat, tiny pieces. She dropped the pieces into one of U.T.M.'s best cream-colored, engraved envelopes, sealed it, and placed it at the bottom of the pocketbook she would be taking to Germany. She had already made arrangements with a courier service in Frankfurt to pick up the envelope at the airport and deliver it to Heidelberg.

The message of the torn letter would be clear to Sean. No words of explanation were necessary. The message from Allison was, *Who needs your sympathy. Stay away. I don't need you. I don't want you.* And if, as Lee guessed might happen, Allison tried to telephone Sean at his hotel, Sean, proud fool that he was, would be too offended to do anything other than give Allison as good as he had gotten. He would refuse to return her call.

Lee walked several paces down the corridor, then approached Allison's door again and knocked loudly. Now for the secret fun of observing Allison's misery.

"Who is it?" called Allison.

"Lee."

"Come in. The door's unlocked."

"Congratulations, Allison darling," said Lee in her most syrupy voice, laying it on thick as she walked into the living room. "Hal told me about the brilliant coup you two pulled off on Cutler's book."

"Well, thanks, Lee. The publishers all seem pretty pleased. You should be pleased too. It makes your job a lot easier."

"Tell me about it," said Lee breathlessly, as if she were waiting for the juiciest of inside stories. The bitch wasn't letting on that anything was bothering her.

"I have a better idea," said Allison. "I'm about to meet Hal in the bar. Henry Spalding's having dinner with us. He's Craig's publisher in New York. Why don't you join us for a drink? While we're waiting for Henry, I'll bring you up-to-date on everything that's been happening."

"Oh, that's a wonderful invitation, but I already have a commitment," gushed Lee, discreetly studying Allison's face. Why waste time with the princess, she was thinking, if the princess wasn't going to give anything away. Where was the satisfaction? "Can you catch me up tomorrow instead?"

. . .

Allison arrived in the bar a few minutes before seven. Hal was already seated at a table that commanded a good view of the entrance and an even better one of the brooding Turner that was one of the prize treasures of the Schloss. There were several other groups of people in the comfortable, elegantly paneled room, but the seating was so well spaced that they had all the privacy they wanted. They had only just begun to discuss some new angles to their selling strategy for the Cutler miniseries when Allison raised her head and saw Henry Spalding. He was standing in the doorway. As soon as he had their attention, he gave them the thumbs-up sign and broke into a smile, and later, at dinner, he agreed to their price without a protest.

The last piece of the Craig Cutler puzzle had fallen into place. Just as the bottom seemed to be falling out of her personal life, Allison couldn't help thinking.

Two days later, on what should have been an exultant return flight to New York, Allison pleaded a headache as an excuse to close her eyes, put on her earphones, and politely escape from Hal's understandably high spirits. The day after the deal with Spalding, Lee had called California to tell them to pass the word to the networks that U.T.M. would be looking for an even larger commitment on Cutler. Now Hal, who had spoken twice again with Cutler, couldn't stop beaming. And for good reason. They had gotten everything they had asked for and more, maybe even enough to impress Hector Frame and his disgusting son.

In spite of their triumph, however, the trip had turned sour for Allison. As busy as she had been in the last few days, only one thought had preoccupied her. Sean. Would she hear from him? And then her time in Frankfurt dwindled to nothing, and what she couldn't allow herself to imagine happening, had happened.

Sean had not returned her call. He did not want to see her. Or even speak to her. She could not fool herself any longer. There was nothing between them, nothing at all.

45

Allison returned from lunch only minutes before Lee Simons breezed into her office.

"What perfect timing, Lee. Sometimes I think you've put a tail on me," said Allison with a show of amusement she did not feel.

"Darling, it's true that I like to keep an eye on you, but only because I worry about you."

"Come now, Lee."

"No, I'm quite serious. You're working much too hard. You've got to take it easy, at least some of the time, and I've got just the right tonic for you. Tonight I'm going with Ed Maloney to a screening of Coppola's new movie. It's supposed to be fantastic. Afterward we're having dinner at Le Dome. Why don't you come along?"

Allison was shaking her head before Lee finished speaking. Lee, pointedly ignoring her, plunged on.

"Ed may not be much of a writer, but he's got a good sense of humor and a set of buns only Leonardo could have done justice to. And most important, he jumped at the chance of meeting you."

"Sorry, but I can't do it."

"You're terrible, Allison darling. Everybody's calling you a born-again workaholic. Don't forget that it's important to be seen out and around in this business. Your uncle was a master at it."

"I like it this way," said Allison tartly. She was losing patience with Lee. This was the third time since Frankfurt that Lee had tried to involve her socially. She could not imagine why. It was not as if any friendship existed between them. Allison tolerated her only because at the moment she had no choice.

"Well, if you change your mind . . ."

"I appreciate the thought, Lee. Maybe next time. Now, if you'll excuse me, I've got some calls to make."

As soon as Lee left, Allison rang Ben Wildman and asked if she could see him. Her lunch had been with Adrian Frame, and it had left her tense and irritable. She loathed these monthly meetings, which, as major stockholders, the Frame faction had the right to demand. She had not mentioned the riding accident in Millbrook to anyone—why give Adrian the satisfaction of knowing she had repeated the story, endowing it with a new life, like a dirty joke making the rounds?—but the fact that something so nasty had occurred made their business dealings that much worse. Adrian always insisted on meeting over lunch, causing the Sturm und Drang of the occasion to be accompanied as often as not by a case of indigestion. Today Allison had been disturbed as well by an urgent feeling that time was running out for her. It came upon her in waves. She would rise above it, shove it away, and then it would hit her again a few weeks later. The Frames had had their claws sunk into the agency for well over six months. How were they ever going to dislodge them?

With Parker Welles taking the lead, they were on their way to restructuring the agency's debt, selling off weak subsidiaries, and cutting corporate overhead. These were all prudent business moves, but they might not be enough.

There was one other approach that had occurred to Allison, though she had not yet decided to pursue it, and Parker was disapproving. It would not be illegal, but it was hard ball, the kind of tough, underhanded tactic the Frames themselves might use, the kind that normally Allison would not. But now, if she must, she would play this last card. She could not be sure it would work, but it might. The one thing she knew, deep, deep down, was that she would do anything to keep the company—Gus Morton's creation—out of the hands of the Frames.

"I've just survived another encounter with friend Adrian," said Allison, when she and Ben were settled in armchairs pulled up to the conference table. "Barely survived. It was quite unpleasant."

"What else would you expect with our favorite corporate terrorist?" asked Ben dryly.

"Exactly. His idea of charm is cracking jokes at our expense, like, our overhead is still so high it could pass for the rate of inflation in Brazil. But seriously, we're getting awfully close to the edge. Unless we can come up with something new, the Frames will be able to do whatever they want to us, and I suspect it won't be pretty."

"You don't have to be so delicate with me, Allison. If you mean they'd use a truncheon on us, I think you're correct."

"Correct, and more than a little desperate. We've trimmed expenses as far as we can. The only thing left would be to cut out personal cars—"

"Not that!" laughed Ben, pretending to be scandalized. "Unless you want to start a riot."

"Well, it wouldn't do the trick anyway. What we need is cash. If we had enough, we might be able to strike a deal with the Frames. What's in the works that we can lean on for more up-front money? For instance, on Cutler, what about pushing the networks even further and asking for an even heftier advance commitment? They love him. They just might go for it. That's the sort of thing I'm thinking about."

Ben nodded. "I agree, though I don't think we can improve Cutler's current deal. How about selling his next unwritten book?"

"Great idea. What else? How is the Mona Lacey package coming?"

"It'll be finished up this week."

"Can we make a similar deal for anyone else? Do some syndication deals a little early?"

As Allison listened to Ben calmly reviewing the status of their various clients, she grew more confident. Of course they could get rid of the Frames. And their secret weapon was right under their noses. It was their clients. The best there were. With these clients, they could put enough deals together to knock the Frames out of the ring. Then she would never have to play that last card. After talking for another half hour, Allison and Ben agreed to stop for now and continue the following day, after Ben had canvased the other senior agents for ideas.

Ideas still were tumbling through her head when Neal came in to tell her who had called while she was with Ben. She glanced at the messages and decided to return Diana's call first. After Gus's death, Allison had plied Diana with questions about U.T.M. and gradually it had become a kind of habit to talk regularly, and occasionally to have dinner or a drink together. It was Diana who chose to keep up the custom, but Allison went along with it willingly.

Diana seemed to have so little left in her life: her family, none of whom she was close to; golf and tennis once or twice a week; the occasional bridge game. She had put her career behind her—its association with Gus was too painful—though she still stopped by the office from time to time. The more Allison discovered about Diana, the more sympathy she felt. She thought frequently of her conversation with Diana about her and Gus's inability to have a child. Was that why they had never married? Had their disappointment killed off the need to make a bigger commitment to each other? It was puzzling, but what other reason could there be? And why had she and Diana not been able to talk about these kinds of things before? Why had they been such . . . well, such strangers? The answer now seemed as sadly obvious to her as it had months ago to Sean: they had been competing for Uncle Gus's attention. They had been rivals.

"I've just made a huge batch of chicken curry," said Diana, "so how about coming by tonight for a bite? If I remember correctly, it's one of your favorite dishes."

"I'd love to, Diana, but I'm swamped. I know I'm going to have to stay late. I'll probably just go to a take-out place on the way home."

"Oh, if you're doing that, I've got the place for you. I hear it's terrific."

"Stop. Don't say another word. Let me guess. You're thinking of Roberto's, right? I read about it last week."

"Yes, that's the spot. Now don't work too late."

"I'll be out before eight."

"Allison, don't you dare stay that late. I'm going to call you at seven to make sure you've left. You hear me?"

"I hear you, Diana. You're as bossy as Uncle Gus used to be," she said, laughing.

At the end of the day, after most of the others in the office had left and the phone calls were down to a trickle, Allison dug into the paperwork that had been piling up on her desk. She skimmed through a stack of memos, deal sheets, and proposals, okayed half-a-dozen contracts Ben had dropped off earlier, and finally started drafting a letter she had been procrastinating on all day to a studio that was trying to renege on a commitment. She had barely begun her explanation of their position, which was absolutely unassailable, when Adrian Frame telephoned. He wanted to talk some more about a couple of issues she thought they had reviewed thoroughly at lunch. As soon as she managed to get him off the phone, he called her right back. Was she free to continue the discussion over dinner?

"Sorry, but I have a date with Roberto," she snapped, nearly gagging at the thought of dining twice in one day with the man.

"Who?"

"Just a private joke, Adrian, but I'm afraid I *am* busy. Can't this wait until tomorrow?"

After agreeing reluctantly to meet him in her office at three the next day, Allison turned back to the letter. She had just worked her way through one more sentence when Lee leaned into her office.

"Night-night, darling. Now you're sure you won't join Ed and me?"

Allison shook her head. "I meant it when I said no before, Lee. In fact, popular me, I've turned down two more dinner invitations since. I'm just going to hit a take-out joint on the way home and leave it at that."

"I hope you're going to—"

"Roberto's. I am."

"Oh, you know about that, do you? Well, I bet I'm one up on you in the dessert department. Ever heard of Sweet Lynn's?"

"No."

"It's a mega dessert scene. An absolute must, especially for their cheesecake. And best of all, it's only a few blocks down from Roberto's. Try it. *À bientôt.*"

Allison listened to Lee's heels click down the hall for a moment, then turned back to the typewriter. She reread what she had written and tore it out of the typewriter. It was all wrong. Better to get out of here now, get some fresh air, something to eat, and take another stab at the letter in the peace and quiet of home. She shoveled scripts and papers into her briefcase, glanced at the time—it was only a little after six-thirty—and then, remembering Diana, picked up the phone.

"I just wanted to let you know what a good girl I am. I'm leaving the office now," she said.

"Now you're talking sense."

"And I'm going to treat myself to a nice big fat dessert, too."

"Sweet Lynn's?"

"What is this, mental telepathy?" laughed Allison. "Lee just mentioned the same spot to me two minutes ago."

"Enjoy it, dear, and give me a call tomorrow."

Half an hour and two detours later (Roberto's for country pâté, seafood salad, and cold grilled vegetables, Sweet Lynn's for the cheesecake), Allison was back in Bel-Air. Even before she put her key in the front door, she heard Tonny barking and, simultaneously, the ringing of the telephone. She dropped her purchases on the kitchen counter and picked up the phone. It was Cynthia Traynor, calling to complain about the treatment she was receiving at her law firm. They had plenty of California clients. You would think that once, just once, they would find an excuse to send this particular junior associate to the Coast to bill her seventy hours a week from the other side of the country—and see her boyfriend. But not these Simon Legrees. As soon as she could break into the familiar litany, Allison put down the phone to feed Tonny, whose impatience at his dinner hour was awesome. Then she switched to the telephone extension in the library and sank gratefully into the soft cushions of the sofa for a long, juicy talk.

When she returned to the kitchen fifteen minutes later, Allison discovered that Tonny had had a good time for himself in her absence. He had pulled the bag from Roberto's onto the floor and consumed all the pâté and most of the seafood salad. Never one to follow a Pritikin regimen, he left the grilled vegetables untouched. It was hard to get mad at him, though, so she merely tossed the remnants of food into the trash can and returned to the library to tackle the contents of her briefcase.

It was going to be a long night of reading. She started with the most promising project, a screenplay, and for the next hour she read steadily, totally absorbed by the writer's idiosyncratic, clever turn of mind.

Casting the movie in her head, Allison padded out to the kitchen in search of something to eat. It was only when she entered the kitchen that she heard it, a low agonized sound that gripped her with dread. There was only one thing it could be. Tonny! Where was he? What was wrong?

She followed the sound from the kitchen, down the hall, into her bedroom, and then, seeing the door ajar, into the bathroom. She turned on the lights and gasped. Tonny was backed into a corner, lying stiffly on his side, his legs rigid, his body shaking with spasms of pain that seemed too big and too violent for his small body. His head was arched away from his body as if he were straining toward some magic pocket of air just beyond his reach. Allison kneeled down and laid her hand on the trembling dog. At her touch, he yelped as if her hand had burned him, then fell back to the floor, panting and gasping.

Terrified, Allison ran to the phone to call the vet. Thank God, he operated a twenty-four-hour clinic. Somebody would be there. Maybe Dr. Jackson himself. It was not yet nine. As she dialed the clinic, she prayed that he would be there, but of course he wasn't. When the man on duty answered, she blurted out that her dog seemed to be having a seizure, she didn't know what other word to use, and that she was bringing him in. Would he call Dr. Jackson? she begged. Please, please call Dr. Jackson!

She wrapped Tonny in a towel and raced to the garage. She placed the dog tenderly on the backseat and drove down to Sunset Boulevard, then east as fast as she could.

"It's all right, sweet puppy. It's all right," she kept repeating, though she knew it wasn't.

When she reached the clinic, she saw that Dr. Jackson had just arrived. He picked up the dog and rushed inside, calling to his assistant over his shoulder as he ran, "Sam, get some phenobarbital. Quick."

Dr. Jackson carried Tonny into the operating room and laid him down on the stainless steel table. The spasms that ripped through him had grown stronger.

"When did this start?" asked Dr. Jackson, as he bent over the animal, checking his vital signs. Allison began to answer, then immediately stopped. Something awful was happening. Tonny was having a seizure that looked as if it might crack open his body. The vet wrestled with the animal, trying to hold him still as he thrashed and twisted and gasped for air, and then as suddenly as it had begun, the convulsions and the rasping ceased and the examining room was plunged into a deadly quiet. The vet held a stethoscope to the dog's chest and listened intently. After a few moments, he stopped, shook his head, and looked at Allison. "I'm sorry," he said softly. "I was afraid it might end this way."

Dr. Jackson waited until Allison had her emotions under control, then, prompting her with questions, asked her to describe the dog's daily routine as well as anything that had occurred from the time she'd gotten home that evening. Was the dog allowed to run without a leash? No. Twice a day, Allison's housekeeper walked the dog. Ernestine had been instructed never to let Tonny off the leash. Was there rodenticide—rat poison—present in the house or on the property? No. Had there been any milder incidents of this kind that might have pointed to a predisposition to nervous collapse? No.

"What do you think happened?" asked Allison, choking on the words.

"I don't know yet, but I'm going to find out. If it's all right with you, I'll do an autopsy. My lab should have an answer for us by tomorrow."

Allison nodded, said goodbye, and hurried out the door without looking again at the dead animal. When she arrived home and saw Tonny's dishes in the corner of the kitchen, as if at any moment he might come trotting around the corner hoping for something more to eat, she began to cry. Angrily, she yanked open the cabinet where she stored his food and threw it and the dishes into the trash. As she thought about the day last year when she and Sean had picked up Tonny and taken him home, she began to cry in earnest, for she knew that she had just lost the last bit of Sean she had still possessed.

Late the following day, the veterinarian telephoned Allison at the office.

"Are you *sure* Tonny couldn't have gotten into some kind of poison?" he asked.

"Positive. I never use any poisons. And Ernestine swears she's never let him run off the leash. I called her this morning and asked her."

"Was there anything new in the house? Anything different? Anything at all?"

"No. Absolutely nothing."

"Then I'm puzzled, Allison. The lab's findings were unequivocal. Tonny died from a massive dose of strychnine in his bloodstream, enough to kill a human being, let alone a dog."

46

Parker?"

"Yes," came the groggy reply.

"I know it's the middle of the night, but—"

"Is something wrong, Allison?" Parker almost shouted into the receiver, now suddenly awake.

"No. Nothing's wrong. It's about the Frames."

"What have they done now?"

"Remember what I mentioned to you the other day? About how maybe the only way we can ever really get rid of them is to get something on them? Some kind of information?"

"Yes," Parker answered in a cautious tone.

"I want you to move on that. Right away. I've just been kidding myself that anything else would work. Get me everything and anything you can lay your hands on that concerns them. Every deal they're involved in, potential exposures, rumors, gossip, the works. Everything they own—or want to own. I want the most complete dossier on the Frames that you can put together."

"That's some job. It'll take time to do it."

"That's the one thing we don't have."

"When do you need this?"

"It's late already, Parker."

47

The more Allison thought later about the phone call she received early the next morning, the more convinced she was that she had finally heard the truth about Tonny's death. Why hadn't she figured it out for herself?

When the phone rang, she had assumed it would be Parker with a question. Instead it was her housekeeper.

"Hello, Ernestine. What's wrong? Are you sick?" Allison asked, guessing she was calling to say she could not clean that day.

"No, Miss Morton, I'm okay, but I need to talk to you before you go. I need to tell you . . ." Ernestine broke off and started crying.

"What is it, Ernestine? Are you all right?"

"It's my fault, Miss Morton. My fault," said Ernestine, choking as she spoke, and then her story came spilling out. She had lied to Allison the other day. She *had* let Tonny off his leash on the day he had died. He was so frisky and happy whenever she let him run free that she could not resist it. She had let him have a good long run that day. At one point she had lost sight of him for a while, but that had happened before and she wasn't worried. He was such a good dog. He always came when she called his name.

It took Allison almost ten minutes to calm down the distraught woman. Of course Allison did not blame her. Of course it was not her fault. Who would suspect that Tonny would get into poison? It was against a dog's nature to be leashed all the time. Allison understood.

As she reassured Ernestine, Allison herself began to feel relieved. The dog's death made sense now. He must have swallowed poisoned bait left out for the coyotes that had become bold enough to come down from the hills into Bel-Air and Beverly Hills. She had read in the paper recently that a child had been mauled almost to death by a coyote only a few blocks from the Beverly Hills Hotel. People, parents especially, were frightened, but, dammit, didn't they ever think through the possible consequences of their actions, leaving poison where any neighborhood animal might find it?

Yes, Allison told Ernestine, she would forgive her. She must try not to worry any more about it.

As the morning progressed, Allison hardly thought about Tonny. Since the dog's death she had been consumed with crazy theories about what had happened, but now she could set them aside and go on to other things, like the agency business she had been putting off. After conferring with Ben and several of the younger agents and dictating a half-dozen overdue letters, she placed a call to Cynthia. This was not so much unfinished business as new business. At first she could not reach her friend, but as she was returning from lunch, Neal waved the phone at her. Cynthia was on the line. Allison closed the door of her office behind her.

"Sorry I couldn't get back to you sooner, Allie, but I've been up to my ears taking depositions. Negligence suit. Ask me anything, anything at all, about drill presses. Too bad it's not a category on *Jeopardy*. But enough of me. How are you?"

"Fine, but that's not why I'm calling. I'm calling to congratulate you."

"Congratulate me? For what?" Cynthia asked uncertainly.

"Your new job."

"What are you talking about? What job? Has all that Southern California sun finally gotten to you?"

"The job that's waiting for you here if you want it. How does associate director of legal and business affairs for Universal Talent Management sound to you?"

"Like a mouthful. Are you seriously offering that to me?"

"Only if you'll accept."

"You're not kidding now, are you? It's the best idea I've heard since I started at this . . . Devil's Island of torts. Tom's been telling me I should quit and I've wanted to, but I thought I had to give this thing some more time. But I've had it. I miss you, Allie, and God only knows, I miss Tom. There. Have I accepted enough?"

"Aren't you interested in hearing your—what do executive headhunters call it?—compensation package?"

"Of course I am, but I trust it won't get in the way of my taking the job. When can I report for work?"

"There's a one-way first-class ticket to LAX coming to you by messenger today. It's good from this date on."

"I'll need a week or so to settle things here."

"That's fine, but the faster the better. I really need you. You know the downside already. You—and I—could be out of work in a month. On my better days, though, I'm convinced that will never happen. Otherwise, I promise you, I wouldn't ask you to stick your neck out this way. . . ."

There was a long silence before Cynthia spoke.

"I'm a gambler," she said. "I can't wait to tell Tom. We'll have to get a bigger apartment than the one he has now, but that's no problem."

"Why don't you come out this weekend and start looking? U.T.M. will treat you to another round trip."

"Okay, it's a deal. But, Allie, there is one more thing I'd like."

"Name it," said Allison.

"A shorter title," said Cynthia with a laugh.

As Allison thought about Cynthia joining the firm, she thought also about their friendship. They had met in their freshman year at college and liked each other immediately. In law school, they became even closer. Allison was the sort of person who liked most people she encountered, but a really good friend was rare. To have Cynthia right here would be wonderful.

Cheered by this prospect, Allison quickly got back into the rhythm of work and that night fell into bed before eleven and was able to sleep as she had not for quite a while. The next day she pushed herself even harder, so hard that she skipped an after-work exercise class, stayed at her office until almost nine, and did not make it to bed until after one in the morning. She was so exhausted that she was grateful merely to be lying down, but when she tried to fall asleep she could not. She tried all the old tricks for coaxing sleep to come, but the more she tried, the more wide awake she became. And then she got hit again by the crazy theories about Tonny that she had thought she had banished. Lying there in the dark, she felt as if her head would explode with the voices inside her, wrangling as if they were fighting over one of the poor dog's bones.

—Isn't it just a little too convenient to blame his death on coyote poison? demanded the skeptic within her.

—What do you mean?

—Well, it sounds to me like the first excuse that popped into your head.

—That's not fair and it's not true. I considered every other possibility.

—Oh, sure. I know those theories of yours. That someone injected poison into his can of dogfood with a hypodermic needle like those Tylenol freaks a few years back. How harebrained can you get! Or that something happened at the take-out places you went to. But don't you think some others would have gotten tummy aches too, hmmmm? Or that maybe somebody even sneaked into your car and planted the poison in your pâté?

—I know that isn't true. I double-checked the car myself. There was no sign that anyone broke into it. And I always lock it.

—Well then, doesn't all this suggest anything to you, or are you totally unimaginative?

—I don't follow.

—Think about somebody you know who doesn't pull his punches.

—Adrian Frame!

—Now you've got the picture. Quite the prankster, isn't he? I have a strong notion that laying out some poison for your pooch is just his latest way of getting to you.

—Oh, my God!

—Is that all you can think to say?

—Dr. Jackson said he found enough poison in Tonny to kill a human being. He must have been after me. He must have wanted to kill *me*.

—Come now. By spreading poison on people's lawns?

—Of course not! I meant, maybe somehow he was able to get at the take-out food. He might have known I was going to Roberto's.

—But you told me your trusty little BMW was tight as a drum.

—Maybe I was wrong. Maybe I just didn't notice. The point is, the man is capable of killing somebody. Don't you remember there was some business involving a murder that his father got him off on?

—True, but you're not kinky enough meat for him. Just relax.

—Relax. Are you joking?

And that was the end of any hope Allison had of falling asleep that night. Adrian's laugh echoed in her ears and she imagined Tonny shaking in her arms again. She switched on the light by her bed and read until it was time to get up and shower and dress for the day—the day, as it happened, that Cynthia was flying in for the weekend.

When Cynthia arrived that afternoon, she drove directly from the airport to the U.T.M. offices to talk with Parker Welles and a few of the other executives she would be working with, as well as with Diana. Diana had decided recently that she wanted to retire completely from the agency, which was why Allison felt justified in offering the job to Cynthia. The two of them would overlap for a few months, then Diana would leave the business for good.

Later Allison and Cynthia drove to Gus's house—Allison still thought of it as belonging to Gus, not to her—for a celebratory drink.

Allison was tired and depressed and anxious, but she did not want to let this occasion go unmarked.

"Parker's as nice as he can be," said Cynthia as Allison opened a bottle of Moët Chandon and poured them each a glass.

"I agree," said Allison, raising her glass to Cynthia. "To you, and a long career at Universal Talent Management. I've wanted you to join me for a long time. I really need a friend here."

"I would say so, judging from what you've been telling me about how things are at the agency."

"I'm not talking about U.T.M. I mean in other ways."

"Something to do with Sean?"

"No, no. He's back from Europe, I hear, but I'm not talking about him," said Allison, her voice trailing off.

"Allie, what's bothering you?" said Cynthia, leaning forward. "Something's on your mind. I've felt it since I arrived."

"You're right, Cynthia," said Allison, looking at her friend intently. "You're so, so right. Something *is* on my mind. I'm scared, that's what it is. I'm scared half to death."

PART FOUR

48

Though Los Angeles was a place of climate rather than seasons—and how Allison yearned for a real fall and spring; sometimes even the thought of a gray slush of winter was appealing—occasionally, when the wind blew steadily off the ocean, there were days of such clarity and brightness as to be almost magical.

This was one of them, and the beauty of the day and of the setting, the lawn and terraces behind Gus's house, was gradually quieting her anxieties. She had had some rough moments lately.

On Friday, talking with Cynthia, she had worked herself into a frenzy of alarm again about Adrian Frame, but looking at the whole thing from Cynthia's perspective, she began to have doubts. As crude and vicious as Adrian was, the idea that he would try to poison the head of a company his father was attempting to take over, and in the process do in his intended victim's dog by mistake, was too bizarre. Even Adrian would not think he could get away with something so blatant. And if by some wild chance he succeeded, he would be in worse shape than before, for then he would have incurred Hector's fury, and rumors abounded that Adrian was terrified of his father's disapproval.

By the time Cynthia had to leave to meet Tom Rosen, Allison had decided that her fears about Adrian were simple paranoia. What really had happened was what *seemed* to have happened: poor Tonny, ravenous as always, had eaten coyote bait. Cynthia said she would ask Tom to check it with the police. Probably they would find that there had been other, similar accidents—and a lot of dead coyotes.

On Saturday Allison went apartment hunting and gallery hopping with Cynthia and Tom, but declined dinner with them that evening, suspecting they would prefer some time alone, and dug into a script that Jake Gillette wanted to do. But then she began to brood again about Adrian, and this time he assumed the proportions of a monster in her mind.

Maybe he was the one who had set the fire that destroyed Gus's house. The police were sure it was arson. The fire had occurred just after Gus had closed on StellarVue, the Frames' company. Since the fire started in the guest house, maybe he had wanted to kill her—and destroy her uncle's spirit by her death. Maybe Françoise's death was not suicide. It was Adrian, after all, who had paid her airfare from Switzerland to California. He must have goaded her into her clumsy actions, which had cost the agency at least one important client, Reverend Horace. Maybe he thought she wasn't being effective enough, though, and decided to get rid of her . . . permanently. Or maybe instead he had gone to the house in search of her, Allison, and had to kill Françoise because she was in the way. Maybe, maybe, maybe. Once into this web of connections, it was hard to break out. The more she thought about it, the more terrified she became, until, mercifully, she simply collapsed into sleep. And the nightmare stopped.

On Sunday she woke up feeling marvelous. Her fears of the night before seemed to have evaporated into the soft, balmy air. It was gloomy in the library, where she usually worked, so she moved outdoors. Looking around at the flower beds that lined the terrace where she sat, a profusion of white, yellow, and red, and inhaling the subtle scent of the lemon and orange trees heavy with fruit, she decided the only problem with the perfection of the day was that she wasn't getting any work done.

Just then she heard a tinkling noise, a bell, a tiny jangle of metal like the sound of a baby's rattle. She turned around and spotted the source of the sound. A light brown puppy, round and cuddly, came tumbling around the corner of the terrace, its feet working with more excitement than dexterity. A red ribbon held a shiny silver bell around its neck.

"Are you lost, little guy?" Allison said, scooping the bundle of fur into her arms. "You don't seem very unhappy. Well, look here, you have a collar. Now stop squirming so I can see who the lucky person is who owns you. That's a good dog, just hold still a second while I take a look at this tag."

The inscription on the tag was simple: *I belong to Morton/Flores, 2393 Stone Canyon Road, L.A., CA 90077/133 Chambers St., N.Y., NY 10007.*

Allison stared at the tag. It wasn't that the words didn't make sense. They did. Absolute sense, but what did they have to do with her? *Everything,* she answered immediately. She jerked her head up just in time to see Sean appear from around the corner of the house.

"I figured this pooch was going to be bicoastal, so I had the collar made out accordingly. Only thing he's missing is a name," said Sean as he walked onto the terrace.

"Sean!" was all Allison could say as she ran into his arms.

They clung to each other without speaking, and then Sean took a small step backward and looked down at Allison. "You feel so wonderful," he said.

"Sean, why are—"

"Shhh, darling. I'll tell you everything in a moment, but not yet." He reached out, touched her lips with his fingers, and slowly traced her face as if he were sightless and needed to confirm her features. Then, moving closer, he kissed her so deeply that he seemed to be trying to get inside her very being.

Late that night, after hardly moving all day from each other's side, Sean and Allison went for a swim. The dark sky was clear and the air was exceptionally soft. The water in the pool, still heated by the day's sun, was warmer than the surrounding night, so that curls of mist danced on the surface. It was soothing, almost amniotic in its warmth, and the two held each other closely for a long time without speaking.

"Promise me you never will let me do that again," Sean finally said. "I was so stupid, so arrogant. So sure I was right."

"I promise. Though I think you made me promise that several times already today."

"Another time won't hurt."

After they kissed again, it was Allison's turn to ask a question.

"When did you say you wrote me about Uncle Gus?"

"Who's doing the repeating now? I told you, right after he died, as soon as I heard. I couldn't stop thinking about you, about how terrible it must have been for you."

"It was. It would have helped a lot hearing from you. I still can't get over your letter coming back to you months later in shreds. It has to have been Lee who did it."

"I agree. She's a monster," said Sean.

"Are you thinking about that pass she made at you?"

"I'm sorry I told you about that. I swore I wouldn't. But no, the key to her is that she's seething with envy of you. That's what drives her on."

"If Uncle Gus were alive, do you think she would have tried something like this?"

"No. She wouldn't have dared, but she would have wanted to. She hates your guts."

Allison, who was holding on to the edge of the pool with one hand, shivered at Sean's words. "Do you really have to leave tomorrow?" she asked a bit plaintively, though she knew the answer already. She had decided not to tell him about her morbid preoccupation with Adrian

Frame. Why worry him when he couldn't do anything about it? And probably her suspicions were a lot of nonsense anyway.

"The time'll go by so fast you won't even notice it. One more week rehearsing in New York, then we start shooting in New Mexico. As soon as we're there, I'll be able to hop back here every weekend. God, I'm happy about this picture. I never thought I'd get to make it. Oscar's a genius to have raised the money. And to think he's directing it. Wow! And I'm going to be in it. He's even got me believing I can act."

"I forgot to ask you, who told you about Tonny?"

"Oscar, of course. You know what he also told me awhile ago? He said he hated it when we split up, because he knew we belonged to each other. Those were his words. He said he'd been plotting ever since how to get us back together again."

"Dear Oscar," said Allison, smiling to herself. It hadn't occurred to her until this moment that if Oscar had not been trying to play Cupid when she saw him for a drink in Cannes, this movie of Sean's might never have come to pass. Probably Oscar had shown her the script only as an excuse to get her and Sean to meet. One of these days she would tell Sean how the movie had been financed. "You know what I'm thinking? Let's name the puppy for Oscar. Do you think he'd like that?"

"I think he'd love it." Sean ran his hands down the sides of Allison's body and his tongue lightly over her lips. "Would you consider a nutty request?"

"Do that again, and I'll consider anything."

"All right. How about letting those shits . . . you know who I mean—"

"The Frames?"

"Yeah, the Frames. Could you possibly . . . well . . . why can't you just let them win the day?"

"You mean, let them take over the agency?" said Allison, her voice rising at the absurdity of the idea. "No, Sean, you know I can't. Why are you asking?"

"Because I'm worried about you. They make my skin crawl. Everything you've said about them makes them sound capable of doing anything."

"It's true, they are awful," said Allison. Again she almost blurted out her concerns, but Sean kept talking, and the moment passed in indecision.

"And this whole business is taking a lot out of you. Do you really need it? You could practice law. You could set up a foundation with what you pull out of the business. You could do almost anything."

"Maybe so, but I'm not going to. Not now. Not until I finish with the Frames."

"Jesus, you're stubborn."

"Wouldn't you be? I can't quit on this until the agency is out from under them. And then I don't want to ever hear their names again. But," Allison laughed softly and lowered her voice, "I admit there is one more thing I want. Right this minute and very badly. Do you think you could come to my rescue?"

"I bet I could," said Sean with a grin, climbing out of the pool and pulling her up after him.

49

Several days later, just before noon, Allison received a call she had been waiting for. She had come to New York to attend the first preview of a musical about Paul Robeson written and composed by two of the agency's top theatrical clients, and not so incidentally to see Sean, who was there in his first week of rehearsal for his movie.

"Our man's in his apartment now," said the voice on the other end of the line.

"Alone?"

"She left about an hour ago. It's the second time she's seen him this week. But our boy is a real worker. Puts in a solid eight hours a day. Aside from her visits, he's always alone."

"That's what I wanted to hear, Mr. Rubino. I hope you don't mind my telling Guy Barnes what a good job you've done."

"Thank you, Miss Morton. By the way, there's one more thing you should know. I've been following this dude in and out of singles' bars for the past two weeks without seeing him have any noticeable success. He might be a touch excitable. You think you want me there, you know, nearby, just in case?"

"There's no need for that," said Allison, laughing. "I'm the dangerous one in this situation."

The building was a white glazed brick box on First Avenue in the low Eighties. An elderly Puerto Rican doorman, dressed in a uniform that seemed a cross between something worn by a Banana Republic dictator and a member of the chorus from a road company of *The Inspector General,* pointed Allison in the direction of the elevator. Since he was in the midst of studying the racing form in *El Diario,* he skipped the formality of calling the tenant to inform him that he had a visitor. No need for that. It was obvious that this lady was a woman of class. *Muy* class.

Her knock was answered almost immediately.

"Hi," she said, as she casually walked past Mike Plesser into a small studio apartment that looked as if it had been furnished during a thirty-minute shopping spree at Bloomingdale's.

Plesser's mouth was still agape, like a guppy's in a crowded tank, when Allison finally introduced herself.

"We haven't met, but I really feel as if I've known you for a long time. My name is Allison Morton. I think you know who I am. I'm here to talk with you about your career," she said, sitting down on a free-form loveseat coated with cat hairs. "Tell me, how's the *The Equalizer* episode you're working on going?"

"Well . . . fine, I guess. I'll be finished in a couple of days," he answered haltingly.

"That's what I like about you, Mike," said Allison as she opened her attaché case, "you're a real pro. You can really turn it out."

"Thank you," he said, smiling nervously.

"Arnie Nelson thinks you're going to have a big future. By the way, I liked your treatment very much. You know, *The Flame and The Mountain.* Too bad the deal fell through. But your work was terrific."

"It was okay."

"What did you say, Mike? I missed what you said."

"It was all right."

"All right? Why, it was sensational. The story. The characters. It was the freshest, strongest thing I've read in a long time. And I look at a lot of scripts. Believe me. In fact, it really surprised me."

"What do you mean?" he asked guardedly as he sat down across from Allison.

"Well, I've read all your other work," she said, dropping a small pile of scripts onto the coffee table, "and it bears no resemblance to *The Flame.* And I don't mean just because these scripts haven't sold. Until *The Flame,* you didn't seem to possess . . . how should I say it? . . . the kind of original mind that one would associate with this kind of story."

"What do you want, Miss Morton? I'm just a guy trying to make a buck. Every word in *The Flame and The Mountain* treatment is mine. I swear it."

"You don't have to. I believe you. Let's switch gears for a moment. I have an offer to make you. Do you have anything lined up after *The Equalizer?*"

"Come on, Miss Morton, don't play with me. You know the last time I flossed. This is the first assignment I've had since . . ."

"Since *The Flame and The Mountain,* you mean? You don't have to answer my question, Mike," Allison said with a laugh. "Of course I know what your assignments are. Or rather, your lack of assignments. You *could* use another job. How'd you like a guarantee to do four scripts for *Welfare Tango*? I think you might have read something about it in the trades. It will be shooting here in New York."

"You mean it?"

"I'm not finished. You could also be the script supervisor. It pays twenty-five hundred a week. The show has a full season commitment, by the way."

"What's the catch?"

"You're a very bright guy, Mike. All I want are some answers to a couple of questions. I'd like you to keep in mind that I run U.T.M., so if you think your answers might get you in trouble with someone else at the agency, I wouldn't worry about it. You understand what I'm saying?"

Mike walked to the window and looked down onto the crawl of traffic on First Avenue.

"What do you want?"

"*The Flame and The Mountain* was somebody else's idea, wasn't it?"

Mike looked directly at Allison for what seemed a long minute and then nodded.

"Why has Lee Simons been up here twice in the last few days to see you? I might be mistaken, but doesn't Arnie still represent your work in our shop?"

"She's a friend," he said softly.

"No, she's not. She came here to tell you to keep your mouth shut, didn't she?"

"I'm not looking for trouble, Miss Morton."

"That's what you'll get if you don't answer me honestly. I told you that I run the agency. Not Lee Simons. She can't hurt your career. But let me tell you, I certainly can. Do you understand me now?"

"I do," said Plesser, his shoulders sagging like those of a broken doll.

"It was Lee Simons who gave you the idea, wasn't it?"

This time he nodded immediately.

50

A nd therefore there's no possible way Gary will do a sequel to *Fate of Iron* without script and directorial approval and five points of the gross. You realize, of course, that Gary is as closely identified with the role of *Fate* as Stallone is with Rocky. We all believe that the potential for *Fate of Iron II* is even bigger than—"

The phone on Allison's desk suddenly rang. She had asked Neal never to disturb her while she was dictating. She still found dictating an unnatural process and needed complete quiet, without interruptions, to go through the two big folders of letters and memos that she faced three times a week.

"Yes, Neal."

"I'm sorry, Allison, but it's Lee Simons. She says she must see you."

"I'm sure she does, Neal, but tell her I'll be finished in forty-five minutes. I'll see her then." Allison carefully put the phone back and then asked Gloria, the stenographer who always took her dictation, "Where was I?"

"*Fate of Iron II* is even—"

The phone rang again.

"Yes, Neal?"

"She absolutely insists that she see you now. She says it's urgent."

"Well, if Lee Simons says it's urgent, then I guess you'd better send her in." Allison calmly replaced the receiver and looked at the stenographer. "Gloria, we'll pick this up after I finish with this 'emergency.'" As Gloria started to leave Allison's office she was almost knocked over by Lee, who stormed in without knocking.

"Some dumb motherfucker is going to be on the unemployment line before the day is out," Lee shouted as she approached Allison's desk.

"What's the problem, Lee?"

"My parking space, that's what!" Lee answered, her voice loud enough to carry out to the secretarial area beyond the closed doors.

"I doubt that it's a matter worth yelling about."

"Oh yeah? Some schmuck painted my name out and put in Ron Lieber's. That twerp Lieber could park that piece of shit Audi he drives anywhere, for Christ's sake. Do you know where I had to put my Rolls? On the street!"

"That still doesn't seem like a reason to get apoplectic, Lee," said Allison, the reasonableness of her tone further goading Lee's rage.

"You haven't seen anything yet," yelled Lee, her painfully thin, pale arms windmilling as much as the confines of her Bill Blass suit allowed. "Wait until I get my hands on the asshole who did this."

"You're looking at that person," Allison said, her eyes fixed on Lee.

"What the hell do you mean by that?" Lee asked, her large, heavily lipsticked mouth becoming immobile, looking suddenly like a wound.

"You don't need a parking space, because as of this moment you no longer have the use of a company car. U.T.M. is hereby terminating your contract." Allison slid an envelope across the desk to Lee. "Our terms, as you will find when you read the letter, are extremely generous. You have nineteen months remaining on your contract, and we're prepared to pay you the entire amount on a monthly basis. That is, until you get another job, of course."

"So, the little heiress has decided to make like a tough CEO. Well, let me tell you something, I didn't get where I am by being pushed around by rich bitches who've had everything given to them. You can't get rid of me that easily."

"Really?"

"The Frames won't let you."

"They've already been informed of it. All the other board members received a registered letter this morning. I'm sure *some* of them won't like it, but there's nothing they can do."

"They're not going to let you get away with this."

"That's what you think. The next board meeting is going to be a replay of the last one, except the Frames have slipped a little further behind."

"What do you mean?"

"They just lost your vote."

"You're not going to have control of that board much longer, you know, Princess Allison."

"We'll see about that."

"Have you thought about all the clients who will demand to leave with me?" asked Lee, her face stretched tight, her voice the file-against-metal rasp of a true snarl.

"Yes, I've given them a lot of thought. Your client list is one of the main pieces of business I've concerned myself with since I got back from Frankfurt. I've been lunching, dining, and meeting with them whenever I could in the last few weeks. Of course, I wasn't trying to compete with you socially. Who would think of trying to surpass the great Lee Simons as a party giver? After all, everyone knows that you're the hostess who can provide her guests with everything. No, all I wanted to discuss with your people was what U.T.M. represents and the very helpful role it's played in their careers and will continue to play. By the way, I was very impressed with how level-headed and intelligent they were. They realize that many of the deals they consider most important to them were made with the help of a lot of people other than just yourself, Lee—even though they all give you full credit for the parties."

"Cut the crap, Allison. What are you driving at?"

"Just this," Allison said, smiling as she held up a fat folder of contracts, festively tied with a green ribbon as if it were a birthday present. "All but two of your clients have agreed to sign new contracts with U.T.M. For three years each."

"I don't believe you," screamed Lee, tearing the folder from Allison's hands and frantically examining the contracts, each one as frightening to her as a lab report describing a fatal malignancy.

"I assure you, the contracts are all in order. If you feel that the only way you can vent your anger is to rip them up, please go ahead. Those are just copies. The originals are in the files. The *locked* files."

"I can't believe you're dumb enough to think you can get rid of me this easily," Lee hissed.

"But what else can you expect from a rich, coddled bitch who's had everything given to her on a silver platter? That's the rest of the sentence, isn't it, Lee?"

"What makes you think the other top agents here won't follow me out the door with their clients?"

"Oh, I just have a hunch they won't."

"I guarantee you George Bellamy will be right behind me."

"I wouldn't place much money on that, if I were you. You'll have to take my word for the moment, since I didn't think to bring a copy here to show you, but George signed a new contract with U.T.M. earlier this morning. And to save you the trouble of asking me, yes, he knew you were leaving. I know George a lot better than you think. I know how you tried to play him against me, too. But George is just as street-smart as you, Lee. He knows what U.T.M. can do for him compared with what Lee Simons can. Any other questions?"

"I'll bet you never heard of the Olympic Auditorium, right? It's a fight place that was built for the Olympic Games in the thirties. They have fights there every week, and I try to get there as often as I can. Lots of Mexican and black kids, hungry and tough. What I love about them is that they get the shit knocked out of them one night and then have the guts to come back another night and bang the hell out of someone else. So the way I see it, Allison, is that you've won the preliminary, but I'm going to come back and take the main event."

"You missed your calling, Lee. You should be writing for the soaps," Allison said, as she reached over and pressed the button on her phone that summoned her secretary. But this time, instead of Neal appearing, two uniformed private security guards walked into the office.

"Lee, these two gentlemen are going to accompany you back to your office and watch you while you gather your personal property. Thirty minutes should be more than enough time for you to accomplish that. Try to do a thorough job, because I've already had the locks changed, and the building security people have been instructed not to let you back in under any circumstances."

Lee stared at Allison, her mouth now a thin scar of hate. Then she turned abruptly and walked to the door, the two guards in step behind her.

"By the way, Lee," said Allison sweetly, "since you no longer have your company Rolls, I've arranged for another car to drive you home. It'll be waiting for you outside when you leave. I wish you luck at your new venue."

"I'll get you, Allison. Bet on it," Lee snarled as she left the office with her uniformed entourage.

Half an hour later, Allison received a call from Neal.

"Thank you," she said, then put down the phone and went to the window. In the parking lot below, struggling under the load of a large cardboard carton, was Lee. The guards led her to a Honda Civic, painted a bright red and as shiny as a gift apple for the teacher. One of the guards held open the door for her. Lee stood rooted for a moment, as if contemplating the final outrage of being a passenger in a car she wouldn't allow her gardeners to park in her driveway. Finally she got in and was driven away.

51

uy Barnes had left two messages for her before Allison was able to return his call.

She had been tied up in a meeting all afternoon trying to get CBS to release Tam Marlowe from his series, which the network had canceled the preceding season. They now wanted to hold on to him just on the outside chance that they had to throw his show, *Mr. Five Spot,* back on the air, since their new schedule was taking a severe beating in the ratings. But U.T.M. had secured the lead in a ten-hour miniseries for Tam that paid a small fortune and was just the career shift he needed. Allison knew she would have to trade something in order to free Marlowe, and so did CBS, so the negotiations were tough and prolonged.

"Progress, Guy?" she asked.

"You bet, after a couple of big disappointments," said the detective. "We struck out on the adoption papers. Couldn't find a thing, even though we checked out all three states, plus Vermont. The adoption must have been private. But your misgivings about what we talked about the other day—you know . . . that thing that didn't seem quite right? It looks like it's paying off."

"How? Tell me, Guy, quick."

"Well, it's all in my report, which is on its way to you right now by messenger. You sure you want me to go into this over the phone?"

"Yes, absolutely. I can't wait."

"All right. We've come up with seven people named Hanson. *E.* Hanson. Any one of them could be the person who chartered the plane. But if you're right about the state and the first letter of the town, I think we have an exact match."

"Go on," urged Allison.

"It looks like the town is Lakeville, Connecticut, not Lyme. Which fits beautifully with Great Barrington. Even though it's in Massachusetts, it's not far away."

"Is there a hospital nearby?"

"In the very next town. I'm working on that now. I think we'll be able to tie that in, too, in the next few days. In fact, I'm sure of it."

"That's terrific, Guy! We're so close now, I really feel it. When you call next time, if I'm in another meeting, I don't care what it is, tell them they have to interrupt me. I don't want to wait a minute more than I have to for this information. Understand?"

"Perfectly."

Parker Welles appeared in Allison's doorway a short while later. He knocked lightly to catch her attention.

"Bingo," he said as soon as she looked up.

"Are you referring to what I think you are?" asked Allison after the tiniest of pauses.

"I sure am."

"Then come in and close the door behind you."

Parker had seen so much and heard so much over the years at U.T.M. that he characteristically exuded the calm, powerful purr of a perfectly balanced and tuned engine. This time, however, he was so keyed up he sat forward on the edge of his chair. "Are you ready to spend money?" he asked. "Big money?"

"For what?"

"For pure gold. The best we could ask for on the inside, outside, and in-between on what the Frames have been doing in the last ten years."

"How much will it cost?"

"A hundred thousand. Maybe more."

Now it was Allison's turn to lean forward. "Somebody *is* thinking big. What will it buy us?"

"Everything. Letter-perfect copies from memory of the financial files on every last thing the Frames have done—and plan to do in the future—from the man who put it all together for them: their chief financial officer, who, in true Frame style, was kicked out on his ass three months ago when he refused to do something that he considered *too* morally repugnant. I don't mean to paint this guy as a Mother Teresa in a three-piece suit. He's a shark. But maybe just a mako, not a killer like the Frames. *Bitter* is too sweet a word to describe how he feels. And he also needs money. Badly. Normally I wouldn't touch this sort of thing, but when you're dealing with people like the Frames, you have to play it the way they do. You have to forget the Marquis of Queensberry. And we don't have a lot of time, do we? What do you want to do?"

"It sounds like a bargain. Buy it. With U.T.M. funds. I love the idea of the Frames picking up part of the tab for doing themselves in."

"Why not? They've been after us to trim corporate overhead. This will trim four leeches off the board."

Allison reached out impulsively to touch Parker's hand.

"It's been touch-and-go lately, hasn't it, but suddenly I feel like a kid on the night before Christmas. I just got another piece of wonderful news a few minutes ago. And now this. I can't wait to open my presents."

52

"Hi . . . Allison . . . I'm . . . glad I . . . caught you. . . . I've been trying . . . to get to you . . . all day," said Ben Wildman, between painful gasps, on the other end of the speaker phone.

"Are you all right, Ben?" asked Allison.

"Never . . . felt . . . better," he answered after a moment. "There," he said, exhaling noisily at the same time.

"What in the world are you doing?"

"Evening workout, Allison. Just finished my abdominals. In the morning I work out with my trainer. Aerobics, Nautilus, and stretching. In the evening I do it myself. Just free weights and abs. You know you should—"

Allison could spot Ben Wildman's favorite pitch—"your body is your temple"—coming on and switched the phone to her other ear and settled back. From the first moment more than twenty years ago that Ben had felt the subtle and not so subtle signs of impending age, he had embarked on a valiant battle to hold the gray, wrinkled, and flabby specter of his future self at bay. He allowed himself no half-measures in his approach. He had spent over two hundred thousand dollars installing a state-of-the-art gym in his Coldwater Canyon house. He exercised like someone training for the Olympics. He had a nutritionist plan his meals and design his mega-vitamin intake, a yoga instructor to monitor his spiritual health, and a daily massage to rid him of any residual tension.

Ben's second concern—a very close second—was his hair. He had started losing it in his late twenties, and in addition to buying artfully crafted hairpieces, each costing two thousand dollars, that usually passed close scrutiny since they made him look partially bald, he was a sucker for any product or treatment that promised a hirsute future. Right now his passion was a new discovery called Rogaine, which he religiously applied to his flapjack-sized bald patch several times a day. Whenever he was alone near a mirror, he couldn't stop himself from edging backward toward it, peering over his shoulder to see if there had been any progress since his last check only hours earlier. These physical obsessions of his were more endearing than narcissistic because he was so open about them. His latest bottle of hair preparation was as likely to be in full view on his desk as tucked away in a drawer, and he did or didn't wear his hairpieces according to his mood, as if they were hats.

"Ben," interrupted Allison, after listening to him tout his newest trainer, "I hate to remind you of this, but don't you remember I missed seven straight appointments with the personal trainer you gave me as a present last Christmas?"

"With a body like yours you need a personal trainer like I need a full-time barber," said Ben with a laugh. "It was just the proselytizer in me that made me give you that. This Christmas I'll come up with something totally sybaritic. That's a promise."

"Promise accepted. Now what's up?"

"Well, this comes out of left field," said Ben, his tone changing suddenly. "I hope it won't upset you."

"What are you talking about, Ben?"

"Well, I guess I've been carrying on this way about exercising because I hate to have to tell you about this other thing. But . . . I think I might have come up with something that'll throw some light on your mother's . . . I mean, Françoise's . . . suicide."

"What, for God's sake?"

"It's probably nothing, but I'm just not sure. You know what a klutz I am when it comes to electronic devices. How I never even turn on my answering machine most of the time. Well, last night I happened to, and when I tried to retrieve my messages, I guess I rewound the tape farther than I realized, and I heard a lot of calls from months ago. One was from Françoise. On the night she died, I'm pretty certain."

"Oh, God, what did she say?"

"It wasn't so much what she said, but that someone else was there with her. I heard the other person say something to her. I think I know who it was, but I'm not positive."

"Who?" Allison asked excitedly. "Was it—"

"I don't want to say yet. I think it's important for you to listen to the tape and judge for yourself, which is why I'm calling. Save me some time tomorrow morning, early, before you get involved with other things, okay? Now I've got to finish my bench work and change and shower. See you tomorrow."

. . .

Ben was almost finished with his bench-press sequence when he heard the front door open. That must be Ramon, his houseboy, he thought. Ramon was early. He wasn't supposed to show for another hour. Probably he'd gotten a lift from his cousin. Sometimes that happened. Ben had asked him to work tonight because he was having a guest for drinks and dinner.

"Ramon . . . get out . . . some . . . ice," Ben said, straining under the 175-pound weight, all the time keeping the count in his head—*four—five.* "And . . . lay out . . . the . . . Brie"—*six—seven.* "It's on . . . the . . . counter"—*eight—nine.* Almost there, he thought, his muscles screaming in pain, his arms shaking as if he were racked with fever chills. "Ten," he gasped audibly. As he was moving his arms back to replace the weight on the rack, a face loomed above his. It was not Ramon at all. It was somebody else. He was about to ask "What are you doing here?" when he saw a blur of hands push hard against the bar. The weight slid out of his hands and, with the speed and inevitability of a guillotine, fell the short distance to his throat. Ben didn't have time either to be scared or to be concerned that he wasn't looking his best. On the other hand, he had all the time in the world. In fact, he had eternity.

53

Late in the afternoon a few days after Ben was buried, Allison's front door-bell rang. She was home earlier than usual because she and Madeleine Neuman, who had flown in from New York, were attending a gala opening that evening of a new play at the Ahmanson and she badly needed to lie down and rest first. Ben's death had punched a large hole in the operations of the agency, stretching everyone to his or her utmost limits, emotionally and professionally, especially Allison. As close as she was to acquiring the ammunition to finish off the Frames permanently, she and Parker didn't have it yet. This work was her priority and nothing the Frames did would deter her.

When she opened the door, she found herself face to face with Sean. She was surprised—and so thankful to see him that she collapsed into his arms. "Darling, I thought you couldn't get here until Saturday," she said, hugging him fiercely. "What happened? Did you leave poor Oscar in the lurch?"

"I would have if I'd had to, but I'm here with Oscar's blessings. He's as worried as I am."

"About me?" asked Allison. His question frightened her because it mirrored her feelings.

"Of course, who else? Now, if you would undrape your lovely self from me for a moment so I can come inside, I would be much obliged. We have some talking to do."

"What's that luggage for?" asked Allison, noticing the two large canvas bags beside him.

"It's for you, Allie, because you're coming with me and you're going to stay with me until we find out what the hell is going on around here. I'm very worried about you."

"You said that already. I'm fine, Sean. Really. There's no need to worry."

"I wish it were that easy, but it isn't. Get upstairs and start packing, and no arguments, please. There's a flight at seven-fifty. We can make it if you get moving."

"I'm not going anywhere tonight, Sean. Except to the theater. I can't leave town."

"Don't be ridiculous. After what happened to Ben, I'm not going to let you stay here alone. I should have come and gotten you before now. It sounds like they killed him so he wouldn't tell you what he knew."

"Ben's death was an accident. No, don't interrupt," she said, seeing Sean's look of pure impatience. "The police are leaning that way. They've seen that sort of thing happen before with weights. Plenty of times," she added for emphasis.

"I don't believe in accidents like that. Now start packing."

"Sean, I wish more than anything I could come with you, but I can't," said Allison, reaching up and putting her arms around him. "I miss you and I want to be with you, but I have some business to take care of in the next few days and there's no way I can do it from Albuquerque. As soon as it's settled, I'll—"

"Involving the Frames? Because if so—"

"Absolutely not," she lied. If she told Sean she was planning to go after the Frames, he would try to stop her. Whenever she thought about Adrian she felt sick to her stomach with fear. Was she a fool to stay here? She was almost never alone, and if she got nervous, plenty of people were nearby. Cynthia and Tom. Parker, Charlie, and Diana. Once the Frames were out of U.T.M., Adrian would no longer have any reason to harm her. Then she would be safe.

"Allie, what am I going to do with you?" said Sean, pulling her closer, running his hand gently over her breasts.

"I'll make a deal with you, darling. Give me forty-eight hours, that's all. Then I'll come to Albuquerque, I promise."

"I'm going to hold you to that, you know."

"I know."

"Okay, but that's it," said Sean, reaching under Allison's dress and beginning to pull down her panties. "Now get this stuff off and let's go upstairs."

"Sean, that feels so good," sighed Allison. "But I don't have that much time before I have to get ready to go out. . . ."

"The show you were going to see has a lousy third act. I read the script. It'll never make New York," he said as he picked her up with the ease of a father lifting a child. "I already told Madeleine you'd be taking a raincheck. And there's one thing I can promise you."

"What's that?"

"There's an absolutely dynamite third act just behind that door down the hall."

54

It was a filthy hot day, well suited to Lee's mood. The distance from where she had parked her car to the office building was short, but still too far for Lee Simons, who was not used to walking anywhere, ever. The air was so heavy that drops of sweat kept springing out on her upper lip and chin like hives. In the elevator to the penthouse offices of Frame Properties, Ltd., she did the best she could to repair her streaked makeup, turning her back on a young messenger who stared at her for a fraction of a moment too long. She wanted to slap him for his impertinence.

"I'm Lee Simons," she said to the receptionist, skipping the nicety of a "good morning." "Tell Adrian I want to see him."

"Do you have an appointment with Mr. Frame?"

"Why don't you just do what I told you to," snapped Lee.

The woman calmly punched a number on the telephone, spoke briefly, then cupped her hand over the receiver as she looked up at Lee with a small, pleased smile. "Mr. Frame is unable to see you."

Lee snatched the telephone out of the girl's hand.

"Is this Adrian's secretary?"

"Yes."

"This is Miss Lee Simons. It's imperative that I see him immediately."

"I'm terribly sorry, Miss Simons, but that's not possible," answered the secretary, with a modulated coolness befitting a surgical nurse. "If you'd like to make an appointment for next week, I'm sure we could fit you in."

"Tell Mr. Frame that if he thinks he can screw around with me, he's dumber than I thought he was. And as for you, Miss Ice Snatch, you can go fuck yourself!"

Lee slammed down the phone and ran out of the offices and back into the equatorial heat, cursing in equal measure Adrian, his flunkies, and the weather. She double-parked her car in front of the entrance to Adrian's building and, in the relative comfort of its air-conditioning, prepared to wait for him to appear. The bastard would have to come out sometime.

It cost Lee an hour's worth of thumbing angrily through *Variety* and *The Hollywood Reporter,* which as chronicles of show business minutiae were a stark reminder of her present, unemployed condition, but shortly after noon, Adrian emerged and climbed into his waiting Bentley. She had known that he wouldn't eat at his desk, since his appetite for rich food was a close runner-up to his craving for kinky sex. She followed his car warily, wondering if he was lunching or simply cruising, until his chauffeur pulled up in front of The Bistro Garden. She entered the restaurant after him, observed that his luncheon guest had not yet arrived, and, before Adrian even had time to look up, went to his table and sat down at the empty place beside him.

"Why, Lee, what a pleasant surprise," said Adrian with a thin smile. "I'm surprised you're not in black. Pity about old Ben. A real Gus Morton loyalist."

"That's the price you pay for a beautiful body. I told Ben that those weights were dangerous. But I was only thinking that he might throw his back out. And cut that crap about it being such a pleasant surprise to see me, Adrian," she said in a low, rasping voice. "Who the hell do you think you are, refusing to let me in your office?"

"I know who I am, my dear. It's you who has the identity problem."

"Don't give me that, Adrian. I think you've forgotten something that's fairly important. You promised you'd take care of me. You said not to worry. You'd kick Princess Allison out of U.T.M. and put me in charge. Well? When are you going to make good on that? My phone hasn't been ringing off the hook with your calls lately."

"Lee dear, we discovered we're going to need a lot more time than I thought to complete the takeover. Did I forget to tell you that? For the time being, my father and I are turning over our interests in U.T.M. to our associates to handle," said Adrian, lying easily and with pleasure. "So I'm afraid I can't do a thing for you. If you need a loan, though, call my business manager. I'll tell him to expect your call. Now," he continued, "I'm expecting a guest momentarily and it might be awkward if you were here when she arrives."

"And who may that be?"

"A client—or rather a former client of yours. Tawny Holmes."

"I hope she's given you a sampling of her herpes simplex, Adrian. She's riddled with it. No big surprise, since she'd take on the kitchen staff here between courses without thinking twice about it."

"You're not funny anymore, Lee. Beat it."

"I'm not leaving this restaurant until you tell me what you intend to do for me. I got bounced for helping you, Adrian. You owe me."

"I'll show you what I intend to do," said Adrian, catching the attention of the maître d', which was not difficult since the man had been watching Adrian's table with growing uneasiness. He started toward them, his grim expression suggesting he was more than prepared to escort Lee from the premises.

"You listen to me very carefully, Adrian," whispered Lee, ignoring the approaching maître d'. "Do you remember that last little party of mine? You had a pretty good time, as I recall. In fact, you had such a good time with those twins, you were literally transported. I don't think you realized it, but the boy and girl were only fifteen. The state of California thinks that's very young indeed. You hurt them quite a bit, you know. Lucky for you, I've been able to keep them quiet so far. No one knows what you did to the girl, particularly the parents. The mother and father are Seventh Day Adventists. Very devout. I don't think they're your kind of people, Adrian, so I've held off introducing you to them."

Adrian, his face flushed, tried to say something, but Lee just raised her voice and continued talking. He waved off the hapless maître d', who quickly scampered back to his post by the door.

"There are others," she was saying, "who *would* love to meet you, though, especially after they view my tape and see how skillfully you administer punishment. The people I'm talking about wear blue uniforms, Adrian, and—"

"What tape?"

"I guess I forgot to tell you about the videotape I made of you. That's right, Adrian darling. I shot a tape of you, how should I say? . . . doing your thing. I thought it would be fun for us to see the highlights of the party again, so I utilized my little video camera. Surreptitiously, I might add. I got the whole thing. You were so busy devouring those beautiful twins that I guess you didn't notice me."

"You miserable bitch," he hissed, with a hatred so cold that his words carried clearly across the room. The heads of other diners half-turned and their necks stiffened. The conversational hum in the restaurant dipped for a moment, then resumed, as the lunch crowd fought their impulse to stare.

"Don't waste your breath with tender endearments, Adrian. There's only one thing you should be concentrating on. Get that U.T.M. deal back on track and me in the presidency or get ready for some publicity. I have my list drawn up of all the people who would enjoy the tape. At the top, of course, are those parents I mentioned. And then there's the L.A. County—"

"Are you threatening me?" said Adrian, grabbing Lee's arm with a fury so powerful that it took all her reserves of self-control not to cry out.

"I'm simply saying, keep your promise," said Lee, gasping in the effort of maintaining an even voice. She looked at her arm. Adrian's fingers dug into her flesh like the metal tongs her father had hung meat from in his butcher shop.

"Listen closely, you filthy pig. You're playing way out of your league. If you don't hand over that tape to me immediately, I'll see to it that you never work again in this industry. I'll destroy you. And don't make the mistake of thinking I can't do it. Now where is it? In that handbag of yours? Give it to me."

As Adrian grabbed for her handbag, he loosened his hold on her long enough for Lee to wrench away from him. He had hurt her arm badly. The imprints of his fingers on her flesh were like the marks of a hungry animal. Lee was frightened, and for a split second she wanted simply to run away, far away, if necessary put a continent between herself and this monster next to her, but the old Lee surfaced again quickly. What did she have to be afraid of? Nothing. Adrian could scream and rave all he wanted, but this time she had the upper hand.

She smiled slowly and, holding her handbag tightly, moved closer to Adrian. She felt supremely confident now and was beginning to enjoy herself. "I have only one thing more to say. I will keep the existence of the tape, which by the way is not inside here," she said, patting her handbag, "a private matter between you and me. But for only one more week. I expect by then to have received some good news from you about my new position at U.T.M. If I don't, you know the consequences. And now, my pet, I must be running along. Enjoy your lunch."

Lee leaned over and kissed Adrian on the cheek before he could turn away. As she rose, he reached up and took her hand. "I have to go to the men's room," he said. "I'll see you to the door."

"Fine," said Lee, gratified by his change of manner. Obviously she had played her cards exactly right.

Adrian pushed the table away and stood up. Feeling better than she had in days, Lee strode out of the room ahead of him toward the front door.

"This way," said Adrian suddenly. He pulled her in a different direction, then shoved her through a door into an alley. It was dark, and the clatter of dishes and Spanish-speaking voices from the restaurant kitchen bounced off the walls of the narrow space. A dishwasher in a dirty apron looked out through a doorway, then stepped back inside.

"What are you doing?" asked Lee nervously.

"You rotten blackmailer," spat Adrian, taking hold of her shoulders and shaking her viciously. "So you think you've got me where you want me? Better think again. You know my reputation, don't you?"

When Lee, who was terrified, didn't answer, he grabbed her by the hair, pulled her face close to his, and slapped her hard. "Answer me!"

"Yes, I know it," she whimpered.

"Make sure you don't forget it. If you persist, I'm not going to hold back. I'll do whatever is necessary. Some people think that maybe Ben's death was no accident. I'd hate to hear that something like that had happened to you. Now I want that tape back and I want it quickly. Understand?"

All Lee could do was nod. Adrian pushed her away and disappeared back inside the restaurant.

Lee fell against the wall and began to retch violently, although she hadn't eaten a thing since the night before. She leaned there, gagging and moaning for she didn't know how long, then stumbled through the alley into the street's blinding glare.

By the time Lee reached her house, her courage and determination were restored. That depraved psycho! she thought, laughing to herself delightedly. Did he really think she would just hand over the tape to him? Lee Simons hadn't gotten where she was by backing off. If he wanted to play a little game of chicken, so be it. She'd show him the kind of nerve she had. If he thought he was more cunning than she, he had a lot to learn. If she didn't wind up in Allison Morton's office fast, then Adrian Frame would find himself wearing a very different outfit in a very inhospitable place.

Lee suddenly felt so good that she called Manolo and told him to open a bottle of champagne. Why not start celebrating right now?

55

Allison placed the call herself. The operator at the other end shifted her from a secretary to a personal secretary to, finally, an administrative assistant, who sounded the way Arnold Schwarzenegger looks.

"Could I have your name again, please?" asked the man.

"Allison Morton. Mr. Frame knows who I am." *And so should you, gorilla brain,* thought Allison.

"What number are you calling from?"

"What has that to do with anything?" she asked, the polite tone of her voice receding fast.

"Mr. Frame doesn't receive calls. He makes them. Now what's your number, or should we both get on to other business?"

Ten minutes later Hector Frame telephoned.

"Good afternoon, Miss Morton. It's a pleasure to finally have the chance to talk to you. I never had the opportunity to establish the kind of relationship with your uncle—"

"I want to see you, Mr. Frame."

"That's a fine idea. Someday I'd love to entertain you here in Toronto. Do you know the city, Miss Morton?" The old man's voice was thin, but there was a powerful presence behind it that even a telephone could not filter out.

"I must see you tomorrow."

"Well, that's awfully soon. I'm actually," Frame laughed disparagingly, "a bit of a recluse. I don't see people—I mean new people—very often. Maybe some other—"

"Perhaps I'm not making myself clear. I have a proposition to make to you in regard to U.T.M. I'm positive you won't be able to turn it down."

"That's very interesting, but I think you're talking to the wrong person, Miss Morton. I'm not even on the board. My son, Adrian, is the one you should speak with."

"Trust me, Mr. Frame. You're the one I have to see."

"You're quite a persistent creature."

"Tomorrow?"

"All right. My assistant will be on the line in a moment. Give him your flight number and one of my staff will pick you up at the gate. Have a safe trip. God bless."

Allison and Cynthia Traynor, who traveled with Allison at her request, were met by a tall, unsmiling man in a white nylon jumpsuit.

"If you and your associate will just follow me, Miss Morton," he said, leading them out of the terminal to a dove-gray Rolls parked immediately in front.

"The liquor is in the cabinet on the left," said the man, opening the car door. "Newspapers are in the rack on the door. If there's anything else you need, press that button by the window. The drive will take twenty-three minutes."

The ride seemed to take a fraction of that time as Allison reviewed once again how she intended to deal with Hector Frame. She didn't delude herself that she was dealing with a normal human being. Whatever decent impulses he had been born with, Frame had almost willfully eliminated. He had ruined so many lives, in ways both cunning and casual, that he must derive sustenance from it. Winning wasn't the only thing for Hector Frame. It had to be coupled with destroying people. Stalin could have used him as a general!

Allison and Cynthia were escorted into the lobby of a large white condominium that could have been located anywhere from Wilshire Boulevard to Collins Avenue. The lobby was deserted save for four men who sat in front of a bank of TV monitors and four others, all over six feet tall, who flanked the front door and the elevator. They all wore the distinctive Frame staff jumpsuit. The elevator took them forty stories up without a stop, directly to Hector Frame's penthouse. There, another pair of uniformed guards stood in front of a set of locked doors. While Cynthia took a seat in the reception area, Allison was directed to Frame's office. As she stepped through the portal, a deafening claxon sounded. The noise was so sudden and intense that Allison almost screamed in fright.

"May I please see your pocketbook, Miss Morton?" asked one of the guards. He quickly inspected the contents and, with a satisfied smile, pulled out a large silver compact. "This looks like the culprit. Would you please turn around and walk through again? I don't think the metal detector will sound this time."

The walls of Hector Frame's office were covered in a bloodred leather that stretched seamlessly around the room as if it had been stripped from one huge animal. A row of windows looked out on the lake in the distance. A narrow door slid open in the far corner as silently as a gesture and Hector Frame entered the room, followed a few steps behind by his son.

"Greetings, Miss Morton. Please take a seat," said the old man, who was dressed in a loose white suit.

"Will you be needing me, Mr. Frame?" asked the man who had met Allison at the airport.

"Just wait outside, Vaughn. I'll ring you when we're finished. God bless."

The old man sat down opposite Allison on a narrow hospital bed canted at a forty-five-degree angle and, after stretching out, pulled a silver fox throw over himself.

"Would you like a beverage?" he asked as he slowly, almost painfully, adjusted his legs.

"I'm fine, thank you. By the way, is it necessary for your son to be here?" Allison asked without looking at Adrian.

"I find that offensive, Allison," said Adrian hotly.

"Shut up!" his father shouted. "You're here to listen. Do you understand that?"

"Yes, Father."

"Please excuse my son, Miss Morton," Hector Frame said, his voice again as serene as the surface of a pond. "But just as you are the living extension of your uncle's dreams for the continuance of U.T.M., so is Adrian both my only heir and my one hope for this entity, Frame Properties, Limited, my creation, to continue after I leave this earth. I've always believed that the best way I could teach my son is by example. Therefore, I must insist that he stay here by my side. But he will only observe, I assure you of that."

"I've come to make you an offer," Allison said, reaching into her briefcase and extracting a manila folder.

"I doubt that you could propose anything that would interest me, Miss Morton. You see, taking over U.T.M. is more than just a sound investment to me. For one thing, the talent business interests my son, and I thought it would be a nice gift for him."

"Thank you, Father. That is the nicest thing you've ever—"

"Did you already forget what I told you? I don't want to hear another word out of you. Now where was I? Yes . . . of course. In addition to seeing my son running the company, I also prize the real estate that the company possesses. And there is yet another reason for my involvement, Miss Morton. Gus Morton betrayed me many years ago. He's not the only one who ever crossed me, but there was something about his smug satisfaction in his high-flown morality that still sticks in my throat. All your beloved uncle had to do for me then was to say I had had dinner with him on a particular night. That was all. It was so simple. But could he do that? No!"

"If you call testifying truthfully in open court rather than perjuring yourself on another person's behalf a matter of betrayal, then the dictionary has been defining that word incorrectly for a long time."

"You're so very like him, my dear," said Hector Frame as he pulled the cover up to his chin.

"I'm sure you don't intend that to be a compliment, but I'll take it as such. My uncle had more integrity in one drop of perspiration from his brow than you've shown in a lifetime. But I didn't come here to listen to you discuss him. Just to hear you say his name is distasteful. I've come here to remove you and your depraved son from my company."

"Brave talk, Miss Morton. Perhaps that's because you have a profession to fall back on. You are, I am told, a, lawyer. Did you know that there are over six hundred thousand of your ilk in the United States? How many do you think Japan has? Remember that they have slightly more than half America's population. Well, they only have twelve thousand! No wonder they do so well. But since you're attractive and not destitute, I can't feel very sorry for you. You'll be interested to know, by the way, that I intend to remove all traces of Gus Morton the moment I take over. My first move will be to rename the company. How does Frame Talent Management sound? Amazing how changing only one word can make such a difference."

Hector Frame started to laugh. He was immediately joined by his son, whose eyes never left his father.

"Is that all?" Allison asked when the two had finally grown quiet.

"Oh, my dear, you really are such an earnest girl. All right. I suppose I have to hear your proposal, since you've come this far. What is it?"

Allison opened the folder and took out an index card. She reached over and handed it to Frame.

The old man stared at the writing on the card. Suddenly his face tightened and what little color there was in it vanished. He tried to speak, but he could not.

"What's the matter, Father?"

This time Hector Frame did not tell his progeny to stop talking. He just sat there, seemingly mesmerized by the card in his hand.

"There's just an address on that card," Allison said matter-of-factly. "Two-three-three Spear. That's the location of a rather nondescript, five-story commercial building in San Francisco. I happen to own it. It's the one piece missing in the land scheme you've been clandestinely trying to put together near the Embarcadero. In case you've forgotten, it's the one that you've already committed over two hundred million to. At rather high interest rates, I'm told. I paid substantially more for this property than you were offering. But you know something? I think I made a fantastic investment. I'm going back to L.A. now. I expect your lawyer to call mine tomorrow before ten in the morning, my time. My terms are simple. I want all your stock in U.T.M. for the property. I know that by morning you'll see how attractive a proposal it is. Good day, gentlemen."

At the door Allison stopped and turned around. "By the way, God bless."

56

The call Allison was waiting for from Guy Barnes came when she guessed it would, while she was in a meeting. It was early in the morning the day after her return from Toronto, and she, Cynthia, and Parker were savoring the details of Hector Frame's defeat. Neal put the detective right through to her.

"Yes, Guy?"

"I've got bad news and great news. Which do you want to hear first?" he asked.

"The bad," answered Allison, the calm in her voice a sham.

"There was no one registered at the hospital under the name we're looking for."

"No one?" asked Allison, unable to keep the disappointment out of her voice.

"You're forgetting something."

"What?"

"I said I also had great news. I decided to run a check on the billing addresses of the patients at the hospital, just in case it turned up something, and it did. Though the name was different, the address for one patient was the same as the Hanson address in Lakeville."

"Are you sure, Guy?" asked Allison breathlessly.

"No question about it. You've found the person you were looking for. Your mother. Congratulations."

57

"Hello."

"Is this phone secure?" asked Adrian Frame in a whisper.

"Is that you, Adrian?"

"What do you think? You ought to be able to identify someone who's been as intimate as I have with you, my dear. Now answer my question."

"What question?" Lee asked, instinctively lowering her voice to match Adrian's.

"The fucking phone! Is it secure?"

"Of course it is."

"Could Manolo be listening in?"

"I wish I had family as loyal as he is. Stop being so mysterious, Adrian. Why are you calling?"

"First off, apologies. I lost my head the other day. I can't believe I threatened you. I hope I didn't hurt you. Am I forgiven?"

"I don't know, Adrian. You hurt me . . . badly. Also you scared the hell out of me. But I'll accept your apologies, even if I can't forgive you. Now what's on your mind?"

"Don't be so bitchy, my sweet, to the bearer of spectacularly good news," said Adrian, his voice suddenly becoming as soft and affectionate as a child's welcome.

"I certainly could use some good news," Lee answered guardedly. She was seated in a chaise on the patio by the pool, the coffee in her Limoges cup as cold as the morning fog that hung over the palms, draping her property like a wet, gray tent.

"I got my father to agree to unseat Allison immediately. It's going to be messy, but there's no way we're not going to win. And you know what that means, don't you?"

"Tell me!" said Lee, sliding her hand inside her robe.

"It's going to play exactly the way we planned. My dear, I'm speaking to the next president of Universal Talent Management."

"You wouldn't kid me now, would you, Adrian?"

"Why should I do that, darling? There's no question about who the best person is to run U.T.M. And now that we're finally sewing up the deal, why would we look elsewhere? This, for the time being, is highly confidential, of course. We wouldn't want Allison to find out sooner than she ought to."

"I could hug you, Adrian."

"I'd like you to do more than that, my dear."

"I'd say you deserve more than that," said Lee.

"It's amazing how cleverly you read my mind, darling. Do you think you could concoct a little scene for tonight?" he asked, his voice barely under control.

"I think Mommy might be able to arrange something along those lines. Let's say my place at nine?"

"Wonderful! And I don't think we'll need too many other participants. I'd like to be able to spend a little extra time afterward alone with you. *Une petite fête après la fête.*"

"I'd like nothing better," said Lee, laughing.

"But one thing, dear," added Adrian. "Try to round up a better-quality group this time. Your last bunch of valet parking attendants and aerobics instructors looked good, but none of them could take any pain. It was very discouraging. I would hate to think they're America's future."

On such short notice, the group wasn't bad at all, thought Adrian, as he sipped a flute of perfectly chilled Perrier Jouet, while a red-haired receptionist with an amazing mouth endeavored to inhale the lower part of his body. In the corner, near a sofa where two busboys from Hamburger Hamlet were greedily sharing a waiter from L'Orangerie, was Lee. She was on all fours, her body shaking, as she entertained a studio C.P.A. wearing a bad rug and a huge Hawaiian whom she had met that very day when he returned her car from a detailing session. A caviar dish that had been filled with cocaine two hours earlier sat on the coffee table with a residue in it so sparse it resembled dandruff. Adrian knew that the good coke was still in Lee's bedroom for later use after the "entertainment" had departed.

"My guests are here for our amusement," Lee had once told Adrian. "First-class coke and libations aren't their thing. They just need stuff that looks like the real goods to get them off. Besides, they can't imagine that *the* Lee Simons wouldn't be serving them the best at her multimillion-dollar Trousdale spread."

By 2:30 A.M. all the others had left. It had been a hot day, the temperature in the low eighties, and now, even with a soft breeze circling the hilltop like the ball on a roulette wheel, the air was still sultry.

"I thought, my dear, that we'd have a short Jacuzzi before retiring to your personal playpen."

"You're just abrim with good ideas tonight, Adrian," Lee said, as she lightly kissed him on the lips.

"My next idea isn't bad either. I'm going to make you one of my famous Frame Buck Fizzes. The recipe for it is a closely held family secret. How about turning on the Jacuzzi while your faithful servant prepares your drink?"

"It's the least I can do, Adrian. I trust you also wouldn't object to a little taste of my private stash. I assure you that when I'm in charge at U.T.M., the quality will be even better. But for now, it's not bad."

"What a marvelous proposal. A little heightening of the senses when the senses are about to be indulged is always welcome. And, by the way, it would be great fun to finally see your little video of me with the adorable twins. I've never viewed my fun and games before."

"Of course, Adrian. Anything for a guest," Lee said, smiling. "There's a TV and VCR on a cart in the poolhouse. I'll roll them out as soon as I fetch our coke."

Instead of mixing Lee a drink when she went to get the VCR, Adrian walked through the entire house to make sure that no one was around. Lee always gave Manolo and her maid the night off when she hosted an "entertainment," but it was just as well to double-check. When he returned to the bar, he made certain he had left no fingerprints on the glass or bottles by handling them with a dish towel. He had made a point of using only one glass himself during the evening and not touching anything else in the house. Now he carefully washed the glass and set it back in the cabinet. Then, holding Lee's drink with a napkin by the stem, he walked back outside to the Jacuzzi.

"I was beginning to think you had pooped out on me," she said. Only her head protruded from the roiling water. Above her, tendrils of steam coiled like jinns into the night air.

"What man in his right mind could stay away from the hottest president in Hollywood? The thought of missing your erotic charms would plunge me into a depression deeper than the Marianas Trench," he said, as he placed the drink down next to Lee.

"I love the way you say that word. Say it again, please."

"You mean *erotic*? Or is it *trench*?"

"No, you silly bastard. You know the word I mean."

"Pres-i-dent. President Lee Simons. It goes very well with your name, my dear. I was thinking that 'chief executive officer' should be appended to that title. What do you think of that idea?"

"I love it, Adrian. As your reward, why don't you slide in here right next to me," she said, reaching up to stroke his inner thigh, "so that I can do all sorts of wonderful, filthy things to you. Take your clothes off and get in here immediately."

"I'd love nothing better, Lee. But first let's see your secret videotape. Is the machine set up?" Adrian asked as he walked over to the cart.

"Just press Play. And hurry up. I'm just too horny for words."

Adrian turned on the set and for a few moments stood in front of it watching the action. The runaway twins whom he had picked up that night were tied together on a bed facing each other. Both were gagged and wore looks of terror. Adrian, naked save for thick studded-leather bracelets on each wrist, stood on the bed above them, holding a heavy braided riding crop. His eyes, made vacant and glassy by drugs and depravity, smiled down at the desperate teenagers. After each stroke of the whip, he knelt down and studied their faces.

"You're not showing enough pain, you little whelps," said his voice on the sound track. "You'll be dumped in a ravine in a minute unless you start showing me something."

"Come on, Adrian. Are you going to watch the whole thing? Get over here, and for God's sake turn the sound off. It makes you seem like you're off your rocker. I got some things to show you now that'll satisfy you a lot more than that kiddie kink stuff."

Adrian turned off the sound and walked back to Lee. He knelt beside her and kissed her deeply.

"That's better," she said. "Much better."

"And now, you miserable, low-life bitch, I'm going to show you something even better," shouted Adrian. He grabbed Lee tightly around the shoulders and pushed the struggling woman down under the swirling waters. "That's it. Fight hard, my dear. Life is a precious thing. It's well worth fighting for."

Lee thrashed like a fish at the end of a line, but Adrian was too strong. Much too strong. She was able to break the surface once, but the tiny gulp of air she swallowed prolonged her life only for a few extra seconds. When she stopped moving, Adrian relaxed his grip and Lee bobbed up and floated away from him like a wreath tossed on the waters. He pulled her back to him to examine her shoulders and back.

With a pleased and practiced eye, Adrian saw that he had accomplished his task with hardly a bruise or a scratch. Her first big swallow of water had taken a lot of the fight out of poor Lee. The police must see this kind of death all the time, he thought. A little too much of this, a little too much of that, and the next thing you knew another misguided celebrant was floating facedown in the old Jacuzzi. It was as commonplace an accidental death in Southern California as hypothermia in the Klondike.

His clothes were soaked, Adrian realized as he walked back to the VCR. But he had anticipated this problem and had left a change in his car. *Yes,* he thought, *I've covered every contingency.* He laughed out loud when it struck him that in a way, albeit a very strange way, his father would be pleased with the smooth manner in which he had executed this little piece of business.

Adrian wrapped a handkerchief around his finger, pressed the Eject button, and took out the tape. It was good to have the damn thing. In the future, he would make sure that he was more careful about who was around for his little scenes. It was when he patted the tape almost affectionately that he noticed the label. He walked toward the poolhouse, where there was more light, in order to read it:

A duplicate of this tape is in the hands of the legal firm of Epstein, Penney, and Lerner, to be turned over to the L.A.P.D. in case of Lee Simons's death by unnatural causes.

Adrian stared at the writing for a long time before walking to his car. He drove aimlessly through the silent streets of Beverly Hills. He handled his car by instinct, unaware of where he was and that a car had been following him from the moment he'd left Lee's house. But even if he had noticed, he wouldn't have cared. He had something much more important on his mind. Finally, on a side street next to his triplex apartment, he pulled over. The car behind him did the same. The lights in the other car went out and the driver just stayed there and watched. Adrian sat behind the wheel smoking cigarettes until the first slice of dawn began to light up the hills. He considered writing a few words to his father, but what could he say? No, it was better this way. Moving deliberately, he took a small, silver-plated Beretta from a compartment hidden beneath the dashboard, put the barrel in his mouth, and placed his finger on the trigger. The short metal barrel felt cold and alien. For a second he touched the opening with the tip of his tongue. *No!* he howled to himself, pulling the gun out of his mouth. *Don't be a fool.* Hadn't his father gotten him out of the trouble in Palm Beach? And that had been pretty bad. There had to be a way out of this, too. His father would know what to do.

∙   ∙   ∙

"So you can see, Father, I had to kill the slut. She was a time bomb waiting to go off. I had no choice."

The old man looked out the window where a line of storm clouds, inky and ripe, stretched across the horizon.

"Of course you had no choice," he finally answered. "But you only accomplished half the job."

"What do you mean, Father?"

"This!" the old man said in a deadly quiet voice. He took a 9-mm Walther from the pocket of his robe and slid the gun across the table toward his son. "*You* are the other half of the job, though it doesn't surprise me you didn't have the guts to go all the way. But you're a lucky boy. Now you have another chance. There's no other way out for you this time. No fork in the road. Only one direction, one solution for you. You've always been a profound disappointment to me, Adrian, but now you can prove to me that you can do something right. I'll return when you've completed the job."

Hector Frame rose and walked to the door. As his hand touched the doorknob, Adrian grabbed him from behind.

"Please, Father! Don't make me do this. I don't want to die," he gasped.

"Take your hands off me," the old man snarled.

"Don't leave me alone. I beg you, please don't."

"All right. If you insist, I'll watch. Actually that idea appeals to me, Adrian," said the old man as he sat down opposite his son once again.

Adrian looked at the weapon for what seemed like minutes before he picked it up. He held it away from his body as if it were alive and poisonous.

"Why do you want me to do this, Father? I'm your only son," Adrian pleaded.

"That's just biology," Hector said coldly, his eyes fixed on a spot far out on the lake. "What I've placed in your hands is an opportunity for you to finally show me that you're a man. Your psychic destiny is there before you. An honorable end to a wasted life is still something."

"There must be another way, Father," Adrian begged.

The old man just looked at him, his face twisted with contempt, his eyes as remorseless as those of a bird of prey.

Adrian turned the gun so that its barrel pointed directly at his heart. His finger started to tighten on the trigger when suddenly his face brightened, as if he had gotten an idea that he had searched for all his life.

"You're absolutely right, my dear father," he said softly, now pointing the gun at Hector. "I don't have any other way out. But I think this is a journey on which you should accompany me. Don't you agree?"

"You don't have the guts to kill me," Hector Frame replied evenly.

The gun kicked upward in Adrian's hand. The report reverberated like a wrecking ball.

The old man sat a little straighter in his chair and smiled at his son.

"Do you think I'd give you a gun with live ammunition? What kind of fool do you take me for? It's time now to end this charade," he said as he pressed a button on the arm of his chair. Instantly the door opened and two of his bodyguards came in. "Dennis, Vaughn, would you please escort Adrian to the conference room? There are two detectives waiting there for you. They'll handle this . . . situation from this point on."

Adrian, in shock, stood up and mutely allowed the men to take him by the arms.

"Oh, Adrian," Hector called as his son was about to leave the room. Adrian half-turned, his eyes cast down to the floor. "I've made arrangements with the authorities to give you more than the usual courtesies in your cell. For instance, they will not ask you to remove your belt. So you still have a chance to make things right. Do you understand what I'm saying?"

Without raising his eyes, Adrian replied simply, "Yes, Father," and followed the men out of the room.

58

We've been through some pretty lousy times lately, haven't we, Uncle Gus, thought Allison, *but now the worst is behind us. I've got Sean back. U.T.M. will stay the way you intended it to. The Frames are just a bad memory. And I've had a wonderful piece of news.*

Allison looked around the office as she waited for Neal to bring her a cup of coffee. Apart from a few personal mementos, which Allison either had given to Diana or taken home, and the addition of the leather-framed picture of Sean facing her on the desk, the office was the same as it had been when Gus Morton was alive. By not changing it, she felt closer to him. As if he weren't dead. As if he might walk through the door in the next minute. It always felt comfortable and natural to talk to him the way she did.

Your timing was always impeccable, Uncle Gus, except for this one last time. I really think you could have held off from leaving me for just a bit longer. To lose you so soon after Sean walked out, well, think about it, that was rough. And then having to deal with the Frames, especially that monster Adrian. I was right about him, wasn't I? They've found things in his car that incriminate him in everything. Ben, Françoise, the fire that killed Maria, even my poor dog, Tonny. And he must have been the one who tried to run down Cynthia in New York. Imagine if he'd gotten away with that! But all that's over and done with now. The company's going to be fine, though it won't be the same without Ben. And I'm very much in love. Sean's flying in late tonight for the weekend. When I think of the future and all the time we'll have together, I know I can survive a few more weeks without him.

I don't think I could have coped with all that's happened without you, so thanks for being here. You're still my guardian angel. I have one last question, though. Would you ever have told me the truth about Diana? I think you would have, though I find it strange that you kept it a secret all these years from me and from her. Well, the important thing is that now I know the truth and finally I can share it with her. You always used to say that in the end things work out. So I have to believe this will, too. You loved Diana very much and I'm going to try my best to also. After all, she is my mother.

"Here's your coffee," said Neal, breaking into Allison's thoughts.

"Thanks, and, Neal, could you please get Diana on the phone for me?"

"That's funny. I was just going to tell you she's on extension two. I'd say that's a real coincidence."

"Diana, you're reading my mind," said Allison, picking up the telephone. "So many things have happened, I feel very out of touch. Are you free for dinner tonight by any chance?"

"That's exactly what I was calling about. There's a delightful new place near Malibu that serves real food. Steaks and chops and fish. No tiny vegetables or 'pasta with kelp.' How about it?"

"Sounds perfect, as long as it's quiet. I can't take any more commotion. Besides, I have something very wonderful I want to talk to you about," said Allison.

"Oh, really? Well, this restaurant's ideal for intimate chats. You do sound happy, Allison. Have you and Sean set a date?"

"Not yet, but it's not Sean that's on my mind. It's something entirely different. Do you want me to pick you up?"

"You're so thoughtful, Allison. I was going to ask if you could. I really can't stand driving on the Coast Highway at night. We can have a quick drink at my place before we leave. Does eight o'clock suit you?"

"Absolutely."

"I have an eight-thirty reservation, which I was lucky to get. If you have good news, it'll be a great spot to be. See you at eight, dear."

It was a clear evening, and as Allison drove up the canyon to Diana's house, more and more of the diamond-bright lights of the city below were being switched on, turning the vista into an earthbound Milky Way. Allison was giddy with happiness. She had wanted to tell Sean and Cynthia, but it was important to speak to Diana first. When she got home that night, Sean would be there—his plane should be landing just about now—and she could tell him everything. Then maybe she would call Cynthia too. She had told Cynthia where she and Diana were having dinner just in case she needed to consult with her. That afternoon Cynthia had gone into what promised to be a long negotiating session with Paramount on the first major deal she was handling by herself. Sometimes these meetings dragged on into the night. Yes, Allison decided, she definitely would call Cynthia after she had told Sean.

.   .   .

Cynthia was in the middle of arguing the last point in Derrick Pritchard's contract when one of the secretaries informed her that she had a telephone call from a Mr. Rosen. She jumped up, delighted to be interrupted. It was already after seven.

"Hey, honey, you're the first friendly voice I've heard in a long while, but what's up?" she asked Tom, after the secretary had shown her to an office nearby.

"Cyn, I don't have much time. I think the jury in the embezzlement case is about to come in, but Chick Emerson, that detective friend of mine from homicide, just called me. It doesn't look like Frame was the killer. Some of the physical evidence they found in the car can't be traced back to him, and it also seems that he was positively—and Emerson stressed this—positively out of the country at the time of the arson job. Also when the dog was poisoned. So we're back to square one. Whoever's out there trying to get Allison is still out there."

"No, don't say that! Maybe all those things that happened aren't tied together after all. Or maybe it's—" Cynthia breathed in sharply and could not say another word.

"Or maybe it's Diana," said Tom quietly.

"Yes."

A deadly silence fell between them, and then a moment later they both started talking at the same time.

"She's having dinner with Diana tonight," Cynthia almost shouted. "At that new restaurant near the beach. It's called . . . John's Place. That's it. She said she was planning to stop at Diana's to pick her up."

"Okay, you drive to Diana's immediately. Maybe they'll still be there. Barge right in. Make up any excuse, but don't leave Allie alone with her. If they've gone already, go to the restaurant. I'll meet you as soon as I can."

"Can't you tell the judge you have an emergency and you have to leave right now?"

"Cyn, you know better than that. Now get going. No, on second thought, there's one more thing. Tim Boyer has been trying to reach me. He's in charge of the Wildman investigation. He left word that he had a strong lead. A possible witness they couldn't locate earlier. I'm going to try to get hold of him right now in case he tells me something you should know. Stay where you are. Give me five minutes—and then, if you haven't heard from me, get right over to Diana's."

. . .

Allison suddenly realized she was coming up too fast on a slow-moving car and hit the brakes. *Wake up!* she told herself. *Get your mind back on driving. Sure you're nervous, but who wouldn't be?*

Hey, Uncle Gus, you there? I need all the support I can get. I want Diana to love me. I want to be the best daughter to her that I can be. I need her and I hope she needs me. I know it won't be easy for her. She must have hated all the attention you gave me. But she's been good to me since you died. A real friend. I think we have a chance as a mother and daughter, I honestly do, and now that that psycho, Adrian Frame, has been put away, we can resume our lives. We're safe now, all of us. If you have any say in these things, Uncle Gus, please make this go well. Please.

The curved driveway leading to Diana's house was lit by floods sunk into the bases of two even rows of palms edging it as precisely as chess pieces. As Allison started to get out of her car, Diana walked out the front door to meet her, carrying her pocketbook and a cardigan in one arm and, looped over the other, a wicker basket covered with a pale blue linen napkin.

"Do you mind if we go along right now, dear?" she asked. "It's such a beautifully clear night I wanted to show you a spot near here that I love. The view from there is smashing. It's on the way to the restaurant. I thought we could stop there for a few minutes and have a little sip of something."

"Sounds terrific."

"Here, look at the treats I've got for us. I was going to surprise you, but I've never been any good at keeping secrets," said Diana, pulling back the napkin to reveal a bottle of champagne, a tin of caviar, and two elegant cut crystal cocktail glasses. She reached into the basket and touched one of the glasses. "These were a present from Gus for my thirtieth birthday. Baccarat. I've still got all twelve. Not a nick on a single one of them. I read somewhere that using glasses without hollow stems kills the bubbles, but I couldn't resist bringing them anyway."

Diana placed the basket on the floor of the front seat and slid into the car. As Allison started to turn toward Sunset, Diana placed her hand on the steering wheel. "No, go the other way. The spot I'm thinking of is off Mulholland."

"Cyn?"

"Why were you so long, Tom? I thought you'd never call. I was about to leave."

"I just talked with Tim Boyer. And, Cyn, he's confirmed it. Ben's houseboy identified a picture of Diana as the person he saw driving away from the house."

"Oh, God, it's true."

"Don't panic. I'm leaving now. I'll meet you at Diana's."

"Thank God. Her address is four-five-five-one La Loma. And, Tom, I just called Sean. No answer. He must be on his way here. I left a message on the machine at Allison's."

"All right, now look, if you get there before I do and no one's there, head for the restaurant, okay? And, Cyn?"

"Yes?"

"Be careful."

"Driving up here always makes me feel like Paul Newman at the wheel," joked Allison.

She and Diana climbed quickly to Mulholland, which twisted for miles along the spine of the ridge like a carelessly abandoned garden hose. It was not nearly as developed as the canyon roads feeding into it, and the traffic on it was sparse, the views unsurpassed.

"Mac Royce asked after you the other day, Diana," continued Allison, to make conversation—and calm her nerves. Her heart had begun to beat rapidly. She had decided that when they stopped she would tell Diana what she had found out. It would be best that way, in the privacy of the car. "He's been offered a big new role on *Timber,* but he's a little gun-shy about television. He's never done a series before. I keep telling him it would rejuvenate his career. The movie roles that had dried up for him would start coming in again after he'd done the show for a couple of years. You know, a call from you might—"

"Allison dear, this is where you should pull off," said Diana, pointing ahead to a small turnoff that seemed to hang over the city like a hawk's nest. "But be careful. Stay far enough back. There's a drop of over a hundred feet, and that little wooden fence there couldn't hold back a bike. Why don't you shut off the lights so we can really appreciate the view?"

Before Allison cut the lights, she noticed an empty car, a Jaguar, parked off to the side.

"That Jag's just like yours, Diana. I wonder why anyone would leave a car like that up here?"

"Probably ditched by its irate owner. All of us Jag owners understand the feeling. You know, I used to come up here all the time with Gus. I was the only one he trusted to drive him, aside from Charlie. He always said I drove like a man. That was a big compliment coming from your uncle. But don't think we used this place as a lovers' lane," she said with a laugh. "It was a lovely spot to talk or just listen to the wind."

"I see what you mean about the view," said Allison. The two women sat in silence for a few moments, staring down at the brilliant expanse stretching out before them. Then Diana reached into her basket and picked up the two glasses.

"Time for some bubbly," she said. "More for you than for me, though. I have to confess, naughty me, that I had some before you arrived." She handed Allison a glass filled almost to the top.

"Don't get the driver drunk," said Allison, with a small, tense smile. She placed the brimming glass on top of the dashboard and watched as Diana poured herself champagne, then bent down to tuck the bottle back into the basket.

"Diana, I've been thinking about something," she began tentatively as soon as Diana looked up. "From the moment I learned that I was adopted I've been asking myself why Uncle Gus didn't want me to know."

"Everything Gus did was for your benefit. He must have had good reasons."

"Do you remember when they went to the airport to get me?"

"I remember hearing about it. But I wasn't there. I wasn't working for your uncle then. In fact, I wasn't even in New York City."

"I know, Diana," said Allison. She hesitated and then went on. "I think I know where you were, though. You were in Connecticut, weren't you?"

"What do you mean, Allison?"

"You know the photograph of you and your sister in your living room, the one where you're standing in front of a stone clock tower?"

"Yes," said Diana warily.

"Well, do you remember it caught my eye when I was at your house a couple of months ago? I asked about it and you said it was taken near your sister's house. In Lyme, Connecticut. But there was something about the tower that looked so familiar I couldn't get it off my mind, and then I realized why. That tower is not in Lyme. It's at the other end of the state, near Lakeville. When I was in school, we used to drive past it on the way to Hotchkiss for soccer matches. It really bothered me that you'd made up that funny story about it, and then it clicked with something else I'd been thinking about. I mentioned it to a person I know, and I discovered a few more things. Your sister doesn't live there any longer, but she did for many years. Elizabeth Hanson was her name then. Later she got divorced and remarried and moved away."

"You're getting into personal business, Allison. Where my sister used to live has nothing to do with you."

"But it does, Diana," said Allison, trying to speak quietly, even though Diana's tone was becoming almost hostile. "It has everything to do with me. When you left New York you went to stay with your sister, didn't you? You went there to have a baby."

"What! How dare you say such a thing!" said Diana, shocked now.

"Please, Diana, just listen," said Allison. "You have to listen. I was that baby. I'm your daughter. You're my mother."

"No! You're lying," screamed Diana, the sound of her voice tearing out of the car into the night air like the cry of a hurt animal. "My baby was stillborn. It died."

"Diana, that's not true. That's only what they told you. They wanted to protect you. They thought it would be easier for you than knowing you had given up your baby. I'm sorry to upset you, but that baby was me. Uncle Gus arranged everything, so I wouldn't be adopted by strangers."

"No, it's not true. Stop lying. I don't believe you."

"Please, Diana, you've got to believe me," said Allison, feeling helpless. What was happening? Diana was not supposed to react this way. "I'm not making this up, I promise."

"You promise! What good is a promise from you? You're the one who poisoned my relationship with the only man I've ever loved." Diana's voice vibrated with hate like the strings of an instrument just before they snap. "If you hadn't come into his life, Gus would never have stopped loving me. I didn't resent all those years of waiting for Laura to die, though only Gus Morton would have stayed by a wife who was a total vegetable. Visiting her every weekend. Celebrating Christmas with her when she didn't even know he was there. I knew he loved me, though, and I understood. But then you came into the picture, and you changed everything. It was not that bad at first. Not when you were very young. Or even a teenager or away at college. But when you came to work at the agency, I couldn't bear it any longer. Gus kept saying he loved me, but after a while I knew it wasn't true. His love for me became 'affection,'" she said, throwing out the word with venom. "I didn't want that. I didn't want him just to 'care' for me. I deserved more. And I would have had more. I would have had everything. If it hadn't been for you. You took it all away from me."

"No, Diana, I didn't take anything from you. Uncle Gus always loved you. His feelings never changed. I can't believe you could ever think anything different," said Allison, beseeching the woman beside her. She wanted to reach out to her with her hand, but Diana's body was taut with rage. She felt a wave of despair. "If only Uncle Gus had said something," she said, "we could have been happy, the three of us."

"What do you mean, the three of us?"

"Gus was my father, wasn't he?"

"Haven't you comprehended a word I've said, Allison?" spat Diana. "Gus wasn't the father of my dead child. He was sterile. The night he ran out on me, I slept with Teddy. Yes, you heard me. Such a lovely, sweet, weak man. Just one night with him and I became pregnant. Pretty ironic, isn't it? Here was Gus, virile, hungry, handsome, and it took his brother, not even a shadow of him, to do what Gus never could accomplish."

"Teddy? He was my father?" said Allison, shaking her head in bewilderment.

"No, not *your* father. My baby's father. My poor, dead baby," said Diana in a distant voice.

Allison stared at her. Nothing was turning out the way it was supposed to. If she was mistaken about who her father was, then maybe she was also mistaken about her mother. Maybe Guy Barnes had gotten it wrong. She felt hot and confused. She shut her eyes, trying to clear her head, then opened them again. No, she thought, Barnes was right.

"Diana, I'm sorry you had to find out all this from me," Allison began again, speaking as calmly as she could, "but maybe it's for the best. There's still time for us, I know there is. If you need proof to believe me, I have proof. The name of the doctor who delivered me. Hospital records. The plane that brought me to New York. I know this must be blowing you away, but the important thing is you don't have to be alone anymore. You have me, your daughter."

"I have *you*, you say? You, Gus Morton's *favorite*, his *treasure*, his *darling*?" demanded Diana, her eyes dark with anger. "What a hideous idea. Don't you see, you are exactly what I don't want. You are what I've tried to get rid of. Yes, you heard me, don't look so dumbfounded. I have no apologies to make for anything that's happened. It's your fault, not mine. You caused it all. Everything. That poor Mexican woman who worked for Gus—she never would have burned to death if you had been where you were supposed to be, asleep in Gus's guesthouse. And—"

"You set that fire?" said Allison, choking on the words. "Then you killed . . . Gus."

"No, I didn't. You did!" shouted Diana. "Didn't you hear what I said a moment ago. Gus's death is your fault, and I hate you for it." Her voice dropped again and she continued speaking as if nothing could make her stop. "And Françoise too. A wreck of a drunk, but I liked her. She had spunk. Too bad she was in your house that day. I had plans for you, not for her, but she got in the way. So did Ben. I never thought of him as nosy, but he discovered too much. I had no choice. And that dog. What did you call him? Some ridiculous name—it doesn't matter. I wasn't after him, I was after you. They'd all be alive if it weren't for you. The only one I missed was Cynthia. Dressed in that slicker, she looked like you."

Allison, transfixed by what she was hearing, said nothing, and Diana continued.

"I must say, one person played right into my hands. Adrian Frame, that disgusting man. I realized of course that he'd make an ideal suspect, so I followed him and planted a few telltale items in his car, just to help the police draw the right conclusions. Keys to Ben's house and to your old place. An empty vial of strychnine. It worked like a charm. Just like a charm." Diana laughed in a tight, strangled way. "For such a talented attorney, it would seem I've been embarrassingly inept at all this, haven't I, but finally I did something right."

"Diana . . . why are you telling me this? Are you making it up?" asked Allison in a barely audible voice.

"No, I am not. And you know I'm not. I'm going to turn myself in," she added bitterly. "Before they come to get me."

"No, you can't. You didn't know what you were doing, did you?" When Diana didn't answer, Allison put her hands on the other woman's shoulders. "That's the way it happened, right? You didn't know what you were doing, right?"

"Let go of me."

"Diana, please," cried Allison, "I want to help. Please let me! You're my mother!"

"Mother?" said Diana, turning and looking at Allison, as if she had never heard the word before. "Mother?"

"Yes, Diana. My . . . mother," said Allison. "You believe me, don't you? Don't you?" She was feverish and shaking, and, catching sight of the glass of champagne on the dashboard, reached instinctively for it. A swallow of this would steady her nerves.

"Don't touch that!" howled Diana, knocking the glass from Allison's hand. As the glass shattered and rained down inside the car, Diana pushed open the door and ran out, stumbling and falling to the ground, where she covered her face with her hands.

Allison raced after Diana and put her arms around her. A car passed on the road, momentarily illuminating the women in its beams, and then disappeared.

"Don't you see?" groaned Diana, struggling out of Allison's grip. "I was going to kill you. I would have succeeded this time. The champagne was . . . You wouldn't have known what was happening. I was going to send you and your car over the cliff. An accident. A horrible accident. I would drive home in my car, and tomorrow someone would phone me with the awful news. That way I would have Gus's memory all to myself. I'd never have to share him with you again." Diana shuddered. "Oh, God, what have I been doing? Have I lost my mind?"

"Don't talk that way, Diana. You didn't know," said Allison frantically.

"My whole life has been a lie. A miserable, rotten lie," cried Diana.

"No, that's not true," said Allison, shaking Diana by the shoulders. "You're not to blame. It's not your fault. It's . . . Uncle Gus's fault. He's the one who lied, not you. All these years. I don't understand. Why didn't he tell you about your baby? Why didn't he tell me? He must have thought it was for the best, but it doesn't make sense. He was a good man who did a terrible thing. Why . . . why . . . why did he do it?"

"Don't ask me why. What do *I* know? I despise myself. But I have an idea what to do. I should have done it long ago."

Diana looked steadily at Allison, then lurched to her feet and ran back to the car. By the time Allison caught up with her, she had raised the windows and locked the doors.

"Diana, open the door. Please!" cried Allison, tears streaming down her face. Diana stared straight ahead as if she heard nothing. And then she turned on the engine.

When she felt the vibration under her hand, Allison became frenzied. She grasped the door handle and pulled on it as hard as she could. She hammered on the window with her fists. She threw her weight against the door, dug her heels into the ground, and yanked with all her might. "Stop, Diana! Don't do it! Look at me!" she screamed again and again.

Diana turned toward her, but even in the darkness Allison knew her mother didn't see her. And then suddenly Diana's eyes focused on her. She stared unblinkingly at Allison and then mouthed the words *I'm sorry*. The engine grew to a roar, the tires spun through the gravel, bits of stone lashed Allison's face, and the car rocketed over the edge of the canyon.

"Diana!" Allison screamed. "Diana!" The shouted name became an ululating cry of horror and rolled around the canyon until it was silenced by the enormous sound of an explosion. Allison collapsed on the ground, the dust from the tires hanging like incense above her head.

Later, the headlights of a car shone in her eyes, but this time the lights did not slide by as the others had. Looking up, she picked out the silhouettes of Sean, Cynthia, and Tom, and then, as her eyes closed again, she felt Sean's arms around her. She pressed her head against his shoulder and wept.

"It's all right, darling," Sean said again and again. "I'm here. Nothing's going to happen to you. It's all over." And in her heart, Allison knew it finally was.

EPILOGUE

M el Starr was happy. The source of his happiness was on a sheet of
paper that he couldn't stop looking at. On it were the Nielsen ratings
that listed *Tinseltown P.M., his* show, in the top ten for the fifth month in a
row. He had a hit. Finally. As executive producer and creator of the program, he stood to make a bundle. And this from a show that was almost
on the garbage heap less than a year ago. His wife was right. They should
look for a bigger house. And in a better location. Maybe in Brentwood.
That's where they belonged. After all, he'd be negotiating a new contract
with the network soon and his agent was going to ask for the moon—and
probably get it. And then there was his piece of the syndication. Can't
forget about that. That could be very major bucks. Then why not also be
looking for a weekend place at the beach? Like at the colony in Malibu.
Why not?

The show started to turn around when they ran a segment on Clar-
ence Teach, the famed sixty-year-old British director of huge-budget
epics: the building of the great wall of China; the discovery of the source
of the Nile; the Chicago fire. *Tinseltown P.M.* revealed that Teach, while a
student at a red brick university in the Midlands, was a member of
Moseley's fascist gang. He also wrote and edited an anti-Semitic rag
called *Troopers for Freedom.* He did not go by the name of Teach then, since
his mother had not yet married Sir Reggie Teach. In those days he was
known as "Brown Shirt Barnswell." The story was picked up by *Time*
and *Newsweek,* and then by every major paper in the Western world. The
show was finally *making* news. The next hit episode featured a profile on
Dr. Jenny Wistman, the warm, vivacious, and hugely popular TV
shrink, who was shown to be a mean and uncaring daughter to her aged,
crippled mother, who lived alone in two miserable rooms in a Detroit
slum. Both Donahue and Oprah quickly booked Dr. Jenny's mother,
along with other neglected parents whose children were rich and famous,
on their shows. *Tinseltown P.M.* was now the talk of the country.

So now the weekly staff meeting of writers and producers had a confident and happy aura.

"Okay, Shep," said Starr to Shep Fairman, an older writer, at the start of the weekly project meeting. "How you coming with that segment on the Randall brothers?"

"Lousy. They both deny that they swapped wives, and neither will talk."

"Have you tried the servants? Let's go for an inside angle."

"I hadn't thought of that, Mel."

"Well, sometimes even an executive producer can get an idea," Mel said with a laugh that was quickly picked up by his staff. "Gloria," he continued, addressing a large woman at the end of the table who was eating an enormous bowl of what looked like pineapple and bran, "what's happening with Rico Marty?"

"His bail is being reduced and he should be released today. The girl he beat up and tried to run over with his Bentley sold her story to *Penthouse*. And I doubt if I can get past his lawyer."

"Dammit. The story's a natural. The guy's been playing a wimp in films for his entire career and in his free time uses broads as punching bags. I got it! Why don't we round up a panel of feminists, you know, people like Gloria Steinem, to discuss it. Call it 'Wimps as Brutes.' It'll add a little seriousness to the show."

"I like it, Mel," said Gloria.

"Yeah, me too," said Mel, as he lit a Monte Cristo. "Now, Barry, you dropped a fucking telephone-book-sized proposal on my desk last night. You can't expect me to read something that long, for Christ's sake."

"I think it's got a lot going for it, Mel," said Barry Hooper, the youngest producer on the staff. I've been working on and off it for months."

"Is this that Allison Morton thing again?"

Hooper nodded.

"Give it to me verbally. If it's any good you can boil it down for me in sixty seconds. Come on. Pitch it." Mel Starr leaned back and blew an immaculate smoke ring toward the ceiling.

Hollywood, Barry Hooper thought, *I love it. Work for months and he wants it in sixty seconds. I guess if Melville worked out here he would have started* Moby Dick *with* "Call me Ish."

Barry plunged into Allison's story, and though in fact it took him almost two minutes, he left nothing out: the explosion in Palm Springs and Gus's death; the demise of Lee and Ben; the Frame takeover attempt and failure; Adrian's imprisonment; the suicide of Gus Morton's longterm companion, Diana; Allison's regaining control of U.T.M. and her success in turning it back into the hottest agency in the business; her marriage to Sean Flores; the impending birth of their child.

"How would you close it?"

"The ending's a natural. Next week she's giving a big memorial dinner for her uncle at Chasen's. All of his friends, which means every big name, will be there. Word has it she's going to announce that she will step down as head of U.T.M.—but only for a while. Seems she's going to create an office of the president that will include the top financial guy who's been there over twenty years, the head of the literary department, a hot young rock 'n' roll agent, and a woman lawyer who's a friend of hers."

"What's this Morton broad going to do after she leaves?" asked Mel, who was now staring out the window toward the dun-colored hills behind the lot.

"She'll be living here, in New York, and on a ranch in New Mexico. She wants to spend time with the baby, but then, in two years or so, she intends to go back to running the company again."

Mel Starr continued to stare out the window.

"Well, what do you think?" Hooper finally asked.

"The ending's too soft for us. The gal ends up happy. Let's forget it."

"Forget it?"

"This kid's had everything handed to her on a platter all her life. For a princess story, believe me, you gotta have Di."